C000103909

Red Heat

Richard Sim

Grosvenor House
Publishing Limited

All rights reserved
Copyright © Richard Sim, 2023

The right of Richard Sim to be identified as the author of this
work has been asserted in accordance with Section 78
of the Copyright, Designs and Patents Act 1988

The book cover is copyright to Richard Sim

This book is published by
Grosvenor House Publishing Ltd
Link House
140 The Broadway, Tolworth, Surrey, KT6 7HT.
www.grosvenorhousepublishing.co.uk

This book is sold subject to the conditions that it shall not, by way of
trade or otherwise, be lent, resold, hired out or otherwise circulated
without the author's or publisher's prior consent in any form of
binding or cover other than that in which it is published and
without a similar condition including this condition being
imposed on the subsequent purchaser.

This book is a work of fiction. Any resemblance to
people or events, past or present, is purely coincidental.

A CIP record for this book
is available from the British Library

ISBN 978-1-80381-455-1

Prologue

BETWEEN MIDNIGHT AND DAWN the First Minister of St. Eleanor, Warwick Constantine, died at his home in *Anse Chastenet*. He died alone.

The Housekeeper discovered him at seven in the morning when she had brought the First Minister his customary morning tea, only to find him, fully dressed but totally oblivious to the world, slumped across his desk, staring empty-minded out of the window. She had put the tea down, crossed herself, then telephoned the head of the special police protection unit who called Inspector Woodbine Parish of the Royal St. Eleanor Police.

It didn't take the Inspector long before he had drawn up outside the *Chastenet* complex. It was pleasantly warm; the languor of a tropical day just beginning. The house lay on a small knoll overlooking Marigot Bay and surrounded by dense jungle. It could only be reached by means of a very dusty, ill kept road. The house itself – or perhaps it should be called a mansion – had been built by a Scot who had inherited the land from his father, an industrialist from Renfrew, who had once had ambitions for making it into the centre of a major sugar plantation. The mansion had been intended as the centre piece of the owner's social status and success but after some initial jungle clearance the sugar project ran aground when the plummeting price of sugar would not justify

1

the massive investment required. The business venture aborted, the jungle began to encroach again. *Chastenet* by 1961 had become the residence of the First Minister.

To Inspector Parish the procedure looked straightforward enough. Warwick Constantine, elected First Minister and Prime Minister designate of the soon to be independent Caribbean island of St. Eleanor, was dead. Parish was appointed simply to process the necessary clean paper work. He would need help. This was to be supplied in the shape of Dr. Ian Fortescue, the FM's personal physician, an Englishman and already on hand to receive the Inspector. It was still early. Only a tiny handful of people as yet knew of the death. The doctor had already signed a medical certificate stating that the cause of death was cardiac arrest. This was true as far as it went.

A strange desolation of death prevailed at *Anse Chastenet* when Woodbine Parish arrived, giving the impression of a place without location, a kind of empty limbo in which he felt insecure. Shortly, however, a black van arrived at nine and removed the body. Subtly the mood changed. Soon afterwards, a black limousine arrived and disgorged Mr Jake Oppenheimer, special assistant to the Governor. All aspects of the death were being carefully covered before any announcements were made. No relatives, no press had yet been informed.

The Inspector questioned the housekeeper. Her answers established a simple chronology of events. The First Minister had returned late having dined out, retired shortly afterwards and not been seen again until this morning. His demeanour? Nothing unusual. He had looked thoughtful and was quiet, impossible to know what he was thinking. If there had been telephone calls in or out, they must have been on his private line. Certainly the servant had not heard anything.

Inspector Parish closed the door on the kitchen and was about to inform his office that his work there was concluded when he heard the clink of glasses behind him. Jake Oppenheimer was pouring two glasses from the First Minister's rum. He handed Woodbine one.

"What shall we tell the press?" Woodbine asked, more by way of conversation than concern.

"Just what the death certificate said. You saw it. Death by natural causes. Cardiac arrest."

"And the post- mortem report?"

"What post-mortem report? There won't be one. He has been taken to the mortuary where he will be prepared for a brief lying-in-state. The briefer the better." Jake was smiling. It was not something Woodbine had seen before; and somehow he didn't really believe in it.

"I see. And...?"

"After a short but decent interval there will be a new First Minister. Everything will go ahead as planned. St Eleanor will become independent on the existing schedule. None of this will become public knowledge. You understand the significance of this I hope, Inspector?"

"I'm not sure I do."

"You have been placed in a delicate position. It could even put you at personal risk. Now you have privileged knowledge of the First Minister's death; all of which you would be well advised to forget." The Inspector was detecting a different Jake now, the real one, showing his teeth.

"I understand Sir."

"Good. I thought you would, Woodbine. You're a good man. We are not really heartless, you know. It's just that we have to have the larger good at heart."

With that, Inspector Woodbine Parish departed, making his way to the car, a certainty forming in his mind. A certainty, cool, hard and heavy that the Constantine affair had the makings of a political time bomb. He was better out of it.

1

NORMALLY I WOULD BE one of the last to accuse colleagues of harbouring hidden motives but I must admit when I entered the Commissioner's office I had wondered what lay behind the invitation. I just had a feeling. Not of doom, exactly. Nor of anticipation. A prickling of the skin, perhaps. Anyway, it was Commissioner Deacon himself who started. I just listened.

"Ah, there you are Cordell. Delighted to see you. I'm sorry you were kept waiting," he said, half rising as he waved me into a comfortable chair on the opposite side of his mahogany desk, itself ensconced in the corner of the turret room where he enjoyed a commanding view of the Thames. A coal fire blazed in the opposite corner of the room. It was a dank November day. I looked out of the window. There wasn't a soul out there. No one. The sky was grey, the Thames was grey and even the tugs sliding down on the tide were grey. I watched, still fascinated by the falling dusk. As a New Zealander the light of the temperate zone still mesmerized me. People talk of the Mediterranean and the tropical light but it is the North which is enchanting: here where day gives way to twilight and you can watch the slow withdrawal of light.

"At my age nothing should surprise me, Cordell," Deacon said, "but I was surprised to hear from the lips of the Minister himself that you were such a great success in West Africa. Remember?"

"It rings a bell."

"Well, yes you did well in trying circumstances."

"I don't know about that Sir, but..."

"Oh yes but I do know about that. Sir Peter himself has put me in the picture in his very cogent way." He stared at me with those cold, blue eyes of his, eyes which he used as a surgeon might use his lancet. They reminded you, if nothing else would, that they belonged to the man hand-picked to command the Metropolitan Police, the world's most renowned law enforcement agency.

"The Society of Leopards?" I asked. "I won't deny it was a tricky business! Oh yes, certainly," my eyes fixed on the cigarette smouldering in the glass ashtray on the Commissioner's desk. "You'll find them all over West Africa, I'm afraid." This was true when I said it but today so much has changed I sometimes have to pinch myself to recall that I didn't dream it all up. "But we got there in the end, got the lot of them in fact."

"Indeed you did." The Commissioner leaned forwards, hands clasped, staring at me as if engrossed, and letting a short pause develop. "You did an excellent job."

Well, in theory I suppose.

I sat back and looked at him squarely, unpleasant recollections invading my memory. "I did what I was paid to do." I judged it best to fall into a subservient role. The Force was more strictly hierarchical in the sixties. Commissioner Deacon was an authoritarian martinet – which again was not considered dysfunctional at that time – so I thought I would keep in my place.

He averted his gaze a moment, smiling slightly. Always well groomed, careful about his health and meticulous about his personal cleanliness Deacon was not always an easy man to make out and you had to take care when dealing with him. I didn't particularly like the man but I couldn't have told you why. He had two grown up daughters who were a constant source of worry to him. Maybe it was those anxieties which made him crotchety. Sometimes he could turn on you like a once-reliable old dog that didn't now care to be disturbed in its habits. His views were decidedly conventional and old fashioned although occasionally he evinced a surprising crankiness; he was, for example, a keen advocate of decimal coinage. He had a pedantic manner which I found irksome but there again it did at least ensure a degree of precision in the running of our operations. He also spoke with a rather cold formality which I could never get used to, something like an actor playing the part.

"How are you liking it, running a desk at Scotland Yard?"

"Well enough, Sir." It was true. Up to a point anyway.

"Good. That shows a willingness to adapt. You mustn't stagnate, you know. But I think you are capable of being a little more audacious. In the tropics you sorted out a problem which would have bogged down many a policeman." he said. "I'm not saying that you're smarter than the others but I've seen all sorts of detectives at work and I know what I'm talking about. You've gained a very valuable commodity there and it all comes down to one word: experience." He stopped a moment and surveyed the top of his desk with its red leather inlay, white note pad and immaculate blotter.

"To revert to the Minister," he continued "the man with whom we must be most concerned. He's had a long discussion with Colonial Office mandarins. It seems they've had a request for assistance from St Eleanor," he said raising his palms in a gesture of openness. "I daresay you have followed the independence discussions in the news?"

Not sure where this was leading and never having been able to state my views to superiors without thinking them through I made a non-committal sound of measured agreement.

"So I will not make a long story of it," he breezed on, "save to say that the First Minister has died suddenly in rather singular circumstances. The gentleman concerned is Warwick Constantine, a former publicist and economist. A good man – or so I'm told. His work was highly rated and he had discreet relationships with our government. As everything is related to everything else even I am not sure where this trail began but in any case the St Eleanor government has asked London if we could second them an investigating Officer. It won't be easy. Whoever takes it on," he said, meaning me, I suspected, "will find the traces have all been kicked over."

There was a lot to assimilate here. Thinking about it, even as the Commissioner talked, alerted me to the possibility that this may not be such an attractive posting. I dimly recognised the name Warwick Constantine but couldn't quite put my finger on him. Moreover I now had sufficient police experience to understand that whatever had gone wrong with the case in St Eleanor couldn't alter the fact that the case was getting older; and everyone in CID knew that older meant colder; and that colder meant harder. No, maybe I shouldn't rush to be positive about this.

Deacon explained that the local police were evidently out of their depth. Some blamed the failure entirely upon the inefficiency of the local constabulary. They were lacking in the detailed experience needed in murder investigations (Deacon was inclined to this view, considering himself to have a wealth of such experience).

"Now, Bruce, the problem is a tricky one." I guessed that his sudden use of my first name was intended to make me feel in his confidence. It didn't. "I want *you* to take this on!" Deacon was nodding his head vigorously, rocking his chair as he did so. His eyes spoke too now, entreating, pleading even. "In my judgement you have exactly the qualities for the job."

I hesitated, not sure what I was getting into. It didn't sound like a straightforward promotion. "You're not serious, Sir?" I said.

"Don't play games with me, Inspector, I am perfectly serious." Deacon continued in a still affable voice. "It's a sensitive investigation. And not only that but an urgent one. I want you to clear your desk immediately and start work as soon as you can. Everything else is to be considered non-essential."

"Yes, Sir." I decided not to argue. I had seen the Commissioner in action and knew he hated to be crossed. Perhaps more significantly, I had even once observed him looking at himself in the mirror, striking one attitude after another and assessing the effect, nearly always, immensely superior. Perhaps he should even have been an actor. Besides the Commissioner was reputed to have an intimate familiarity with the confidential meeting rooms of Whitehall. There was no point in being uppity.

Suddenly a smile lit up his face. "It'll only be for a few weeks. Six weeks at most. With any luck you'll even have some free time to enjoy the place."

"You mentioned our own Government, Sir. Where do they come in, exactly? I thought the idea was to leave as much as possible to the locals until independence?"

"I haven't been given any solid information" Deacon answered. "But I understand this fellow Constantine was thought a safe pair of hands to steer the island to independence. Now there's uncertainty and what with Castro taking over in Cuba the Americans aren't too happy. So there is some concern across the road in Whitehall. You know what they're like. They are supposed to be so discreet but, it seems to me, they run around like a lot of headless chickens whenever anything unexpected turns up. That's it really! They don't like the unexpected and there was no reason to feel Constantine may have been under threat. Now that it's happened they would like to know something about the origin and nature of what went on in St Eleanor that night. Just in case there is more to it than meets the eye. Probably nothing special. But either way it's an unexpected death which needs examining. In a discreet sort of way. The local police have turned up nothing. That's why they are happy to give us a try."

"Can you give me a few more details, Sir?"

"I can indeed. It happened without warning as such events always do. The First Minister was found dead at his home on 27 October 1961. Detective Inspector Woodbine Parish made an exhaustive study of the incident, concluding that it was a tragic accident, occasioned by an overdose of barbiturates. This may well be the case but considering the significance of the case everyone would be happier with an assessment from Scotland Yard. You'll be given the full report, of course."

For a moment the Commissioner glowered at me with an expression which was presumably meant to instil respect. To me it looked a little pompous but I thought I'd better play along. "You want me to do this, Sir? Well then, of course I'd be honoured to carry out your instructions." He smiled benignly but I couldn't help feeling I'd replied exactly as he wanted.

"Will you be sending anyone along with me?"

"No" he admitted his eyes bleak and remote. "You'll be on your own but of course you'll co-ordinate with the local Royal St. Eleanor Police. In this case, Superintendent Frank Worrell. If it becomes political no doubt the Governor, Godfrey Faed, will have something to say. But no one else from the Yard is to be involved. They have a new First Minister, Bob Jamieson of the United Workers Party but I don't expect you to be involved at that level."

His expression planted a query in my head. Was there more to this than he had indicated in his edited version of events? "And yourself Sir?" I asked.

"I'll be incommunicado. I have no remit there. And one thing, Cordell: this is a potentially touchy subject. *Do* make every effort to be diplomatic. Leave no stone unturned but don't ruffle feathers unnecessarily."

2

LATER THAT AFTERNOON I was in my office gazing out of the window wondering how I was going to give my wife the mixed tidings, i.e. I had been given a plum posting to the Caribbean but she was staying home. It's a strange thing but I can still remember everything so clearly. A few figures scurried along the Embankment but mostly I was just looking at the line of parked official cars. My tea cup, on the desk, was still half full but long cold. It was an ordinary moment in an extraordinary day. I was just considering how I would pitch my news when I heard someone slip into my office. I turned around.

"Ah Ken. What are you up to?"

"What are *you* up to more to the point?" It was Ken Briscoe, the office wag and long-time friend, the old timer who had befriended me when the rank and file could give an outsider a hard time. Leaning against the jamb of the doorway, Briscoe eyed me curiously. In his late forties he had been something of an unofficial mentor to me when I first joined the Met. Briscoe was someone I had always been able to count on so I took our friendship seriously. Not that that wasn't uncontroversial. Briscoe was not especially popular with all of his colleagues. He was often running down the Force and casting aspersions on its administration, darkly hinting that they hindered the fight against crime.

He would, however, speak up for Britain's growing coloured population, a point of view far from being that of the majority. Yet Ken knew everything a copper should know and more. It was Ken who was a dab hand at setting up his grasses; and it was Ken who had a sixth sense when a petty thief would have links to the Mr Big of London's sinister East End.

Right now he was looking at me intently with steely blue eyes, a raincoat hung nonchalantly over the crook of his arm. "Hear you're off to the Caribbean," he said. "Great news." But he didn't sound as if he meant it.

"How the hell did you know about that?" An unwritten protocol required that I should look astonished so I duly obliged.

"Just by keeping my ears open. Something you should do. Fancy a pint? Tell me about it?" As Briscoe spoke the office lights seemed to burn more brightly as the dark of a November's evening descended. I could hear shouted farewells and clocked that the typewriters had fallen silent.

"There's not much to tell." For once I was almost at a loss for words but he gave me a plaintiff look and I could hardly deny him.

"You look a bit rough 'round the edges if you don't mind me saying," Ken said. "Difficult meeting eh? I daresay a pint would do you the world of good." Ken was a policeman of the old school who would never get used to paperwork. He was always more at home asking questions, out and about. We were not obvious friends: the contrast was partly one of age but also of background. Heavy and slow, he was not an educated man but retained a native shrewdness honed by years of diligent investigation into London's underworld. In short he was unusual in possessing, unlike all too many of his colleagues, an invaluable commodity: the capacity to think. I enjoyed my banter with him. Besides I felt like wetting the whistle.

In a few minutes we were out in the bleak winter air sniffing in the cocktail of industrial pollution that was central London's air in those days, battling alongside the homewards bound office workers, and working our way towards Whitehall from Scotland Yard's embankment home. A winter fog was laying itself across the city shrouding buildings, traffic and individuals. We turned into Whitehall from the embankment, the condensation creating a beadwork of drops on my coat. Cars, red buses and honking taxis inched their way down from Nelson's column.

Ken became jaunty and talkative, his complexion the usual ruddy colour, as we made the short walk to the pub. He had grown a little flabby, probably the result of too much office work and a consequent lack of exercise but he still walked with the rolling gait of the ex-mariner which he was. The air felt muffled under the gathering fog and I felt relieved when we turned into the warm fug of a tolerable public house. We looked round the gloomy interior where there was a scattering of early evening customers, both standing and sitting, drinking beer. Ken got the drinks in and in no time he'd cut to the meat of what was on his mind.

"Well fancy you getting a plum job like St. Eleanor. You'll be the envy of many a Yard man!" Briscoe's eyes seemed to drift to a far off place as if he were contemplating a holiday on a sun soaked beach somewhere. "Care to tell me about it."

"I daresay," I smiled. "Well, in to every life a little sun must shine or so they say. A trip to the Caribbean should do me very nicely, thank you. I guess it was just my turn."

"Maybe but maybe not. It won't be all plain sailing you know. You know very well it's the first days after a murder which are the most important. This one has long gone cold." I expected a measure of scepticism from Ken: it was his style. He applied to the world a mixture of cynicism, Christian morality, fierce loyalty and common sense; and would have benefitted my career enormously if that had been in his gift.

"Murder? Who said anything about murder? Besides, the local investigations have got all the essential information. It's not so cold," I said.

"I hope not for your sake. Murders are rarely easy and they say this one might be political. You might find yourself walking on egg shells. Have you thought of that one?"

"No. Why's that?"

"A poisoned chalice, I'd say." With that Ken sipped at his pint, allowing the thought to settle.

"How so?"

"Look below the surface and I'd say you're more likely to get trouble than plaudits. Are there any suspects?"

"It's far from that stage. Looks like an over-dose, pure and simple. Besides, I've been asked to start afresh."

"That doesn't mean anything. You may find there are suspects aplenty when you get there. Have you been polishing up your charm skills?"

"Well, now you mention it I can't say I have. But oh yea of little faith! I'm not without diplomatic skills."

Ken smiled. "It might be more than a polite word or two. Accusations may have to be made and there could

be more at stake than simply finding the culprit."
I stared at my beer a moment. I wondered what Ken
was hinting at. Ken affected not to care about Met
politics but his detailed knowledge of inter-office politics
stretching back over many years implied otherwise.
"And another thing," he said. "Are you sure you're not
being set up. You know the Commissioner doesn't really
care for you."

I let out a jovial laugh. "Give over! We have a good
working relationship." I glossed over my own doubts
with some brazen good cheer but I must admit he'd
spiked my curiosity. Ken was fixing me with his beady
eye. Every few moments the door opened and a few
customers arrived; others left.

"You don't really believe that do you? You know he's
never really forgiven you for *North Star Investments*
and the way Greencroft got you off the hook." Ken
helped himself to another swig full of beer

"Oh for Christ's sake, Ken! *North Star Investments?*"
I exploded suddenly angry. "That's all done and dusted..."
That fiasco was not something I wanted to go into.

Assistant Commissioner Goss had rebuked me
ferociously last year. I'd made a silly mistake in
ensnaring a group of 'businessmen' bent on a corruption
scam involving senior staff of *North Star Investments*,
who had a majority share in a pharmaceutical company
which were billing the NHS well over the top for a new
tranquiliser. Although I had some knowledge of white
collar crime this was much more than fixing the books
and had involved setting up a whole front organisation
based in Portugal, *Tarragano*, who were allegedly
producing a key ingredient. This proved to be a skimpy
organisation turning out very little but absorbing

hundreds of thousands of pounds a year. It should have been an open and shut case but the *North Star Investment* directors had been careful to set everything up carefully to meet legal requirements and put a lot of distance between themselves and those with "dirt" on their hands.

It turned out that when I moved to arrest the suspects I'd entered a tangled web in which 'evidence' I'd thought was cast iron was not admissible in court. A case, months in the preparation, had gone awry and it was my fault. Hands up. I'm not denying it. I'd been green then and I had a lot of amends to make. I could have lost my job and Goss had hinted that maybe I should look for a job more suited to my talents when Detective Superintendent Greencroft had put in a good word for me. Greencroft was highly regarded in the Force and was known to possess good judgement. It probably saved me. Argued that the blame should have been shared. So I wasn't sacked, just shunted on to the sidings.

Since then I'd carried out a number of assignments, done a lot of in-house training and best of all, built up a steadier detective record but I still needed a big success to put the past behind me. This had probably put Peter Goss in a difficult position when I'd been recommended for the St Eleanor investigation; but he'd evidently backed me. Now Ken Briscoe was putting a fly in the ointment. I thought he was wrong but you never could tell. If Deacon were hostile, he had masked it well. But there again, you don't get to the top of the pole without knowing how to dissemble.

"Well, don't say you weren't warned. If you make a mistake here they'll bring all that up again, you know. Sure you're not being set up?"

"Naw. Sure." I said smiling and projecting a self-confidence I did not feel. The truth was I could do with a change and hadn't expected to be offered one as appealing as this. I'm sure he didn't believe me but I was telling the truth, convinced the job would be a good career move and one spiced with a bit of Caribbean heat.

"Mark my words. It all looks great today but it will count heavily against you with the Met bigwigs if you screw up again."

"A lot of people would be damaged if I screw up."

"Worse than damaged, in your case."

"I'll take the risk."

"Well, you know what I mean. It's a trick of management. There are so many bosses they can diffuse the blame but the guy at the bottom has no let out clause. Forget the tropical island stuff. This'll be no holiday. It seems to me that the Boss has handed on a lot of shit to you. The local police can't handle it so what makes him think you can. So, he is taking you for a fool. You take it on...and if you're not careful you'll find yourself up the proverbial creek without a paddle."

"I think you're being overly cynical, Ken," I said. I would have been angry at Ken's suggestion but I knew he was a good copper, a good egg. In time most policemen finally grow inured, disgusted and thoroughly discouraged until they are downright cynical, emotionally shielded. But somehow old Ken Briscoe had managed to preserve a heart.

"Well it may work out better than I feared but don't you forget Bruce whatever happens you're not on your own. If you want a quiet word you can always give me a bell, if it comes to it. I can maybe do a little digging this end if you need it." At this Ken tapped his nose solemnly to indicate that all exchanges between us would remain confidential. I'll say this for him. He had balls. Some said he was just a plodder, lacking in imagination but they were wrong. Ken had insight.

3

It is a sad confession but I have to admit I've taken some seriously wrong turnings in life. It had all began so innocently and with such high hopes. Everybody had said I couldn't do it, shouldn't do it and wouldn't do it. The idea of leaving New Zealand and exchanging life there for that of a poorly paid police officer in London was probably an odd one but I do know where it originated. I was born in New Zealand – in Nelson, South Island to be exact – but I never tired of sailing off our coast where the seeds of a lust to see the world were sown. So when War came I volunteered easily enough and was just in time to see the tail end of the Burmese campaign, serving under General Slim's luminous command. Not many people talk of those times. The only significant film made of it was about a Japanese camp for British prisoners yet it was the site of Japan's biggest land defeat in the Second World War, courtesy of the British Empire. There was no US involvement so, of course, no films. But there's another reason why not many people know about it, Britain's so-called 'Forgotten War.' Even the veterans don't like to talk about it, not the details.

Me? I had been demobilised in October 1946 at the age of twenty one with the rank of Lieutenant and a cheaply made tin medal which was so coarse I was almost embarrassed to wear it, HMG's reward for a wasted youth in a devastated land. With the end of the War I moved to England, under the false impression that this would soon become a booming economy brimming with opportunities for a man of my talents ready to try his hand at anything. I had not reckoned that I had also become a bundle of raw emotions, many of which I struggled to understand.

I was not idle in any way; just not too successful. First, I put myself to car mechanic work, finding a job at *Buists* in Cricklewood, north London. It didn't pay well but offered some satisfaction for a while, but not enough for me to justify to my parents my sustained stay in Europe. Then, I tried my hand at selling motor-cars but found the constant pressure of selling not to my taste. After that I put myself to copy-writing for an advertising company but though this was better, found the inane creative requirements of advertising too demanding on my patience and finally my temperament. So I'd signed up for the Met police in search of a more action focussed career.

Not long afterwards I had met Katie who was intelligent and good looking in an open confident sort of way. I had seen more and more of her, pursuing her whenever I could but somehow, though the longing had been there from the first, not recognising that I was in love with her. Then when I overcame my self-deception and realised that I had loved her from the first, it was a joy to find my feelings reciprocated. I adored her open enthusiastic nature, her Northumbrian country accent, the unpredictable swerves in her interests and her shining almond eyes which made me feel enclosed in her love whenever she looked at me. God, how much I had loved her that first summer and in time we had married. I had never felt like that before or since. Two children had come along and all seemed set fare but ten years later had found us at breaking point. After the early joy, work had wrought some strange and subtle changes. Katie had found that marriage had opened the door out of work and innumerable friendships into a species of solitude. But she was my lodestone, exerting a tremendous power over my emotions and my conscience. I could not lie to her.

That's why I wasn't overjoyed to be giving her the news I was off to the West Indies without her on a special assignment. It did make me feel guilty. Katie wasn't the manipulative sort, at least not especially. Of course she could be manipulative but it wasn't her default pattern of behaviour. She was more likely to blow her top which I found extremely unpleasant. But she'd have to be told. She'd think I was off on a joy ride. Couldn't really blame her but she'd have to be told.

Mind you, I'm not saying I wasn't pleased. I had been getting pretty fed up with things. Here was I, thirty six years old, still in pretty good shape but restricted to the banality of investigating and grappling with low-lifes. To add to it, the weather was damp and the talk of the ordinary Londoner parochial. Since I'd been working at Scotland Yard, I'd fallen into a regular routine but that Friday night I was an hour later than usual in getting home because of Ken Briscoe's intervention. Our house was a large Victorian one with its own name, Lynwood, on the borders of Wimbledon, part of the vast aggregate of London with its insatiable appetite for provisions and suburbs. It was a handsome stone-built house with an arched porch and a glass inner door decorated by engraved birds of song. We loved its feeling of home and hearth. To tell the truth I was struggling to keep up the heavy monthly payments on it. But it wasn't only that. I felt as if the days here were running out. Life at Scotland Yard had been far from what I'd expected. What kept me going were my family: my wife, two children and the need to earn. These were my salvation but right now even these were looking pretty thin. They had not yet become a deep habit of my life. More surprisingly perhaps, commuting back and forth had given me something, a yearning perhaps. Here in London you still felt the great strength of this immense city struggling through countless misfortunes. It was just that I felt powerless to do anything and needed again the call of action.

Yet it was the first proper home I had enjoyed since leaving my parents, most of it Katie's work. It was a real home, a serene place I could feel safe in without much trace of any of those inner demons from the past. Here I felt I could hold my past securely inside my head. Lynwood was furnished with a miscellany of things which had mainly belonged to Katie's family. They were heavy handsome bits of furniture but often scuffed and marked. The heavy Victorian oak wardrobe was worth something but the walnut table had ring marks, the Parker Knoll chairs needed re-upholstering and the kitchen dresser's doors kept popping open unaccountably if you didn't continually wedge them with pieces of paper.

I had always meant to take the furnishings more in hand and upgrade the house but aside from the money issues I'd been putting things off not because I was a prevaricator by nature but because my life had always seemed so transitory, so temporary and unsettled unlike those of normal people. I don't think Katie understood this but then I didn't really either.

That evening I had arrived home to find Katie and the two children sitting around the kitchen table, laughing, talking and eating. Laura, as cute as only a small child can be, led the demands for attention as she had done ever since she had displaced Andrew as the darling of the family, a position he had occupied until Laura had come along. But Andrew's boisterousness could never be ignored for long while Laura's delicate forget-me-not dress only emphasised her vulnerability. It was amazing how quickly they had grown into little people. If anybody had said to me only a few years earlier that I would become besotted by small children I would have said they were daft. But there it was. Andrew and Laura both had developed a charm and will of their own which was irresistible.

It was a familiar family scene: tea was spilled on the table and there were crumbs everywhere. Katie got up and came towards me, smiling. She was wearing a smart royal blue suit. Though she'd had it a while the suit had lost none of its original freshness and still preserved the brightness of its original colour. She put her arms around me and kissed me lightly on the cheek. It seemed as if she knew instinctively that something was wrong. Was there a reluctance to my embrace?

"Are you all right?" she asked puckering her brow.

"Yes. Of course. I'm fine." But the forced smile could not disguise the slight irritation in my voice.

We wandered into the living room. It was spacious but cold in winter. The walls were painted a pale green, a colour which had looked so relaxing on the paint chart, but in winter added its own layer of chill. A large Victorian fire place, complete with a polished brass fender and blue tiles decorated in the Dutch manner, dominated the room. Usually I found its look of permanence re-assuring but not today. I struggled to light it. Scrunched up pieces of paper, charred sticks of wood and numerous expended matches lay in the grate, reproofs to my ineptitude. An acrid smell rose from the fire place. At last when I was close to giving up, the fire ignited but joy was short lived as billows of smoke blew back from the grate into the living room because the chimney was still too cold to receive the flames. Finally the coal crackled and blazed; the air cleared and with it the mood of the room lifted. I loved living here.

WE ATE OUR SUPPER EARLY. After all it was Guy Fawkes' night and the children could hardly contain their enthusiasm. But we savoured our lamb chops and some simple plain vegetables. On the radio they were already talking about Christmas, about how much people would spend this year and what tricks the stores would get up to, to get us to spend more. One of the speakers was worried that the true meaning of Christmas had been lost.

Later, Katie washed and I dried.

"You know I always talked half-jokingly of getting away to a desert island," I laughed. Of course I'd been rehearsing what I was going to say but it didn't make it any easier. Now there was nothing for it. So I told her. *Bim-bam-crunch*. At first she was delighted for me, thinking that my efforts and steady application were now being repaid after the highs of Cyprus and Ghana and the disaster of the *North Star Investments* affair.

"Could I not join you?" she asked seizing on the moment. "You know I would love to see the world. And – oh, I know I would love this – I could watch things and help you in your work."

I frowned. "You know that's impossible," I said at last. And she knew it too. It was utterly impractical from every point of view. Then I saw her jaw drop. She saw only problems in having to cope with two small children on her own and no support whatsoever, neither practical nor emotional from her husband.

"You should have given him a good talking-to. God, you can be irritating sometimes. Does he realise you have a wife?" She wasn't cross, more flabbergasted, really.

"I'm sorry if I mishandled things but it's only for four weeks or so, darling."

"A bit more than that I'd say...Oh, I suppose it doesn't matter that much," Katie said in a conciliatory voice but failing to contradict me. "It's just what am I supposed to do? These aren't easy circumstances, you know. Looking after the children single handed causes me a lot of problems. You never think of anything. You only think of yourself." She was glowering at me now, arms akimbo, ready to be belligerent.

"You'll be alright," I said as if that would re-assure her. I put my hand around her shoulder and said quietly: "I do love you, you know. In the end I'm doing all this for *us*."

"You're always too ready to do whatever he asks," she said, ignoring my aside.

"The Boss is ok. He's got his orders too," I said relinquishing my arm. Truth to tell, it was hardly what I thought as Katie knew well.

"You sound like a typical man when you adopt that sulky tone. You don't usually give up so easily."

"Eh, well…"

"Oh, it doesn't matter." She grunted but seemed to accept my point. "Bruce. You're such an idiot. You play the Great Detective but you don't read yourself well and me not at all. Of course you're gagging to go. I know that. I don't begrudge you your chance but I don't think you've given me and the children any thought at all. It's going to be huge pressure on me and you haven't even tried to pin him down to a time limit!"

"Well, it all depends…"

"I know it depends but there have to be limits. I am going to have a hundred and one things to do. Did you ever think of that? It's bad enough that you do so little anyway but now it's going to be a nightmare for me and you just seem to take it all for granted."

"No, I don't really but the way I see it there are only two ways ahead. I tell the Boss that I can't complete his assignment and wait for my career to hit the buffers or I go ahead, put my back into it and fulfil my commitments as best as I can. What else can I do?"

Katie looked at me sceptically for a moment then her face lit up and she walked over and embraced me. "Promise me that you'll think of me and the family and try to get back as soon as possible" she said.

"I promise."

She smiled; and when she smiled it was like her whole face was lit up by a flash of gold. "And try to remember that your bachelor days are long since over."

"I'm trying."

"You can say that again. I don't know anyone as secretive as you are. I had just about decided that you aren't hiding anything when you come up with this. But there isn't anything else, is there?"

"No, I don't think so…"

"Meaning…people may be hiding secrets from you?" She sighed and looked at me reproachfully.

"Too true. But it's only Ken spooking me. I've no reason to think there are more secrets being kept from me." Even as I said it, I was unsure. The journey from one brain to another is the most difficult we ever make. Most of the time we live in some sort of Cartesian prison; it can be hard enough to understand what dark fish are swimming around in the darkest pools of your own mind without expecting someone else to understand. That's why Katie's trust was so priceless. I smiled to reassure her. "Look…if it turns out to be longer than expected I'll arrange for you to come out as well. Maybe turn it in to a holiday. We have some savings…"

"Don't make promises you can't keep."

"You'll see."

She shook her head slowly, her expression suggesting exasperation but I sensed there was a residual affection beneath the surface.

I stepped forwards and wrapped my arms around her waist. "So how was your day anyway? You know you look beautiful, as ever?" I kissed her on the back of the neck and she smiled. "Ken reckons there might be a spot of promotion in it for me if I do a good job."

"He would say that wouldn't he? He's your friend," said Katie as she plunged her hands into the soap suds and began violently scouring the grill pan.

"I've got to pull this off. Not least for my own sake. Ours that is." I was almost pleading.

"Well, just see you get back in one piece," she said, her voice softening "and maybe we can run to a caravan holiday on the south coast somewhere....Oh, you'll never guess," Katie said as she washed a brightly coloured ceramic. "I've got some news for you too. I'd nearly forgotten myself but I had the strangest encounter this morning."

"Who was it this time? Nanette wittering on about some new project of hers or news from the Church? Or both?"

Katie smiled, put her hands on her hips. "There you go, jumping to conclusions. Not very good for a police detective, dear. If you were more attentive you would appreciate I was trying to give you some useful information."

"Go on," I said.

"Well, I left the house this morning to do some shopping. Nice and frosty it was. You know that feeling when everything is crisp and clear? Everything looked brighter and fresher, somehow more real. It was like a good omen when I almost bumped into the little man. Middle aged, fattish, dressed inconspicuously but well, I suppose. Nothing special about him. Except, poor man...he looked exhausted. Anyway, he apologised, saying he was just checking off house numbers, hadn't been paying attention to where he was walking. And do you know what? He was looking for our house. I looked more closely at him and I saw him differently, His eyes were deeper, thoughtful. You know what I mean? Something to do with the eyes. Reminded me of the Mallam we once met..."

My blood ran cold at what she said, recalling the Mallams as they called their holy men on the Gold

Coast. It brought another palindromic name back to mind: Renner. That is what chilled me. Renner had been like a dark cloud hanging over us. The rarely seen dark suited man from MI6 who had popped up unexpectedly in Accra and Nicosia, like a harbinger of doom: Nemesis.

Katie was saying, "– so I told him he could ring one evening this week."

"But it wasn't Renner was it?"

"Idiot!" Katie said. "You haven't been listening to a word I was saying. Well, I'm not going to tell you if you're not going to pay attention."

"Sorry, love," I said. "My mind wandered. It was you talking of Mallams. Sent my mind off to West Africa and Renner. Anyway what did he say, this man?"

"Well, it turned out he wanted to speak to you quite urgently but he wouldn't say what it was about. I pressed him but then thought better of it and just gave him our telephone number. He was ever so grateful."

"Urgently, you say?"

"That's what he said. But he wouldn't say what it was about. In fact he kept looking around. Very fidgety, as if he thought he was being followed. I thought you might know what it was about."

"Me? No. Haven't a clue." I must have sounded confused.

"He didn't give his name. Can't you even guess who he may be?

I rubbed my forehead and made a great effort of memory but nothing came. "No. He doesn't sound like anyone I recall. Well, I'll have to wait until he rings. It'll probably turn out to be something incredibly mundane."

"Would you like to bet on that?" Katie asked. "Come on, let's get those fireworks off."

And so saying she dried her hands with a sudden flourish and flounced off into the hallway to dress the kids for the frosty night. I wasn't entirely pleased by her attitude. I was a police inspector but my wife's sarcasm reduced me straightaway to the status of a child. Come to think of it, in nearly all of our verbal interactions there's almost always been an element of put-down. What, I wondered, gave her the right to talk down to me as if I were a boy? Walking into the passageway I found that even *Mandu*, the children's black and white cat, was irritable and out of sorts, jumping quickly out of my hands when I tried to pick her up.

Still, the thing to do was to redeem myself by putting on my best Daddy act for fireworks night. The temperature was dipping when we ambled out across the frosty grass into the back garden. The rush of cold on my cheeks was invigorating. Winter had arrived and no mistake. Gone now were the scent and colours of our little garden plot which I loved so much. The scent especially was something I missed over the merely picturesque. Still, the gloom was brisk and alluring. The children were excited, a veritable handful alright, but they seemed to have got the message that they had to take great care with fireworks and that these things were best left to Daddy. So their mother's exhortations had given me a free hand. It was one of the rites of fatherhood I enjoyed performing like pushing them on a swing, deliberately losing to them at cards, shouting *Snap!*; or even, more recently, plunging into the open pool with them.

We passed the greenhouse and the potting shed and then stepped beyond the hydrangea bushes towards the thick hawthorn hedge which separated our house from a neighbour's. Stepping past an upturned watering can and armed with a torch and a box of *Swan Vestas* I set out the rockets in their jam jars and admonished the family to stand back as I lit the blue paper. The touch paper flared into life and then suddenly with a whoosh the rockets went up, soaring into the night sky before exploding into a myriad of bright stars. Green, red, golden, they were captivating and I was relieved the damned things had worked out well. I stole a moment to look at the entranced faces of the children, eyes open with wonder, and briefly illuminated by the efflorescence of the rockets. God knows where they were at that moment. They seemed to be living in a dream world of magic and fairies. It made it all worthwhile.

I lit the sparklers, Katie and the children taking them with a look of reverence, holding the little metal rods with marvel as they spat sparks of light all around them. The air was full of explosions from neighbouring gardens as other parties' rockets shot out into the night sky, exploding into fountains of colour. I started lighting the volcanoes now which I had lined up near the hedge and stood back to watch with relief as they burst into flowing, effulgent cascades of colour. Others spewed out torrential showers of golden sparks. For the first time I saw the children from a neighbouring garden look in at our display, their faces mesmerised by the spectacle.

Katie squeezed my hand. She was smiling warmly at me. "Isn't this wonderful, Bruce? They are all so happy. We are such lucky, lucky people."

4

THE NEXT MORNING I was in the bedroom listening to the Home Service, watching millions of motes dancing in the sunlight, when I heard the doorbell go. A bit of a surprise but at this time of the morning it probably heralded a parcel delivery. I waited, quite still. You see, you could keep a check on things here. The bedroom opens on to the landing. Half way along, the staircase leads directly down to the hallway where the front door is located. It can be quite convenient knowing when someone is there. This time it wasn't so handy because in a few moments I heard a heated exchange in progress. Normally, I wouldn't be able to make out the words but normally people wouldn't be yelling so much. Clearly, Katie was not happy about something.

My reverie broken, I skipped downstairs to see if it was anything I could be of assistance with. Sunlight slanted across the hallway, dividing the smooth wooden opening into two halves, one bright, the other shaded. Sure enough, the front door was open where Katie, chestnut hair tumbling over her shoulders, was remonstrating with the postman. Between them stood what looked like a child's push bike.

"You'll never believe this," Katie said, half turning to face me. "Someone has sent us a wheelchair."

The postie, a lean dark uniformed figure, was brandishing his paperwork. "There's no mistake," he said, pointing to the address which clearly showed our home and above it, my own name in block capitals: **MR BRUCE CORDELL**. Well, that settled it. We had no choice but to accept the article and the postman, job completed, went on his way. My eyes followed. It was not an encouraging vista. A lot of rain was pouring in a peculiarly persistent way. Opposite, a van was being unloaded and a dog was snuffling about. I returned to the issue at hand. An unwanted gift. Now I had a chance to examine it a little more closely I could tell that what I'd thought was a push bike was obviously a folded wheelchair. I stretched the dark blue cloth wide so that it folded out into a neat looking chair complete with two foot rests which I had mistaken for pedals. There was also a brake which could be controlled from the rear. But the wheels were large, obviously designed to be self propelling, an observation reinforced by its manufacturers' insignia, **HAMILTON SELF PROPELLING WHEELCHAIRS**.

"Well, of all the ridiculous things..." I said, totally flummoxed by this unexpected turn of events.

"If we don't hear from someone in the week," Katie said, "then we'll have to find a good home for it. I know what. Perhaps the hospital could do with one."

"I daresay," I said, raising my eyebrows. "Very level-headed of you. I imagine they'll always appreciate a useful donation."

So saying, I folded the wheels back up and reluctantly propped it up in the hallway while Katie returned to some Saturday morning chores in the kitchen. I pulled on a jumper and after a visit to the downstairs loo, picked up my copy of *The Times* and dropped into the lounge to catch up on the world's events. But my mind was in turmoil. An accident? A mistake of some sort? That's what Katie had readily assumed but my experience of the criminal underworld had taught me much about signs and signals. Gradually the horror of it wrapped itself around me. My insides lurched. Why? What had I possibly done to induce somebody to send me such a gruesome message. Mentally, I did a checklist of possible enemies from the past but though it had been a pretty chequered one I still couldn't imagine there was someone harbouring such a bitter grudge against me. From the present, then? Much more likely. A warning. Some sort of caution about how I should handle the Caribbean assignment. I considered I should preserve the evidence. But it had just gone and I would look very silly chasing after the post van for a delivery note I did not want. I thought darkly: let this not happen to me. But what exactly had happened?

I searched my mind for any significant ambient features. Was there anything else which could widen the meaning of this strange epistle? The date, perhaps? The sixth of November. Hard to see anything in that. A letter out of the blue with some oblique allusion perhaps? A surprise visitor? A new friend? Wait... what about the mysterious man who was trying to find our house the other morning but who never accepted Katie's invitation to phone. Could he be significant? But every time I tried to construct some sort of coherent message out of it all, I had to give up again. All I was left with was this slightly sombre feeling that I had been warned.

A doleful beginning but perhaps it could not be otherwise.

But it was only to be the first of two surprises that morning. I had gone into the kitchen, put on the kettle, taken down the tea-pot and begun the search for the tea caddy when the telephone rang.

"Hello," I said. "Wimbledon 252."

"Mr Cordell. Bruce Cordell?"

"Yes....who is..."

"I'm so glad to have reached you. I was looking for you yesterday but you weren't in. Met your good lady and she kindly gave me the number."

I half wanted to hang up on him but half of me was intrigued so I answered: "Yes. She told me but what's this about? Are you responsible for the delivery?"

"What delivery?"

"Alright. Maybe not. Well, could you just tell me what you do want?"

"No snap answer to that I'm afraid but...could we meet perhaps? Then I could explain properly."

"I'm afraid I'm tied up at the moment..."

"I know. Going to St. Eleanor. That's what I wanted a word with you about. How about this afternoon. I have a proposition to make. Say, three o'clock at my place."

"And where's that?"

"Thirty four Belgrave Square."

The address did it. Perhaps I have latent snobbish sympathies – though I don't think so – but I couldn't resist an invitation to one of the capital's most exclusive residential areas. I was impressed and greatly intrigued. "Alright. Three o'clock it is but what's your name?"

But I'd been slow off the mark. The line had gone dead.

IT WAS NEARLY THREE when I made my way up from the South Kensington Underground station, swivelled behind Harrods into a quieter backwater and then into the immensity of Belgrave Square, perhaps London's grandest and certainly the capital's most valuable piece of property. By the time I found myself making my way to number 34, sandwiched between various assorted embassies and institutes, I had completely forgotten about the incident of the mis-delivered wheelchair which had passed much as an ephemeral breeze fades from memory, leaving no trace.

I rang the bell and in moments the doorway was filled by a portly figure dressed in a dark jacket and pinstriped trousers. Well oiled, dark and greying hair was swept back from a broad brow. A stout middle aged man, he looked me up and down before smiling affably. His darting blue eyes betokened a deep lain wariness. Somehow the man oozed money but I couldn't have told you how.

"Onslow-Bell", he said extending his right hand towards me.

Something about the man encouraged an equally brisk: "Cordell. Bruce Cordell."

The shutter of my mind must have stayed fully open that day because I can still remember every detail of that scene. The hallway was floored in white marble. To the right a wrought iron stair case centred with a red carpet wound its way upwards. My host ushered me inside and I soon found myself sitting in a comfortable, high ceilinged, sun-lit lounge. The windows looked out on to the square's private well-trimmed gardens, replete with mature lime trees. The room itself was elaborately decorated. The walls were covered in watered silk wallpaper and the paintings which adorned the walls could have been family heirlooms; they were certainly originals. But I tried to focus on my host, the person with whom I should be most concerned. It was not difficult. Onslow-Bell exuded a sense of power and I soon felt unwittingly deferential. Although he was clearly carrying a lot of fat he also looked as if he had once been muscular. His face was ruddy and focussed, his eyes small and intent. I can't say I could have docketed him easily into a category but he looked as if he were used to getting his own way. Yet his eyes had an unsettling bleakness about them. Maybe his life was not so comfortable as it seemed. A middle aged lady, I took to be some sort of maid, appeared and placed a silver tray replete with tea and scones on the low marble topped table.

"Glad you could make it," he said in a deep voice, still standing. "When I learned you were going to St Eleanor I quickly decided you would be just the man to help us out, to do a little sleuthing on the side so to speak. Do help yourself," he said gesturing towards the tray as he dropped into a chair opposite me. I took my cup of Darjeeling tea as Onslow-Bell sat back, took a business card out of his waistcoat and slid it across the table.

WALTER ONSLOW-BELL
International Project Assessment
Consultant

34 Belgrave Square, Tel: 368

There was, however, no hint as to what the owner might be a consultant in.

"I feel I must ask how you know of my posting to Saint Eleanor. It's not for public knowledge."

He smiled. "Don't worry. You see I used to work for the Foreign Office and still get asked my advice from time to time. So it's not too surprising that this information came my way. But this little confidence is safe enough with me, I can assure you. It will go no further. However, it did occur to me that you would be well placed to render IPA a little assistance."

"What is it exactly that you have in mind?" I asked. "I must confess I'm very flattered by all the attention but not a wit wiser." I smiled at him defensively but it was not infectious.

"The business interests I represent believe you are well placed to deliver what they want."

"I will not do anything unlawful."

"No. Of course not. My dear boy, I'm certainly not suggesting anything of the sort."

"Then what?"

"Quite simply I wish to solicit your help in a confidential matter," Onslow-Bell began in a soft and winning manner. "You see I represent certain business interests in the Caribbean who are very concerned about the region's development and the prospective Federation. These interests are taking soundings as to how things are developing and are likely to develop. It's perfectly normal. Big businesses run big risks and they like to minimise them. That's where we come in. I'm part of a panel of analysts who are able offer international companies that kind of information. We call ourselves International Project Assessment. One way we help is by future profiling. We do profiles of suspect areas. A kind of SWAT analysis. Strengths, weaknesses, challenges – that sort of thing. By doing this we can assess how secure their investment is and what measures they may need to take. Nowadays, it is a standard due diligence procedure to ensure they are looking after their investors' money responsibly."

"An expensive way of doing it, I'd say."

"The future's such a hostile planet you'd be a fool not to take advice and go armed into it if you thought the advice was good, wouldn't you?"

"I dare say."

"St. Eleanor is a good case in point. Independence creates uncertainty; and our clients don't like uncertainty. What we would like to see is a report – not necessarily long – in fact definitely not long. Busy executives haven't time to read long reports. The report itself might be 6,000 words but the key is the Executive Summary which should be on one side of Imperial foolscap paper. Your assessment should focus on the present state of political and economic threats to the viability of the St Eleanor economy in the short and medium term."

"I'm no economist," I smiled.

"Nor should you be. We are looking at political assessments. We think that in the next few weeks you will be well placed to talk to some of the most important people on the island. You will have your own professional reasons. That of course is only right and proper. But you will be well placed to do a little side line."

"Sounds interesting but what exactly do you mean? I have my own work to do and that will be time consuming." I asked in an unjustifiably aggrieved tone.

"It's simple. Keep your eyes and ears open. Ask a few pertinent questions. Your initial focus is to start with the possibility of massive political change on the island. Wholesale nationalisation, Cuban alignment....that sort of thing. A long shot but you should cover the ground if only to dismiss it. Then focus on the more immediate likely changes perhaps with some reference to the key personalities concerned. Pro-Western biases and ideological hostility – that sort of thing. Sum up with a very simple assessment of the threat to the business environment. Your key categories would be 'insignificant', 'low', 'medium' and 'high'."

I shook my head slowly in disbelief. "Sounds great but I'm not sure I am really cut out for that sort of thing or how compatible it is with my work."

"Very compatible I should say. You can't be working all the time, you will be meeting many key people and you are bound to find yourself mulling over these questions anyway. The island is in ferment. The report will be anonymous, of course."

"And what exactly are you offering me?"

"Five thousand pounds."

"Five thousand pounds!" I almost shouted in disbelief.

"Half payable now. The rest on completion of your job in St Eleanor. And by the way I will help with the editing. So you need not worry too much about the format."

I was still reeling. This was truly big money. More than I could hope to save in a lifetime. I must admit I'd thought myself that I was invulnerable to money offers but failure to get promotion and a sequence of financial misfortunes were making me vulnerable to the idea of easy money. "Its probably no surprise to you to know I could use the money," I said, "but you need to explain – ."

"Explain what? It's simple enough and you will be able to pay off that mortgage and still have ample to spare."

I was still confused but it was too much to ignore. Besides, I couldn't see anything wrong with writing a short confidential report. What could go wrong? There was nothing illegal about such a proposition; and indeed there was no need for my employers to know. Let's face it: if Ken was right they didn't even care for me that much.

"I can show you some samples if you like. Help give you a bit of an idea. I've got some in my study." So saying Onslow-Bell levered himself out of his chair and began to walk towards the hallway. I followed. The journey was not a long one. Onslow-Bell led me to another room, one crammed and cluttered with books and papers. There were boxes of files and the shelves overflowed with material. Yet the desk at least looked well-used and a place of earnest endeavour.

"Let me show you," said a smiling Onslow-Bell as he picked up a bundle of very slim blue files. I could see they had been individually commissioned by companies operating globally in key sectors: finance, motor cars, chemicals, petroleum, pharmaceuticals... He let me look through some. Although impeccably typed, bound and presented, they were quite flimsy. Less than twenty pages and always with a very concise Executive Summary, sometimes no more than a paragraph. I whiffled through them. The titles themselves were illuminating: *Pressures and Strains in Post-Colonial Africa*, *The OAS Campaign to Destabilise France*, *The Satellisation of Egypt*, *Indonesia's Konfrontasi* and so on. I'd seen enough to get the picture. This looked good stuff, analytical and thoughtful reading, as close to scrutinised and weighed reality as you could hope for, with allowances for all the variables. After all, there were no absolute guarantees in this world.

"I don't think I could write to this level at a first draft but you'll edit and revise, you say?" I asked.

"That's it. I want to be on top of the material myself."

I hesitated. "But then there is the whole question of the research. I very much doubt that I will have the free time to do it."

"You may not need as long as you think and you will be well placed to ask the right questions of the right people. We have someone on the island to liaise with. He should be able to help if you have problems. Besides if things don't pan out well you are free to withdraw..."

"Well, Mr Onslow-Bell. On that basis, you've got yourself a deal."

And we shook on it. I suppose I should have thought more deeply about it, should certainly have checked with Katie. But I didn't and that's the simple truth of it. And so it was agreed; and, yes, you could say it was too good to be true. From his desk he then produced a stiff sheet of white paper which he handed to me. It was covered in small heavy black type printed closely together.

"Your contract," he announced. "Sign this. A little formality but it protects us both. And guarantees your fee as you will see." It took me a long time to skim through the paper and work out what I was looking at. It was short but didn't commit me to anything I couldn't do. All I had to do was write the report and there could not even be any guarantees about its quality. I signed.

"Good,'" he beamed as he took the paper back. "Well, if you don't mind, Cordell, I have to prepare for a conference. All a bit of a bore I must say but one has to do these things. Know what I mean?"

"No. Not sure I do, Sir. But I don't doubt you're right."

"Rightio," he smiled. "See you when you get back. Oh...and everything will be alright with your charming wife, I trust."

"Yes. She is very supportive." I had no clear idea why he had asked after Katie but presumably he wished to convey a sympathetic interest in someone who mattered greatly to me but who was not his responsibility in the least.

"Good. That's what I like to hear. And I have that name you could use as a useful contact when you get there. He does a lot of work for us, is something of a businessman himself and can give you a general briefing to start you off with. After that its up to you. You should meet most of the island's luminaries anyway in the course of you work."

"Who is this contact?"

"One Rufus Halliday. A singular name, I must confess but there it is. He's a long term resident of the island. Knows it well. He may ask for a little additional help for one of our clients. A few words to the wise, you know, that sort of thing. But he's better equipped to speak to you about that sort of thing."

"Where do I meet him?"

"No need to worry about that. He'll know where to find you. Leave it to him."

And that was all. It really was incredible how quickly my life was to be transformed. I left Belgrave Square floating, as it were, on air and feeling that I had moved into some sort of ante-room for Heaven. I managed to shrug off the excitement by the time I made it home though my legs were still trembling. But I was being filled by a calmer energy now and Onslow-Bell was receding somewhat into the background like the memory of something hardly experienced or only experienced by a part of me no longer present.

Back at home I walked straight into the kitchen and made myself a cup of tea. I drank it slowly, conscious of the comforting warmth moving down my throat. I smiled to myself the smile of the smug. It had all seemed easy enough, perhaps a little too easy and mysterious but so long as I was careful to keep my eyes open and not get in to anything more than Onslow-Bell was proposing I could see no harm in it. We should indeed be very much better off. What I thought then, no, rather the feeling sweeping over me was that he's got inside my head. What I had absolutely no idea of was that I was being completely out-manoeuvred.

LATER THAT DAY I explained the deal to Katie. At first she questioned me eagerly and made me repeat my story again and again. A scepticism crept into her voice and I could tell that familiar nagging suspicion that something was not right was taking hold.

"You know," I said, "There are lots of people who earn a little money on the side. It's not that unusual; and it isn't as if it interferes with my work. It's just by way of sniffing the air."

"Yes but it isn't a little money on the side. It's more like a small fortune!"

"And money for old rope if you ask me." I smiled.

"That's what worries me. Too good to be true. Are you sure this wonderfully generous man didn't make any other demands?" She asked this in a tone of voice more reminiscent of a mother teasing the truth from a recalcitrant child than a wife chatting to her spouse.

"Absolutely certain."

"And you are being honest aren't you?" Katie's words revealed an unexpected access of suspicion, justified perhaps but actually contradicted by the facts. Onslow-Bell had made no additional or unreasonable requests.

"Of course I am." I found myself shouting indignantly at her suspiciousness. "He spoke with such confidence it's got to be true and its hard not to be swept along."

"But who is this man and what does he want? If I were you I'd just forget about it. It'll never happen."

"What makes you say that? What he asked for was straightforward enough. And five k is hardly to be sneered at."

Katie hesitated. "No...it certainly isn't. And I suppose if we don't accept we'll always be wondering. We can't unmake what's happened."

"Exactly. I don't see any other solution. We've got to explore this opportunity. One way or another our lives have been changed by this. Maybe not much but maybe a lot. They'll never be quite the same again."

I could see she was about to explode but, thinking quickly, she refrained. Instead she smiled and said: "You can't ask your boss?"

I was exasperated both by her sound sense and the fact that I had put myself in the wrong by shouting. "All right, all right," I lied. "I'll clear it with the office first." Lying was out of character but the self-reproach flitted away in a moment. Something deep within me was evidently determined to have the money. But I knew I couldn't possibly raise the issue at the office; I would be in deep trouble.

"Well then, everything should be fine if it's ok with them," Katie said. After that she continued to probe a little more but with diminishing enthusiasm. Gradually, even my recollections grew a little confused. And in the end there was the money. Katie too was lured by this. Make no mistake: it helped the whole thing mightily. Where she had been hostile now Katie became positively keen. Like me she remained a tad suspicious but the thought of so much money for a very modest side line was too much. The idea quickly rooted. In a couple of days she was downright enthusiastic.

So the morning I left Lynwood, 2 December 1961, came much easier than expected. For Katie that is. Now that the time had come I was full of self-doubt as to my ability to solve a mystery where on hand investigators had failed. Still, I was determined to give it my best shot. But corny though it may sound I felt a sense of real loss, similar in its suddenness to that exhilaration of my first meeting with Katie all those years ago. We embraced tenderly and then trying to cover my feelings with a show of comic light heartedness I left with the words: "*For lust of knowing what I should not know I take the Golden Road to Samarkand.*"

There was the wheelchair incident too, of course. But I couldn't think of anyone or any gang who might harbour such a grudge against me. A nasty message but what was the point of a warning I couldn't understand? Perhaps the best thing would be to forget about it, get on with my work and ignore the whole thing.

5

I ALWAYS FEEL IN my element when I go on a long journey. Flying in a heavier than air machine still gives me a rush of boyish excitement, a feeling of being on the edge. I had not told my friends or any of my neighbours that I was off to the Caribbean. Already, for reasons I couldn't fathom, there was something a bit furtive about my assignment.

The flight couldn't be done in one leap. And it was long. I found myself spending interminable time looking down on the blue sea, corrugated with waves, watching it recede at 600 mph, giving me a feeling that I had compulsory leisure to do anything I fancied but of course I could do little more than read. I had Robert Louis Stevenson with me. Something about his love of desert islands must have communicated itself to me.

Stevenson and work, that is. I had brought my brief with me and dry though it was I tried to bring myself up to speed with the case. The facts of the First Minister's mysterious death were plain enough but what did they prove? So who was this man, Warwick Constantine, this man on whose head, were I a painter, I would have to focus all the light? I pulled his photograph from the file. The face that looked back at me was unmistakable: the self assertive jaw, the set mouth, the thick trenchant nose with its distended nostrils, the wide lively eyes beneath the heavy eyebrows conveyed the face of a man of determined will but it looked a kindly face too. Why should anyone want to kill him? There was no apparent motive.

Constantine had a good reputation among the locals. He was community spirited, always supporting the local communities whenever he could. He appeared to have no enemies but maybe this was not the case. Maybe someone hated him enough to kill him. Was there something about the First Minister we did not know, something important not in the files? Constantine was an activist. So what were the political issues on this nearly idyllic island? The British wanted St Eleanor to join the newly set up West Indian Federation but it seemed that many of the natives preferred Home Rule, if remaining a Crown Colony were no longer to be an option. Added to this confusion were a miscellany of disputes: the US Navy wanted an anchorage and other facilities; there were continuing arguments about the best forms of investment; and endless rows about the future of the island's only strong cash crops: bananas and sugar. And, of course, just across the water Castro had declared his allegiance to the Russians. In sum the political situation here was baffling, complicated and a recipe for trouble. Had Constantine become an obstacle to something which wasn't wholly legitimate? Could there be subterranean pressures at work? His death must have been to someone's advantage. I saw that the First Minister's last engagement, cited in my backgrounder helpfully put together by Woodbine Parish, had been a dinner with some English friends, the Quillhams. Quentin Quillham was a successful journalist and publicist, his wife an artist and owner of a very successful arts gallery on the island.

Mulling these things over I fancied that Inspector Woodbine Parish had got it right. The old man was in the habit of taking barbiturates to help him sleep. This time he had inadvertently gone just a wee bit too far. His heart, no doubt under strains of office, had simply expired. It had been a terrible tragedy. I continued leafing through the file as methodically as I could and, I'm afraid, in occasional lapses drew little faces in the margins. I was glad of my refreshments at Antigua and then I found myself to be one of only a small group who was taking the onward flight to St Eleanor that day. It was all going according to plan.

Finally, I was relieved to find myself peering at the island itself as we circled for our descent. It looked very green surrounded by a sea of turquoise and fringed with surf. On second thoughts the rain forest looked forbidding, primeval and largely untrodden. I could make out the white sands of the beach. A few buildings, mainly thatch by the look of them but some concrete, looking like upturned sugar cubes. Abruptly, the humming of the engine changed as the plane banked for its approach run, becoming a roaring as the braking flaps began to open under the wings. Soon we were gliding down.

The sun was disappearing over the horizon as our little plane touched down on a runway lit by amber lights. Using engines in reverse, we gradually came to a gentle canter. The airfield proved to be a single strip of tarmac complete with a hangar and a small administrative block. Beside the admin block I could make out some huge propellers, presumably wrenched from some long dead plane. Elsewhere there were heaps of engine parts and nowhere an intact craft to be seen.

Our aircraft came to a standstill outside the small terminal and a rickety looking set of steps was wheeled out to us. Suddenly everyone was up, pushing and jostling as they tried to remove luggage from the overhead racks. I too grabbed my bag and made my way with the other passengers to the dilapidated looking offices. A battered sign proclaimed in huge letters WELCOME TO ST. ELEANOR but it looked like it could do with a lick of paint. You could hardly call it Customs and Excise so perfunctory was the inspection but I suppose that is what it was. The Customs Officer handed me a list and asked if I had anything on it. He asked me to open my case and proceeded to go through it with an air as if to say he knew this to be a deplorable breach of manners. Then I was on my way through. I found myself instinctively patting my breast, reassuring myself the passport was still there. In only a few minutes we were out through the other side and I was bidding a thankful, silent goodbye to the other self-absorbed travellers. While I made my way to the exit, a bevy of tourists scrambled inside a waiting bus, middle aged ladies clutching hand bags and sketch pads, an old man complaining of a missing item and up front, on the pavement and perspiring gently, a genial looking guide held aloft a placard announcing a hotel name.

It was muggy alright, just as I had been warned. I noticed that my travelling companions had cars waiting for them and quickly disappeared into the night while I had barely reached the pavement. I was ready for a stiff drink, a shower and bed. My shirt was becoming clammy. I looked around for my reception committee but there was hardly anyone there now. The road was quiet. For the first time I found myself wondering what a police car might even look like out here. I strolled out to the road, dumped my bag and let my eyes drift up to the first pin pricks of light, now appearing in the tropical sky.

"The night sky is something you can always savour in this part of the world," a disembodied voice with an extraordinarily pleasant timbre said behind me.

I turned. A tall, gangling man unpeeled from the darkness and came forward in an ungainly stride. "Worrell's the name," he smiled as he extended his hand. "And you must be Bruce Cordell."

"Superintendent..."

"Frank, please. I insist. Very pleased to meet you." He gave me a gentle handshake, his dry hand quickly slipping away like a discarded glove. Yet the squareness of his jaw and his firm eye contact lent him a look of complete control and great self confidence. "You must be tired after all that flying. Here. Let me take your luggage. The Land Rover's over here."

I followed eagerly, already set at ease by the man's amiable manner. Clean shaven with a thick fleshy face he looked a homely sort of man. Only his sad eyes, not wholly explained by his facial structure, hinted at a life which had maybe seen too much of the underside of humanity's behaviour. Clearly he was off-duty, wearing a cheap looking checked shirt over baggy trousers, dark socks and sandshoes. Nonetheless, I suddenly felt aware of my crumpled suit and poor shave after my long flight.

"How was your trip?" he asked as we sauntered over to an old Land Rover parked near the main door. "No sickness, I hope?"

"No. None. Thanks for asking. Just plain tiring. This is not the easiest place to get to."

"Just two flights a day in from Antigua."

"Must make things dear."

He looked at me suddenly, startled then laughed. "No. Not especially. Our stuff comes by boat." He opened up the back and dumped my bag inside.

The Land-Rover moved off quietly. We made a wide circle on to the tarmac road, the only one so far as I could see, then we sped along an avenue of palms towards the smudge of rain forest I could make out against the evening sky. The road was barely one vehicle's width but although there were passing places, it was clear that any hope of rapid progress over the rutted and twisting roadway was out of the question. The moon had risen quickly, its light falling on the steering wheel and showing up calluses on Worrell's hands. Perhaps stirred by the headlights or the bouncing of the Land Rover a strange nocturnal population appeared before our eyes. Lizards and night birds sped out in front of us and fruit bats cut through the air.

"Jungle?" I asked finally, pointing at the forested area.

"Yes. Rain forest really. We don't have many dangerous animals, other than the human sort," he laughed. "Just pythons, rashly imported from South America in the last century. Otherwise it's pretty harmless." He laughed again.

"Just as well. I've never cared for the jungle since the war. How are we doing for time?"

"Quarter of an hour or so. Don't worry. We're on schedule."

I was glad to hear it. My clothes felt sweaty and uncomfortable against my skin. I was looking forward to a wash and an early night. The Lord knew but I was tired. I imagined the cool feel of linen against my skin. It was a very reassuring day dream.

We rounded a bend and suddenly I saw a line of lamps shining from across the bay. I made out a few boats at anchor in the bay below the stars. "Soufrière," Worrell announced as if I would know this little place. At last we broke into a more inhabited area and then a distinct small town. I gazed at the little streets we had suddenly entered, streets almost entirely composed of two storied buildings, self contained but not detached, and broken here and there by the intrusion of a little shop. At that hour people hung around on first floor wrought iron balconies, curved and elegant, talking from building to building which overlooked the little square, lit only by little specks of light from the rooms behind. "Soufrière," he said. "Used to be the capital of the island under the French. They set up a guillotine here during the Revolution. Abolished slavery too. Then the British came. Reinstated it. But there's always been something a little French about the place."

There did indeed seem to be a whiff of the Mediterranean about the place – and a tang of salt hung in the air – but I was in no mood for whimsies. It didn't take long before we had passed through the small township and begun a long ascent up a small hill before finally drawing up in a very dark roadway.

"This is it! Your Rest House." He brought the vehicle to a halt, not far from a steeply rising grass bank topped by a long wooden bungalow and a scattering of trees. "It's getting late," he said. "Can you see? Here, let me help."

Frank produced a powerful torch, stabbing the darkness like a sword and disturbing great bats that wheeled and circled above us. We got out together and unloaded my luggage from the back. By our headlights I saw a path snake up the bank side. Frank helped me bring up my bags. A lengthy wooden cabin stood before me. A wide low-eaved veranda was hung with cooling ferns. To my surprise all the windows were open. "Don't worry," said Frank. "You're too high up for the mosquitoes. Enjoy the quiet!"

So saying, Frank produced a key for the front door, opened it and deposited my luggage, gesturing his hand inside. I looked cautiously about. The glow from Frank's torch lent the room a curious, watchful feeling as if I were intruding. I groped for the electric light switch near the door, found none. It suddenly occurred to me that, of course, there would be no electric light here. A glow of light suddenly appeared from the table where Frank had lit up an oil lamp. "There you are," he said. "That's better. I expect you'll need to catch up on some sleep. You look dead beat." He smiled. "So I'll leave you to it."

"Thanks for everything. Nice meeting you...Frank."

"And I'm very happy to meet you, Bruce. At last, I may add. You'll find we've a lot to talk about. And I'm sure I'll be very glad of the assistance of the Metropolitan Police but it can all wait till the morning. Sergeant Aldridge will pick you up at eight. Well, I'll leave you now. See you in the morning. Then we'll get down to business."

I watched him go. The moon was high and bright against the darkness. A million stars shone above. The surf boomed in the distance. Perfect. The frogs sounded as if they had been reinforced by a thousand companions, adding to my sense of being somewhere else. The Rest

House was laid out to government specifications: everywhere was the smell of old, worn timber, a folding screen marked the division between dining room and living room, an experienced black enamelled iron bed and a hideous yellow wardrobe lay screened off from the rest of the room which comprised two rattan chairs, a plain table and a wooden chest of drawers on which a mirror gazed back at me. A colourful rug was the only adornment to a plain wooden floor. A small bathroom adjoined at the back while a WC lay just outside the dwelling.

I unpacked my things. In the wardrobe I detected the faint scent of a departed woman and in a drawer was a sheet of paper on which a vanished traveller had scrawled out a forgotten shopping list. They were such personal things when the room was supposed to be impersonal that I couldn't help but wonder who had passed this way before me. By a gas light I cooked myself a simple omelette and salad from the supplies which an invisible hand had left me. I stripped and showered beneath some metal work which leaked from every valve. Exhausted, I sat on the edge of the bed and rubbed my hands through my hair, a sudden wonderful optimism flooding through me, a feeling that life is complex, infinitely exciting. From the rain forest outside I could smell the whole rich distillation of a wild Caribbean night. Was it possible that only this morning I had been in London? The day had lasted an eternity. But what, I wondered was my next move going to be?

6

THE NEXT MORNING I awoke to a changed world. Dressing as well as I could manage I locked the door behind me and walked down the path, attaché case in hand, to a bright new day in a bright new place to await Sergeant Aldridge. The morning shroud was retreating now, revealing distant rocky peaks, pinnacle by pinnacle, until a phantom horizon of surging volcanic summits gazed down on me. I could smell the closeness of the rain forest too, felt an early touch of warmth in the air and heard the chatter of alien bird life. The sun was ascending with its promise of a day of invincible heat. Everything which had been emitting such tremulous sounds during the night had now sunk back into somnolence. Tendrils of mist still wriggled wraithlike through the grass, a light breeze lifted a torrent of bougainvillea against the cabin. Great care was evident in the nearby planting. There was a scatter of tall conifers but the cabin itself was surrounded by looser plantings of fern and palm. The paths, lined with white lilies, were of crushed sea shells.

Right on cue at 8.30 I heard the drone of a motor vehicle making its way up the hill. In a moment, a Police Land Rover drew up right outside my residence. English, tall and lithesome, Sergeant Aldridge wore a pressed neat uniform with a safari hat and a polished brown leather belt. I let him take me away. The earlier drift of rain had moved off as we took the coastal road, the only real road on the island, and skirted the turquoise sea making our way east towards the capital. I enjoyed the vistas the drive afforded us, the clear morning light gentling the granite mountains as they shouldered their way out to sea. They were not like mountains I had seen elsewhere and I would be pushed to say why not. Perhaps the light over them was different. At any rate I was grateful for the moment of contemplative privacy in our small floating world. We were nearing St. Jacques when suddenly we forked off the main road into a smaller branch which led towards an imposing white mansion overlooking the bay. Its dome sparkled with a piercing whiteness in the tropical sun. Indeed, Police HQ proved to be much larger than I expected. Larger and grander, like a politician's election promises, some sort of relic of an older age: it had a real *"We are here to rule you"* look.

As I climbed the steps, the main doors stood open, creating a hint of a cooling draught. Everywhere there was the scent of jasmine which seemed to waft into the most unlikely crannies. There was not a person in sight. In a moment though, as if she had heard me, a civilian woman came out of a door, still talking to someone inside. "Chief Inspector Cordell?" she asked. "Superintendent Worrell wishes to speak to you."

"Very good."

She showed me straight to Worrell's office. He sat impassively at his desk, in a halo of blue smoke, evidently a chain smoker when the mood took him and intent on some papers, looking strangely changed from last night. The office was decorated in a Spartan fashion.

No frills, all basic functional stuff: a desk, two chairs, some filing cabinets, a metal waste paper basket and a side table. Nothing that would trap the dust.

"How were the digs?" He sounded like an old friend so I couldn't help warming to him, trusting him even. Besides he had a comfortable, easy charm, an islander trait as I was soon to discover. His ready smile helped, lending him a sophisticated air as if life itself were a bit of a joke.

"Great. Thanks for setting me up."

"Penelope will be coming in to do the cleaning. And she'll cook you an evening meal at seven."

"Nice touch. Much appreciated."

There was a brief silence while Worrell leafed through some pages in front of him and I listened to the ceiling fan slicing through the air.

"So I see you're a New Zealander," he said. "That's great. You'll have a feel for island life I dare say. Don't worry, I'm not looking for miracles but I hope a fresh perspective might throw up new patterns. For the moment I'm going with the public statement that it was an accidental death but I'm keeping my mind open." Worrell evinced an air of relaxed competence. You had the feeling that he was an experienced old fox.

"Ah yes. An overdose. Yet in the file I saw he had been in the habit of taking the same dosage for quite a long time."

"Yes, you are right. And all the people close to him were carefully interviewed in the hope that someone, somewhere, may have seen or heard something out of the usual but no dice! We certainly seem to have run out of other ideas. But the government wants a hush-hush look into things."

"The investigation looked pretty thorough so far as I could see."

"Thanks. It's not the impression people here give me. Every functionary on the island knows more about policing than I do," he complained. "I get advice all the way from plumbers and teachers and firemen right up to the Governor himself. I get tips from the Doctor and complaints from the public health. Why, I've even had the clergy telling me the best way to catch a crook. It makes you sick." But his laugh belied his words.

"How about the politics?"

Worrell gave me a weak smile. As he explained it soon became clear he had good reason to be concerned. Rumours about the Federation abounded, some wild but some plausible. What was certain was that the new amalgamations would mean different demarcations. A running feud between those who were likely to lose their positions and those who stood to gain enhanced status and power was now reaching critical mass. Unfortunately Constantine had been in the middle of all this. Continually trying to placate people and trying to get some to accept the unpalatable, had he gone too far?

"You've read the file?"

"Of course," I said, busying myself lifting papers from my case. "But you'll understand that I may want to interview some of these people again."

"Naturally. We told everyone concerned that this was only a preliminary interview and that our detectives may wish to follow this up further. You must know I'm not satisfied with the back-up we've been getting."

I said that was why I was there.

"I hope you make the most of it. It'll all be a little strange. You'll have to do much of the interviewing yourself. I can't spare much PC time...sorry about that...and I hope you begin to understand that this island could go places. The last thing it needs is a reputation for unresolved murders, especially at the top. So mum's the word." I guessed too that Frank, my new friend and colleague, was capable of performing the difficult feat of being familiar and discreet at the same time.

"Of course. I want to help in any way I can. To tell the truth – one of the things which disturbs me – if you know what I mean, isn't so much the statements but some of the portraits that come through." I held up the wodge of papers. "Too good to be true." Frank laughed. He knew what I meant. The written work is sometimes given too much authority, as if they were temple doors to some sacred inner sanctum of truth. Reality is hardly ever like this. Don't get me wrong. The reports were all well written, models in their way: precise signed statements, referenced sources complete with detailed observations clearly delineated from facts. But not one suspicious character, not a hint of ill intent, never mind foul play. It didn't add up. No group of humans is as straightforward as this. You never truly know anyone. No one.

"Everything in Warwick Constantine's file suggests that he was a careful operator. There is nothing in his record to suggest that he would make rash judgements."

"Exactly," Frank suddenly looked severe and full of gravitas. "Constantine was well liked by most people. He was a Federalist but then so are many people. He has been guiding us that way. He was quite tactful about it, knew his limits. There was nothing to suggest that he was provoking any particular enmity over this.

We haven't got to the bottom of it yet." Unexpectedly, Frank's words had dislodged a memory of what the old German Chancellor, Konrad Adenauer, had recently said: that there were an infinite number of ways of telling lies but there is only one truth.

"One thing," I asked. "There doesn't seem to be a lot of thought given to a private motive."

"Oh but there was. I can assure you. Trouble was, none could be found. His colleagues are adamant that he had no personal enemies. But don't take my word for it. In fact I suggest you make them among your first port of calls."

"Family?"

"He was a widower. Two grown up children. Neither have lived on the island in years. There is a sister in Saint Jacques but I don't think they were so close."

"What about Constantine's own personal file. There must be one."

"Must there? Well, there's not one that I'm aware of. The Governor's office may have one but you'll have to ask there."

I nodded acceptance though I was a little surprised. Still, there were bound to be some new procedures. This was my first morning after all.

"But first we need to get you properly inducted." Frank must have been reading my mind. "I imagine you could do with a little guided tour of the island. I'll get Inspector Quick to take you out directly after this and just let me know if there's something special you need to get an eyeful of."

"Thanks Frank. I'd appreciate that. Right now my priority is still familiarising myself with the background to the case. I'm not indulging in any speculations."

"Quite correct!" Worrell sat back in his chair musing. For a moment I had the disquieting feeling that he might have been thinking that this is one colossal waste of public time and money but if so he was keeping mum. Instead, he remained encouraging. "Well," he said, "we'll speak some more when you're up to speed. It's just I can't help feeling there's an issue here which we just don't know about. Something which has just got out of hand....Aha! Tim, come in!"

We were interrupted by the arrival of a thin spidery looking young man, aged about thirty, in a short sleeved light blue cotton shirt and regulation navy blue trousers. His eyes, bright as pins, swept around the room but settled on myself. He scrutinised me eagerly, his face lit up by a lively restlessness. Then he threw out his hand with a brisk: "How do you do Chief Inspector Cordell." We shook hands. Too late I discovered his was a bone-crushing hand shake. He broke into an infectious, rather mad laugh.

Frank explained "Inspector Quick. Tim knows all about the case and in fact I want him to be your liaison officer. You'll understand I am available but perhaps not all the time. So much admin and so many meetings." Frank held his hand to his head in mock agony. "But Tim – Inspector Quick – will be happy to help you with most day to day queries you may have."

"Thanks. I'm sure that will be fine." Tim looked like a lively fellow with a ready smile on his face, perhaps too easy going for the rigours of police work.

"Please. Never mind about Inspector Quick. A plain straightforward "Tim" will go down better. But from what I heard about your case, it's a dud." Tim didn't sound too encouraging.

"There's always a chance for a new approach," I said hopefully.

Tim nodded agreeably. "Certainly if it comes from Scotland Yard, then we're all ears as the Americans say. If I can help in any way, do say! I know the lie of the land here. But I don't envy you. It always seemed to me that Constantine was quite an uninteresting person really."

"Except for one little detail."

"You mean that he's dead."

"Precisely."

"Touché."

Worrell told Tim to show me around HQ introducing me to colleagues and then to take me for a look around St. Jacques and some of the island. We would catch up with one another later in the afternoon. Then he rose, bundled up some papers and made to leave as if on urgent business when a young police woman came in, her shoes making a slap-slap noise as she walked across the floor, dropped a file on to Worrell's desk and shot me a smile. She was a neat woman of medium height, a round face and open, surprised looking eyes. I saw at a glance that she was some strong force of nature. She walked out again. I could almost feel the bright smoothness of her skin.

"You like her?" Tim asked when we left Frank's office, observing me with a mischievous grin across his face.

"Yeah. Well, she's quite a looker isn't she?"

"She's kinda sexy you mean." Then Tim made an expansive gesture with his hands perhaps delineating the size of her breasts. "That's Lucy. You'll have plenty of time to get to know her. Come on. Let me show you your new cubby-hole."

It proved to be plain and functional, about twelve by twelve with two tall windows staring directly on to the car park. The bare walls and desk looked fine. I could live with that. There was also an empty filing cabinet and a book case with empty shelving. The only personal touch was a handmade model of a speed boat which adorned the window ledge, an overlooked legacy of a former occupant.

Tim then started me on a whistlestop tour of the building. It was all smiling faces and pressing of palms but a necessary induction. Down in the basement I saw the cells and the interrogation rooms complete with a brand new panoptical cell for special prisoners or those suspected of being suicidal. Then Tim informed me that time was getting on and that I needed to start my island tour. There wasn't time to visit the Crime Room but that could be done on my return. This was mildly disappointing but no worse. The Crime Room would be essential for my desk bound research. All major police stations, in those days, had a crime room where crime reports and intelligence on the locality's crime had to be sent. It was the beating heart of criminal investigations.

"You see, I have to show you around the island," Tim was saying to me. "But I must be back by six to finish some Court work."

"Let's get going then!"

7

I DIDN'T KNOW QUITE what to expect that afternoon as Tim drove us into Saint Jacques, watched by lizards flickering on the rocks. Saint Eleanor is almost crescent-shaped. The smallest of the Windward Islands, it is about thirty miles long and from north to south about eight miles deep. St. Jacques was almost on the easternmost point of the island overlooking a narrow bay. As we beetled along the coastal road in Tim's asthmatic Vauxhall I saw mountain roads winding their way up to large looking dwellings perched high along the rim of the hills, probably above the mosquito habitat. In fact the higher the road, the larger and farther apart were the houses. These, I imagined, would be where the owners and rulers of the island lived. Beyond them still lay big, dizzy mountains.

We came on St. Jacques quite suddenly from the hills. It was almost dancing in the liquid heat, framed by coconut palms, a flurry of boats and ragged shacks roofed by tin. More comfortable dwellings dotted here and there spoke of a little wealth. There can be few towns anywhere in a lovelier setting than St. Jacques. We passed rivulets by whose pools women whacked cottons on the rocks; and went on down by the naval fortifications of Admiral Rodney which still commanded the harbour. The sun was like a torch, illuminating every detail. Every boat, every anchor glistened brightly. Individual flowers seemed to shout out from the shore line with their vivid yellows, reds, cerises... St. Jacques had sprung up from around the original sheltered anchorage, huddled up beneath the hills and bathed by the Caribbean. Seventeenth century ramparts shielded a busy little port and a cluster of vertiginously zigzagging dark alley ways which constituted the town centre.

We glided past a steepled church, or it may even have been a Cathedral, and around an open green space in the heart of the town. Opposite the camel necked church the names of former citizens who had sacrificed their lives in 1914/18 and 1939/45 were inscribed on a grey marble monument. It was probably just as well that Tim loved driving and it showed. We motored assertively through the narrow streets, dodging honking cars and manoeuvring firmly past little knots of people clustered around busy intersections and children playing in the verges. The old town was a complex of blind alleys and narrow lanes. Dogs, cats and mules with porters vied with cars and trucks. It looked a busy place with shops, booths and stalls all doing a good trade but litter and rubble cluttered the narrow alleyways beyond. Lizards stalking flies, crawled over the walls. Difficult to police, I figured. I put this point to Tim.

He looked back at me earnestly. "I know what you mean. It's a proper rabbit warren of a place. You'd think a man might be robbed, stripped bare and the culprits run away down a network of alleys. But the strange thing is it's just not like that. St. Jacques is a law abiding place with nothing of that sort going on."

It was difficult to take all that in. Bolt holes all over the place if things got difficult but the people full of goodwill. The boisterousness, the clamour, the vivid colours of the women's dresses were all alluring. I was sure Tim knew what he was talking about: crime was just not a big problem. Fire might be, I guessed, with all these wooden structures though some had steps down to basements hinting at coolness; but Tim didn't speak of it. Nonetheless I was glad Worrell had fixed me up with a cabin in the hills.

My background briefing paper told me that St. Jacques had been a French trading post as early as 1680, and before that it was a Spanish colonial outstation. Then Admiral Rodney took it for Britain in 1778 before it reverted to the French in whose hands it stayed until the British took it back again in 1808, this time for keeps. There was little visible sign of French influence though I understood Creole was still spoken by some of the Islanders.

I watched the stir of life from the solitude of Tim's car. In the town's market place hundreds of people, apparently with no road sense, were moving around creating a great babbling chatter. The air was full of the whining of beggars as well as the cries of fruit sellers and other stall holders selling baskets, carvings, spices, LPs, T shirts and all sorts of *bric à brac*. It was only as you got closer to the harbour front that you became aware of St. Jacques's more commercial side with a panorama of docks, freight offices and cranes idling by, all with a supporting cast of refuse and bottles. There was a line of houses, rotting picturesquely. Here too a few fishing boats bobbed at anchor. St. Jacques was evidently a muddle of accretions centring on the harbour. Unromantic, glistening, circular petrol tanks stood nearby the harbour while, not far away, a line of coconut palms swayed slightly in the sea breeze.

Most offices and the large central market were close to the dockside. So too was a lively fish market, slaughterhouse, some bars and gambling dens along with garish shop fronts daubed in bright colours. I noted a bank, a pharmacy, at least one grocer and the inevitable, ubiquitous Coca-Cola signs. We parked up and climbed out of the Vauxhall to help me catch the pulse of the place. Straightaway I winced in pain as my face and forearms took the full force of the tropical sun.

There was little traffic around the harbour itself which stood idling. A handsome cargo ship was docked; big and imposing, it awaited its goods. The flag at the masthead, sporting a resplendent blue anchor, lifted gently in the breeze. Far away I caught a glimpse of tiny islands, looking like tiny rocks in the sea. A scattering of men stood by the dockside in the shade of harbour buildings, chatting and evidently waiting for something. In fact they looked as if they had wholly mastered the art of waiting. Abruptly, I realised I was quite unfamiliar with all this, afraid of the enormity of the task that lay before me, unsure I was up to it. I knew I must do better than that. Vaguely, across the harbour from us I had the impression of unusual movement among the crowds but I was too new and too far away to attach much importance to it. Tim was casting his eyes over the women, radiant in their flamboyant costumes.

"Looks a nice place," I said, smiling affably. An understatement. I drank it all in, feeling now a deep intoxication of living, a warmth even for the low life.

I was still too young to be gripped by cynicism or a yearning for home.

But Tim, who had started treading heavily up and down, was not in the mood for exchanging pleasantries. "I'm glad you think that way. If only things were so simple. I'm afraid we'd better be going," Tim said. "The demo is due here soon. I'd rather we didn't get mixed up in it."

"Whatever you say. What's it about anyway?" I asked, hearing for the first time the cries of fierce, indignant voices, my eyes still glued to the colour and movement of the crowds.

"Plantation workers," Tim said. "They've set up a co-operative on their own but now *Allied Fruit* have stepped in, doing deals with the shipping companies. They've stopped the co-operative from exporting. Unless they can get someone to carry their stuff they will go bankrupt and pretty damned quick at that."

I was flabbergasted. *Allied Fruit* were a big banana company of course, importing vast amounts into Europe and North America but it never occurred to me that they would stoop so low to crush rivals. If the locals couldn't get the crops out and on sale in Britain, then it wasn't going to be long before everything was lost. The workers were facing ruin and whole communities with them. I said as much and Tim grunted. "The old, old story. 'Love of money is the root of all evil.' The Bible's right. But there's something else too. Some of those fat cats at *Allied Fruit* don't give a fuck about plantation workers. For two pence they'd go back to the age of slavery. It's racialism plain and simple." Tim's small, circular eyes blazed ahead, his usually frivolous temperament contradicted by a serious mood.

"So how's it work?" I asked, solicitous.

"Usually? Simple. The plantation owners reign at the top, often from afar. Then come the estate managers, the real hands-on directors of the plantations who supervise the work. They're white. The plantation labourers are black. They have little job security and poor pay but have to be grateful for what they can get. That's the norm. But a sympathetic landowner gave land to the workers at a knock-down price and they set up a co-operative. It's really bugging *Allied Fruit*." His face changed as he spoke, becoming harder, more trenchant. For the first time I was conscious of a great energy beneath his emollient attitude.

Just then I thought I heard something, the grinding of brakes coming to a halt. A black Cadillac had slid up behind us. The door opened. A tall black man, immaculately suited and sporting a pair of sunglasses emerged. He straightened himself up, looked at me as if the look alone were a message, then he averted his gaze, staring instead at the bobbing water craft. The figure was doing nothing wrong but I felt a shiver run down my back as my intuition told me that the presence of this man was no coincidence, that he was looking for me. He was so out of place. Not just him and his smart city clothes but the expensive American car. It was some sort of statement. A statement I felt was for me. Surely not. Yet I couldn't stop a sudden cold prickling feeling running across my skin. A small part of me wouldn't stop whispering a warning that someone was looking for me, following me, maybe even hunting me.

"See that!" Tim said, nudging me, his eyes focussed on the horizon. I turned back to follow his gaze, dismissing the silent figure behind. There was nothing at first but then I heard something, the grumble of a crowd in the distance. For a moment everything was still as if waiting for some sort of confirmation. It made me uneasy. I looked around. Huddles of people were standing around, gossiping, gesticulating. It looked almost like a normal crowd but not quite. Tim was looking up the street anxiously. A police van zoomed by. I could feel the tension tighten around the milling crowds. Another rumble and then the spell was broken. Now we could hear the voices of distant chanting crowds, their clamour growing louder, a dull rumbling like the low growling of a dog which might turn dangerous in an instant. Then a flood of protestors poured towards us, their cries growing more distinctive. "*Allied Fruit* Out! Out! Out!" over and over again. Placards proclaimed "*Right to Work*" and "*Let Our Produce Out!*"

Urged by a friendly prod, I got back in the car. Tim wasn't taking any chances. Even he had turned his attention from the women. Instead, he slipped the car into reverse, did a three point turn and exited the way we had come. He was barely in time. A wall of angry young faces surged towards us. Crowds were pushing near us. A handful, not many, started throwing anything they could get a hold of at the Port Authority offices: flower pots, brickbats, bottles, broken chairs... the lot. A stone pinged off our bonnet. As we made our escape a different feeling came over me: a sense of exhilaration, almost of freedom, of living life at the edge.

As Tim swung the car northwards my eyes looked again at the waterfront with its colourful main squares and streets plumed with fir trees; and the imposing Old

Fort, its walls covered with cracks, political scrawls and weeds. Then it was gone and we were speeding northwards, moving away from the capital as the sun beat down on scores of corrugated roofs.

8

"Sorry you had to see that, boss. I wasn't meaning to put you in harm's way," Tim said as we cruised down the road.

"No harm. I want to get the island's pulse," I said truthfully enough. "At least now I know there's real anger out there."

"Sure thing." Tim smiled, raising his eyes to mine, ambiguously innocent and knowing. "Just goes to show: there's always an upside to everything."

I laughed but I could see that this was serious stuff especially for a small place like St. Eleanor. What I couldn't afford to lose sight of was that by heritage all St. Eleanorians were part of this story. The plantations had been fostered by the colonial authorities and black people had worked round the clock, six days a week to sustain them. Feelings were bound to run high if anyone tampered with plantation business. Things may be getting better but even that wasn't sure. The island's economy was improving: sugar, cashew nuts and pineapples were harvested; tourism was developing, if only because jet travel was growing; new glass offices were nurturing a different type of worker in the capital. But it was the newly fought-for and so proudly defended workers' co-operative which symbolised the battle for the souls of the islanders. This could be a protracted and bitter conflict indeed.

I was pondering this when after only about fifteen minutes of easy driving we came to the village of Babonneau, huddled in to the central hills on outcrops of rock and scrub with lots of fresh water on hand and sweeping hill views. There could be no denying the magic of the place. Even the bedraggled little houses with their rusty roofs looked as if they hugged a delightful secret life of their own, the scene reminding me of a Monet painting with the street of bright colour painted on to other blocks of bright colour. Tim brought us to a halt near a small café called simply *Chez Ginette*, suggesting it was time for something to eat. We made our way over, slaloming between some stalls of cassava, papayas and peanuts.

"Good afternoon...what can I get you?" a middle aged woman enquired politely before her face broke into a smile as she recognised Tim. "Ah, it's you...I didn't see you there," she said, talking to Tim. The lady, Ginette, was the proprietor but also Tim's aunt. Her hair was adorned by a *tignon*, a popular knotted female head-dress made from cotton and patterned blue.

Tim leaned his face closer to mine and said in a stage whisper: "Relax, Bruce; enjoy yourself while you're here. I don't mind telling you Auntie Ginette once taught me an important lesson in life. We are all free to choose our attitudes."

Ginette laughed boisterously and said: "Oh he was a fine young tearaway!" But right now it was she who radiated such an air of vitality, helped by her bright eyes and the thick black hair which sprang from her head in such profusion. After a few moments of banter she went back with her order. Tim went on talking about his youth, his mother's early death from cancer and his estrangement from his father, a tough ship worker and how he was bleeding inside. Tim had become something of a delinquent but Ginette's shrewd stewardship had turned him around. He had made it his mark to make all well with his father while he was still in the world and had even joined the police. Ginette returned soon with our fresh soup and a warm smile.

We had sat down at an outside table with a view of the tropical forests on one side and of the ocean on the other. Tim smoothed his hair down with his hands, making sure nothing was out of place. Palm trees littered the shoreline, and beyond them the glittering, blue sea. A sweet fragrance of jasmine hung in the air and bright red bougainvillea fell over the wall of our café. We had barely finished our vegetable soup, when Ginette served us with fresh fish, caught that very morning.

"You have never been in the tropics before?" Tim asked.

"It's really very good, mmm…very tasty…Yes, I have been in West Africa, a brief sojourn in Accra but that was all very different from here. I've wanted to see the Caribbean for a long time. This place your Aunt's you say?"

"Yes. Auntie Ginette runs one of the finest eating establishments on the island. I like to visit whenever I have a chance. I'm a real St. Eleanorean you know."

"You come from here? That's what you mean?"

"Born and bred as they say. I guess that's why Frank wants me to show you around. I know St. Eleanor well. You'll find it's not a community, just a nest of rattle-snakes…" But he was smiling at his own quip as he said it, contradicting himself. I took a liking to Tim. On first acquaintance he appeared carefree, lightweight even.

But there was a kind of remote professional detachment behind the easy smile as well.

Around us was the buzz of a happy meeting place with its multiple conversations, the clinking of glasses and the shifting of chairs. I was relaxed by the cheery atmosphere, pleased that Tim had brought me here. Suddenly I got a start. It was the curious figure from the Cadillac, the one who had appeared so out of place at the harbour. We were being followed. It was creepy. But wait a moment. Could I be wrong? He looked similar but maybe it was someone else after all. A lookalike? Maybe. I relaxed and decided not to say anything to Tim. Something about him niggled though. The man who had appeared that morning was like a harbinger of an ill-omened fate. He had been intent on some mission, probably not his own. There would have been something altogether freakish about his sudden re-appearance. Yet here the diners were all focussed on their pleasures, their meals and drinks, chatting, laughing. It could not be less sinister. On the other hand, look again, what would I know? The whole place could be crowded with crooks of all stripes and I couldn't tell. It just went to show that if the First Minister had been murdered all the murderer had to do was keep his mouth shut and he'd be in no real trouble. Don't talk, don't explain, say nothing and no one will catch him.

Finally, sated by our lunch and our chat we resumed our trek. Scattered trees appeared, offshoots from the jungle mountains, overshadowing the road for many furlongs. On my right rose mighty jagged volcanic mountains, silent now and wisped with cloud; on the other warm and gentle sandy bays fronted a sea stretching into infinity. As our road rolled eastwards along the coastline we could see white cascades falling straight down from the distant mountains, as if drawn by a single brush stroke.

Wild ginger perfumed the air, mist boiled up out of the valleys, tropical colours startled in their intensity. Vivid splashes of red and purples crowded under overhanging expanses of green; and beyond them the ultramarine of the sea and the endless blue of the sky. Only a few people were out of doors and nothing stirred yet still I found the villages – fishing ones mainly – delightful in their way, with remnants of French provincial architecture in view and restful tranquillity on offer. All human habitation seemed to be focussed around the coastal margins. Some magnificent tree ferns too, relics of prehistoric times.

The interior was given over mainly to dense equatorial rain forest, occasionally lit up by the orange-red blossoms or darkened by a mighty mouthed hollow. The forest was often hilly too, especially in the West where there were the huge volcanic mountains, visible from my cabin. Here and there, perched high in the hills you could glimpse a rich man's house. Less agreeably, there were often half completed concrete skeletons of buildings, begun but never finished. Dusty trails led into the wild interior.

Strangest of all, I once saw a huddle of houses way up a mountainside, well above the treeline on lime green hills bathed in lemon light. I asked about them but Tim only laughed, explaining that they were built by drop-outs, people well beyond the reach of taxation and society's demands.

"Broken men," he said "with no visible means of support, no home, no allegiances."

"Criminals?" I asked.

"Not really. They live on the margins and everyone is suspicious of them. They can be put in the frame for anything but that's just talk. They don't harm anyone."

"Looks pretty inaccessible to me. How do they live?"

"They can grow a few things, I guess, but some of them do come down from time to time. Look over there!" I followed the direction of his pointing finger. "You see that torrent. There's a very rough trail that climbs up just beside it. It can be pretty well used all year round. You would be surprised how many times people make the trip up to *Libreville*. That's what they call their little shelters."

I looked at the waterfall opposite, and saw the outlines of a track, winding up a very steep mountainside until it got lost in the folds of rock. We drove on. Occasionally the hills were intersected by little villages which, here and there opened onto broad, fertile valleys cultivated by plantations of bananas, pineapples, sugar cane and cacao. For a while, I stared captivated by the rows of bananas and the little figures who patrolled the aisles, tending them. It was getting to late afternoon when we turned tail for home. The sun had begun to glow orange and the jungle reflected back a luxuriant spinach green against a rust laden sky.

BACK AT THE STATION I found the bright sunlight of the day giving way to a wearisome heaviness. There was no breeze now, only heat. While enjoying the reviving qualities of my cuppa I pondered once more the street disturbance and Tim's words. Of course racialism was at the back of this. Racialism as well as greed and it went back, way beyond the present banana dispute. In St Eleanor this had been marked by a kind of racial hierarchy with the whites at the top, coloured people next and the black population at the bottom. By the time I was there in the nineteen sixties this regime had been well and truly battered but many retained the same social attitudes and resentments. There was still much simmering hostility to the traditional arrogance of the British and against the local whites. Who could blame them? Would it prove relevant to the death of the First Minister, he who I had heard Worrell say was an outspoken advocate of Federalism.

This gave me another unpleasant thought, one which I decided to have out with Frank at the outset rather than have it pollute our relationship. Until very recently black people had not been promoted to inspector rank as a matter of policy. Of course this was neither my fault, nor something I would ever have supported but no doubt these things rankled. West Indian constables at that time rarely even had the benefit of a good secondary education. So it would not be surprising if there were sometimes a latent hostility beneath the surface of things. Yet I needed these people if I were to get anywhere.

"Tell me, Frank," I asked once I was ensconced again in a rattan chair in his office, "is there any resentment here. In the local Force, I mean, to my coming out here to take over the investigation. After all, I wouldn't be too surprised and I would like to know the ....." My words were broken off by the sound of Frank's laughter.

"No," Frank said. "Guys like Tim and my colleagues are just relieved to pass the baby. This is a political case. There's been too much blasted complacency about this case for my taste. You Scotland Yard guys – we've heard all about you – you have the know-how, you'll settle the mystery for us and you're welcome! Make no mistake! And we'll be glad to get back to our work with drunks and vandals and bicycle theft!"

I was relieved and found myself rubbing my brow only to see Frank staring at me intently. "Look. Racialism matters but there's other things more important which you might mistake for it," he said. "I hope you won't take it amiss if I give you one or two words of advice which I know may sound obvious." He looked momentarily embarrassed. "But there again what's obvious to us may not be so obvious to Europeans and I don't want to take chances. So no offence meant."

"None taken," I said. "Just assume I'm as dumb as they come. You won't be too far wrong probably anyway! So fire away."

"Well," he said, leaning forwards as he pulled his damp cotton shirt from his back. "Please remember to respect local customs and folks' homes, however humble; and don't ever go into the jungle unescorted. Some people have done that and never found the way out again. It may be a small island but I assure you it's big enough to get lost in!"

"I can believe that."

"There's another thing. A small thing perhaps but one you'd do well to remember and act on. Scotland Yard assigned *you* to us. You're their man, not ours. Frankly, even I don't know exactly who you are. Of course I've been sent some information by London but it doesn't really reveal anything about you, about *who* you are. You'll have to work at it to get on with people but no, there's no real hostility to you."

"Don't worry; I won't be giving myself airs and graces", I said. "I need you. I need your expertise. As for me: who am I? Well, I suppose there's no simple answer to that. In fact I've been trying to work that out most of my adult life. You know how hard it is to understand another person fully. We're all a bit of a mystery. It's not like we're characters from fiction. But we'll get to know each other well enough. Let's just give it time. I'm not going to be keeping things back from you."

"Well then, Bruce, don't worry. I'm sure we'll get along just fine."

I was relieved. This would take some careful handling if I were going to build a relationship. Perhaps my knowledge of Europeans would even be of assistance. Deacon believed that some of the Europeans had deceived Worrell, and that there may have been a conspiracy which the local police, unfamiliar with the dark science of white evasion, had not seen. "You'll see," Deacon had promised, sure of his own cunning, but I was not so certain.

LATER THAT EVENING, after a delightful casserole prepared for me by Penelope, I sat watching the shadows assembling over the coast, feeling as if I had stumbled out of my life into someone else's. It was very pleasant but strangely troublesome. Despite the pleasure of the afternoon I found the memory of that tall figure in the Cadillac would not go away. A strange pricking sensation of being watched had accompanied me on my return to the Rest House. Looking around, I saw nothing to worry about and berated myself for being so neurotic. Yet the feeling lingered. I had long learned to trust such feelings whether borne from ancient primeval instinct or experience or a mixture of the two. But today's uneasiness was surely the exception.

After all, I was certainly being well looked after. Penelope's meals were good hearted and cheerful, the bed was comfortable, the room adequate and the shower worked. It was all I needed. Stirring myself I thought that really I should phone Katie and try to say something sufficiently pleasing she could maybe feel it on the other end of the line, when suddenly the telephone rang. Damn and blast! Just when I was feeling so relaxed. I made for the side table where the telephone was and lifted the receiver. There was a brief crackling of transatlantic buzzing before I heard the voice on the other end.

"Bruce! It's me Katie. Not too late for you, I hope."

"No. It's fine. I was just turning in."

"Turning in? You mean you weren't going to phone me."

"Of course I was. Just a figure of speech. Anyway, here I am."

"I just wanted to check everything was going alright. Had a good flight? Settling in well and all that? We didn't have much chance to talk yesterday."

"Yesterday? I thought it was today." Oh God, would it be tomorrow there?

Katie laughed. "Transatlantic calls are cheaper during the night."

"I see," I said, momentarily remembering that Katie would be thinking of the cost of living, watching the electricity and the telephone so that the bills didn't rise too high. "Yes. Well, anyway, I'm fine. Everything's going well. I had a good flight. Today I've just been meeting people, getting to know the ropes and all that...A beautiful island."

"Good. But I'm not convinced you're that pressed for time that you couldn't have phoned."

"It's my work keeping me distracted."

"If you ask me, your work is much more likely to suffer if you don't keep in touch with your family."

"How are the children?"

"Laura and Andrew send you their love. They're asleep now." There was a brief pause while I imbibed these facts. "Look Brucie," Katie spoke more softly now. "You haven't forgotten your promise. Don't take longer than it takes..."

"I won't. Never fear. The mosquitoes are killing me." The one thing I was certain of, hearing Katie's voice over the long trans-Atlantic telephone line, the ghost of a voice whose inflections I knew well, was that Katie was not being overwhelmed by her single handed combat with domestic responsibilities. We chatted inconsequentially and I felt a stab of homesickness.

"Alright," she said at last. "That's enough for now. Next time, you ring me and put it on expenses. OK?"

"I'll do that small thing. Bye, love."

"Bye. And Bruce, one other thing. I thought I'd keep the best till last. He's been as good as his word."

"Who has?"

"Onslow-Bell of course. Two and a half thousand pounds paid into our account."

"My God! I can't believe it..." There was a short pause.

"Yes, it's true. Our problems are over."

I really was stunned. Though it was in the agreement the reality was of a different order. We weren't just solvent again: we were rich.

9

THE NEXT MORNING DAWNED bright and clear. Buoyed up by last night's good news I drove down the steep descent into Marigot Bay, to *Anse Chastenet*, official home of the First Minister. I'd fixed up the visit yesterday evening as soon as I could, more to get a feel for things than in the expectation of finding something not already in the files.

It was pleasantly warm; the languor of a tropical day just beginning. The residence was located on a small knoll overlooking Marigot Bay and surrounded by dense jungle. An affable housekeeper, the deeply bronzed Mrs. Dorothy Miller, greeted me bright eyed and smiling on the mansion's forecourt. I flashed her my warrant card but it wasn't really necessary. She was expecting me. Mrs. Miller took me over a short flagged path to the high glassed main entrance door. The outside walls were beginning to flake under the unceasing heat but it was clearly a handsome building. I lingered momentarily admiring the cerise bougainvillea before entering a long reception hall.

Dorothy Miller, who was still in residence, began by asking me what I wanted to see. I could tell that, middle aged though she was, she was used to exerting a certain authority around the house. She was quite tall and strongly built. I explained what I was doing and she told me she'd already been notified to expect me. She eyed me curiously. "I thought Woodbine Parish had already carried out that investigation?"

"Just checking up on a few things." I smiled.

"Sure you're not coming here to lay the blame on someone?"

"Nothing of the sort...Now, if I could have a look around, please."

She let it go at that which was just as well. Though I was keen to move on, I understood what her words implied: tongues had been wagging and doubt thrown on the real purposes of my investigation. But Dorothy proved helpful enough, taking me on a whirlwind tour of the house where I savoured the mansion's delights, its perfumed wooden interiors, the beautiful sea views, the long garden receding down the hill side, the study where Mr Constantine had breathed his last, a most extensive room running almost the whole length of the building. The floors were of beautifully waxed woodwork and the spacious windows looked out to sea, admitting bright sunlight. A richly embroidered carpet from India lay in the centre of the room. The rosewood desk still radiated a sense of power and mystique. Dorothy was keen to show me the locks to the building, obviously of unusual construction and opened by keys of which there were only two.

"Who else has a key?" I asked.

"Nobody. Nobody except the Police Protection unit. If there was a murderer he got in by some other means." All of this was in Woodbine Parish's original report and I had no great wish to go over all the details again. Suddenly I became aware of Mrs Miller's eyes scrutinising me closely. "Do you think he was murdered?" she asked. "That's what people are saying, you know. He was as strong as an ox."

"But he wasn't so young was he? Living isn't as easy as the young think. There are so many things which can kill us. I'm afraid we never know who may go next, the when and the why. Maybe he did well to make it so long."

Mrs Miller shrugged. I didn't linger. Instead, I took a turn outside to examine the setting. *Anse Chastenet* sat well up the hillside and was accessed only by a narrow road to the south. The sea lay to the west and pretty dense tropical forest on each side. A stream tumbled down from the east. In other words the First Minister's residence was enclosed by the hill behind it, a stream to the east, and jungle and sea elsewhere. The main entrance faced the road from the south east. I began a circumnavigation of the property from the entrance gate. For the first time I became aware of an imposing fence which bounded the property, high but not insurmountable. Dorothy had told me that the gatekeeper shut the gates at six and that there was always a policeman on duty at the gate lodge. The cleaners had a clearly defined time frame and were closely supervised by Dorothy herself. Walking up the hillside to gain a better view of the property I crossed the little stream and followed the dust laden path until it became very narrow, taking a sharp bend towards a stand of trees. Soon I came face to face with a large pond. A young woman shod in oversize rubber boots was cleaning debris and vegetation from the water. I stopped a moment and stared into the water's murky shallows.

"Are you the gardener here?" I asked.

"Yes. That's right. Leonora Peabody. Pleased to meet you."

I smiled what I hoped was encouragement and went on back down to the house where I re-joined Mrs Miller in a sitting room. Dorothy, who retained a beguiling but suitably humble demeanour had made a pot of tea, bringing it in on a tray along with some biscuits. We sat on blue cotton covered armchairs looking out on the sun lit morning. Dorothy became quite talkative, speaking neither too emotionally nor too briskly; and I was content to let her ramble.

"It's hard to understand in a way. I mean Mr Constantine not being around anymore, not being anything but the world still going on."

"Will you be staying on when Mr Jamieson moves in?" I asked. Apparently the new First Minister had shown no eagerness to relocate to the official residence, preferring to linger at his home in St. Jacques.

"I don't know. I doubt that Mr Jamieson would want me. He has his family and probably different arrangements. But Government House asked me to stay on and look after the place in the meantime. So that's what I'm doing. We shall see."

I nodded, smiling. Who would want to vacate this place quickly if there were no need? I didn't like to discommode such an obviously kindly lady but I had to work through the routine. The local police had already subjected Mrs Miller to a lot of questions. Describe exactly what happened in your own words. Was the First Minister looking well? Were you aware of any personal rows? Had he had any issues with his dosage before? What had he last spoken about? No, you are not under suspicion. We have to ask these questions.

What was he working on at the moment? Describe how you found the body. Start again at the beginning.

"Well, it was a normal morning, just like any other. He liked an early morning tea at seven. I made up the tray and brought it to Warwick's study where he usually had it. But when I entered there he was! Sprawled across the desk. I knew straightaway he was dead. It's a funny thing life isn't it? When it's gone, you just know don't you? You know it's left. Mind you that didn't stop me. I shook him and when there was no response I phoned for an ambulance. Then I phoned the Duty Officer of the Police Protection Unit."

"The one at the gate?"

"That's correct. That is standard procedure if anything untoward happens. But the next thing I knew it wasn't the police who came it was a doctor, one assigned from Government House. The policeman, Woodbine Parish came a good half hour later."

Everything Mrs Miller said simply confirmed what she had already told the police but with different phrasing, nothing rehearsed, usually an indicator of honesty. Between midnight and dawn the First Minister of St. Eleanor, Warwick Constantine, died at his home in *Anse Chastenet*. A widower in his early sixties, he died alone. Dorothy, the elderly long-serving domestic, discovered him at seven in the morning when she had brought the First Minister his customary morning tea, only to find him, fully dressed but totally oblivious to the world and staring empty-minded out of the window. She had put the tea down carefully, crossed herself, telephoned the head of the special police protection unit who had then evidently telephoned Inspector Woodbine Parish of the Royal St. Eleanor Police.

"Well thank you very much, Dorothy." I smiled. "I think that about wraps it up. I needn't impinge on your time any more." I half rose to go when some activity beyond the windows captured my eyes. A small huddle of gardeners were working in a shady part of the garden not far from the mansion. Following my gaze Dorothy explained that two of them were rescued drug addicts in the wreckage of their youth ostensibly assisting Leonara, the incredibly thin, wiry gardener. The saved youths were there on the ex-First Minister's insistence but I could tell they were of no use to the real gardener who was struggling to make the simplest of instructions understood. Sadly, insensitive to the incredible fertility all around them, they saw their travails only as chores to be skimped.

"There's one thing, though, that puzzles me, Chief Inspector," Dorothy was saying.

"And what's that?"

"Who killed Warwick?"

"The death certificate says cardiac arrest."

"We all die from that," she laughed. "But who poisoned him?"

"There is no evidence of foul play."

"Then why are the police still asking questions?"

"Just routine procedures, Dorothy. We have to do these things. Mr Constantine was a very important man. The tees have to be crossed and the ayes dotted." I smiled but I could see she wasn't convinced. A wise old bird, this one. She knew very well that many of our procedures were built on sand and were as movable as the tides.

"I'm not convinced you'd come all the way from England just to follow a procedural point. No, I can't believe that's true. Life has taught me, Mr Inspector, that nothing is straightforward. Nothing is simple"

I smiled sadly, wondering if Dorothy had said this as naturally as it had seemed or had she been pondering Constantine's death and wanted in some way to plant ideas in my head? As his housekeeper she had acquired enough experience of him and his ways to suspect that something was amiss.

"Well, Mrs Miller, as you raise such a disturbing possibility, do you know if Mr Constantine had any enemies?" I asked as conversationally as I could manage.

"Not that I know of. But I do know that Warwick was a good man. I think *Anse Chastenet* may have been the only place where he could truly relax."

"Could you explain that a little more?"

"Well, just that. He was out at work most times either in the office or touring around people and places. Sometimes he went to London. Sometimes to Kingston. But the pressures always seemed to fall off him like a discarded coat when he came back. You see, he could be at ease here. He liked my plain cooking and we accepted each other at face value. He could really unwind here."

"I can believe that. And nothing more at all to say about your recollections of that horrible day?" I asked.

"Well no. Of course not. Just a shock. The overdose I mean. He took sleeping pills most nights. Its strange that he got it so wrong. Perhaps eating out hadn't been a good idea. Maybe the wine confused him. Then there's yourselves of course. Police asking so many questions. That makes you wonder what had gone on. And what has happened to Woodbine Parish? He was a good man. Then there was the removal of his papers –"

"What? What papers?"

"All his personal papers were removed from his desk. I never saw anyone do it but they've all gone."

We returned to the study. I examined his desk. It was clear. There remained only an address book but very little else. The drawers were empty. I didn't doubt she was right. Somebody had been through his desk.

"So who took them? Someone from his office? Do you know?"

"You did, of course. Must have been."

This threw me. I must have looked non-plussed for she immediately added: "Not you personally of course. But I think it must have been that young man from the Governor's Residence, Mr. Oppenheimer."

This puzzled me. I could see that the First Minister's Office might need to recover any official confidential documents but from everything Dorothy had said his desk was full of personal papers. Besides, Jake Oppenheimer, so far as I understood it, worked with the Governor not the First Minister; and the British were disengaging. "Are you sure about this?," I asked as casually as possible. "Maybe he had thrown his papers out."

"Never. Mr Constantine was more anxious about the safety of his papers than he was about himself."

We paused. "What is it you are getting at, Mrs Miller?" I asked. "Why are you so certain papers were stolen?" It was only then that I became aware of something else in Mrs Miller's manner which I had not noticed before, something hurt and wary, suggesting she had more awareness of the evils of the world than I had thought.

"Oh, I don't really know. Don't worry," she said. She looked blank. Then she turned away from me slowly and looked out of the window but she wasn't focussing on anything in particular. Gone now was the polite deference and veil of diffidence between us: something new had entered our conversation. We were alert and keen to get to the bottom of things.

"I've given a lot of thinking to it and, you know, I think we never fully understand someone else even when we have known them for years. And you know what I think?" She tossed her head as she spoke.

"No but please tell me."

"I think there's something else to this sordid tale that we have no inkling of."

"I daresay you're right but we'll get there in the end."

"No, Chief Inspector, you misunderstand me. I think the intruder may have stolen something else from this house on the night of the murder after all."

"But you said nothing was taken, that you'd checked most meticulously."

"So I did and that's what I told Detective Woodbine Parish but I've been thinking since then that there's more to this than meets the eye."

"What do you think it was?"

"I really don't know. I searched and could find nothing out of order. He kept no official secrets here, I'm pretty sure but something was taken. That's what I think anyway."

"But you have no idea what?"

Dorothy shook her head sadly.

"And why do you think something was taken?"

"His study was ever so slightly disarranged."

"As if someone had been looking for something?"

"Precisely."

"I see no reference to that in our records."

"Probably because I said nothing to the police at the time. You see the disturbance was so slight I couldn't be certain that Warwick himself was not responsible."

"Aha. Yes, that would be unfortunate. And in the event, you are not aware of anything missing apart from the papers on his desk. And that was later."

"No but if it were some secret sort of papers then I suppose I wouldn't be."

So that was it. Probably as far as we could go for now but we had perhaps discerned the shadow of a tiger in the room, a tiger no one had noticed before now but one ready to pounce. Yet where could I go with this nagging suspicion? For the life of me I couldn't see why Oppenheimer would take even his official papers, never mind his personal ones. I would have to ask him outright. But then a picture of Briscoe's warnings in that dingy London pub floated back. Yes I was supposed to be the investigating officer but I'd better tread carefully or I could be dealing with matters well above my pay grade. I could contact the Governor's Residence and ask to speak to Oppenheimer but that might carry explosive consequences. I certainly could not afford to let it be known to a wider audience that the First Minister's papers were missing. That would provoke more unwanted questions about his sudden death and burial. And, of course, there were people in the Residency including Oppenheimer himself who could suffocate and bury me forever in silence and cotton wool if they took against me. Despite what Briscoe had said I had indeed learnt some lessons from the *North Star* fiasco.

"Do you recall what these papers looked like?" I asked.

"Well, I wasn't snooping but they were official papers and personal ones, I think. He often worked on them at home. Nothing I can specifically recall but there was a sky blue coloured file he had been looking at for several days. What it was about I have no idea."

"Thank you Mrs Miller. You have been most helpful. And who had Mr Constantine been dining out with the previous evening? Some big occasion?" I asked. It was a blind of course. I already knew. The answer had been in the file compiled by Woodbine Parish.

"Hardly. That newspaperman, Quentin Quillham."

I LEFT *ANSE CHASTENET* feeling exhilarated that I was doing something worthwhile and looking forward to meeting the Quillhams. I swung out past the police guard house and back on to the road leading north west to the capital until I came to a point on the hill high above the First Minister's residence. Spotting a rough patch by the roadside which had obviously served as a kind of lay by I came to an abrupt halt and climbed out to observe the landscape more closely.

I breathed in the sea air and looked down on *Anse Chastenet*, nestling below and shining like gold against the dark drift of the surrounding tropical forest. For the first time I noticed to its rear a store house, expansive garages and a garden shed. The whole complex was more to conceptualise than I had initially thought; and that brought with it a myriad of possibilities. To the right the estate abutted the jungle, its border defined by a stout six foot high chain link fence, rusty perhaps but firm. But it probably was scaleable; and approachable from here. On the sea side of the house, gardens cascaded westwards and beyond that, a short expanse of open ground until you reached the unscaleable cliff tops. The view brought mixed feelings. The place certainly looked impenetrable but that was all. I sighed. A possibility of foul play would mean that I must examine some of the minutiae of West Indian politics; and that kind of thing always risked stirring a hornets' nest.

10

WHEN I REACHED ST. JACQUES I drove through the town centre, soon finding myself in the Hawke's Bay area where sprawling, comfortable bungalows, mown grass and bright gardens presented a little enclave of order in defiance of the casual sprawl of the capital; a correct, suburban island in a sea of unconcern. Most British and other foreigners lived hereabouts, near or around the island's premier golf course where colourful squalor gave way to colourful opulence, the narrow streets to wide newly tarmacadamed roads. Bright pink, green and yellow houses, many with lime green shutters dotted the hillside. Expensive looking hotels clustered near to the old harbour where halyards slapped against the flag poles in the gentle sea breeze. Lucy's instructions had been very clear and it wasn't hard to find my way to *The Spyglass*, a substantial two storey house set in a new but mature street behind large, lush cascading hill gardens.

I hadn't said anything more about the Quillhams to Dorothy but Quentin had been cited in my backgrounder put together by Woodbine Parish. Warwick Constantine had dined with the couple on his last free evening. I parked nearby, almost opposite the Quillhams' substantial residence. There was a high white wall around it. Bougainvillea creepers covered large parts of it, cerise flowers gleaming in the sun. Hardly a breath of air stirred and the sunlight dazzled me as I made my way to the whitewashed building. It all looked so innocent. As I stepped on to the yellow path I noticed another Land Rover, older than mine, parked nearby. An elderly European man sat in the rear, reading a paper. I thought nothing of it. Then just as I reached the door a white woman – a young woman – came tearing out in a great hurry. She was dressed in tattered jeans and a rather scruffy T shirt with a safari hat pulled down over her eyes. I scarcely had time to take the huddled figure in before she crashed past me. As I turned to see where she was going she jumped into the Land Rover and a moment later it had made a U turn at speed back to the main road. I shook my head, puzzled; and knocked.

My jostling thoughts were further disturbed when the door swung open and a dark haired woman stood before me. "Chief Inspector Cordell?" she asked.

Straightaway, my preconceptions were blown away. I had expected to meet a woman perhaps grey haired and dressed formally. She was in her mid-forties, her eyes sharp and cutting. After the exchange of introductions Mrs Chantelle Quillham smiled and stepped aside. Briefly her gaze flitted between my face and my shoes as if she were weighing me up in some peculiar way of her own. "Please come in", she said. "Thanks for coming. My husband will be down in a minute. This way, please." I wiped my feet and followed her into a bright sunny drawing room festooned with cacti and other thick leaved green plants. Shadows reached across the wooden floor from the garden, the trees outside looking as if they wished to rest their burden there. Otherwise it was a living room which could have been anywhere in the Home Counties complete with stereo, upholstered sofa and lace curtains. Only the brightness of the daylight betrayed its real venue.

"Please take a seat," she said, gesturing me towards an armchair. I sat down. A slim young black woman appeared soundlessly. "Tea? Coffee? What's your pleasure Inspector Cordell? I've got some *Lapsong Suchong* left...."

"Oh, that'll be lovely. Yes, thanks." The young woman disappeared as quietly as she had entered. I noticed for the first time how tidy the room was, if cluttered, but she evidently had a housekeeper. "But I'd just as soon get straight on if it's all the same to you. Thank you for seeing me. I know it must be an awful business for you as it is for everyone. It's just the pair of you who were the last to see Mr Constantine socially..."

"That's alright. No need to apologise. Here we go again! Ever since Warwick's death people have been asking me about him. I must have met a dozen people and it's been Constantine this and Constantine that. What on earth do people expect me to tell them. But don't worry, Chief Inspector," she put her hands up in mock appeasement. "I wish to help you as much as I can. Your assistant explained everything on the phone and I'm not a child. Sudden deaths are bound to hurt everyone involved. I know that. And yes, we considered ourselves to be among Warwick's friends. I must admit I'm still having difficulty coming to terms with it. I suppose it's the way it happened. Such a shock and, you know, it's not as if you could say 'Goodbye.'"

"No, indeed. A terrible business. He was a friend?"

"I hadn't put him down as a close one but I suppose, yes, he was." She looked solemn, reflecting perhaps that Constantine's death represented the loss of a friend as well as a First Minister. Myself, I was unable to find anything else to say but I sensed her grief was overlaid by something else: a hardness of mind if not of expression. I studied her intently for signs of dissimulation or guilt but there was a mystery in her face which I could not decode. I felt she had something to tell me but, as all policemen are trained to do, I would have to wait until she told me in her own good time.

A silver platter of tea, milk, sugar and cups appeared and were set out before me. Chantelle poured out two cups of tea through a strainer. "No sugar for me. Thank you..." I took a sip of tea and purred with delight. It was no doubt considered refined and fragrant. "Lovely, Mrs Quillham. Just the way I like it," I said as I sipped it. Looking around the room with all the pleasing furniture and paintings I couldn't help but feel that pleasant though it was, it all really belonged back in England. What was she doing here? This was no ordinary household. The Quillhams employed a housekeeper who doubled up as a cook, a washerwoman, a gardener and had even been known to hire a chauffeur on a part-time basis – all, of course, on the low wages which were prevalent at that time. Yet for all that, Chantelle was evidently a woman of progressive views, an avowed enemy of prejudice and well disposed to everything new that she considered 'progressive'. On the coffee table I noticed a copy of the *New Statesman*.

"I don't know what's keeping him!" Chantelle said suddenly. "Honestly, Quentin is a workaholic. He knows very well you're waiting for him. I'll get him!"

She made to stand up but I gestured my palm downwards. "It's alright, Mrs Quillham. I can wait while he finishes what he does. Besides I'm more than happy to talk to you about how you became friends with Mr Constantine and in fact, how on earth, you ever ended up in this little corner of the world."

Needing no more prompting Chantelle gave me a short autobiographical account of herself. Originally from Alton in Hampshire she had met Quentin Quillham while he was working in Fleet Street shortly before the War. She herself had enjoyed a short-lived career as a graphical artist with a small printing company but had rather buried her talents on becoming, first, a married woman and then a mother. Only in recent years had she revisited her early enthusiasms, opening an art gallery in St. Jacques which had proved surprisingly successful, and now helping to start up a new publication, *Caribbean Currents*.

"An art gallery!" I asked, a little surprised.

Chantelle smiled. "Well, more a kind of anti-art gallery," she explained. "We stock all sorts of things. Our focus is on Caribbean art of all sorts. Paintings, carvings, trinkets, wooden constructions..." The gallery was not only drawing visitors but, by encouraging local talent, had become popular with St. Eleanorians. Now its exhibitions and artist launches were firmly established in the capital's calendar. "We like to think it has become the focal point for arts on the island. The islanders love it. But when a cruise ship comes in the first thing they want to do is hit the bars and shops. So it's become an earner as well..."

"That sounds like good business."

"You must visit some day, Chief Inspector. You'd be most welcome."

"Thanks. I'll take you up on that." Yet I couldn't help observing that despite her loquaciousness she hadn't been too anxious to give me a detailed explanation of her work. I asked about their new magazine. She said it had grown naturally from her art work. From there they had started to put together the basis of a new magazine for the island community. It would be a ground breaking magazine written largely by West Indians for West Indians and mixing glamour, sex, arts and international political issues. At least that was the plan. And that is how their acquaintanceship with Warwick Constantine had grown and prospered. He was a keen supporter of the concept, seeing how it could help build local self-confidence, combat false stories, and provide support to aspiring local students, artists and politicians.

Next she indicated some family photos on the sideboard. There was one of Chantelle and Quentin together with two young people. Their children, I guessed. I asked about it. Chantelle remembered when the picture was taken. They still lived in London then. Yes, there were two children, the youngest of whom, Anne, had made a lucrative marriage into a commercial family, lived in the Home Counties, and had two children of her own. Michael was a moderately successful accountant in London. Suddenly, I heard a bellow from the top of the stairs; immediately accompanied by a heavy tread. A middle aged man with iron grey hair poked his head in the door looking around slowly in a watchful almost reptilian way. I jumped up and thrust my hand out saying, "Chief Inspector Cordell. So pleased to meet you!"

He grasped me warmly and we sat down again but I couldn't help noticing that Quillham was breathing heavily like someone who was out of breath but trying to disguise it. Chantelle took this moment to absent herself, busying herself with something in the house. Was it something she always did when her husband went into a confab with a visitor? "Understand you want to know what we talked about with the old boy, the night before he died?" Quillham asked rather brusquely when we were alone.

"Yes. I think that might be helpful. We've already talked about it – your wife and me I mean – but I'd like to hear what you have to say."

"Well first of all I take it this bit about a sleeping pill accidental overdose is seriously in doubt is it? Interesting." He emanated doubt.

"No. It isn't really" I explained. "We just need to check out everything. A sudden death of the First Minister doesn't happen every day. There are a lot of loose threads we have to tie up if government is to continue smoothly."

Quillham suddenly looked a little withdrawn, contemplative even. Only his eyes were alive, bright and lustrous, strangely penetrating. But he sat quietly while I explained in more detail what it was I wanted; what it was they had spoken of during that last fateful evening, if there were important aspects of policy he was particularly immersed in, if indeed he had any grounds to believe anything was seriously amiss with the First Minister.

"You see we have to ask certain questions. Why, for example, would such a successful and accomplished man take his own life or, more likely, be so reckless with the risks of such a large and lethal use of sleeping pills? But first, if you don't mind, I'm interested in how you became friends of the First Minister."

"What do you mean?"

"Well, it's not obvious why you should get together for such a friendly dinner."

He shook his head and smiled. "Some detective you are, if you don't mind me saying. Don't you know anything about my past?"

"Tell me."

"Simple enough. After the partition I was doing a lot of odds and ends for a number of Fleet Street papers. There was a growing consensus that the Empire was finished. I did one or two pieces on emerging African leaders and while I was doing them I found it useful to go along to the Royal Commonwealth Society in the West End. It's more like a Club really, you know what I mean. Anyway lots of emerging African leaders used to visit there, passing through London. Anyway, I hung about the bar and made a few useful acquaintances. The King of Swaziland for one. He was only a kid then, of course. It's amazing how easy networking is in a place like that. Anyway, once over, Warwick Constantine was staying there, probably attending some conference. It doesn't really matter but that's when we met. Well, we kept in touch even when he moved up in the world. It may even have influenced our decision to move here rather than, say, St. Lucia or Grenada. Naturally, when we arrived we contacted the Constantines and I'm pleased to say they were happy to renew our friendship despite his workload. Then, of course, we came up with this idea of an arts mag for the West Indies. The rest as they say...is history."

"I see. Thanks for filling me in on that. Most interesting. So going back to the last dinner could I ask whether he said anything at all which showed his preoccupations that evening?"

"No and yes."

"No and yes?"

"He didn't say anything out of order...no confidences... nothing like that. The dinner was at our invitation but I think he was glad of a little respite from his work. I had written a little piece for a London paper on St. Eleanor's prospects after independence and I wanted his clearance. I didn't want him to feel misquoted. I showed him the copy and he was happy enough with it."

"Nothing more?" I prompted.

"No. But since you contacted me I've been giving the matter more thought. He did ramble on about the sea. The sapphire sea...he was a bit of a poet you know...and did I ever consider the exotic life which pulsed and shimmered beneath it...and he spoke of an underwater channel deep below." Quillham laughed at the memory. "I didn't rate it particularly at the time but he seemed to be making a point of it. Maybe he wanted to...maybe he knew how things would work out."

"Did he strike you as depressed?"

"Not clinically but yes, perhaps, he had succumbed to a certain weariness of spirit. Depression if you like but only in the everyday sense. Nothing drastic. I asked him outright. I said you strike me as looking a bit down. No, he said, it was just work tiring him. That's why he was dining with us. He needed a little bit of light relief, a bit of fun." But I noticed a kind of catch in Quillham's voice, a disharmony which often means someone is concealing the truth.

"Nothing else?" I asked.

"He mentioned some papers he'd been absorbed in earlier that evening. A bit worrying but he wasn't that bothered; more intrigued, I'd say."

"Did he elaborate? What were they about?"

"No, and it didn't seem right to embarrass him by probing too much. But he was in a state of mind that was understandably despondent," Quillham stated finally.

"How so?"

"Warwick was a supporter of the Federation. He opined that though this would undoubtedly mean a degree of dependence it would also spread our risk a bit better. Certainly St Eleanor would gain some advantages from economies of scale and shared facilities such as use of Kingston University and a joint currency. A free trade area should help..."

"I daresay so why was this particularly depressing? Surely the Independence lobby was just part and parcel of normal politics. I imagine that would hardly have surprised him."

"No. Not in itself. But there are some odd influences coming into the island now that everyone is gearing up for the British withdrawal. The banana companies are out to close down our independent plantation and that's gone down like a lead balloon. You know they have got the shipping lines to black their produce. Even got the local one on the job. And as if that's not enough there's a big push by a Miami consortium to set up an entertainment complex here and that stinks of the Mob if you ask me. Now they've been pushed out of Cuba..."

"Wait! Are you saying Mr Constantine seriously thought organised crime was trying to get a foothold on St. Eleanor?"

"Thought so? Knew so! Those guys stink."

"Was he going to stop them coming in?"

"Easier said than done. It's not the 1930s. These people have the best lawyers and reps money can buy. If you say anything bad about them in print they'll sue you. They also work through a battery of front companies so it's almost impossible to pin anything on them. You know that."

I was nonplussed by this. But it was the step forward I was looking for. Was there anything else? "What did you talk about the night before? Did he indicate anything else on his mind?"

Quillham seemed to ponder this a while then suddenly he asked: "Do you know what Warwick said to me?"

"That's part of what I'd like to know."

"He asked *me* if *I* felt threatened."

"And did you?"

"I said no. I meant it at the time but suddenly there's a lot of water gone under the bridge. I'm not so sure anymore. Can I know what killed him?"

"I don't see why not. For Warwick a dose of *Dial*, ended his life."

"And what's that?"

"A barbiturate used as a sedative. He had been prescribed it, *Dial*, that is *diallylbarbituric acid*. Taking it carried risks. Exceeding the prescribed amount could cause death. He knew that."

Quillham snapped. "That stinks! Sounds to me like a professional job, to me. Very neat. Simple. Plausible. Who are you looking for? A murderer or the people who paid him? This isn't conventional police work, if you ask me. This requires an intelligence assessment."

"Okay. Well that's more your line from all they tell me. Let's play with a few thoughts. Who do you suggest might want to kill him?"

"Well, what you have to remember is that Warwick Constantine was an honourable man, what he said he'd do he'd do even if he had to bust a gut to do it. Of course, he was careful not to give too many hostages to fortune, as you'd expect...after all, he was a politician. But once he was committed, it was always going to be difficult to stop him."

"I see but where did that take him?"

"Ha! Well, he wouldn't want the mafia and he was sympathetic to the plantation workers but ...everything was still in the air. There were too many external factors at play limiting his room for manoeuvre. He was still keeping all the balls in the air so far as I know."

"But you spoke of murder."

"Pure speculation on my part, I suppose, but the whole thing stinks to high heaven. Well, without a clear motive it's going to be hard, Chief Inspector. And we can't really deduce a motive from such scanty facts, can we? The mafia could be contenders but there are others who may have found him difficult. In the end maybe it even really got too much for him."

"But if we were to follow your speculative line of thought then there are some important contextual facts, aren't there? If what you suggest is correct the murderer would surely have to be well organised to tamper with his pills."

"Organised. Right. Who? A local group? Foreigners? British? Mafia? Cubans?"

"Well, as you say, Constantine was fairly conservative, favoured by the British. Does that help?"

"Maybe it does. It seems to rule out the British."

"So the question is what would it be about Jamieson's taking over that someone would like?"

"Impossible to guess but he leans to independence rather than a West Indian Federation." Quillham mused for a moment as was his wont. "Hard to believe though that that would be a motive for murder."

At that I straightened up and pulled out my card which I presented to him. "If you recall anything, anything at all which might suggest Constantine had enemies...real enemies...or might have been suicidal let me know. You can contact me there."

WHEN I GOT INTO my home late that afternoon I saw a scurrying cockroach but managed to kill it before it made its cover. I smiled to myself, thinking I was beginning to adapt to life here; and would soon have some stories for Katie. At that moment the telephone rang. I was a little startled. Who could that be? The office? Something I'd forgotten. Surely not the right time for a call from across the deep blue sea. I picked it up.

"Cordell."

"Ah, the very man. Rufus here. Rufus Halliday. I'm sorry to bother you. You were told to expect a call from me I understand," he explained abruptly.

"Yes...I remember the name."

"Well, it's time to meet up. One o'clock at the Barracuda alright? Expect you know where it is by now," the voice asked in the same rather harsh tone.

"Okay. One o'clock. But how will I recognise you?"

"Don't worry. I will know you. See you then."

He hung up. Well, things were certainly acquiring a momentum of their own. I hadn't cared for the man's bossy tone but there was no hostility in it. Some people are like that. A telephone voice is not a good guide to someone's character. He may be a much more agreeable character. Hard to know given the brevity of the conversation.

Restless, I took a turn outside and soon found myself walking up to the fringes of the Wild. The hot tropical climate was not quite so oppressive here, there was fresh water in abundance, and fruit and flowers grew readily, radiating a lush primordial grandeur. I stumbled over the stones but it didn't bother me. Stooping to touch a leaf, I pressed its wet sinews between my fingers and released an intoxicating scent. I felt transported. It was only for a few moments but they were enough.

The glass was definitely half full that evening. As for the First Minister's death one thing especially fascinated me. It might be important; it might not be important. The files told me that though everyone had known Constantine and had spoken well of him and of his insightful flair, what they had really encountered in him was a locked door, an impenetrable reserve which had made it impossible for them to get close to him. Mr Constantine was a man of secrets. Of that I had no doubt.

11

THE NEXT MORNING I did some brisk exercises before going in to work through the files on local crooks until lunch. It was nearly one but I felt completely relaxed. I was beginning to get the feel of the place and was rather enjoying myself. Why not? Life here was congenial. I had my own adequately equipped home, atop a hill with views over the sea on one side and to the *Deux Pitons* on the other. The encroaching wild added an allure of its own without any of the threat it may once have implied. As for the locals, they were indeed charming just as legend had it. The Caribbean voices were so full of life, it was hard not to be drawn to them. And if it was difficult to resist their charms then it was impossible to deny the attractions of the sharp brown eyed girls with hair blossoming like thorn bushes. Of course I could have done without some of the begging but what can you expect when you stay in a fundamentally poor sort of place? Paradise it wasn't but for wealthy European visitors it was all too easy to see how they could succumb to such an idyll.

So, feeling virtuous, I was free to meet up with my new-found business acquaintance, Rufus Halliday. All in all, the encounter was almost by way of mixing business with pleasure. So I was pleased that lunch time to take myself over to the well known watering hole overlooking St. Jacques. But the meeting was tinged with a little foreboding, a feeling that I was engaged in something a bit illicit. Should I really be writing up a report for business interests? It seemed harmless (and lucrative) but was it right? So I drove down to the Club, puzzling over Halliday's arrangements.

I got there just as the sun hit its fiercest heat. On entering, the place wasn't too prepossessing but it was already filling up. The Club mainly consisted of one long room with a bar and piano. I imagined it could double up as a dance hall. Elsewhere there was a card room for bridge replete with a billiards table. In fact at first glance, the Barracuda Club looked exactly like the sort of place I detested. The surfaces were full of fussy little trays containing walnuts and almonds; and Perry Como was singing away at full blast. It was a kind of unofficial refuge for Europeans. There were no black people there apart from those serving at the bar. Almost straightaway I recognised my quarry, looking just as he had advertised himself: a tousled and red haired man sporting an open necked white shirt and tanned trousers lounging in a bay-window armchair gazing out onto the town and the limitless blue sky. I made my way over to him, gin and tonic in hand. "Mind if I join you?" I asked.

"Not at all, Old Boy," Halliday answered, beaming a smile right at me as he waved me into a chair opposite. "Cordell wasn't it? Never forget a name. Halliday. Rufus Halliday." He extended his hand in welcome and I shook it firmly. His eyes were warm, glowing like sunlight. Halliday possessed an effortless charm to which I responded, relaxing and listening to his almost musical voice. But I shouldn't count on it, I told myself, business people are often like that. They develop a veneer of easy charm which turns out to be deceptive.

"That's right. I remember yours too. Small world?" I said as I sat down in the chair opposite. I was surprised at myself. I never would have expected that I'd slip so easily into the totally deceitful pose of long term acquaintance.

"Small island come to that. You don't have to stay here long to see the same familiar faces popping up. Especially here...the Barracuda Club."

"That sounds promising," I said, my gaze wandering down to the harbour where a handful of bare-masted boats bobbed in the sunlight. The mountainside across from the waterfront was a complete lush green but for one plot high above the town where the police headquarters had been built and whose white edifice frowned down on the town.

Halliday peered into his glass. "In fact you know it's too British really. A certain type of Britishness too. You know what I mean?"

"Can't say I do."

"Well...it comforts a certain kind of person. Most of the Whites pop in eventually. A bit like Piccadilly Circus if you know what I mean? Whisky, gin and tonics. It reminds them of the Oxford Union, the Travellers Club, public school...That sort of thing. Lots of self-important people spouting utter nonsense."

I found this a bit unsettling but said the opposite. "Really? Glad to hear it. I'd like to meet up with a few more of the British community here."

He gave me a half smile. "Stay here long enough and you should see 'em."

"I'm sure you exaggerate or you wouldn't be here yourself. You a regular?"

"Not really. Got to be back in London next week. Back and forth, you know. But I'm afraid it's not always true that you meet interesting people at the Club." He sighed. Just then, a whiff of scent distracted my attention. Rose, myrrh and sandalwood. Subtle, evanescent, brusquely intimate, the fragrance briefly transported me into a dream world like a bridge suddenly thrown across to an island, taking me by surprise. I turned and saw a young European woman, tall with long dark brown hair and a sparkle to her face, standing nearby chatting amiably to her companion. I was startled. I felt I *knew* that face from somewhere. I was sure of it. Or thought I was. Well, that was a welcome change from London anyway. Women allowed! Puzzled but reassured I returned to Halliday who was smiling and in a moment she had become part of the furniture. "I've travelled around a good bit," Halliday was saying, "at the fag end of Empire but wherever you go you find the British have set up watering holes for themselves – sounds a good idea I know – but so often they're full of crashing bores who just want to drink gin and talk nonsense all day."

"Well, I imagine they feel safe in their clubs, insulated from the natives. It's not always a good thing, I agree." There was an uneasy pause. "So where do the locals go when they want to relax?"

Halliday raised an eyebrow. "All sorts of places, you know. But the Big-Wigs come here just like the rest of us. There's no colour bar you know?" Halliday's eyes shifted uncomfortably as if he were anxious to avoid someone.

I looked around at the sea of white faces. "You could have fooled me." It was a code of conduct from the late nineteenth century and it was taking a long time for people to see how outdated it had become. But change was finally coming. Attitudes would take a little longer.

"No. I kid you not. They come here as well. It's not South Africa or the Southern States but there's a money issue. Only the more senior locals can afford the rates here."

"Ah, I think I see now. That must keep out a lot."

"All you'll get here is the *crème de la crème*. You know what I mean," Rufus Halliday said, eyeing me shrewdly. "These are St. Eleanor's big decision makers. I don't mean so much the politicians. I mean people who make the real decisions. Like what really matters. They are our best brains, our best businessmen. They know how to make money. And they know how to make an independent St Eleanor work if the island is to have a future. You know what I mean? They have ambition. They want to better themselves but most of all they want to better themselves for the sakes of their families. They want them to have a future too."

"Sounds good. But I don't see any here today," I said wondering what the *'crème de la crème'* could mean on a tiny island of only some 100,000 people.

"Oh, there'll probably be some here later. I can't say there wasn't a fight to admit black people. A lot of bloody nonsense but we won in the end."

"Care to tell me about it?"

"Oh the usual. Bigotry. A lot of people viewed the locals with scepticism, with racism even. Although the population is black with maybe ten, fifteen per cent having mixed blood of white and black, the truth is the blacks have always been at the bottom of the heap. That is until now."

"British attitudes?"

"Not entirely. Even people of dual race are often snobbish about their mixed colouring. It dates back to slavery, you know. Ever since then those of mixed race have always claimed superiority over the ordinary black. Anybody'd have thought the blacks were still making dugout canoes! It's an attitude which has taken a long time to die out. There were really comparatively few white people permanently resident here and they are either wealthy retired settlers or holding on to most of the best jobs. Of course not very long ago it had been policy to give the best jobs to whites. But that's changing and changing fast now that independence is on the way." Halliday shuffled in his seat and looked at his watch.

"Well that's for the good, I guess. Personally, can't say I don't like the place. It looks stunning. It catches your breath. I don't know what it is. The people, the sun, the beaches, the jungle...or maybe the little villages...but whatever it is; it smells alright and turns your head." Something about the man's furtive looks forced me to lower my voice, speaking almost conspiratorially. "Now then...Walter Onslow-Bell tells me you may be able to help me with a few queries he has about the future of the island."

"Yes, yes. Of course I know all about that. It has an interesting future, no doubt. Some good cash crops – bananas, sugar, nuts, that sort of thing. The politics should be stable enough despite all the hoo-ha provided there's no interference from Castro or Uncle Sam. The big question mark is around tourism development. There are great opportunities of course but it could be a nightmare if..." I had pulled out my pen to make some notes and was reaching for my briefcase when Halliday stopped me, planting his hand heavily on my forearm. "No need. No need," he said. "I've written up a few notes for you. You can have it. It's all there...and much more detailed." He paused. "Dash it all if I haven't left it at home. Tell you what though, I'll drop it around to your place tonight right after work. Say six? Would that be ok?"

"Fine by me but do you know where I am? I'm a bit tucked away from the beaten track." I then went on to explain where my Rest House was, Halliday taking it all in without notes, apparently quite happy to drive by. He resumed his little lecture and I listened as he held forth about the island and the ways of its people, who mattered and who didn't, where the best eating houses were to be found and how the plantations operated. Mostly it was the small change of a small country's life but I gobbled it all up. I didn't fool myself that it made me an expert on the place but I felt at least as if I were sniffing the wind.

"Do you have any suggestions for people I might see while I'm here...for the report I mean?"

"Don't worry. I'm sure you'll come to the right conclusions. And who knows? A good report might open other doors."

"I wish I could share your optimism. I don't want to come unstuck on it."

"Certainly not. I'm here to help in any way I can. And I certainly don't want to see you end up in a wheelchair."

He must have seen my teeth clench. "A wheelchair?" I said.

"Just an expression." He looked at me oddly and added, "I'm sure there's no harm will come to you."

With that I tried to push my worries to the back of my mind but there was no doubt that the wheelchair incident had left me with a numbing distant fear, heavy like bad indigestion. "I think you'll find my analysis is pretty thorough," Halliday continued. "But it may be an idea to talk to one or two people around the island. Maybe the Anchor company can give you some insights into trading issues....the Governor, of course, I tell you what, what about seeing Jamieson, the new First Minister? He's also the main Independence advocate. There's little goes on in the island he doesn't know about."

"Jamieson? Okay. I'll need to have a word with him anyway. I'll bear him in mind."

He smiled. "Now these things are two way of course. A chap like you ferreting around beneath the surface could be really helpful."

"Thanks. Of course I'm happy to pass on any tid bits which I can but I don't think I'll be doing a lot of what you call ferreting. I'm really here to help with the reorganisation and advise on any training needs. Simple task for a simple plodder."

"Well, all the same, let me know if you come across anything interesting."

"Such as...?"

"Well. You chaps must get a feel for the way the wind is blowing. Unions, gossip, street talk, security precautions, that sort of thing."

"Concerning anything in particular?" I asked, genuinely intrigued.

"Politics, that sort of thing." When I pressed him Halliday lowered his voice and seemed to be talking out of the side of his mouth. "There's one chap we are interested in doing business with but he's a bit of an enigma. We could do with more gen on him before we approach him. Perhaps you could help?"

"Who is he?"

"Matthew Forrest, the manager of Anchor Marine. Do you think you could help?"

"I daresay. It's a bit irregular but I don't see the harm. I'll ask around."

"Good Man! You see there's a spot of bother. Nothing for you to worry about but it needs attention."

"What sort of bother?"

"The sort of bother a man in your position may be able to help with. Before investing our client wants to do a little more project development work. Your report is part of that. It's early days but let's say they want to look at how the public responds, how it reacts to the new product. It includes implicit as well as explicit responses, measuring levels of customer appetite etc., etc. These things can get quite complex. And we at IPA like to be thorough. One thing we like to do is to take soundings of key players."

"Sounds reasonable but where do I come in? And what's the flap about?"

"Oh, surely you understand that you can be a great help with the sort of level of access to people and information that you have. As for the flap, these clients of ours may pay well but they are also very serious people if you get my drift. They must be taken seriously."

"Alright. I'll do what I can. But can you elaborate a little on what you want me to find out from Forrest? I thought you knew everyone here."

"But not necessarily well enough. OK I've met him a couple of times. Nothing more. Matthew Forrest. We need to know more. Tall, thin guy. Runs *Anchor* shipping as he calls it. Its a small company based in the Windward Islands, registered right here in good old St. Jacques. Small profit lines, strictly local freight only but he does well out of it. He seems to be branching out. Some people speak kindly of him, others don't. We'd like to know a bit more about him and we figured you might have a little more on him in your records room up on the hill over there."

"Such as...?"

"Anything really. He gives nothing away about the family business. Whether he's straight as they come or if there's a darker side. It's tricky to say. Maybe you could help give him a clean bill of health or dish the dirt on him. Either way it would be helpful to know. If he's clean he might be a good man to do business with. If you can get a natural opportunity maybe you could ask him if he'd mind shipping a few extra articles that wouldn't appear on a Bill of Lading. But only conversationally...you get me...don't push it"

I hesitated. It was a bit close to the bone. Police records are confidential. Yet I knew of officers who had gossiped when they shouldn't have. Also it was easy to do. A few minutes work would probably suffice. A doddle. And this man was going to hand me a report needing next to no extra work for which I have already been paid handsomely. "Okay," I said. "I'll see what I can find and get back to you a.s.a.p."

"Thanks Bruce, I really appreciate that. That'll be a big help." He paused a moment then went on. "The thing is," he said, "there is a big feeling for change here and that's important. The islanders want a bigger say in their own destiny and I'm all for it. It can't be done

120

overnight of course but there has to be more of a partnership in decision making. Good thing too!"

"Sounds ok to me too," I said. "But complicated."

"I can see you're a man after my own heart, someone who likes to get to the bottom of things, to find out what's been covered up. Once you do that – expose everything that seems mysterious – we discover our own strength"

"Well, it certainly helps to put an end to the confusion of things."

"Now, I'm afraid we shall have to cut short our interesting little discussion for I have another appointment. But we shall speak again. Six tonight. *Caille Blanc.*"

At that Halliday got up, leaving me to my thoughts. It was then that a thought suddenly popped into my head. I hadn't remembered her face at all. It was the scent. It was the same scent I had sensed my first night at *Caille Blanc.*

12

"A TYPICAL BUSINESSMAN, MID-FORTIES, I would guess. Arrogant," Lucy was saying, "with a lovely younger wife he doesn't deserve. They run a shipping line if you can call it that. One freighter and two smaller vessels for island hopping. The good thing about them is their house."

We were back at the station, in my office to be exact; and I'd been quizzing her in as nonchalant a manner as I could muster about Forrest, the man of Halliday's concern. Lucy was proving an agreeable colleague, willing and always smiley.

"Any particular reason for your interest?" Lucy asked. Her tone said that she understood him and I didn't.

"No. Just a name I'd heard in a different connection."

"The shipping boycott?"

"Yes. It's pretty toxic. I was wondering what pressures had been brought to bear on him to make such a decision."

"You and half the island! But I imagine he's fearful of losing other contracts."

"I suppose you are probably right but he's wrecked his popularity here." We let the matter drop and there was a short pause before Lucy brightened again.

"Ready, then?" Lucy prompted, smiling.

"Ready! Well, it's about time I saw the crime room, Lucy. Care to show me the way."

We walked down corridors until we come to a large chamber, festooned with archives. Usually, I like archives. They teem with millions of good, rich stories and insights into all manner of lives. This time I groaned inwardly. There was just too much. Or was there? I found the Constantine case had its own filing cabinet which for all its size had only one drawer containing all the raw material which had been distilled into the summary report composed by Inspector Woodbine Parish, a copy of which I had already been studying. The details of all the interviews and scene of the incident information were kept here. I spent the afternoon sifting through the papers. It was a meticulous record. Inspector Parish had interviewed everyone involved, carefully distinguishing between facts and observations. In the end it was impossible to disagree with his assessment: death by overdose.

I opened up the case file again and looked at it intently. Constantine's friends and associates could all be accounted for. If it were foul play, it had to be someone from outside his immediate circle. There had to be people who knew Constantine – such a public man – but who were just not showing up on the radar. And then, of course, there was the Quillham conspiracy theory. If it were that I was unlikely get anywhere. Yet I wasn't downhearted. All experience told me that patience was a virtue in detective work; and that when you felt something was significant it probably was, even though you couldn't put your finger on it. So I spent a good part of the afternoon making marginal jottings and not getting very far, still stuck on that missing blue paper.

Interesting as the evolution of my thoughts was I certainly needed more information and there were two important interviews to set up. First I put a call through, briefly to Government House and asked to speak to Mr Oppenheimer, Jake Oppenheimer. The lady at the other end sounded as if she hadn't ever heard of the man and I feared no progress would be made but then, quite suddenly, a man's oleaginous voice came on the other end.

"Oppenheimer here. Who's that?"

"Me. Chief Inspector Cordell here. Recently seconded to the Royal St. Eleanor Police. I'm so sorry to bother you at work but something's come up. And I think you'd be in the best position to help me."

His attitude relaxed a little, the tone of voice softening. "Well, it's a bit difficult at the moment. Can't it wait?"

"No. I'm afraid not. But we shouldn't be long. Half an hour, tops. Initially, at least."

"Well, it can't be today, that's for sure. How about tomorrow evening? Can you make the Barracuda for eight?"

"Eight it is."

I replaced the receiver and sat looking at my desk blotter for a moment. A slippery one, this, I reflected. And not just his oily voice. Come to think of it, that's the kind of description you get in fiction but don't encounter in real life. Yet here he was, Mr Oily Voice. How does one develop that? Perhaps he's been perpetually trying to disguise his voice. *There's nowt so queer as ....*

With Mr Jamieson, First Minister-designate, it proved bizarrely easier. He was still operating from his former office, *Windward Islands Solicitors,* which I now phoned. I expected it to take an unconscionably long time to arrange a meeting and was pleasantly surprised to be informed I could meet him the next morning at nine thirty. I marked down Bob Jamieson of *Windward Islands Solicitors*, and now First Minister designate, for immediate attention. He might be a man who could fill in useful details. I got out his file and got more than I bargained for. On leaving school Jamieson had begun as a clerk in the Registrar's Office for the usual small salary. He had a good basic education, was willing and soon became a dab hand at the typewriter. But for a man of his colour there was not a real career. That was the plain fact of life for many West Indians of that time. He had moved from there to the Education Office where much the same story ensued. Then he had got a job at a Solicitor's Office; and suddenly he had had a stroke of luck. The partners had liked him. He had won a grant to study law in England and he had gone with their blessing. Since his return he had not looked back. The *Windward Islands Solicitors* had started life as a Legal Partnership between two of Jamieson's contemporaries, Killen and McMorris. It had begun, strangely enough with a slightly left wing agenda, committed to being socially responsible and its cases full of compensation, matrimonial work and even a commitment to those with mental health problems. On Jamieson's return from England he had been taken on as a partner but as the years had slipped by Jamieson's partners had departed to set up their own practices while he himself had moved into the more lucrative field of company work until he had discovered there was more money to be had working with wealthy investors.

Hence he was fronting up several overseas companies in St Eleanor. Quite a career. Looked a wee bit on the slick side for my taste but we were all learning that the pace of life in the former colonies was quickening and that the turnover of leaders was rapid. I dashed off a brief telegram to the Yard indicating progress was being made but not giving any hostages to fortune.

I had been feeling buoyant about things when Frank dropped by and enquired how I was getting on. I reassured him that progress was being made then just as he was going I called after him. "I won't be in first thing. I'm going straight out on a call," I said.

"A development?" Frank asked lightly.

I grimaced. "I wish! No, but it's too hot to sit and fester so I'm going to do a little research." Then something prompted me to ask: "The new man. Jamieson. Could you tell me a little about him? As a man, I mean. Politics aside."

"Jamieson?" he said. "Watch your step."

"The new First Minister? Why? Not a pleasant guy?"

"Charm itself but watch yourself all the same. He's a slippery customer but don't quote me on that."

"One of Constantine's more significant enemies?"

Worrell shrugged as if to say he was a political rival but it didn't signify. "How can I put it? He's the sort of man you shake hands with and you'll feel you want to check you've still got your watch. You'll be relieved to find you have, only to discover when you get back that he's taken the shirt off your back." With that Frank disappeared down the corridor.

Lawyers eh? Instinct warned me that a solicitor was nearly always a person of doubtful integrity. As the new First Minister he was the obvious gainer from

Constantine's demise. Plus he was a man to go places when the British pulled out. There should be some threads worth pulling around those facts but, all the same, Briscoe's warnings floated back. Just as I'd come to this point Lucy made a re-appearance. "How's it going there? It's nearly five. Did you find anything?"

I looked up. "Nope. It's what I didn't find really? I mean: Why am I here? Your Inspector Parish seems to have wrapped up everything pretty satisfactorily."

Lucy remained standing, silent. Then her face crinkled into a grin. "You'd better not let people know you have your doubts, Sir. Everyone is expecting results."

"Indeed?"

"The whole of St. Jacques has been talking about your visit. Your name is being spoken of everywhere in the streets."

I shot a quick glance at her only to be instantly reassured that I was not being paid some pointless compliment. Well, so much for a confidential assignment.

"Will you tell me something, Lucy?" I asked her after a pause. "Frank gave me a garbled story about Woodbine. I couldn't understand it at all. Why haven't I been introduced to him?"

"Do you think I know all his secrets?"

Secrets? Freudian slip, perhaps, I thought to myself. Hoping to learn more I went on. "Listen, Lucy, we seem to get on. Tell me what you know of him."

"I can't say anything because I know nothing. Nothing much anyway. I must admit I'm rather surprised you weren't introduced to him when you arrived."

"Well, tell me what you know anyway."

"Not a lot. I didn't work with him personally. He's kind of old," Lucy replied. "All aches and pains and joints but he had a good reputation in his day as a solid sort of policeman. Retired now. Lives on the hills like a hermit."

"Retired but not too senior?"

"No. No black people were not allowed above the rank of Sergeant in his day," Lucy smiled, taunting me perhaps. Insolence or friendliness, hard to say. "Come to think of it, it's not that long since the rules changed," she went on. "Woodbine had it in him to go all the way to the top but the rules changed too late to help much. Still, he made it to Detective-Inspector and that was pretty smart."

"A good detective, you think?"

"Hard for me to judge if I'm being truly honest but he had a retentive memory and was pretty shrewd about people. I don't really know if he's still like that."

"Well, that's encouraging at least."

"It wasn't his fault you didn't get to see him."

"Whose fault was it then?" I asked as casually as I could.

Her face dropped into a frown. "I don't know but there are arrogant people around who like to interfere. Look, why not just go and have a word with him?"

"Don't see why not."

Lucy smiled and then burst into laughter. "But take care!" she added.

"Why?"

"I hear he likes a captive audience. He tells stories. Over and over again. You'll never get out unless you are ready to fend him off." Lucy rolled her eyes in imitation boredom. But I only felt a lively curiosity to see the reclusive Woodbine Parish and his cliff top retreat.

"Thanks for the warning but I think I can take it."

"But that's only when he's decided he likes you, otherwise he's a bit standoffish. Been on his own too long I reckon. And maybe the Force wasn't altogether a good influence. It destroys your faith in human nature. Woodbine doesn't trust people too much at first. But once you're over that you'll be fine..."

Suddenly she smiled mischievously, as if enjoying the teasing advantage of knowing a secret the other doesn't. "Guess what?"

"What?"

"You've an invitation from the Governor. Personal one to one. Quite an honour." As she spoke, she handed me an opened letter. "I've just come from Frank's office. He told me to give it to you."

"The Governor?" I asked, exasperated.

"That's right," Lucy said, flicking the letter over to me. "Take a dekko." I did so, standing motionless, staring at the paper. She went on talking as if the letter itself were a mere adornment to the news. "You'll have to go. You can't turn down an invitation like that."

I nodded. "I thought that." It was a beautifully embossed letter. Quite regal in its way. That and a meeting with the new First Minister tomorrow morning. Must mean something but I didn't know what. "To tell you the truth, Lucy, I don't know what a Governor is. Is he the top man or more like a school governor?"

"Well neither really. You see, he's in-between. Constantine...Jamieson, I mean... and the Assembly really run the island now. The Governor is more pre-occupied with the handover arrangements. They're preparing to become the High Commission. More like an Embassy, you know."

"I see." But I didn't.

13

THAT EVENING I DROVE back, before a freshening breeze, towards Soufrière, a flood of sparkling light pouring over the great blue sea. Eastwards stretched the green of the rain forest while to the west a thin line of foam creamed upon the finest of white sand. The tide dented the coast, forming bays, pools and lagoons where the water lay at rest embraced by the arms of the land. I shut the engine down outside *Caille Blanc* and walked up to the rest house. The air had a sparkle in it like dry, tingling wine. But here, beneath the umbrella pines the shadows were pleasantly cool and heavy. Inside, I discovered an evening meal of fish pie, green beans and apricots had been left for me by the mysterious Prudence. It was like being attended to by a generous spirited Elf.

At six, right on cue, just as I was finishing I heard with no surprise the purr of a limousine outside. It was a smart black *Vanden Plas*, probably the only one on the island and certainly not the sort of car I would be driving up this beaten up old track. It was a very large, sleek vehicle for this part of the world. But Halliday didn't seem perturbed as he emerged from his luxurious car, a cheroot in one hand and a slim file in the other.

He smiled as he joined me at the door. "I was rather interested to see where you live as a matter of fact.

Never been to this little corner before. So it's another one down to experience, I suppose." I gestured him inside as he continued, "One thing I never asked you about. I leave all this sort of thing to the London end normally but do you do much writing? I suppose you must. Reports mainly, I guess?"

For the first time I noticed that he was older than I'd first registered, his lower face seeming to have a texture of putty or was it a relic of some disease he'd once contracted. Either way it left his complexion resembling a bunch of shrivelled grapes.

"Reports? Yes. That's right," I replied dryly. It sounded odd here. It made me feel like some embodied ghost of bureaucracy. "Too much police work is pen pushing. It's ridiculous. But enough of that. It's good of you to come," I said. "Let me get you a drink. Gin and tonic ok?...I see you brought the notes you spoke of."

Halliday smiled and handed me a neatly typed manuscript of about twenty pages. "You'll find everything you need there. Just really needs a little editing, a bit of freshening up and your own personal imprint and that should keep Onslow-Bell happy." Halliday looked around him with an air of *bonhomie*. "It's nice here, isn't it," he said. "Tidy, peaceful, orderly. Everything is well arranged. A bit like St. Eleanor itself. Anything which would disturb it is thrown out."

Handing him his gin and tonic we began chatting and I was surprised how easily Halliday opened up about himself. It turned out Halliday had lived in many of the Caribbean islands and had ties with central American countries. "I don't pretend to be an expert," he said, "but I think I know my Caribbean." And he spoke of going over to Tobago to stay with an old friend and of proceeding to St. Lucia to pursue a business acquaintance. With St. Eleanor where he usually lived, he was thoroughly familiar.

"Your wife likes the life here too?" I asked.

"My wife died two years ago. Cancer."

"Oh...I'm sorry to hear that."

"I'm over the worst and my work keeps me busy." But his conversation soon shifted back to his concerns for the island's future. The British Government, Halliday said, was keen to thrust independence on St. Eleanor whether the islanders wanted it or not. Federation had been the preferred option but alone if they insisted. With independence the British would quietly jettison their exchequer grant after a short transition period. The island politicians had twigged that of course and knew they would find little succour in federal plans for the West Indies. Much of this was new to me but Halliday's perspective was unsettling, offering a glimpse of dark abysses compared to which my case was a garden flower-bed.

A lot had changed since the first heady talk of independence. The winds of change had turned into a tornado sweeping all sorts of early ideas out, leaving a political impasse between Federalists and Independence politicians. Federation might have offered some hope to St Eleanor but Jamaica and now, Trinidad, had no desire to spend their hard earned lucre baling the little islands out. So the Windward islands were likely to be thrown to the wolves.

Just how were they going to pay their way? It was not obvious. St Eleanor had a handful of cash crops: bananas, pineapples, sugar, cashew nuts. None of them were big earners. Visitors from North America were now seeping into the islands, bringing with them a spending power the British had never approached. Everyone thought there was potential in tourism development but there didn't seem to be many people offering to put their money down. Then from nowhere the Americans had announced that they were interested in having a naval facility on the island. For the British it was a Godsend. A commitment like that would enable them to get out of the island with a little dignity. But it seemed not everyone saw the offer as entirely welcome. I must have looked a little bemused by this avalanche of facts for Halliday offered to help me by throwing light, if I should need any, on the country's customs and the character of its people.

"That's very good of you," I said, smiling. "Well, you're certainly being very helpful, I don't mind saying. I've put out a few feelers about Forrest."

Halliday raised his eyebrows. "Quick work."

"Didn't see any point in hanging about. Well, there's no police record but colleagues know him. Reasonable business reputation. What the bankers would call '*highly respectable.*'" Halliday smirked. "A bit on the arrogant side I hear" I went on. "No real nuances yet but they'll come no doubt."

"Thanks old man. There's no rush. I wouldn't want you embarrassing yourself with your new colleagues."

"No, indeed. Well, I won't."

"You're a breath of fresh air, I don't mind saying. You've only been here a few days and its clear you're no stick in the mud."

"Thanks."

"Haven't you noticed? They just don't bloody well care, these Whitehall guys. They've obviously got some bloody deal going with the Yanks and they're planning to spin it to the islanders that it's some Godsend! Have you heard? The Americans have been allowed to hold military exercises here next week. Exercise Swordfish! It's a bloody disgrace! They treat Britain as a colony, never mind St. Eleanor. But just you watch! Once the Yanks get a hold of things they'll bloody well wreck the place, if you ask me."

I wasn't sure what to say to that. Instead, I frowned sympathetically. "I suppose they've got a job to do."

Halliday's eyes narrowed then suddenly he guffawed quite unexpectedly. "You're a one. I can tell, Bruce. Keep your cards close to your chest, don't you? Very wise. Don't blame you at all. I can see we'll get along just fine. Well, I guess I'd better be getting along. Leave you to your supper."

I smiled. "One small thing, Rufus. Where exactly is this naval base...anchorage...whatever...going to be?"

Halliday leaned over and picked up the file he'd delivered. Leafing through it earnestly, he stopped at a page map of St. Eleanor. He stood there poring over the little map as if it were a nautical chart. For the first time I became aware that the tropical dusk was falling. I flicked on the gaslight. Halliday's signet ring positively flashed in the light as he stabbed at the map. "Yes," he shouted. "That's the spot." I bent over beside him following the line of his index finger to a cove not far north of St. Jacques: *Schooner's Landing*. It all looked innocent enough. Were Halliday's concerns so well founded, I wondered? What, after all, could possibly spoil the beauty of such a place when it felt so good to be alive?

"When you've filed your report with Onslow-Bell there's another little matter we'd appreciate your help with." Halliday's face, lit up by the oil lamp, seemed to be aglow from within, full of an intense understanding. "IPA has been asked by a client to look into the island's tourist potential. If you could pick up any straws in the wind that would be useful."

"Straws in the wind? You must be joking! The potential is vast! Any fool can see that," I said.

"Ah," Halliday looked a little pensive. "Well, you see it's a little more complex than that. Our clients are looking at various islands to expand into. We are talking top notch hotels, shopping malls...maybe, theme parks. These things cost a lot of money. So they need to be sure they are backing the right horse. They need reassurance about all sorts of things which may happen after independence. What will happen to the infrastructure, for example. That airport would have to be expanded. The roads too are very basic. St. Jacques can take liners but only just and nowhere else can. Also what about tax plans? Big companies need to make big profits. Not everyone understands this. They cannot function, cannot invest huge sums unless they can be assured that they can take the money out. We are not sure where Jamieson stands. Sometimes he sounds quite socialistic. Pally to the Cubans even? That's where you come in."

"I don't know about that. I'm a policeman, not an economist or a politician."

"Nonsense. A man of your calibre can soon ferret out the information. Access to the Governor, access to the First Minister...why, there's no stopping you. You'll become IPA's researcher. And that's big money. Far more than a policeman's salary. You must know that."

I nodded non-committal but all the while I was thinking of Onslow-Bell's thousands clicking up in our bank account. "I'll see what I can do," I said after a pause. "I should have some time. The First Minister's death looks to have a straightforward explanation."

We strolled amiably together back to his *Vanden Plas Princess* where I once more admired the bodywork before it oozed its way back down the hillside in the direction of Soufrière and the island's ring road. I watched it go idly for a few moments vaguely aware of the tropical languor creeping back over me and the breeze kissing the trees above. Back inside I returned to Halliday's file, reading it more closely and cross referencing it with what little experience I had. I soon sensed that this was the real McCoy and that my work for *International Project Assessment* had been largely done for me: it was perceptive, acute, reflective and informative.

Suddenly it occurred to me that maybe my meeting with Halliday had meant something a little more after all, his comments more measured than they had seemed. Had he been preparing me for something, and if so what? I found myself going over his conversation again. What was it...eastern Caribbean...Forrest...business development...a new client...more money than a policeman earns...damning the British and the new US anchorage to hell. There was something more to this but I couldn't figure it out and I guessed I wasn't meant to...not yet, anyway. And as I began to wonder, I felt a certain chilling of the evening air. Despite having made a decision to support IPA and for good reasons too, I found myself pondering whether or not I had been right. But this was the sort of decision that couldn't be easily unmade. It wasn't like taking something back to the shop.

There was a jangling of the telephone. I picked up the receiver.

"Chief Inspector..."

"Bruce! It's me. Katie. Is it a good time to talk?"

"As good as any. How are you keeping?"

"Fine. I'm well. And the children."

"That's good. I'm ok too. No big news here but I'm getting a better grip on things now."

"Does that mean you'll be coming home soon?"

"Whoa there..! Not so fast. But I am interviewing most of the people I need to. And I think I understand things better. Its looking like a genuine overdose. I just have to eliminate one or two other possibilities, to be sure then I might be heading back."

"Great! That's wonderful news. And this Onslow-Bell stuff? Will you be able to complete it ok?"

"Yes. I think so. Things are falling into place better than I'd feared. It should be ok. Any news at your end?"

"Not exactly big stuff either. But I've been thinking..."

"...and?"

"Well, I think with this money we can afford a new car, a proper one instead of the old banger."

"Oh yes?"

"It can wait until you're back but there's no reason for any further delay. I've advertised for someone to help with the cleaning and once I've got someone I'm going to start driving lessons."

"Good for you. That's an excellent idea."

"I thought you'd approve."

"Of course I do but look! This is no good. This haphazard stuff. We must fix a time when one of us will call and then take it in turns." We duly made arrangements for more regular communications at an unearthly hour of the morning, twice a week.

Some of Katie's thoughts lingered long after she'd hung up. We were rich now. Not that this was a reason for extravagance but we weren't church mice any more so why live like them? Then suddenly my meditation was interrupted again by the telephone. Had Katie forgotten to tell me something? I picked up the receiver.

"Chief Inspector Cordell speaking."

"There's going to be a murder," an unfamiliar woman's voice announced. It took me a moment to readjust. It was no voice I recognised.

"Who is going to be murdered?" I asked noncommittally.

"The writer, Quentin Quillham...he's going to be shot."

"Who is going to shoot him?"

"I don't know. That is all I know."

"Who else is involved? Why...are you still there? Hello? Hello?"

The line was dead.

She had spoken with a foreign accent. Foreign to me that is. It didn't sound local but I couldn't be sure. Youngish but its hard to tell on the phone. In the end there was simply nothing for it. The message required a quick, robust response. Nor should I allow myself to be radically redirected. Tomorrow morning I had an important and hard to re-schedule meeting with the new First Minister. This could not be re-arranged. Instead, I rang the Police H.Q. and spoke to the Duty Officer, explaining briefly what had happened and requesting that Tim and Lucy visit Quillham in person and inform him of our concerns. There was little more I could do.

That night I struggled to sleep, slipping from one distressed position to the next. I don't normally set any store by dreams, forgetting them as soon as I wake but one proved more lasting, haunting me to work the next morning. I had dreamt that I had stolen some gold or some such which I had carefully hidden in a black case and taken it on board a sleek modern train so powerful it gave the impression it was really going places, evidently in the USA. I stowed my case in the racks alongside some identical black cases belonging to some travelling musicians. So well was my treasure hidden that I had a spasm of anxiety that someone might take my valuable contraband without even meaning to. Then I relaxed, adopting the more carefree *mien* of the musicians and sat down in the carriage whereupon almost immediately two undercover black FBI agents, dressed in the uniforms of Confederate officers arrested me.

14

WINDWARD ISLANDS SOLICITORS had their gleaming glass and chrome offices in St. Jacques on Hawke Square. It was one of a couple of modern office blocks adorning the quayside. Most of the island's businesses were grouped here, well away from the rutted tracks which were the hallmark of most of the town. The next morning I climbed the stone steps at the imposing front entrance, soon finding myself in a small reception area presided over by a matronly middle-aged receptionist.

"Can I help you?" she asked.

"Chief Inspector Cordell. I've come to see Mr Jamieson. He's expecting me."

"Oh? Please take a seat." She rose, crossed the floor and disappeared into another room. I sat down on a leather sofa. By my side a dusty leafed cactus tree stood in a pot of soil studded with cigarette butts. Opposite, a large globe stood on a mount, hinting at broader vistas. Glass walls overlooked the harbour. The sun outside wasn't pleasant any more. It was a blazing inferno. But the view was superb, the visibility clear. The waterfront lay spread out before me like a child's model. Sounds of the town filtered in – honking cars, barking dogs, distant shouts.

The receptionist returned, silently resuming her position behind the typewriter. Time passed. I stood up, went over to the globe and placed my hand on it, watching as the world turned around. First the Atlantic slid past, then the Caribbean, then the States. Suddenly, another woman, younger and all in green, came to collect me and I was guided through a large office which evidently housed the typing pool before she gestured me towards a high ceilinged private office. The door was open but I tapped on it nonetheless before entering. A tall thin man clad in a neat, well trimmed light grey suit was standing by the window gazing down on the St. Jacques market.

"Chief Inspector Cordell?" he asked as he turned to face me.

"Yes. Mr Jamieson? I'm pleased to meet you."

"Yes. Do come in." He moved over to his desk which was strewn with a disorderly mess of paperwork, shook hands with me, then sat down. "Do take a seat, please?"

I flopped down opposite him, wriggling my back comfortably into the chair while noting that it was one of those offices where the guest's seat was deliberately kept at a lower level than the host's. The desk itself was fairly cluttered with paper but no more than you'd expect for a working executive. The wall behind his desk was plastered with certificates of achievement. Yet it must be said, now that I had a good chance to look at him, Jamieson wasn't quite what I had expected. He was black as ebony and his teeth were bright like upturned grave stones; and the whites of his eyes positively sparkled with intelligence. He talked quickly and laughed a good deal, welcoming me to his office. He positively beamed goodwill as he offered all his assistance to the police. Yet his appearance was slightly marred because he was so thin, his skin seemingly stretched tautly across his face giving you the illusion of his having, as it were, especially deep-set sunken eyes. Brushing some imaginary crumbs from my knees I started out by outlining my area of enquiry but trying to make it sound as routine and boring as possible.

I was struck then by what a polished operator Jamieson had become. A staid conservative he was not. The very acme of charm and vitality, he was a native of the island. Yet there it was, if I doubted it, a gleaming golden Rolex strapped around his wrist and a constant reminder to anyone who needed it, that Jamieson was a seriously wealthy man. And now First Minister.

I looked up. "So you're now First Minister, Mr Jamieson. Congratulations. Are you planning to run the island from here?"

"No." Jamieson smiled. "I'm giving them a little grace to sort things out at *Anse Chastenet* but I expect to be moved in there before the month is out."

"So let's be clear about this. You have no reason to believe anyone would want to kill Mr Constantine?" I asked.

"Absolutely none at all. It was a great shock to everyone. His passing I mean. But murder – no – I doubt that. He was using sleeping pills and it all went wrong. That's everyone's guess and mine too for what it's worth."

I smiled ruefully. "But we have to make enquiries, you know. Tell me, Mr Jamieson, was there any politics below the radar, so to speak, which could have been bothering him?"

"I don't think so. The big issue was pretty up front. Independence or Federation. You know the issues. He backed the Federation. He also kept an eye on the economy. The *Allied Fruit* dispute, investment...that sort of thing."

"Ah yes. Investment. I've heard something about that. Can you fill me in? By way of background."

"Sure thing. There are some wealthy American business interests who would like to develop the island for tourism. Many of us think that's a great idea. That's what *Alpha Omega* are really about. Bringing together a consortium to invest in this island, to give it investment it has never had. Their plans will bring diversity and lots of American dollars into the island, something we badly need."

"Do you really think it would work here? This is not Barbados or Jamaica."

"Why not? I think there are a lot of people who would be interested in investing in St Eleanor's future. Our island is one of the most enticingly exotic, hottest, blackest and basically safest places in the Caribbean. Of course people would want to visit. Here, take a look at this." Jamieson got up, went to a work shelf on the wall and picked up a glossy brochure. He threw it over to my side of his desk.

I picked it up and started leafing through, to see what he was getting at; and, I must say, I was surprised. It was some kind of business prospectus. It had obviously been put together by a PR outfit, by the spelling I would judge it to be of American origin. It envisaged the development of a quiet shoreline called *Schooner Landing*. I could see its glitzy look would impress many of the legislators. An artist had sketched out a picture of how the Island front would look after development. A glittering façade of majestic hotels gazed out on to miles of golden beaches where waiters plied their iced drinks among throngs of golden skinned holiday makers. Off shore a few yachts dotted the horizon. It looked beckoning and surely there was an implicit message of jobs, investment and money for the Islanders.

"See what I mean?" Jamieson was smiling now. I could see he might be on to something. Signs of the encroaching commercial world were already appearing on the island: St. Jacques now boasted a Hilton and a Sheraton. Who could say what the future offered?

"I take it *Alpha Omega* is one of your clients?" I asked.

Jamieson laughed. "*Was*, you mean. I have to sever all ties now I'm First Minister designate but sure I like their ideas. Everyone knows that. This place could do with a real good shake-up. They may even figure in my election prospectus. You know what I mean?"

"And American money is the way?"

"You bet it is. Investment means jobs and that's what people want. If we get the US Navy base then St. Eleanor will move up mightily in American perceptions. The future's ours for the taking."

"Are the shareholders all happy with this?" I asked. "It looks like a very speculative business to me. It's an awful lot of money to put up front when the market hasn't matured yet. Maybe never will. You've got a hell of a lot of established competition already in the Caribbean."

"Well, Chief Inspector, you know as well as anyone that sometimes you have to sanction big investment in order to strengthen the strategic position of the group long term, forgoing revenues in the short-term. A focus on rapid returns would be very unconstructive. Sure, there will be some shareholders who are not so happy with this approach but most will understand it. At least that's what I've been led to believe."

And clearly Jamieson's Arcadian vision of American investment saw no implicit threat to the islanders' welfare. Money would bring happiness and an untroubled balm would descend on the island. He suddenly put his fists on the desk in a clear indication that he was a busy man who needed to get back to his work. "Do you require any further assistance, Mr Cordell?" he asked, deliberately mispronouncing my name, thereby inserting a discreet put-down into the normal civil code of politeness. But his desk did indeed indicate that he had a mountain of legal papers to read.

"No. That's all for now, Mr Jamieson. Thank you very much for all your help. You know where to get me if you suddenly remember something else of significance."

It had become a professional routine, a habit, even a game, to observe people, their little idiosyncrasies, attitudes and responses. Put them together and you could build up a picture of them and even begin to predict how they would behave in certain situations. The problem, of course, is the deceit people weave into their personas to make them seem better and to disguise the bad. I could see I was going to have difficulty with Mr Jamieson. I rose to my feet. Jamieson rose too and smiling, shook my hand. Suddenly a memory of the dream I had the night before was triggered by something I saw. Now the memory of that dream came back to me abruptly for as I looked across Jamieson's desk I saw there, clearly as a bell, a small but unmistakable Confederate flag. What the hell did an island politician want with that?

"Tell me, Mr Jamieson," I nodded as I made my way to the door, smiling as I spoke. After all, I mustn't be seen to take this too seriously. "Why does the upstanding newly appointed First Minister keep things like Confederate flags on his desk." I gestured towards his desk top and his eyes followed my gaze. The smile disappeared from his face. For a fraction of a second, no more, he looked startled. Then I could sense his brain racing to retrieve the situation. Which would it be? A straight lie or some other labyrinthine story?

"Don't think I joke about things like this," he said testily, "but that's what it was. A joke in very bad taste." So saying he picked up the miniature flag and dropped it in the waste paper basket. Then he shook his hand as if cleaning it of some kind of contamination. "Not a joke I appreciated very much. In fact it was probably not so much a joke as a mistake," Jamieson smiled. "You see I have been talking to this man – an amiable enough American in most matters – who may be persuaded to invest a lot of money here if we play our cards right who puts a high store on what he calls 'heritage'. As if that word could cleanse the damned thing! Well, he gave it to me as a little present among a bundle of other things. I spotted it straightaway, of course. Now, I was about to tell him where he could put his flag when I remembered the money and the island's need, then I thought of discretion. That's me to a T. Mr Discretion. So I accepted his present. I've only just opened things up now. Doing a little sorting out before you arrived, you see. But *that* goes straight into the bin!" He laughed again. Evidently moral fastidiousness did not harden into rebellion if his financial interests were at stake. "Now if you forgive me Chief Inspector,"

Jamieson said, walking me to the door. "I have a very important engagement this afternoon and I'd better get home and changed.

"A business luncheon?" I asked as we shook hands in parting.

"Not exactly," he said touching his nose and then played an imaginary but unmistakable off drive to the window.

I laughed and bade him farewell. I smiled back, content to let him think I was no further forwards. But that wasn't true. I'd gleaned something from our conversation. There must be people who'd know who Jamieson's backers were. There had to be.

15

A FEW MINUTES LATER I started back to the Station.
There was something wrong with the new First
Minister's explanation. But what, exactly? I reckoned I
had better confide in the team as soon as possible. So it
was that that afternoon we made an earnest threesome
in the cramped confines of my office. Lucy doled out
iced tea and biscuits.

"What should we make of this?" I asked after I had
summarised my morning's discussion.

"I was hoping you might be able to tell us," Tim
mumbled.

"Do you have any special reason for asking us? What
strikes you as suspicious?" Lucy asked. The truth was
that there was very far from being anything overtly
wrong with Jamieson's explanations. Yet I was *suspicious*.
It had struck me that there was something a little bit glib
about the whole waterfront vision of wealth and jobs for
everyone, *Schooner Landing's* own very specific
development projects and Jamieson's airy dismissals of
personal gain. I put that observation to the others.

"I see what you mean. Unlikely, if you ask me,"
Tim smiled his disbelief. "I would never put any faith in
a politician's honesty. But crime? That's another thing."

"My feelings too. It's not easy to dispute anything
he says. I suppose we'll just have to put the meeting

on record and wait and see if anything contradictory turns up."

"I don't have a great faith in that strategy either, honestly quite frankly." Tim looked at us solemnly as he spoke. "Don't get me going about politicians! He's an affable guy to a degree, especially if he doesn't feel threatened by you and he's after your votes. But smiling nicely like an advertising model doesn't turn a scorpion into a kitten!"

Lucy had been looking pensive throughout this exchange. "It might," she suggested, "be worthwhile taking a look at the companies working on the *Schooner Landing* construction project and those who are due to set up shop there when the new premises are ready."

"The actual businesses you mean? He didn't mention any details on that."

"I don't suppose he would but it must be central to the plans. Are they all tourist shops and hotels? What else do they have in mind? We should find out more about who is going to be behind any new ventures," Lucy said.

"Certainly should. It looks as if you've got yourself a job."

THE BAR AT THE Barracuda was noisier than it had been during the day: a certain raucousness had crept into the bubbling chatter of the evening. I picked out Jake easily enough, his long legs sticking languorously out from under a corner table, his whole demeanour aristocratic and somehow disdainful, his suit a light cotton one but grey and formal nonetheless. On the pale wooden table beside him the light struck a glass full of a brown-amber iridescence. Leafing through a copy of the newly launched *Caribbean Currents*, Jake's eyes seemed intent on the print but they looked up as I approached.

"Mr Oppenheimer I presume? May I join you?" I asked as I pulled a chair out.

"Ah, Chief Inspector. Be my guest," Jake smiled. Dressed as he was and enclosed by the wooden backdrop of the Barracuda bar, Jake Oppenheimer could have been sitting in London club land so far as appearances went. "Let's keep it simple," he said after I had settled myself down, his intensely cold blue eyes scrutinising every detail of my face. "I'm a busy man and I don't have much time for socialising, Chief Inspector. So let's get down to business. Did I detect a faint anxiety on the phone? Some unanticipated concerns, perhaps?" I could feel the sneer from across the table.

"You could put it like that. It may not be important but I'd appreciate it if you'd indulge me. A lot of our work involves raising improbable scenarios, examining them and then knocking them down again. Constantine's housekeeper tells me that he was in the habit of reading and annotating files at home. But on the morning he was found they were all removed. Do you know anything about it?"

"Government property. I picked up all those papers that very morning. They weren't exactly top secret but they weren't for anyone's perusal either. I collected them for safe keeping. Later I handed them over to the new First Minister once he'd been sworn in. You get it?"

"I get it alright but could you give me any idea of the contents, Sir?"

"Do you think they have any relevance?" Jake laughed and banged his whisky glass down on the table with a clunk. His tall bearing and thin chiselled mouth all lent him an indefinable air of cold authority, one not accustomed to being questioned. "Well, as it so happens I can," he said, plucking at the lobe of his ear. "There was a situation report on the plantation workers' strike, an update on the forthcoming Colonial Secretary's visit and a fairly detailed report on the proposed US Navy anchorage."

"That would be at Dolphin Bay, just north of St. Jacques. And quite close to *Schooner Landing*, *Alpha Omega's* planned leisure complex. I suppose they hope to capitalise on a future permanent American presence."

"I daresay you're right."

I gazed down momentarily at my glass of tawny port sitting on the dark table top as I mulled his words over; then back at Oppenheimer. And there I had him. The mask had slipped. He was scrutinising me wholly differently, his expression one of profound puzzlement. But then it went as quickly as it had appeared; and he was back to his superior but slightly amiable self. The mask had slipped only for an instant but that had been enough. Friend Oppenheimer was a skilled play actor. Had probably even been trained. There was certainly something else on his mind.

"Do you know anything about a sky blue paper he may have been reading?" I asked.

"Sky blue paper?" Oppenheimer smiled. "It may have been among his papers but I don't remember it. The colour denotes nothing significant, I'm sure."

"And nothing else?" I asked innocently.

"No. Nothing. I'm sure of it." Oppenheimer glowered at me as if I'd rather spoiled his evening which I probably had. "You know, I don't envy you,

Chief Inspector. Investigating this mess is a pretty thankless task. Disasters ...like the First Minister's death... are just things which happen from time to time. You're probably just wasting your time trying to make sense of it or explain it away." He smiled while giving me a nod of friendly complicity as if he were saying that of course he understood why I was properly following up my concerns but that there was nothing in the matter to be a cause for concern. The effect was to elicit a small sigh of resigned acceptance from myself. Another dead end.

"One other thing," I added before we wound up. "I was talking to the last person to speak to Mr. Constantine before he died and he insisted the First Minister was also very wrapped up with concerns about Cuba..."

"I daresay," Oppenheimer drawled. "I would think most of the Caribbean and Central American countries are keeping an eye on Castro but I would hardly think it would have had any bearing on his demise....Who were you talking to?"

"Quentin Quillham. They had a meal together that last evening. They were friends."

"Well, there you have it. Quillham was probably digging for an angle for one of his stories." He smiled broadly and I felt dismissed but sure I had perceived a tiny but significant sub-gesture in Oppenheimer's bearing, one denoting something more than the man's customary condescension.

"I hope that gives you a way out of your difficulties," he said finally.

But he had rather added to them. Yet I guessed I'd got just about as far tonight as I was going to. "I think it clears up that point," I said emphatically. "And yet..." I added enigmatically.

"And yet?" he echoed, clearly curious.

"Ah, I think it opens a way of enquiry, Mr Oppenheimer. We shall see." Disclosing nothing more, I felt at least I'd nudged him off his supercilious self confidence.

16

I LEFT THE BARRACUDA in a simmering rage. I had no way of forcing Oppenheimer to tell me anything useful but I had a strong sense that he was holding something back. Nothing definite, mind you, but years of experience had taught me a lot about how to read people. And Jake Oppenheimer was a man of unfathomable confidences and secrets. He was not telling all.

Outside it was inky dark. I was glad to make it to the Rest House though my mind was in such turmoil, sleep was not a possibility. Instead I tossed ideas around. Nothing Oppenheimer had said could have accounted for the sky-blue reading matter that had so interested the First Minister. At that moment I made a mental resolution to query Quillham some more.

By way of distraction I took up Halliday's draft report on St. Eleanor, my little moonlighting venture for *International Project Assessment*. The money may have been paid into my account but I'd better make some effort to master the contents and put my own *imprimatur* on them. But, head still buzzing with suspicions, my concentration proved weak. It soon proved pointless so I flicked through to the conclusions, my eye falling on one paragraph.

"St Eleanor is heavily dependent on the price of bananas", it read. *"Economic collapse, should it occur,*

has the potential to pitch the country into chaos, further boosting the potential for enhancing Cuba's influence. To achieve domestic stability, Britain favours a spread of risk through the island's adherence to the much mooted West Indian Federation. Indeed the UK is likely to help the Federation strengthen its position by supporting policy, economic and institutional reforms. But if St. Eleanor sought to go it alone the newly independent state would have an opportunity to diversify its economy and adopt a nuanced approach to diplomacy in the region. However it might also prove more vulnerable to Cuban sponsored subversion and blandishments."

This puzzled me but I decided I was in no mood for political speculation. Sufficient unto the day. I pushed the papers away and let my mind wander. For the first time the thought crept out that Oppenheimer was probably simply being protective of government confidences. He struck me as a self important individual, just the sort to play blind man's buff about a blue newsletter even though it were a matter of no importance. I'd maybe over-reacted. The more I thought about it, it was most improbable that a newsletter would provoke a First Minister's suicide. A bone weariness settled over me so I took myself to bed. Yet despite my weariness it proved difficult to fall asleep and when I did it wasn't to be for long. I soon came round again, gradually aware that the telephone was ringing.

I groped for the phone, feeling more like a stunned fish than a Chief Inspector. For a moment I could hear nothing more than crackling and buzzing on the line then the voice of the Duty Sergeant came on the line. "Chief Inspector Cordell. We've got a body. You must come immediately."

"A body? Whose?" I answered stupidly. "Where are you?"

"I'm at HQ, Sir. But Mrs Quillham has just rung in. She is in a state. Quentin Quillham has been murdered. In their own home. The Spyglass, St. Jacques."

It didn't take me long to dress and climb back into the Landover. When I drew up there were already two police cars and a mortuary van. I climbed out slowly. After the torrid heat of the day I found the air unexpectedly cold. A police constable was sitting in one of the cars, his peaked hat tilted forwards, but he paid me little heed so I walked into the house.

I was relieved to find the lean figured Tim already there, waiting in the hall and taking charge. "Mrs Quillham is in the lounge. In a bit of a state. A police sergeant is with her," he was saying. "I imagine you have been told the basics. It's Quentin Quillham. Just as you warned. Writer, journalist. Acquaintance of the ex First Minister. That's why we thought you should be called in. Head battered from behind with a blunt instrument. Probably about midnight. Found in the early hours by his wife. Exit, and probably entrance too was by the front door. The culprit probably left in a hurry. The door had not been closed properly. Quillham was last seen alive shortly after ten when Mrs Quillham went to bed. He was here in the study working. No visitors were expected but there again," he said, "anyone may have come in."

Tim took me into the study. Quillham was lying on his front, fresh blood spreading in a congealing pool on the mat beneath him, his head cracked open like an egg shell. I knelt down beside him but more as an act of respect than a useful action. The photographer had just finished his work; the police surgeon, Dr. Ian Fortescue, a lean man in his forties, cigarette drooping from his lips, was winding up his initial investigation. No doubt he would perform his duties more thoroughly in the mortuary. Dr Fortescue introduced himself.

"Nasty business, Chief Inspector. Blunt instrument. Used repeatedly on the back of the head and neck. Awful way to die. Not been long dead. We'll be able to give you a fuller picture after we've done the autopsy...which reminds me, may I introduce my assistant, Hennrick Straughan, bright young man, knows his stuff."

At that point a rather reserved looking, heavily built young man extended his hand towards me. His fingers were dry and bony in my hand. "Well, you must have a stronger stomach for this kind of thing than I have," I said grimly. "Best to get on with it. I'll look forward to reading your report." Almost immediately Dr. Fortescue and his assistant started to remove the body. The print man was still busy, moving unobtrusively from desk, to door knob to lock and sundry other points around the room.

"You knew Quentin?" Tim asked. His voice, suddenly abrupt, had a hollow tone, his gaze a wary, wounded look. "You had an anonymous warning."

"Yes but nothing more. I didn't take it seriously enough... We need to go over a few circumstances."

"Mrs Quillham found him about an hour ago. He'd been working late. Too late. She woke up to find he still hadn't made his way up so she went down to investigate and that's when she found him. Just as you see."

"Nobody saw anything?"

"We are doing door to door queries."

I nodded grimly. "Is Mrs Quillham in any condition to speak."

"Yes. She's talking alright. Maybe it even helps her." So saying, he led me into the living room where I had spoken to Mrs. Quillham in more congenial circumstances. She was very pale, sighing and with a dropping of the shoulders. A pot of tea had been hastily prepared for her. Her gaze looked older than only a short while earlier, as if she'd seen too much of life's miseries in her time. And now she had. "Nothing really prepares you for it, you know, nothing," she said. "Of course, I suppose I always knew it was a possibility but the fact of his death. Well, that's something else. Never to see him again, never to hold him, never to see his smiling face again. Oh my God, it's all too much." Her resolve faltered and she wept openly.

"At least he was doing what he wanted to do." I patted her awkwardly on the shoulder. "He loved his work and he loved the islanders, Mrs Quillham." My words were inadequate but such situations are always difficult. She needed a moment and I willingly gave it to her.

Mrs Quillham picked up her tea and took a sip.

"It was such a shock," she said. "Seeing him like that. Lying on the floor. It was horrible, simply horrible. The whole thing's a total nightmare. I wouldn't say Quentin was a reckless man and I wouldn't have thought he had any enemies.... Not to the extent of wanting to kill him anyway. He had no enemies," she said, "because he understood people. He had a great capacity for empathy. And St. Eleanor was his country. He was one of the very few British who felt they belonged here," she said.

"Very true, I'm sure. Tell me," I asked, "what did you notice first?"

She frowned, backtracked, and then said, "The silence, I think. It wasn't natural. Even at that hour I felt something was wrong."

"That's while you were still upstairs. Did you notice the house had been broken into?"

"But it wasn't. The door was unlocked. Nobody had forced an entry. When I came down just after four I found him in his study, lying on the floor, face down, feet splayed, arms out straight and a nasty growing red stain. It was terrible."

I gave a tight lipped nod to this. Having survived the war I thought I knew better. Luck, fate, providence – call it what you will – but whatever it was that decided when your time was up, it took no notice of how careful you were.

"Did your husband ever receive any threats?"

"No. Or at least none that he told me of. But I think I'd have known if he had serious worries like that. He just laughed at the police warning."

"Would you say he was anxious or especially worried during the last few weeks?"

"No, I really wouldn't."

"Indeed not. And there was nothing else out of the ordinary in the weeks preceding. No bust-ups? No new friends?"

"No. Nothing like that. Just the meal with Constantine. But we've told you all about that."

"So you can't account for your husband's death in any way?"

"No. I can not."

"This must be terrible for you," I said. "Do you need any special assistance? Would you like us to contact anyone for you?"

"No...I'll be alright. It was an awful shock but I know terrible things happen. I learned that lesson as a child."

"Would you mind if I just had a look around the place?"

OF COURSE MY REQUEST was just a formality. But already there were some odd features to the killing. It did not sound like an assassination or even a pre-planned murder. More like a burglary gone wrong. But was it? How strange that he had been a personal friend of the deceased First Minister.

To my surprise Mrs Quillham offered to show us around. Perhaps it was a distraction.

She was as good as her word and gave Tim and I a guided tour of the rest of the house. Dawn was breaking, giving an unreal quality to our tour. First, she ushered us into an adjoining room which she proclaimed as the conservatory, pleasantly cool and continually ventilated by a ceiling fan. An enormous palm grew from a large Chinese porcelain pot, decorated by fiery tongued dragons. Oriental draperies hung from one wall and strings of beads covered the doorway. The French windows opened on to a garden bursting with colour and lush outpourings of plant life. Flowering plants had overgrown pathways and lawn borders. At the bottom of the garden there was a small boat, tethered and bobbing on the sea.

Then we came to his study. Quillham's body had been removed. But the chalk outline still had the power to shock. I had been at murder scenes before but even I found this gruesome. Blood had pooled over the matting, staining it into a strange pattern resembling the map of a make-believe country. But it wasn't only that. The room was an austere workplace dedicated to writing. It also looked as if the occupier had only popped out for a moment, it was so obviously Quillham domain. His presence hovered about the place and it was unlikely that Chantelle intruded much there.

"Nothing has been touched", she said unnecessarily, as if to confirm my thoughts. "His study is exactly as it was when he was killed."

"But its…"

"Cool? I know. It's the only room in the house with air conditioning." I stood there a moment in awed contemplation. In the early 'sixties air conditioning was the height of luxury and a sign of sophistication. How wonderful it must have been for Quillham to have got back from his visits and cooled off over a long drink.

"What about the safe?" I asked.

"The safe? Ah yes. His strong box. He'd only had it put in a few weeks before his death."

"Weeks? That could be important."

"I don't think so. He'd often spoken of getting one for his confidential documents but even when it was finally installed he still hadn't got the habit of using it. It was always empty….. and unlocked."

Examining it more closely I could see that it was indeed little more than a strong box though it had been fixed to the wall and had a combination lock. It was certainly empty now apart from a few specks of dark grime; and its door stood ajar. I could see the tears welling in Chantelle's eyes.

"Thank you for everything Mrs Quillham. Do you think we may…?"

"Yes. Of course. Be my guest. I'll leave you to it."

With that she departed, leaving us free to look around Quillham's den. The room seemed to be completely sequestered from the world. There was no noise from early morning traffic, from children, from domesticity. All was perfectly still. The rosewood desk itself was meticulously tidy. One of the walls was full of maps, maps of St Eleanor and the Caribbean, detailed large scale maps. I went to his desk and quickly leafed through the drawers. There were piles of stationery, luggage labels, certificates, letters, a few out of date bills, pencils and pens. Little clue as to the personality who had once lived here, except perhaps a tidy one but I sensed, nonetheless, a strange stirring in myself, the first tremors of the excitement of an investigation on the move.

Was it possible that someone came to the *Spyglass* not just to burgle but to steal something very particular, so unique that maybe even his wife and the police would not be able to identify what it was? I considered the room. Quillham had fallen forwards headlong when he had taken the blow. This would be consistent with the intruder theory. I stood on the spot where he must have been standing. He would have had a good view of anyone in the hallway but not much more. There was a different way of looking at it, of course. There always is. Perhaps he knew who the visitor was, had even invited him in and felt no threat at all. Not that is until the visitor had felled him.

Then I turned and studied the bookshelves more closely. One wall mounted shelf was obviously his working library. It teemed with yearbooks, heaps of economic statistics and some general history books. There was a tray of typing paper on the desk alongside an ash tray and several stacked telephone directories. In the corner stood a filing cabinet stuffed, drawer after drawer with copies of past editions of his newsletters, going back some years. Rows of suspender files contained copies of reports which I presumed had already been dispatched to clients. There were also reading notes, cuttings of news items which had caught his attention, records of conversations. Others contained memorabilia of the mundane trivia of daily life: bank statements, receipted invoices, correspondence. Much of it was well out of date.

"Find anything?" It was Tim.

I shook my head. "I didn't expect to find anything. But it's interesting. I'm just familiarising myself with the subject at the moment: his routines, his friends, his interests...that sort of thing. He spent most of his time here?"

"I should say so." We both gazed silently on the room, almost reverentially. It was one of the most comfortable rooms in the house as well as being a working office. In addition to the desk, filing cabinet and book shelves there were two deep armchairs, replete with brightly coloured chintzes which looked as if they were changed regularly.

"A nice room," I said at last. "But perhaps not as many books as I'd expect to find in a study."

"No? I suppose he studied a lot of periodicals; and maybe he did a lot of work talking to people. Books, you know, were maybe not so important. Besides, if you're not very careful, books soon become mildewed in this climate....and you're satisfied here?"

"For the moment. I may be back."

Then an unusual item caught my eye. Wedged between the books on the bottom shelf was a small box. Pulling it out I saw that it contained a Kodak instamatic camera.

"Oh what's that?"

"It's nothing. It's just his camera. Doesn't look very used. Maybe he wasn't very proficient or even very keen." Tim moved to the window and gazed out absent-mindedly. I was fiddling with the box, removing the camera and adjusting the back when I noticed with a start that there was still a film inside it.

"Do you know there's still a film in here? Is it his?" I asked.

"Well it must be," he said. "I'll ask her. We'd better take it. Take a look. Probably nothing but you never know. She'll get it back of course."

I smiled and tucked the Kodak box under my right arm, looking at Tim with a deepened respect. He appeared carefree at first acquaintance, lightweight even. But there was a kind of professional detachment behind the easy smile. "Let's have a peek upstairs?" Tim nodded. The stairwell was covered with prints and I paused to examine them. Attractive, a bit arty, they looked like souvenirs from sundry visits in a well travelled life but they gave little away about the occupant's own life.

The upper floor proved to be surprisingly different in tone. A bare wooden surface opened into all the rooms. The walls were adorned with original paintings, mainly of local scenes, brightly coloured and joyful, redolent of the island's rich flora and strident light. Not, however, quite what you might have expected from the choice of a professional connoisseur. The record player alone was his, I was told, and this showed some enthusiasm for classical music. All the big names were there. Privately I thought I could not recall a victim's house revealing so little of the man's private life.

In the bedroom I found his wardrobe still apparently untouched. Quickly I ran my fingers through the pockets of his suits. I hoped to find a letter or note of interest slipped away in a pair of trousers but there was nothing. Then on the floor I spotted a piece of paper which had worked its way loose. It was a folded map of Miami. I looked at it with wonder but could see nothing in it of significance but quietly placed it in my pocket. I'd done as much as I could for now and told Tim as much, remembering just in time something I should already have said.

"Inspector Quick," I said. "I must commend you on the efficient way you have conducted this investigation. You have seen to everything in an exemplary way."

"Thank you, Sir."

"And we'll catch up on this later ..."

Mrs Quillham was waiting for me at the foot of the stairs. She was twisting her wedding ring, moving it up and down on her finger. We thanked her for her co-operation, promised decisive action and cautioned her not to discuss the matter with anybody else. We didn't want hearsay evidence clouding the investigation, I explained. And I thought: Chantelle, you are having a terrible time of this.

"Yes, I'll be careful...good luck", she said with a smile that came and went. After that we left. It was just as well. My contrived professional equilibrium had quite evaporated.

17

ON THE WAY BACK TO MY *Land Rover* I caught sight of
an open area almost opposite, shielded by trees and a
crumbling sun-baked wall, a bare earthed, dirty area
with a sparse scattering of gravel. Not having clocked it
when I first arrived, I had simply parked in the road
beside it. The morning light shone at an angle,
illuminating the space and helping me to spot the tyre
marks. The rain too had played its part rendering the
terrain easier to read, neither too wet nor too dry, the
moisture providing enough give to the tyre pressure but
still sufficient firmness for the shape to hold. I stood and
pondered the situation. Was it significant or was it not?
Discretely curtained by trees even the sound of cars here
would scarcely penetrate to the houses opposite.
Intrigued, I followed the tyre tracks to the bend where
they joined the road. The back wheels as always left
their marks inside the tracks of the front wheels as the
vehicle had turned right taking the road westwards
towards Babonneau. I tossed my bag into the back of
my guano-gathering vehicle and drove off, pondering.

AT THREE THAT AFTERNOON we all assembled in the
police headquarters' only conference room for the
formal commencement of the case review. Frank sat at

the head of the table as the presiding officer. Tim, Lucy, myself and a third officer called PC Gary Slade whom I had not met before comprised the rest of the company, informally known as the murder team. Worrell began with a summary of the case so far.

Quillham had lived with his wife in a fairly luxurious home in St. Jacques. He was fifty two years old, ran financial and travel newsletters which were pretty successful, albeit sometimes controversial; did consultancy work for a number of companies and was himself celebrated as something of a workaholic. On the day in question it had been business as usual. He had worked at his desk from early morning until late evening with short breaks for refreshments. In the afternoon he had gone for his fairly customary daily constitutional walk around the old harbour. Later, he had slipped away for a drive for purposes unknown. In the middle of the night, about four in the morning, he had been found dead by his wife. He had been assaulted with a blunt weapon and bled to death quickly. There was no sign of a break in; and there had been no noise. The surrounding area had been searched thoroughly in a grid pattern but no murder weapon had been recovered. The murderer had instead disappeared into the night without a trace. Perhaps an escape route had been pre-planned. So had the murder been premeditated? Perhaps. The killer had evidently come armed yet in the apparent absence of a motive, suspicion had focussed on the idea of a burglary gone wrong. Nothing had been stolen. Frank stopped and looked around at his colleagues.

Silence.

Then he resumed: "About the killer himself we have nothing, nothing at all, unless you could say it was done by someone who leaves no trace of himself." He paused. "Because of the victim's close relationships with Constantine and the telephoned warning he had received, I want Bruce to be the lead in this case." Lucy and Tim exchanged glances. "He has already brought himself up to speed with the deceased's background", Frank went on. "He will be following this up with a tour of the main people involved."

"I have met the widow this morning along with the Inspector," I added by way of confirmation. "I would like to know much more about the victim. Everyone seems to agree that he possessed some very strong convictions: pro-Federalist, pro-the plantation workers, objective but partial to the Western Alliance. He travelled a little bit but mainly based his newsletters on his own reflections and analyses of trends and events. That's certainly very unusual in itself but I want to know more about his tastes and enthusiasms; his likes, his strengths and his social life. He must have had one. I want to know about his friends and his enemies."

Lucy had a different point and a more ingenious one at that. "And his weaknesses," she said firmly. "They're very important too."

"Yes, I agree", Frank said in the tone of a man who did not normally agree. "Weaknesses that may have made him vulnerable in some way." There was another pause while I took on board that I'd been upstaged by Lucy in the mid-flow of my performance. I glanced over at her. Our eyes met, then parted.

"Any thoughts?" Worrell asked.

"No. Not at this stage. Just the obvious of course," I said. "What I find so worrying is that the files are so thin. There is no context, no motive. Violent crime is extremely rare in St Eleanor. I can not believe it was just an interrupted burglary yet there is no apparent motive. In fact, apart from the widow, there are shockingly few people to interview."

No one said a word.

"The files are very thin, I agree," Tim said as he poured himself a glass of water and slid into his more thoughtful demeanour. "And I agree we must build up more about the victim's whole social and working life. One of the reasons the usual lines of enquiry are not working here is because murders are often not committed by criminals. At least not by our normal run of criminals."

"Agreed," I said. "And what I'd like to get to grips with now is exactly that. I have not yet had an opportunity to investigate anyone who might be involved to spot irregularities, hidden motives. If the crime is more than a disturbed burglary then that is the way we have to go." I said this easily enough, not reflecting on how a murder investigation always changed people's lives, how the very act of asking intrusive questions added drama and depth to ordinary lives.

"Has the news of the killing been released?" Lucy asked.

"Yes. A very brief announcement," Worrell confirmed. "At this stage it's better we tell the public as little as possible. The more we say about what we think the more we help his killer or killers." No one said a word but there was clearly unanimity. "Well, there we are for the moment," Worrell continued. "Of course, Bruce is primarily drawn into this because of Quillham's friendship with Mr Constantine. Especially the fact that Quillham dined with Constantine only the night before the First Minister died. A very singular fact but it may be coincidental." Worrell spoke in a low voice, almost conspiratorially. "There's one other thing. I have arranged for a direct line to be put into Chief Inspector Cordell's office, reserved exclusively for his investigations. It may be useful for informants, ...that sort of thing." Worrell broke off and looked around the table. Everyone was quiet as they absorbed this new piece of information. Worrell resumed, "I have no further information, no lines to pursue so I have nothing for any of you to get stuck into but please keep alert and this may change suddenly in the course of the next few weeks. Is everyone happy with that for the moment?"

There were nods of confirmation all round. With that the meeting was concluded. I was just clearing up my files from the desk as the others were leaving the conference room when I became aware that Lucy had sidled up to me, showing an inclination to linger and to talk. She passed me my Parker pen.

"Ha! Is that where it's got to! Thanks ever so much. I'm very grateful Lucy but where did you...?"

"To tell the truth..." She leaned close to my ear and whispered. "I'm very worried, Bruce."

I caught her confidential tone. "What is it? What's bothering you?" I asked, surprised by her manner.

"Nothing and everything. Everyone speaks well of the dead. It's the usual pattern. Natural causes or death. People always make out the deceased was a paragon of virtue." Her bright eyes were on me, weighing my response.

I smiled. It was true enough. People were always reluctant to speak ill of the dead. To listen to them you'd never have believed these people could possibly have had such murderous enemies. Yet they self-evidently did. "I know what you mean, Lucy," I said. "We just have to work through that."

"No," said Lucy. "There's a bit more to it than that. I was thinking about what you said. You're right of course. The files just shouldn't be so thin by now. Something's wrong. Information is being suppressed."

Her readiness to engage with responsibility whenever and in whatever form it took, impressed me. "You think so?" I asked.

"I know so. Why is so little known of his movements? St. Eleanor is a hotbed of gossip. Always has been. Always will be. People always know things. That's the main reason crime is so negligible here."

"Come again?"

"It's more effective than policing, you see. You are never wholly alone. Someone will always remember your car; recognise your face in the dark, the sound of your voice. You can't do anything here without being noticed. Sooner or later someone will report your movements to someone else, your family, your best friends..."

"Or your worst enemies? OK Lucy, do you have any other angles?"

"Well, as a matter of fact I do. I think it'll be all the better if you come along tonight to a public meeting of the plantation co-operative."

"The demonstrators, you mean?"

"Well, yes and no. It's a public meeting. Supporters really. They are going to discuss what they can do to help. But there'll be plenty of activists there too. Why not go along? After all, both Quillham and the First Minister sympathised with the plantation workers. I'm going. My dad works there. I'm going to show him some support. But for you, it would also be a great chance to see some of the other side of St. Eleanor life."

"A workers' meeting? I doubt they'd allow it. I'd be lynched."

"Don't be silly. We can leave early if you don't like the way things are shaping up."

I pondered. St. Eleanor and its people were proving to be a bit of an enigma.

"What's the meeting about?" I asked.

"They are trying to set up a broad coalition with other groups on the island. A *Common Purpose* campaign."

"*Common Purpose*? Sounds serious and very political."

"Maybe but it's also a good way to test the country's mood." She could well be right. Perhaps it could be a short cut to taking the island's pulse. St. Eleanor was filled with hidden lives and unanswerable questions. Gossiping in the streets, queuing at the bread counter, its inhabitants mulled over the mysteries. Have you seen the price of veg? What do you make of the rudeness of the pastor's wife? Is so and so's girl really pregnant? No. There could be something blowing in the wind. One had to get involved to find out anything of worth.

"Do you have a plan?" I asked

18

"Simple. relax." And I thought I detected just a hint of a smile as Lucy continued, "We'll go in. They know me but they know me as one of them. I'll introduce you as someone who is sympathetic, someone who wants to understand. It's nothing but the truth anyway. Look, the plantation co-operative is a bit like a family. Everything is done by discussion and negotiation, cricket matches, dances, outings..."

"One big happy family?"

Lucy laughed. "Well, people are stupid to imagine a family must be happy. Do families conduct themselves in a gush of kisses and embraces? The best families are ones which squabble and fluster. They're the ones who instinctively know what to do in a crisis. And that's our plantation co-operative for you." I shook my head doubtfully. "Trust me," she went on. "Two sets of eyes are better than one. It's called teamwork." And then she laughed. And I laughed too.

Allied Fruits' decision to force shipping companies to black the co-operative's produce was a disaster for many islanders and it was impossible to see what good could come from it, except of course to *Allied Fruits*. As a policeman I couldn't ignore it. So we set off early that evening. I changed and donned a pair of sunglasses; Lucy too had added a wide brimmed hat to her appearance. We drove over through the little capital with its stores and shuttered white buildings, palm trees and purple creepers. We parked two streets away. A white van drew up across the way. I looked over. Memories of that sense of being tailed in St. Jacques seeped back. No one got out. I tensed, half expecting to see again that tall, lean and sinister figure I had glimpsed that first day. And perhaps it was the shared tension, perhaps our shared preoccupations but whatever it was Lucy must have received the same message telepathically. She tugged my arm and nodded to get out. "He's no trouble," she said.

I relaxed and climbed out. The community hall loomed up, unmistakable in its bulk. We walked in. It was pretty quiet. After the dazzle outside it took a moment readjusting to the arrangement of laid out chairs and rubber plants. It was like Community Centres the world over: the brown wooden floor boards, stained and worn by years of use. Countless meetings, dances and wedding receptions had left their mark. Metal framed folding chairs were still being set up when we arrived. Lucy was obviously well known but I was a subject of curiosity. Nearby, four or five men and a couple of women were clustered around talking quietly to each-other. One of them was white. I was startled. It was a pastor.

"Pleased to meet you, I'm sure," the Pastor shot out a hand as he approached me. "My name's Strangeways, the Rev. Strangeways." He was a tall, thickset man in a sombre suit which didn't belong here. We shook hands in a formal cold greeting. A small crowd of the curious quickly gathered around. I felt very uncomfortable, conscious of my position and conscious too of my skin tone.

Lucy stepped in. "Meet Bruce. He's the most important man in the office. He does all the big think jobs and pulls them all together...we'd be lost without him." She smiled broadly as she often did and it was infectious. The others smiled too, good naturedly.

After a momentary but intense consideration I said, "Not so hot in here is it?"

One man nodded, smiling. His name was Julian. Although a youngish man he confined his judgement of me to a downward sweep of the eyes and then shook my hand effusively as if welcoming the Prodigal Son. "No, cooler than outside. Well, Chief Inspector, are you here to find ring leaders? You'll be disappointed if you are."

"I'm not on official duty," I said. "And anyway we're certainly not against the plantation workers. That's all perfectly lawful. But I do want to know more about the Co-op's problems."

"You must be joking. To tell the truth, you all knows *Allied Fruit* are doing everything they can to shut us down. They think they lose out bad. They think we're a threat to them...They don't even own a plantation here but they're determined to drive us out of business. *Allied Fruit*, they signed a new deal with *Anchor*. They don't need them. It's just to make sure the only shipping company on St. Eleanor blacks our produce. Without a shipper we have no future. We don't sell enough locally to pay our workers and overheads."

"So you'll have to sell out to *Allied Fruit* and for the least cash possible. A very bad deal," Lucy put in. Well, I thought, at least these were certainly not yet a coerced or dispirited people. Observe and listen! Note the anger, the undercurrent of suspicion and unrest.

"Everybody do agree. But we don't give up easy," Julian said.

"Dammit! I know," the Rev. Strangeways who had been listening in, roared. "You could lose everything. They'll not only buy you out at bargain basement prices but they'll pay your people so bad you'll be no better than slaves. As for a Union, you wouldn't have a prayer." Then he added in a more level voice: "May evil come to he who seeks evil."

"May I ask what your particular interest here is, Reverend." I said.

"This is the Lord's work. And meetings like this are absolutely vital. In meeting rooms and Churches and Church halls ordinary people get together the world over to discuss local issues, social problems, unemployment, injustice. The list goes on and on. Christian protest, that's what it's called."

"I see."

Julian interjected: "Constantine promised to help. He said he would supply the shipping for the crop. He really did. There must be a paper trail about this."

"Unless he changed his mind," Lucy put in.

"Is that it?" Julian exploded. "*He may have changed his mind,*" he repeated, mimicking Lucy in a childish voice. "Doesn't it bother you that *Allied Fruit* may have had the First Minister bumped off?"

"You should be careful about making such accusations. The First Minister died of an overdose," I said rather primly.

Julian screwed his face up in an expression of disgust. "You're surprised? You expect a world of calm, good order? Rubbish. You must be blind to reality. Of course they would kill him if he stood up to their greed.

Its time to open your eyes. The world is changing. I've no use for your order, for the upper classes and all their hangers on ...There's only one class that matters now. The working class!"

Julian glared at me but Lucy broke us up. "He's not your enemy, Julian. We have to go with the facts. We have no reason to believe the death of Warwick Constantine has anything to do with the co-operative's predicament."

The woman to her right smiled. "No honey, he wouldn't have changed his mind. He was concerned about our co-operative and besides he was frightened the Americans would be too much for us when the British left. He wanted us to develop ourselves first. He once said that American influence would be like a great leafy tree which would stop us from seeing our own sky and sun."

A trickle of people began to seep into the meeting room. We sat down and waited as the hall slowly filled up. A large man sat down beside us. He turned a suspicious face towards me but said nothing. I said nothing either. A little embarrassed, I turned to Lucy. "You recognise many people?" I asked.

"Loads but nothing exceptional." Yet she was smiling and exchanged little waves with incomers, evidently enjoying the occasion.

Proceedings began. The atmosphere was hot, close and intense. Several people got up to cheers of support and attacked the condition the shipping boycott was putting them in. The speakers were sure, speaking to their supporters. Everyone was keen to help the stricken families in any way they could. They were all talking about it and angrily too because circumstances had conspired to prevent any other action. No one wanted to see the workers succumb to the immense pressures which were being brought to bear on them. There were many offers of support to the food bank which had been set up to assist the workers. For me, it was educational as I learned about the hard life of the plantation workers, leaving on me indelible traces. Even years later I could never contemplate eating tropical fruit without recalling the hardships of plantation work.

Suddenly I was startled. Julian elbowed me roughly as he climbed up to speak: "I agree with the speakers. But we need to be more focussed in our campaign." He wheeled around to speak to the larger audience at the back of the hall. "*Anchor* must be prevailed on to ship our crop. God knows they've made enough money from the islanders down the years. They shouldn't be allowed to refuse us. Any fool can see they've been kicked by *Allied Fruits*. We mustn't let them get away with it. You mark my words, if we let the capitalists get away with it there's even worse to come."

There were cheers of support for Julian as he sat down. A burly, bossy looking woman from the floor said: "We're not going to take this lying down. We are not just going to form an orderly queue and go down to the dole office. We are going to shout and scream and make a big damned nuisance of ourselves." Everyone cheered at this. In the end the meeting agreed that a deputation from *Common Purpose* would be assigned to attempt to meet with *Anchor's* bosses once again to appeal to their consciences and to force them to lift their blacking of the co-operative's produce; and also to meet with the new First Minister to plead for his support. The evening's proceedings gave me much to ponder.

The dispute was another resentment to add to their seamless multitude of sorrows. Divisions such as these become a state of mind, a permanent resentment. As for myself I could take cold comfort from the fact that I was not hated though I personified authority. But for now we'd heard enough.

"We're leaving," I said to Julian. "But, if you ever have evidence of crime you are free to come and talk to me or Frank Worrell at any time. Thanks for the information about *Anchor*, by the way." I pulled myself to my feet. Lucy and I said our goodbyes and made our way to the door.

"And remember," the pastor was saying sternly to anyone who would listen. "You'll be committing a terrible sin if you bear false witness."

THAT EVENING WHEN I returned to *Caille Blanc* I was greeted by a little surprise. Putting my hand on the handle, the door slipped ajar. But how? I hadn't unlocked it. Surely I had secured the blasted thing before I left for work. I would have anywhere but out here you wouldn't leave your door unlatched unless you wanted a snake or a mongoose coming in from the wild. It made no sense. No sense at all. But even as I thought this I distinctly recalled locking the door that morning. Just then the door slammed shut behind me, sucked closed by a sudden gust of wind. I jumped, startled. I drew it open again and stood in the doorway a moment peering out at the treetops. Then I went back inside, drawing the door closed again. As I fumbled for the lamp I felt the crunch of something beneath my feet. Something else was wrong. Badly wrong. The light revealed a shattered plate by the doorway. Well, that most certainly wasn't me. So who was it? And why? A message of some sort? Quickly I searched the house. Nothing. Just their little leaving card.

Behind me, a dark tree branch, stirred by a sudden breeze, knocked on the glass. Were they watching me now, I wondered? Had they visited just to show they could? Perhaps to see what I would do, perhaps to make me go to someone I should not. Someone I should not trust. Was someone trying to get inside my head? To break me from within? Make me scared? Because scared is easy to control. Then the telephone rang. I froze despite the heat. I picked the receiver up. It was Katie. Relieved, I began an update of events but not wishing to alarm her, understated developments.

"Yes, Bruce, I understand but we knew when you signed up for this that there was something a bit iffy about it," she said. "You can't be surprised if you meet some dodgy characters. More importantly," she went on, sweeping aside all thought of further discussion, "I have news for you."

"What's that? Is there something the matter."

"Laura is missing you badly."

This made me feel uncomfortable. Guilty, even. I had certainly received my reminder that I should not be dallying here. I was needed at home.

In the meantime I had a job to finish.

19

When I got back to the office the next morning I went hunting for a cup of tea and instead found Lucy at my desk, hunched over a wedge of papers, staring at my initial findings with a concentration so intense it reminded me of how a doctor, suspicious that there might be a malignant growth, might examine an X-ray.

"What do you think you're doing, Lucy?" I said as I walked up to her.

"Excellent, Sir. Excellent work." Lucy beamed a smile at me.

"I think I'm beginning to understand you, Lucy. You only flatter me when you're up to no good."

It turned out that Lucy had been mulling over my words. "After what you said I started looking at Quillham's financial position again. It wasn't just that top of the range house they have but he did frequent trips abroad, mainly to Florida, but even to Europe...... plus he had a sports car, a yacht, a good life cover and some other investments. I know the guy was a workaholic and his wife runs a business but all the same it looks like an expensive lifestyle for someone who at the end of the day was only a journalist."

"So you're saying his money came from other sources..." So much for Chantelle's testimony, I thought. Did she really know so little about her husband's work or was she lying? I hoped to hell I wouldn't have to proceed on the basis that everyone was lying to me.

Lucy pulled a face. "I am not saying anything. You're supposed to be the detective. Quillham had a good reputation but so what? It might just mean that he was careful to keep some of his social circles well segregated. No one seems to know if he were up to other things and that in itself is unusual for Saint Eleanor."

"Other things. Working in other areas?"

"Well, why not? We know he was a bit of an entrepreneur and his speciality was finance. Maybe he was well placed to earn a little unreported income." As Lucy spoke she moved a little closer to me and I noticed how flawless her skin was for the first time.

"Doing what exactly?" I asked.

"Well, I just thought it was an angle that maybe hadn't been fully covered."

With that Lucy left me to my thoughts. She could be right. Quillham had been a man of many secrets. We just didn't know him. The polite fastidiousness? The diligent researcher? Perhaps he was someone quite different. That raised the possibility that Quillham had somewhere upset someone best left alone? Something didn't seem to tally. Perhaps he had stumbled on something sinister, something bad enough for others to want him dead. Or a bogeyman from the past, perhaps? What about that safe? Had someone stepped in and terrified him? There wasn't any help from forensics either. No prints. No murder weapon. No broken glass. No window levered. No locks forced. In fact no evidence of a break-in. It would be easy to suspect a disturbed burglar but if so the man must have entered through an unlocked door and was surely aware that someone was up.

I sat back and looked out of the window.

There was something missing in this dry account of his life. What a step to have taken, to have hazarded all on the quality of your own analyses, to earn a living – and a good one at that – by selling news through a particular set of lenses. It must have been a passionate pursuit. No wonder when he was on to one of his famous scoops he could disappear for days on end before emerging tousled haired and secretive with a completed manuscript to spring upon the world.

But the critical questions went unanswered. Who would want to kill him? Who gained by his death? There were no surprises in his Will which gave the house and most of his wealth to his widow, Chantelle, and substantial cash settlements for his son, Michael, and daughter Anne. There had to be another motive, as yet buried, and it was my job to bring it to the light of day.

I returned to the pathologist's report on Mr Warwick Constantine. It had taken a lot to get a hold of, unnaturally so considering the status of the investigation. But it didn't add anything new. And it did not confirm any sinister suspicions. A thumping great overdose of barbiturates in the victim's organs. The First Minister had just gone to sleep and stayed asleep. The report was long and exhaustive. But there was one thing which struck me. There was whisky in the victim's body. Not a lot, rather a small residue.

I told Lucy about my trawl.

"I suppose it's always easy to kill an unsuspecting victim. Even a First Minister," she said.

"What do you have in mind?"

"Well, you know. It's rather suspicious. Isn't it? Detection its called. The interpretation of unrelated details."

"Go on. I'm interested."

"Death by excessive barbiturates. His normal bedtime drink was whisky, ok? But maybe this time his nightcap was spiked. And I don't suppose the whisky glass was properly examined. A fishy business."

"There's no such suggestion in the First Information Report. And you always insisted Inspector Parish was nothing if not thorough."

"Perhaps you should talk to him?"

"Perhaps I should indeed."

THAT AFTERNOON I VENTURED into St. Jacques with a view to clearing my head and revisiting the environs of the *Spyglass*. The town was busier than usual and I stopped at the kerb to let a passing cyclist by when, to my surprise, there was a slow grinding of brakes and he came to a halt just in front of me. "Ah, we meet again," he said. It was Julian from the *Common Purpose* meeting. I'd almost forgotten about it. I asked him if they were making progress. "Some," he said. "We're gathering our strength and getting ready to use it now. The vultures will not get their way."

"You have got another shipping line in?"

He smiled. "Something like that. But we have had so many kicks in the teeth we are not holding our breath. We've got a Tramper agreed to take a load to Liverpool."

"Sounds good but forgive my ignorance: what's a Tramper?"

"It's what it says it is. Follows the cargo, goes round from port to port looking for goods to pick up."

"Very good, I'm sure. Good luck with it all. But who do you mean by the vultures?"

He gave a shrug of his shoulder as if he were casting away some malodorous clothing. "Surely you know. After all, the police and the capitalists are all in cahoots...." I stood there awhile wondering if he were serious. "Oh, come on man! Don't shed your crocodile tears for us. I know the police don't care about us. You have to be rich to get any help from the police and that's a fact!"

"It's much more complicated than that," I said wearily.

Julian must have guessed from my expression that I was genuinely at a loss. "*Allied Fruits*," he suddenly announced. "They have made an offer for the co-operative's land. It would be the end. But they'll not get it. The workers are united. Those bastards are up to every skulduggery to close down our co-op. It's everything many people on this island worked for. It was the whole life for pa and ma. Its ruined them, this bloody cooperative struggle. It was everything, their lives, their family, their hopes, their fortune..." He looked as if he were going to sob but he straightened himself up and barked: "But we won't let them!" And on that triumphant note he pedalled off.

I stared after him and repeated his last words to myself. His family's life, their hopes, their fortune. Immediately my eyes filled with tears. I had put myself momentarily in their place and that was enough. For a second or two I suffered what they suffered. Julian had not said so much but it was as if I had read them all into his tone, and joined up the gaps in his suddenly weary face. Shaking my head, I resumed my idle wandering but after a few minutes I had a light bulb moment. Of course, the independent banana plantation had to be the key.

It was just too much of a coincidence. *Allied Fruit* were too determined to take the co-op. Quillham had been on to something. It was while I was considering this that I became aware that, quite by chance (or was it in response to some unconscious prompting), I had found myself outside the City Hospital, St. George's. On impulse I entered. An interview with Dr. Fortescue, the pathologist was long overdue. And there was no time like the present. In the interior the smell of medicines mingled with that of cleaning detergents and cigarette smoke. Above, ageing fans struggled unsuccessfully to move the still, humid odours which wafted along the corridors and wards. I should have known that in a hospital for the sick there would also be the odours of a barracks.

It was off putting and after that initial but hesitant reconnaissance I resumed my short walk back down the main street of St. Jacques. I don't know how many times I walked up and down before returning to the hospital entrance. I still hadn't a clue as how to go about this. I stopped to think about this doctor a moment. I had no appointment which would have made everything easier but I wished to be done with it now and didn't want to wait a moment longer. Besides, there might be some advantages to a discreet off the record meeting. I recalled Fortescue was only a pathologist on Mondays, Tuesdays and Wednesdays. The rest of the week he was a surgeon or working on bowel problems. Today was Tuesday.

I asked for Dr. Fortescue at reception but didn't get any encouragement. Instead, I had to wait with others, sickly patients largely silent and morose, preoccupied with their troubles. I was keen to be gone when suddenly I saw a white robed man at the end of the room chatting to one of the blue smocked nurses. I recognised

Dr. Fortescue straightaway. He was a man in his forties, with a drawn angular face, the tired look of an overworked doctor and a cigarette in his lips. I leapt to my feet and dashed down the room just as he escaped through the swing doors into the corridor beyond. Catching up with him I hurriedly re-introduced myself as we walked. He gave me a long leery look and then said I'd better come into his office. I apologised for my hasty intrusion. I said I knew he must be busy.

"Doctors are always busy," he said.

"Do you have an emergency?" I asked, genuinely concerned.

"Maybe not." He visibly relaxed. "Truth to tell, it's not as bad as general practice. Do you know I've had to deliver a baby during a Hurricane and once I performed a tracheotomy in the open air. No...all in all I prefer hospital work. What can I do for you?"

He was smiling now, looking much more relaxed and amenable so I cut to the quick and asked him about the First Minister's death, suggesting that there may have been some concerns he didn't feel he could commit to writing. But Dr. Fortescue was careful and adamant that he'd put a lot of thought into his report. The First Minister had died from an overdose of barbiturates. "I've seen the report. It looks thorough," I told him. "But I just wondered why no proper post mortem was done on him. He was the First Minister, after all." As I spoke, I recalled my first impressions of the mortuary in Cyprus during the EOKA emergency. Since then, my lasting impressions of an autopsy had always been morbidly grisly and tainted by the ubiquitous smell of formaldehyde. The doctor looked decidedly edgy, casting a moist and malignant eye over me.

"It was cut and dried," he said. "There was no need."

"But surely there were further points worth exploring. You would surely want to be as thorough as possible."

He was inflexible so I told him of suspicions of foul play. Fortescue looked startled but not shocked. "Well, that's one for Dr. Kildare I think. Absolutely not a word of truth in it. I can only tell you what the medical data says. Everything was consistent with an overdose of barbiturates. Nor was there any sign of violence." I considered this. "You've got a hell of a job, I know", he went on. "But someone has sold you a dud for whatever reason. It was the Governor's office itself... Mr Oppenheimer....who ruled there was no need for a post mortem. So, you need have no worries on that score. If I can think of anything which may be of interest, I shall let you know."

THAT EVENING, RESTORED TO my cabin, the air was windless and calm, the heavens filled with a marvellous amethyst glow. I was about to squander my time, seduced by nature's charm when I remembered one other thing I had to do. Lucy had a good point. But who might be the missing link? And why was there evidently secrecy about it? It was strange to me that a man who built his work largely on a world of contacts and networks should have so few friends. For all his connections with relatives and London-based acquaintances these ties had largely been severed by distance and the growing rift in the habits of life. Quillham did not seem himself to have made a single intimate friend unless you counted Chantelle herself. Yet she seemed to know nothing that bore on the circumstances of Quillham's death.

Could the old country still be the source of lucre? It was then that I remembered Ken's offer of assistance. I picked up the phone to a hiss of static. Momentarily, I was transported to childhood when on my brother's prompting I had put a seashell to my ear in the sure belief that I would hear the sea. It was what I heard now as I began to dial. I was relieved to get through on the first attempt. They could be the very devil, these transatlantic calls. Briscoe – my helper and my hinderer – which role would he play tonight?

"Hello, Bruce. Great to hear from you. Marvellous. Thanks for the early morning call. Its three here you know. How's it going, old bean? Soaking up the sun?"

"Not much chance. Look Ken, I haven't much time. I want you to do something for me?"

"As a favour you mean?"

"Exactly. Strictly off the record. Not a word to anyone."

A short pause. "Flying below the radar are we?"

"Has to be like that. Are you in?"

"Fire away."

I explained something of the second murder; and of the background and connections of Quentin Quillham. "I want you to look into Quillham's London end a bit more. The files are very thin. We are totally focussed on a local murder but is there anything in his work in London which could have provoked crime? I would like to know."

"Sounds reasonable, Bruce but it's a tall order. How much time do you want? I'd have to ask the Guv'nor if you expect..."

"No. Nothing like that just yet. It's only a hunch. Whatever you can spare will be fine. Even a little desk work might throw some light on things."

"Can't you give me any sort of lead to follow?"

"The money would be good. If you can access any accounts."

"That vague. It could be a lot of paperwork to plough through."

"Well look for exceptional payments – especially if they are anything like outlandish consultancy fees."

"I'll see what I can do. Anything else? Maybe a bit more straightforward?"

"His family. Start with his family. He has a son. Lives in London I understand. His name is Michael. Michael Quillham. Have a chat to him. See if it leads anywhere useful. There's also a daughter, Anne Gardiner. Lives in St Albans. Look into her too."

"Okay. Will do. But don't expect miracles. I'm up to my eye balls....And, anyhow Brucie, you will take care?"

"I always do. That's why I'm still alive."

"Ah, but do you have sufficient cunning....?"

The phone went dead.

20

A GREEN PARROT BANKED slowly, turned and glided away. That morning I had sketched in a visit to Mr Woodbine Parish of Slippery Hill, as advised. I left directly from home and was confident I was unobserved by the world as I throttled the Rover. The road itself was a veritable dodgem track, potholes and craters communicating themselves to me by means of bone jangling bumps. Yet it wasn't long before I breezed along the fifteen miles or so it took to get me to one of the more idyllic bays on the island, my thoughts about the case growing more complicated as the trees became more numerous. Something else too was bugging me: a faint buzzing noise, growing in intensity. I glanced back in the rear-view mirror; and saw something little more than a dark smudge closing rapidly from behind. My private reverie was well and truly shattered. Especially as...Wait a minute. He shouldn't be doing this. The sedan came shooting up, well over the speed limit. The road was barely wide enough for two abreast but suddenly he was at my shoulder, forcing his way past. I jerked into the verge. The driver tootled his horn as he sped past. But in that split second there was a flash of recognition, something familiar about him. Yes, that was it. The same man I'd seen by the docks that first day in St. Jacques. The same man we met again at Auntie

Ginette's. My shadow. Who the hell? But try as I may, no connection would come.

Instead I peeled off the road in search of Woodbine's retirement retreat and some sort of enlightenment. Exactly what, I didn't know. Perhaps it was the intuition that there was something, something important which the retired detective might know but which wasn't in the files. Perhaps it was just the thought that I had to keep doing things, anything, in the hope that something would give. I swerved sharply into a narrow track which became rough the instant I departed the tarmacked road. I slowed down to avoid the potholes and the boulders washed up by the rains. The car swiftly became a sauna and I reflected that it had to be a very simple life out here, almost primitive. The track certainly didn't look as if it were used to much traffic. The ruts were deep and the way was pock marked by stones. I progressed further up the precipitous ascent, through the dense woodland, for almost a mile. Seeing a wooden house on a rocky promontory up ahead, beyond the reach of even this pitted track, I brought the Land Rover to a halt; and got out.

Quiet.

I couldn't see a soul but the greenery was so dense someone could easily have been observing me. Fallen tree trunks loomed out of the dense woodland, resembling petrified bones from the Jurassic swamp. A few steps in and you could be lost forever. Take-it-easy, I said to myself. There was nothing to worry about. Then I stepped out towards Woodbine Parish's home, surely a place for painters or hermits rather than retired police officers. A fresh breeze travelled down the hillside towards me, bringing me some relief as I covered the last few yards to his home.

There was little need for polite enquiries. The ex-policeman, a night's growth of white grizzle clearly visible, was standing at his front door. Approaching with a smile, I sized him up. He was tall and thin with a wart on his neck and round metal framed spectacles over his eyes. I could see now that he was an elderly man with a head of hair the colour and texture of wire wool. A cigarette hung from his lips, conferring on him a mocking appearance. When I approached he shuffled from one foot to the other, smoothed down his shirt and greeted me though he looked weary, his downturned mouth adding to the impression of someone who had faced a few hard truths. I introduced myself and showed Woodbine my identification which he contemplated with the sort of critical attention you might think more appropriate to a connoisseur of fine art. He shook my hand warmly.

"Morning, Chief Inspector. I'm Woodbine Parish. Pleased to meet you." He spoke with a surprisingly cultured voice which seemed to belong to earlier times. "Due some rain," he added.

"It'll come, soon enough," I smiled and found myself looking into a rather battered face in which a pair of bright almond eyes twinkled brightly. An iguana scuttled by, briefly stealing our attention. "I'm glad to meet. I am sure we can talk. Yes, you know I've been invited to look into the Constantine affair again." A quickening in the old man's eyes suddenly alerted me to the fact that Woodbine wanted to be back, to be someone again. The life of leisured retreat was not for him. He was not yet ready to grow old or to die.

"Constantine, you say? Good. That's what I wanted a word about. Yes I know that case well. We don't get many murders hereabouts." Woodbine smiled again. Then he started to talk; and as he did so he became quite loquacious. The old detective evidently had a taste for murder; and told me in some gory detail of the murder of a local girl who had been murdered on the perimeters of the beach below. The girl turned out to have been pregnant. Many malicious mutterings implicated the family but nothing was ever proven. He held me riveted for a while, sending my synapses whirring with possibilities as I considered that there may be a totally different killer on the loose who murdered Quillham for quite startlingly different motives to those we had suspected. That is until I realised that the old man was talking of events of half a century ago. My heart sank. This was far worse than Lucy had intimated.

When Woodbine stopped, all was very still except for the cluck of a hen. I threw a glance over my right shoulder. It didn't seem right to be talking police business in the open but all was just a tangle of trees and bushes. Nothing moved. A huge heap of wood was stacked against one wall. It was hard to imagine a purpose for it in this unremitting heat.

"You parked nearby?" the old man suddenly asked, casting his eyes around.

"Just up there," I replied, gesturing up the track. He squinted as if he was having difficulty spotting my transport though it wasn't fifty yards away.

"I'm still setting the place up. Someday I'll get 'round to the roadway," he smiled broadly. Whether the smile was in self-mockery or not I did not know but I doubted the road would ever get built. But I was ready to go along with the fiction if that's what he wanted. I was beginning to understand that despite his evident friendliness Woodbine was not a man to be rushed. I would have to go slowly.

"Do you know how much it would cost to make this track accessible to traffic?" he resumed.

"A lot."

He nodded. "It's terrible. They clean you out. The tax man, the machinery, the workmen..."

"You wanted a word?"

"You handling that damned Constantine case. I thought you could do with a few words with the old guy who well-nigh broke his damned skull in trying to work it out."

"You spoke of murder."

He nodded again. "It always reeked of something rotten." He stopped, then seemed to search his memory and began again. "You see when I got that phone call that morning it was odd in itself. Straightaway I couldn't figure why someone of such humble rank was selected for the task, and suspected it was perhaps because it could only be a thankless one. When I got there that morning I had hoped a simple procedure was all that was necessary. I looked around. It was a bit creepy, you know what I mean? A strange kind of desolation prevailed, giving the impression of a place suspended in time, like I had fallen into a kind of empty limbo." The old detective paused and then resumed in a manner reminiscent of a written police report. "The study looked functional but warm and comfortable. The desk was plain but the paintings were antique and there was a long Chinese rug with a dragon motif. But there was no doubt that Warwick Constantine was dead. He was slumped over his desk. Evidently, I was appointed simply to help with the necessary clean paper work. I would obviously need help. This was to be Dr. Ian Fortescue, the FM's personal physician, an Englishman and already on hand when I got there. It was still early. Only a tiny handful of people knew as yet of the death. The doctor had already signed a medical certificate stating that the cause of death was cardiac arrest. That surprised me but it was true as far as it went. Cardiac arrest had been caused by an overdose of sleeping pills, self-administered.

"Nonetheless, I felt compelled to go through my routines. I asked the doctor if he knew when the First Minister had died. I recall he said 'Not exactly. Not yet anyhow but *rigor mortis* is already setting in so it was probably late last night. We should be able to be more precise later today.'

"Well, as if on cue a black van arrived shortly afterwards and whisked the body away. I sensed that the mood had changed. Soon afterwards, a black limousine appeared and disgorged Mr Jake Oppenheimer, special assistant to the Governor. Have you met him yet? I hope he's not a friend of yours because I've got to say I found the new visitor's haughtiness distasteful. There was no hint of sorrow or regret in his demeanour. It was as if nothing much had happened. The First Minister's life had already ceased to be part of our lives, reduced to a check-list. All aspects of the death were to be carefully covered before any announcements were made. No relatives, no press had yet been informed. So far, so good. At least, I think that's how Oppenheimer thought.

"At that point I excused myself to question the housekeeper, Mrs Miller, a matronly woman who was weeping, her head in her hands. She was the only resident domestic. She had been the one who found him when she brought a morning tea, as she did habitually. Her answers established a simple chronology of events. The First Minister had dined out but returned before ten, retired shortly afterwards and not been seen again until that morning. His demeanour? Nothing unusual. He had looked thoughtful and was quiet but not out of the norm, impossible to know what he was thinking. If there had been telephone calls in or out, they must have been on his private line. Certainly the servant had not heard anyone. When she arrived the First Minister was still in his study, fully dressed, slumped over the desk. It was a big shock, she said.

"I didn't doubt it and had to prompt her to continue. She said: 'I knew straightaway he was dead. Funny thing, life, isn't it? When its gone, you know, don't you? It wasn't just sleep. Life had left him.' I kept having to prompt her.

"Well, she said she had her procedures, you know. Just like the police. She had followed them. The ambulance was soon there but so was Dr Fortescue; and he dismissed it. He'd been there a bit. Then there was me and now the man from Government House. I asked her who else apart from the First Minister had keys to the house. She said only herself so far as she knew. It was difficult. She had answered between sobs. So I closed the door on the kitchen and was about to inform the office that my work there was concluded when I heard the clink of glasses behind me. Jake Oppenheimer was pouring two glasses from the First Minister's rum. He handed me one.

"'What shall we tell the press?' I asked, more by way of conversation than concern.

"'Just what the death certificate said. You saw it. Death by natural causes. Cardiac arrest.'

"'And the post- mortem report?' I asked.

"'What post-mortem report?' he said. 'There won't be one. He has been taken to the mortuary where he will be prepared for a brief lying-in-state. The briefer the better." I asked about the First Minister's family. He's a widower, you know but I believe he has a younger sister. She would have to be informed. Well, Oppenheimer wasn't worried about that. He told me not to fret. He'd take care of all that. Then he said a most unusual thing. You know what?"

I said. "I've no idea. Do tell me."

"Well, he said: 'After a short but decent interval there will be a new First Minister. Everything will go ahead as planned. St Eleanor will become independent on the existing schedule. None of this will become public knowledge. We are not really heartless, you know. It's just that we have to have the larger good at heart. You understand the significance of this I hope, Inspector?' I said I did but I didn't. Oppenheimer must have sensed it. He then warned me that I'd been placed in a delicate position the details of which I'd be well advised to forget.'"

Woodbine paused for effect, letting the words sink in.

"So what did you conclude?" I asked.

"Conclude? Its been bugging me ever since. There is no conclusion but that morning a certainty had formed in my mind. They don't want the police to uncover anything, nothing at all."

21

WOODBINE'S DEMEANOUR HAD CHANGED. I could tell his was a humorous and kindly nature, mixed with a certain melancholy but right now he looked wary as well as weary. "I'll readily admit that I was very uncomfortable with that. I hesitated but decided to look more closely into his death. There was a dearth of information but I examined that case from top to bottom and I could find no enemies of the victim, no motives...Everything, they said, added up to a tragic accident." Woodbine scratched his chin before continuing, "But I never bought it. There were too many odd factors."

"Odd factors? Well, tell me about them. What do you think happened? Speculate away. I don't mind."

"You know how it is. The sudden death theory suited everyone. Oppenheimer pushed it from the outset. Just about ordered me to quit. So they all settled for it. Even pushed for it. It's much neater and easier that way. But I wouldn't have it. It didn't add up. So I pointed out the inconsistencies, the unlikelihoods..."

"And paid for it with your job?"

"And was rewarded with early retirement," Woodbine smiled dolefully. "What happened is another thing and I don't claim to know the answer to that but I agree you might benefit from an exchange of views."

"I've read the files."

"Files be damned," he laughed. "There are things and thoughts which don't get into the files. You know how it is. There's always little things that don't get into the records. Good reasons for that, of course but sometimes it's the little things which turn out to be more important than we first thought. So it's maybe time for a chat."

"Well, I haven't been able to glean much more but I do know that his last known meeting was a dinner engagement with the Quillham. Now, you see Quentin Quillham too has been murdered. I can't help wondering if there was a link. Quillham was carrying out some financial investigation into *Allied Fruits* and more particularly, *Anchor Shipping*. Now, I'm not saying that's significant but it could be and it's not in the files so I want to look into it a little further. After all, *Allied Fruits* are a bit controversial right now."

Woodbine shook his head. "Controversial is hardly the word," he said slowly. "But that's trade union business. It's politics even. It's nothing much to do with Quillham. That man lived in a kind of cocoon on the island. He mixed mainly with the Europeans. Travelled sometimes to America, sometimes to London. He wasn't that involved really with our concerns. If you asked me to imagine Quillham taking an interest in our local difficulties, it would be with the Governor-General or.... with Constantine himself." Woodbine's voice bespoke bewilderment.

"I have a witness. Thinks Quillham had found problems."

"Did he say *what* kind of problems?"

"No. My witness had nothing more. Just said he was troubled."

"Since when?"

"Just a few weeks."

We fell silent but I was aware Woodbine had been listening intently. That was significant in itself, suggesting he may once have been a good investigator. Few people bother to listen properly. Or at least not for long. Usually, they crash out of a conversation while they formulate what they're going to say as soon as the other person stops. Woodbine was taking in every word I said, weighing them up not so much to work out what he was going to say but considering the angles. I could see now that the man's openness concealed a great complexity of character and experience. His age, his gentle manner and his personality all signalled a non-threatening person. But his mind was still sharp, a danger to criminals and fools alike. The lines on his face seemed to have grown more severe and stark like the crevices of a rock face.

"Well," he said presently. "Is there anything special you expect of me?"

"I don't expect anything breath-taking, just a talk. You can never tell. I have examined the file but as you say, sometimes not every thought is in the file. They are locked away in people's memories. So I just wondered if you had more to say. Like *Allied Fruits*? Or anything really? Something might just pop up which gives us a whole new perspective."

"I'm afraid there's nothing much but I can't see that talking can't do no harm."

"Well now Woodbine, may I ask a few questions?"

He smiled. "Be my guest. It's been a grim business. But police business has its share of grimness. I thought I'd seen the last of it but life is full of surprises, isn't it?"

Suddenly the old man looked at me closely and then appeared to have reached a decision. He leaned forward conspiratorially, before saying, "Come in. Come in to my house." A brief gesture of welcome, but words full of meaning, so warm and pleasant that they were quite disarming. "I want to show you something," he added.

"What exactly?"

"Nothing much, maybe. But it means something to me."

I followed him inside.

"Like a coffee?" he asked amiably as he led me into a small kitchen. "I've just got some on."

"That would be great."

Woodbine Parish took his time preparing the coffee, executing all his movements with great deliberation. He was not used to company, I guessed. He filled up two large mugs, handed me one then led me through to the front, whistling as he did so. We passed into a space adapted into a workroom. Models were scattered all over: cars, little steam locomotives, boats...I knew now where my office model steam boat had come from. The room was not pleasantly furnished, colonised as it ways with boxes, half broken wooden chairs and other bric-a-brac. But the old man panted his way through, pushing open another door. Suddenly I had one of the finest views in the world. From his front window you could see the entire expanse of the Bay below. The brightness of the sun repelled any glumness that the little house may have held. Woodbine looked into the distance. He said, "It's very restful here. That's the great thing about St. Eleanor. Have you ever been here before?"

"No. This is my first visit." I too looked out on the horizon. It ran in a kind of sea shell shape with two arms of land either side protruding outwards. A scattering of birds floated on the thermals. It was a revelation. Whenever I had previously driven around the coast I had only seen a part of the bay, on turning a corner, another part but then I had no longer been able to see the first. But from the heights of Slippery Hill it all looked very different, unified and even spellbinding.

"What a wonderful view," I said. "I envy you."

"I had the house built here for it," Woodbine said smiling. "I saw it first when I was young. Had to negotiate the purchase but people didn't see the advantages in those days, only the difficulties. Got it for a song. I was only 28 at the time. Couldn't do much with it for years but I never forgot about it. Then not long before retirement me and a few friends went around cutting lumber. Took us two years and a lot of graft to build but we did it."

"You spend a lot of time here?"

"Course I do. I never wanted to travel or join things. Just build this house and live in it."

Woodbine gestured to me to sit on the sofa. Now I had time to take in the room itself. A battered wooden dresser, a red and white striped pouffe, boxes crammed with papers, pencils and unfinished chiselled bits of wood he'd been working on...carvings of wild animals, some samples of home-made pottery and even a potted palm made up the rest of the furnishings. This room was way better than the other but still cheaply furnished. For the first time I noticed the loudly ticking wall clock and the smell of stale tobacco mixing with that of polished wood. "Make yourself comfortable," he said.

"Cosy place you've got," I commented as I sat down.

He laughed. "No need for that. It's a tip. I know that but I don't care. It's home for all that. Now you tell me what it is you want to ask about." Woodbine settled himself down to listen. Quickly, I summarised the state of the investigation and my concern at the paucity of leads. But right at that moment I was thinking Woodbine could have been all manner of things: country recluse, ageing drunk, gentleman eccentric. I didn't know him yet but I couldn't help warming to him. He offered me a cigarette which I declined then lighted up himself. We must have passed a full half minute without saying anything, Woodbine seeming to smile at me thoughtfully behind little clouds of smoke. I decided to let my host set the pace, tell me things in his own good time. Sure enough he began to open up but not about the case in hand. Instead Woodbine told me some remarkable stories about islanders he had known – none of them relevant to the case – looking at me all the while with his bright eyes, glowing with life. He told me stories of the wild and of the sea, the strange creatures of the rain forests, and the secrets hidden by the locals. After a while, fascinated though I was, I sought to draw him back to the investigation, to the matter that should have all our attention.

"Listen, Inspector. I am trying to help. You know how it is," Woodbine was speaking softly. "An understanding of our islanders is necessary if you are to get anywhere. You have to get into rhythm with the drumbeat of the people. Murder investigations are always difficult. You can't get involved at any level without getting hurt. Everybody senses that; and they're right. So if you're wise you haven't seen anything. You know nothing. And carry on as usual. If anyone comes by you look as normal as possible. What I do is my own business. What you do is yours. Why get involved? That's how it's done." He seemed almost to be wincing as he imparted this little piece of folk wisdom. "Am I right?"

I nodded slowly.

"In my work I saw many things, met many interesting people." I listened, waiting for him to go on. At that moment he was almost confiding. "They were both happy and unhappy days but all certainly memorable."

Quietly I sipped my coffee, only to find it had an unexpected kick in it. He had laced it with rum or worse. Probably a local *hootch*. In the distance a ship, made tiny by our cliff top eyrie, was pulling steadily away from us, churning a ruffled white wake behind it.

"There was one peculiarity I wanted to tell you about," Woodbine said quietly.

"Which was?"

"I talked to all the ministers, all of Constantine's associates. They were all agreed that there was nothing especially untoward troubling him at the time."

"I know about that. It's in the file. You found that there was nothing irregular. I was hoping you might have something which was not in the file."

"Steady on. Just listen to me. The file doesn't say everything. It doesn't, for example, have thoughts which were in the back of my mind."

"Okay. What did you find?"

"Constantine *was* sympathetic to the plantation workers. He didn't like what *Allied Fruits* was doing at all...not at all. But there was something else. I see Jamieson didn't tell you. Well, he wouldn't. He acts for *Alpha Omega* or did until recently, anyway. But Constantine was also growing mighty suspicious of the

Schooner Landing project. There's nothing written down. Leastways, nothing I could find but he had serious doubts."

"Could be. Probably, even. But where does that get us?"

"You know as well as I do that some rumours have it that *Alpha Omega* are a front for the mob. In that case what was Jamieson doing taking a fee from them?"

"That's the thought that was bugging you?" I asked feeling leery and thinking that if police officers took their lead from street gossip, the world would be a madhouse.

"That's the thought that was bugging me."

"Look I hear what you're saying, Woodbine, but that could well be mistaken. As for the mob, well, people gossip and come up with all sorts of tales. Even if the criminal connection is there I doubt that in itself would prove much. Lots of honest people deal with *Alpha Omega*. You know how it works. It's not the Chicago of thirty years ago. These people are careful to run straight businesses now. Especially cash businesses like entertainment. They are more likely to hit you with a writ from some posh legal firm than with bullets from a berretta."

"But that's my point. The mob is making inroads here. The new First Minister worked for them, for God's sakes....Corruption could be close behind. That's why you can't get a word out of anyone. Besides...." Woodbine hesitated as if struggling with something he didn't really know what to make of. "According to Mr Constantine, Quillham had confided in him that he'd come across something which had profoundly disturbed him and cast doubts about the intentions of *Alpha Omega* towards the Islanders."

"Well, that is puzzling," I said. I just didn't like this leap into pure fancy but he might have had a point. "Let's say your theory's right, just for argument's sake – it still wouldn't explain Constantine's sudden death or why Quillham was killed."

"It would if he'd been talking too much." As he said this Woodbine raised his hands, palms upwards, in an age old gesture of helplessness. But, I wondered, perhaps this was it, the quirky angle I was looking for. It was highly speculative. No wonder it didn't merit an entrance in the file but it *could* mean everything.

"What do *you* think?" I asked finally.

"I don't know Bruce. I just don't know. But I'm glad I left you with the thought. Constantine was a formidable opponent. He was removed. Quillham had serious doubts but he didn't publish them. Maybe the Mob knew about them. Maybe they didn't. Maybe something could still show up in his papers."

"His papers? But we've all been over them thoroughly," I said.

"From his study, yes I'm sure you have. But you know what writers are like. They often have notebooks....bits of work here and there. What makes you so sure he kept everything in his study? I wondered if he didn't have a safe deposit, a reliable friend, something like that."

"But nothing showed up when the whole island was in uproar."

"But a man with secrets would not have left them lying round for anyone to find too easily." He looked away with a modest curl of his lip.

"Ok. I'll bear that thought in mind. Is there anything else?"

Woodbine spread his hands in an expansive gesture. "Well, otherwise I guess I'd follow up your line on *Allied Fruit*. Sounds promising, if that's what Quillham was working on before his death. As for Constantine himself, who knows? In any case feel free to use me as a sounding board. You know I'll not be playing any office politics with you at any rate. I'd just like to know what happened. It was always a bad case. Went down as a sudden death. Had to. But I always knew it was wrong. No trace of anything else at all. That always made it look different. But it's your job to investigate, Inspector. You carry on."

"And Quillham? Any other thoughts on who may have killed him? You say you know all the locals who could be suspected?"

Woodbine looked down, shaking his head. Suddenly he asked, "Do *you* know a man called Julian Maddox? He'd been seen with Quillham, hadn't he? That's a strange coincidence. You see he'd been a visitor to Constantine in his last days. I'd always been surprised at that association. And I don't really believe in coincidences."

"Nor do I. Maddox? No. But wait a moment. I think I do. A union man...Yes, I have met him. Of course I have...But he's not under any suspicion. His name is not on the files."

"No good reason why it should be." Woodbine sounded reflective. "Common enough sort of name I suppose. But it was one of the odd things that bothered me. Maddox was a nobody, a street agitator but he had been in touch with the Quillhams some time back. He went to Jamaica shortly afterwards...Nothing odd about that either, by the way. Lots of folk been leaving but I always wondered if there was more to the connection than anyone realised. He's probably not important anyway but there again I saw him in St Jacques a few days ago and then that got me thinking again."

I shrugged. It wasn't much.

"You see it's something you may not yet know about this island. Its hard to live a wholly private life here. No one's interest is peculiar to himself. Here islanders are anchored in a certain commonality. So any question of murder will quickly raise the same names. There are none in Quillham's case? Well then, Maddox is the only mystery I can think of. Otherwise you must look to incomers for your suspects, especially the Europeans."

"OK. I nodded. "It might be worth looking a bit more closely at him." I had long made it a practice to judge the man rather than his story but I knew improbable hunches could sometimes turn out to be true. And I had put Woodbine down to being a sharp, restless man who wanted to get to the bottom of things: reliable. "I'll give him a try," I said. "Any idea where he might be reached?"

"As a matter of fact I do. He's known to associate with two others, both rum customers. One goes by the name of Murray. He's a car mechanic of sorts down in Soufrière. The other's one Valentine. He runs a small craft shop specialising in Caribbean folk art. Its called *Windward Curiosities*, a small shop in St Jacques. Maddox has been a supplier. Maybe this Valentine could put you in touch."

"I'll give it a go. Anything else?"

But there was nothing else. Yet when I got back to the office shortly afterwards one thought obsessed me.

I've found a name. Julian Maddox. That constitutes the end of an important phase of my investigation. Someone evidently of some knowledge of the underworld. An underworld connection with Quillham. A political activist too. Not probably a major actor but perhaps a small fish or rather a tributary feeder to a great river. I wanted him.

22

No one paid me particular attention when I arrived at the police station that afternoon. I had become just another member of staff. I started with the telephone directory. Nothing. Not a great surprise nor a great disappointment. But a lot of police work involves the elimination of lines of enquiry. Lucy and Frank were talking in the corridor, just outside the Chief's office. Remembering Lucy's astonishing grip on local grass roots talk, she was my natural first contact for information on Maddox, the suspect to whom I must return. I went out into the corridor and loitered. In the background a phone rang. Frank turned back to his office and made his way slowly over to the phone as if to show he was not going to run for anyone's sake. I said nothing but Lucy sensed something was up.

"How well do you know Julian Maddox?" I asked Lucy.

She nodded affirmatively. "Not that well. The guy you met at *Common Purpose*? He dabbles. A bit of a troublemaker. Can't say I was surprised to see him getting involved with the plantation workers. He used to work on building sites. Carpenter. Self employed now. Makes bowls, figurines. Dabbles a bit in Voodoo shapes for the tourists. That sort of thing. Lives alone, never married. Attracts some malicious rumour but that's just because he's a bit of a recluse. I must admit we've had to call on him now and again because people point the finger at him but he always comes out clean. He could be a much maligned man. On the other hand...What about him?"

"He was seeing Quillham before his death. At least that's what Woodbine told me."

She nodded thoughtfully. "How often?"

"I don't know. Woodbine thinks it might be important. I rather agree. I want to follow it up but there's no trace of him. What do you know of him? Do you know where we can get him? Is he capable of murder?"

Lucy grimaced. "Maddox? He's certainly always in the frame. Probably never had much of a chance. His mother died when he was an infant and his father was a petty crook. Even as a child he chose his pals from the wildest kids in the neighbourhood. Then I guess he just got wilder than the worst of them."

"Good grief! How could someone like that possibly become an acquaintance of Quillham's?"

Lucy laughed. "Well, he has his good points. They say he is a good wood turner and when he gets control of himself he seems to have had some charm, believe it or not."

"I believe you. Psychopathic behaviour. And much more commonplace than most people realise. Woodbine says he trades with the local St. Jacques curiosity shop."

"Could be. That would be a natural thing to do. That's Valentine's place. Now, *he* could be trading illicitly. Wouldn't surprise me. He's kinda shifty. Won't look you in the eye. But I wouldn't have thought it was anything serious."

"Well, let's get along and see Julian Maddox. It looks as if he's going to be worth interviewing. Can you look him up and see where he's hanging about?"

"Sure. Will do." And Lucy charged off, business-like. But I had barely returned to my desk work when she was back. "No luck with Maddox I'm afraid. He probably has no fixed abode," Lucy said.

"No worries," I said but it suddenly struck me that even finding the folklore shop without Lucy's help might be problematic. "We'll have to try this curios shop. See what we can find out. Have you met the proprietor before?"

"Yeah, once but I was in the background. Valentine, you mean? I don't like him. On the surface he's a successful retailer, majoring on the tourist market. All smiles and helpful but deep down he's a ruthless money grubbing bastard."

"Well, be that as it may he could lead us to Maddox."

"First, I'll telephone. It may save time," Lucy suggested. It seemed a good idea so I waited while she quickly found the number and made the call. She got straight through to Valentine, saying she was a cousin of Julian Maddox, that she'd just arrived from Jamaica and would like to see him but, sadly, didn't have an address and she wondered if the shop where he traded might have it. Unfortunately, it was a while since they'd done any business with Maddox, Valentine said, and he had no address.

"Well, it was worth a shot. Do you believe him?"

"Not as far as I could throw him."

"It's not far. Can't be. Let's try a more direct approach."

"Just a minute...." Lucy left but was as good as her word, returning quickly, brandishing a wooden figurine.

She flashed me a smile. "Just a little keepsake he can value for me. Valentine loves these kind of things. It'll help establish our *bone fides*."

I raised an eyebrow but she tucked the strange object under her arm.

I needn't have worried about finding the shop. It proved easy. The shop sat on a small turning off a main road from St. Jacques. A large sign, illustrated by a huge picture suggestive of great riches inside, hung over its gable end announcing "*Windward Curiosities and folklore*". The alley where it stood wasn't paved and I stopped the Rover well short. The building itself had little to commend it. Like most other buildings in this area it was built of adobe, or mud bricks. Neither was it well placed for trade yet oddly its very dilapidation lent the building a kind of picturesque air with its sun worn shabbiness and look of decay. A couple of goats broke off chewing grass to stare suspiciously at us as we climbed out and made our way over. The area was deserted but for a poor woman who sat cross-legged near the door. She was short and at first unremarkable looking. She was neither ugly nor pretty, no longer young but not yet old. She gave me a searching look as we stepped past her and for some indefinable reason her features were burned into my memory. I would have said something but the press of events sped me on. We went in.

Immediately I was struck by its otherness. It was a shop unlike any other. Poorly lit with virtually no daylight, it reminded me of nothing so much as a giant cave. Slowly the shadows began to form themselves into more distinct shapes. Garishly ornamented masks hung from the ceiling. Charms made from stone or feathers, yet polished and tinted like sea shells, leered up at me.

Candles, curiosities and locally crafted wood lay on the shelving. A young man's face looked up as we entered. He was wearing a creased T shirt patterned with parrots and intertwined branches. His nonchalant pose and disdainful expression suggested an altogether more self-confident looking man than you might have expected from his somewhat rumpled appearance; or, indeed as Lucy assured me from his reputation as running a lucrative side line, managing cock-fights.

"Good afternoon Sir," he said to me in a breezy voice. "Is there anything I can interest you in?" My eyes were still sweeping over the shop's contents, taking in new arcane articles with each glance. The whole place smelt of smoking and tobacco. An ash tray stood on the counter, bursting with cigarette butts. "If there is anything you don't see," the young man continued, "just ask. If we don't have it in stock we might be able to get it."

We stayed silent a moment and the young man continued to stare at us. Indeed, I had the unsettling feeling that he had judged me and evidently thought I might be good for a pound or two. He proceeded to show me some of his choice goods and we spent a few instructive minutes learning about local crafts. Business was good, he told me. They were even developing a mail order business. Looking around I could hardly credit that but I bought a small gift for Katie, a nicely carved wooden locket on a chain of finely woven thread.

"Is Mr Valentine in?" I asked while he took my money.

"He's busy right now. Can I help?" he asked slowly.

I told him I'd come on important business and must speak to Valentine himself. The young man relented and led us to a door, beckoning us through it. The first thing I noticed on entering the next room was its lack of normal furnishings. Tables, chairs – that sort of thing. Instead there were boxes and spilling out of them all manner of goods that looked as if they could furnish a museum. But a desk sat in the middle and from behind it an elderly man scowled up at us, obviously not welcoming the intrusion. After the briefest of introductions the assistant left, closing the door behind him.

Valentine never spoke but waited for me while moving some paper into a desk drawer. We sat down in chairs opposite the desk and Lucy held out her carving. He took it from her, examining it only momentarily before flicking his dark eyes contemptuously. There was something about the old man which puzzled me, frightened me a bit even. And his face looked horribly intelligent.

"It's a fake," he said. "Quite newly made. I doubt whether it has any special properties."

"I daresay. I'm more interested in the man who made it," I said letting my words sink in. "Actually, I'm here on police business." I flashed him my card. "I thought you might be able to help me with some information about his whereabouts."

He shot us a hostile glance, his eyes dancing around nervously. Clearly his experiences of the police had not been wholly agreeable. Yet I couldn't help recalling Lucy's observation that when she'd approached him, he couldn't meet her eye. "Ah, yes. The young lady, I recognise. Well, what can I do for you?"

"It's about a man who makes things like this. He's not in any trouble," I added hastily. "It's just we think he could help throw light on a few questions. In his legitimate line of work, I mean. Julian Maddox?"

"I don't know him. He comes in from time to time but I don't really know him." But he was too fast with his answer, not genuinely searching his memory. A shade aggressive.

"If someone wanted to get some voodoo trinkets made on this island would he be a person to could go to?"

"Maybe," he said, shrugging his shoulders in a deliberate, exaggerated gesture. He smiled slowly. I couldn't have put my finger on it but there was something about this little inter-action which was bugging me, something in his voice almost unnerving. It was almost as if he had been expecting us, keeping something close to his chest.

"Well, I'll be more precise. Where would I go to find the man who made figures like this?" Here I waved expansively at the carved figure on the desk.

"You want a good luck charm?" he responded bluntly.

"No. I'd like your advice on where Maddox may be hanging out," I said.

"My advice?" The man sounded surprised then looked at me suspiciously. "What would that be about, now? Advice is free but it comes without guarantees."

"My colleagues are convinced you are all talk and don't really know much about the making of these magical figures." I probed to identify any illuminating hinterland Julian might have.

"Which is not your opinion or you wouldn't be asking!"

"Not exactly true. I want to know specifically where Maddox is."

"Well he might be someone who could help with voodoo enquiries but I'm not offering any guarantees, like I said."

"Fair enough, but where is he? And who is he?"

He shot me a look then focussed his eyes on a tiny spot on the desk. You could see he was weighing up his options, almost sense the movement of the man's cogitations. Clearly he didn't want to help me at all. He wished I would go to hell but maybe, he was thinking, it was better not to antagonise the law. He didn't want to be involved in police work but that didn't make him bent. Lots of people are like that.

"I don't know anything about him," he said finally. "But as you suggest maybe he is someone you should talk to."

My pulse was starting to race. "What do you know about him?"

"Well built. Forties. Tallish. Doesn't smile much."

"We don't mean physically," Lucy interjected. "Is he honest to deal with?"

"I'd say so. Not bad. A bit off-putting at first but he's alright when you get past that."

"Okay. So where do I get a hold of him?"

The dealer said nothing but turned and started leafing through some papers stacked behind him. It was a smallish room cluttered with arcane goods and strange looking keepsakes. A phoney oriental rug covered most of the wooden floor. From above, a huge picture of some monstrous tropical landscape glowered down on me. Comfortless trees, lone yellow piercing eyes of some unidentifiable beast and a melancholy twilight spoke not of St Eleanor but somewhere quite other. Africa, perhaps. The dealer finally finished rummaging and produced a large dog-eared book. He seemed to know his way around because in no time he had copied out a name and an address in Soufrière. I took it gratefully but he was keen to shoo me away.

"Now Sir, I'm afraid that's all I have. If you don't mind, I'd rather like to lock up. That is unless you actually want to buy something. Perhaps I could interest you in some of our figurines as you have spoken of them..."

THERE WAS NO TRAFFIC as my Land Rover wheezed down the road towards Soufrière that afternoon. I had the track to myself. Descending to the coastline I kept an eye glued to the rear view looking for the unexpected. After a final bend I reached the coastline, parked and got out unobserved to walk the final half mile or so into town. It wasn't far but it would take at least ten minutes, long enough for something untoward to happen so I kept my eyes alert. But, no, I was not one for letting gloomy thoughts get to me, as I strode down the beach that January afternoon, taking in the leaning palm trees, the sound of seabirds, the scorching sun, the white sand. Fishermen were sitting by the waterside, looking for a sudden darting flash in the clear waters. A couple of men with knives were working with dogged intensity on a shark, about four feet long, its line of jagged teeth retaining a look of menace. A small motor boat, *The Lazy Suzie*, coughed into life and pushed off from the pier, her bow ploughing into the quiet waters of the bay. I spotted the outboard motor, registering that it was a new aluminium boat with a cargo capacity, I would guess, of nearly half a ton. A scattering of fishermen's huts lay nearby, close to the golden sands and palms. A fisherman was hauling on a boat line. A group of girls were playing tug in the sand, their slim bodies twisting and turning as their cries of delight cut across the faint sound of distant traffic. I reached the jetty with its flotilla of pleasure boats and solitary catamaran, listening to the soothing sigh of the water beneath.

Coming to a few tumbledown houses, lean-to's and empty sites I reached the town proper, once a French settlement where a guillotine had presided, a proclamation ending slavery read out and a bastard form of the French language survived even after a hundred and fifty years of British occupation. Testimony to the crumbling of empires, somehow such a rich history deserved something better. But then who cares about the history, the stuff yelling at you from the books and the media. It's all a bit of a blind, a nothing. It doesn't tell you about real life, the secret order of things. Today, Soufrière still served as a centre of sorts. It was still the place most local people would go to for their groceries, to pay their council bills, to get their ailments fixed, their teeth pulled out or their motor mended. That's what mattered.

An elderly man scrutinised me through dull eyes from behind a small stall of lemons and bananas. A few other onlookers stood around smiling; no one sullen or withdrawn. They eyed me curiously, not aggressively, but it was hard not to see the poverty, impossible not to detect the signs of despair. It reinforced my respect for Lucy and Tim, my islander police colleagues, who had worked hard to make something of their lives. The disarming noise of children laughing and chasing one another floated on the air. It was a convivial little town with not only a general shop but a post office, a chemist, a bakery and an extensive fish-processing business; all infused with a gentle French colonial style, the town square bounded by two storey houses with long windows and wrought iron balconies. I came to a dead-end. A wished-for turn did not present itself. I thought of finding someone to ask but feared that a misunderstanding would soon arise. From an upstairs room a baby cried.

Then quite suddenly I came upon the exact little lane, Garden Street, which I had been looking for. Strange but perhaps not too strange. These odd things did sometimes happen in small towns. Garden Street had only one strip of houses and opposite was a patch of scrub land, and beyond that was the sea. I ambled down and sure enough the garage was just where it should be, plumb in the centre. I found Murray working on a clapped-out looking car in his garage. He had his shirt off but being by trade a mechanic he was wearing long blue overalls reaching almost to his shoes. His side-pockets bulged out with the presence of some much used mechanical tool. Right now, he was busy with something under the bonnet. Beneath him, deep black oil stains soaked into the crevices of a concrete floor. The whole place stank of oil and cleaning fluids.

I cleared my throat.

He stopped and looked up at me. "You looking for somewhere?" he asked. "You look lost."

"Gilbert Murray?" I smiled. He nodded but stayed quiet, looking like a small animal caught in the gun sights of hunters. "I'm Cordell, Bruce Cordell. I'm looking for someone", I went on. "His name is Maddox. Apparently, he can help me. I've been told you may know where he is. Do you know where I can find him?"

"Well, I guess you've been told wrong. Haven't seen Julian Maddox in a good many months. I would think he'll more likely be in St. Jacques. Or even out of the island. He's often island hopping on business. Used to be, anyway. Is it important?"

"Could be."

Murray seemed to relax and gave the impression of having everything under control. "Well you could try Windward antiques," he suggested. "That's a curio shop in St. Jacques. I know he sometimes brings them items."

"Thanks, Mr Murray. That's a great help. I'll look them up sometime. You sound as if you know him a little. Do you rate his work highly?"

Murray looked a little surprised. "His work?"

"His craft work. What he sells."

At that Murray let out a great guffaw. "Not a tinkle," he said. "Julian buys and sells. He doesn't make anything. Not that I know of, anyway. Seems to get by on it though."

"I see. Well, I'll check out *Windward Curios* next time I'm in St. Jacques. Thank you for your time, Mr Murray."

I felt he was being honest enough so business done, I went in search of some provisions although the nagging circular thoughts returned. The walk gave me time to think. You see this could have been an example of the sort of thing which was puzzling me. Was Murray being straightforward or not? When you look at people going about their day to day business it's hard to make out any pattern, impossible to believe anything important is afoot. But maybe I was circling something bigger. I came to a dead-end. The post office presented itself. There was an air mail letter from Katie waiting for me along with another undistinguished brown envelope and another from the Met. I opened the one from the office and put the other one down. It wasn't serious. Just my monthly pay slip. The wheels of bureaucracy grinding on...Then I opened Katie's letter and stood riveted as I read. It was written on pale blue air mail paper, and the handwriting was meticulously looped and curved as though it had been written by a child.

Dear Bruce,

I don't know how long it takes for a letter to reach what sounds to be your very remote location but I think the answer may be to write regularly rather than wait for each other's letter. Transatlantic calls are so expensive they can't be entertained on a regular basis. I envy you the warmth rather than the work. The children are well and both missing you.

Katie then began a long discourse on what the children had been doing and how much they had enjoyed the blessings of a day's outing on the Sussex downs. Despite the wintry chill, daffodils and snowdrops had been poking their way through and the watery sunshine had made the trip a great success. Andrew, however, had been cheeky and rebellious; Katie had had to give him a good dressing down. But briefly, Katie's amiable ramblings transported me back to all that was best of home, nearly three thousand miles away. I had been very lucky with Katie. Everyone liked her and it was difficult to imagine why a woman like her should marry me yet we had got on extraordinarily well together. But right now I had to admit that amidst all the turmoil I had hardly given a full heart for her and the children.

23

DUSK WAS FALLING WHEN I got back to *Caille Blanc* accompanied by the whining of the mosquitoes and croaking of frogs. I sat down, re-read Katie's letter and finally struggled with a reply. Writing had never been my forte but diligently I penned a few lines. It seemed to me that I couldn't be very detailed, partly because my work was confidential but also because I did not want to worry her. Yet once I got going I was surprised by the emotional force which suddenly found voice.

Dear Katie,

Thanks for your letter. It is late as I write this and the moon is high. It is very still but never quiet. The constant croaking of the frogs is unremitting and has to be heard to be believed. The whole island is a revelation. The cooling sea breezes, the salty tang of the air, the great carpets of foam on the beaches and the screeching of sea gulls above make this a quite unique place yet I should like to be home. I should go to bed now but I don't want to go because you are not there. I have not been a good letter writer partly because part of me wants to put you out of mind until this business is over. But its no use. You keep coming back to me. Perhaps the truth is that you are never so utterly absent from me that I am totally without you. I dearly want to be done here and back home but it is going to take some while yet, I'm afraid.

My colleagues are very helpful. All that could be asked for, really, but I feel isolated so it is especially good to hear from you. So much is expected of me and I don't seem to be making much headway. There are puzzling things about the case apart from the obvious. I'm finding it harder than usual to work out the relations of the people to one another. Social communications here are not as clear as you might expect. As a result I am not getting a wholly convincing picture of the personalities at work. I meet them but the picture is like an outline on a blank piece of paper drawn with rather faint and neutral colours telling very little. I see smiles and angled faces but no inner turmoil or secret purposes. Yet I have no doubt that it's all there somewhere. I fear I am learning too slowly but I'll get there in the end.

I then studied her report on the children's activities with rapt attention. Fatherhood should be about togetherness. Yet here I was on the other side of the world. Back home I was used to having my personal life hijacked or even obliterated by the buoyant explosive lives of the children but in the perfect still of this remote corner it was almost possible to feel again the solitude of life before parenthood. Andrew was often difficult, I knew. He was getting moody and needed new activities but little Laura was the energetic one. If anything went wrong she screamed. It was amazing our eardrums were still in working order considering the decibel level in the house. Pushing aside such thoughts, I then penned a few lines describing the island of St. Eleanor as best as I could, careful not to give the impression I was having a whale of a time while she was slogging away. It was the best I could do. My mind was elsewhere. Then I sealed it up and put it on the end of the desk, ready for posting.

THE NEXT MORNING, SATURDAY, I returned to Saint Jacques on personal business. Deciding that a touch of the normal and familiar was in order I went to the *Green Parrot* café. The pavement tables were all occupied, the cafe full and noisy. I spotted a vacant table and went over to it. It was good to be one of a crowd amid a swirl of customers, enjoying an innocent coffee and some biscuits, which looked like they had been designed by a modern art student. So good that I lingered there longer than necessary as my host gave me such a warm reception. A native of Trinidad, originally from Bridgetown, he never stopped saying how happy he was to welcome someone from Britain. He still tended to view colonial influence as beneficial and I hadn't the heart to explain to him how times were changing. We had a long chat about how business was faring, interrupted by customers' orders, especially those of a group of youngsters who quickly drank down their coffee and then threw their empty cups in the air to be caught by our host. He pretended to be amused but when they left, he made a rude gesture and cursed them under his breath. Couldn't say I blamed him. Left to my anxieties about the job in hand, I thought, at least I had the IPA money. So Katie was quite right. A new car would be in order. Just then there was a clattering of china which made me look up. Passers-by were idling outside but nearby two women were engaged in an animated conversation, oblivious to my prying ears.

"What time did you say you woke up?" asked a rather burly thirty something.

"Four o'clock...if I hadn't, the whole house would have been ablaze."

"Good Lord! What a thing! That bad? I'm finding all this hard to believe. I would have thought he was so reliable."

"It doesn't matter," the other said. "On some things he can be so peculiar. He's often playing pranks. It's pathetic really but this time he's gone too far!"

I looked out of the window and took a deep breath. The world and its problems churned on, releasing their torrent of emotions. My eye caught a familiar looking face, that of a young man earnestly reading a paper while supping a large breakfast sized beaker of coffee. For a moment, I wondered if it were one of my off-duty colleagues; but, no, it was young Hennrick Straughan, Dr. Fortescue's doughty lieutenant. I hadn't recognised him at first in his multi-coloured T shirt and sandy trousers but it was Straughan alright.

"Mind if I join you?" I asked as I sidled over, coffee in hand.

"Be my guest," Hennrick's young face smiled as I sat down opposite. "I could do with some company. I've just popped out for a little break."

"I can imagine you need a respite from all those stiffs!" I said with a grimace.

"Are you anywhere near a conclusion on that writer chap's case or shouldn't I ask?" he answered. "It's just that it's stuck in my mind ever since that night. Such a horrible business. It's etched on my memory. Blunt instrument. Used repeatedly. An awful way to die."

"I don't need reminding. There was an awful lot of blood. I saw it myself. What a night to remember.

Someone must have hit him on the back of the head very hard indeed."

"Not necessarily as hard as you think. He had one of those thin skulls. Some people do. It's just one of those things."

"I know. But at least the First Minister's apparent cause of death has been confirmed. There are no suspicious circumstances. Death by an overdose of barbiturates."

Straughan suddenly spilled some coffee on to his lap. He stared at me blankly, not moving a muscle. At that moment anyone would have thought him a madman. "You can't be serious!" he said at last. "We did the autopsy. We were all told it was terribly hush-hush. But there is no doubt his death was caused by a lethal injection of air. *Air embolis*, we call it. You see, the brain cannot take a long shot of pure air. It's an easy weapon but it cannot be self administered. The mark of the syringe was still visible."

"You sure about that?" I said, trying to stifle my excitement. 'There was no post mortem."

"A secret one. Yes, we were all sworn to secrecy. But I presumed the police knew. Well, at least the investigators...I mean they'd have to." Straughan had the look of a wild man at that moment but I had nothing to say. Well, that was that. What was Fortescue's game? Well connected though he was, he had quite irresponsibly evidently tried to put a genuine investigation on the wrong trajectory. Or was Fortescue simply doing as he was told. I looked at Straughan and let the silence grow between us.

As soon as I emerged into the daylight again I was smiling all the way. I had no doubt about it. Constantine had been murdered and Maddox may hold a key. I couldn't wait to get back to the station to tell Lucy and Tim. Walking along the dockside towards the pier I had a positive spring in my steps. This would be the making of me. I scarcely noticed a large vessel which was being loaded, loaded with the co-operative's bananas. Behind me, a lorry was beetling its way behind me to the ship's side. Strictly normal port traffic. Then I picked up the quieter tones of a more expensive engine. A black limousine swept along the front before disappearing at the far end. I stepped off the pavement and the same instant I heard the roar of an engine to my left. A dark shape shot up on my left and it took only a split second to clock that it wasn't stopping: it was aiming straight at me. I jumped forwards, just in time as the car swept past, missing me by inches.

Shaken, I sat down on a stone wall. Already, the dark car had skidded round a corner, disappearing into the urban labyrinth. Was I turning paranoid or had someone just tried to kill me? I had been lucky. No doubt of that. I stood up again and found the crowds interested in less exciting fare. A man clicking spoons between his fingers commanded an audience at least five people deep. Some American sailors were laughing and strolling about, come ashore from one of the ships involved in *Exercise Swordfish*. Further on, a small water burst had attracted a crowd of onlookers. Others were watching a small boat being unloaded. I walked on. People were jostling and laughing, noisy and swarming like bees in the brilliant sunshine. They were clustering around clothes merchants with their lengths of colourful dress material and also around tables piled high with heaps of jewellery and junk.

"Pain!"

I knew the French word right enough, easily detectable amongst the Creole, still widely spoken on the island. At first I couldn't make out the beggar's face. He had repeated his mantra automatically enough, ever alert to the presence of a white man. Now he thrust out his cupped palms. I reached my hand into my pocket.

"Get yourself a jam sandwich", I said, handing a few coins to the shadowy figure.

"Thank you Sir," said the voice in English, devoid of emotion. He leaned forward for a moment and for the first time I caught sight of his face. Intelligent eyes set in a weary face stared back at me. He had an air of deep sadness. Good Times would never come again if they ever had. "It's no use," he said.

"What's no use?" But the figure shrank back, laughing mirthlessly; and I walked on. An enormous apprehension descended on me, contrasting with the excitement of my morning find. I walked on disconsolately, lingering on the pavement. Recently, I'd acquired a habit of eating a piece of chicken from Giselle's, a stall housed under the wooden hall of the great market. Munching as I went, I slalomed between the stalls of pineapples, yams, cassava, papayas, and cashew nuts until my gaze fell on a mother who was with her child, a child making a lot of noise. The mother, about forty, her hair brushed perfectly, wore a heavy blue dress which masked her figure. She was becoming exhausted by her boy, careering around with a toy car and some small change he kept producing from his trouser pocket. He did everything his mother told him not to do, to keep her attention, spreading out everywhere to mark his territory, like a king, a conqueror, expressing what adults learned to mask: a love of money.

When I stopped watching the child, I looked across to the busy street and my eyes fell on a figure approaching with rapid steps, his face earnest, grim. Then I recognised him. It was him: the man in the red T shirt and jeans, the man Woodbine had directed my attention towards. Julian Maddox. He was walking quickly towards me, one hand nonchalantly in his trouser pocket, the other busy with a cigarette. Thin and athletic looking with just a hint of a swagger, he stopped at the pavement's edge to take a drag on his cigarette and it was at that moment that our eyes met. There was a good fifty yards between us. I started towards him but he dived into the dense throng. A large lorry freighted with pineapples passed between us before I could dart across the road, just about able to keep my eyes on the man's rapidly disappearing back, dodging through the crowds.

"Police! Stop! Stop that man!" I bawled, feeling like some stage comedian. Heads all turned in unison like a flock of geese changing direction together. But the fugitive was running well ahead. Nobody was impeding him. I was closing the gap when a foot suddenly appeared from the crowd, sending me sprawling. I hit my right knee hard on the ground. Dazed and grovelling I cursed, got to my feet and started moving again but a pain shot up my leg. It had only been seconds but they were enough. The figure was already heading out of the crowd towards the mean alley ways. I followed him round the corner but there was no sign. Instead, two scrawny children, playing in the street, looked up at me in amazement. A series of doorways mocked my quest. A maze of narrow alleys wound their way up the hillside and down to the harbour. St. Jacques folk must live on top of each other, densely packed. There couldn't be much privacy or quiet here but I knew it was pointless to make enquiries. I didn't give up that easily, of course. I searched the side streets but only found fractious children, yapping dogs and somnolent pensioners. There was no sign, no trace of Maddox but he'd been here alright.

I shook my head sadly. No use here. It would be madness to hope to find where Maddox was hiding among this riot of buildings, some of them not even proper houses. I turned to make my way back when I fell victim to a sensation of being watched. I suppose a stranger, a foreigner and white man at that, will always be a subject of interest in a closed community but I felt uneasy. Looking up, I saw a group of men looking out from an overhanging window. I retraced my steps but although the lane behind me was deserted I felt a stab of tension in the back of my neck. I turned. No one. But for the first time I regretted my solitary pursuit, without colleagues into the more backward streets of the capital. But it was already too late. Two men were walking purposefully towards me. Glancing over my shoulder I saw two others had cut off any hope of retreat. The street suddenly had grown eerily empty where before there had been passers by. Only moments earlier it had been a proper thoroughfare, not truly busy, but certainly not deserted either. And now, no one. I could see myself being knifed before I could do anything.

Desperately, I backed myself against the street wall looking for any opportunity to escape. I heard some rubber soles making swift running steps. Frantically I looked around for any projection which might give me some shelter and spotted, to my left, a door. I leapt down to it and turned the handle. It opened. Thank God! I breathed more deeply, filling my lungs for action. Ahead the little hallway was dark and sombre. I guessed this was an entrance to a block of flats but I wasn't such a sitting duck. I crossed the floor to an inner door, standing slightly ajar, just as my pursuers burst in. I didn't knock. I put my shoulder to the door and barged inside. Then I fell upon a scene that I can't find words to describe, which I smile about now, but which, at the time, startled me sufficiently to make me almost forget the blades of the criminals.

I had come upon, not a stairwell as I had anticipated but a small courtyard. In front of me about a score of women were sitting, quietly reciting a prayer. My breathless and dramatic arrival attracted almost no attention at all but I, not content with interrupting their holy ceremony, tripped over an upturned stone, cursed and sprawled out over the floor. I felt ashamed even in my own danger. What could I say to these women? How could I explain myself? But I didn't have to say anything. One of the younger ladies took me by my elbows and helped me to my feet.

"Excuse us, Sir, if we finished our prayer before assisting you. But take a seat over there," she said, pointing to a chair beside the wall "and wait for us if you will."

Her friendliness was reassuring. I looked back at the door, just in time to see it closing. My pursuers were in retreat. Strange but maybe not so strange. There were too many witnesses here. Momentarily unsure what to do, I followed the lady's advice and went to sit at the rear. I didn't have to wait long. A small group of women returned and contemplated me uncomprehendingly.

Then the lady who had spoken earlier said: "If you wish to join our prayer group you are more than welcome. We are ready to receive you. But if you are simply a passer-by then its not for us to discern God's intentions."

Not knowing what to say I thanked her again.

"Are you interested in our literacy project?" she asked, looking faintly puzzled.

"Yes."

"We need all the help we can get." She took me over to a table festooned with children's books, mostly with a Gospel message. "You see these books are so old! We need modern up to date literature. Do you think you could help us?"

"Yes, I do," I said with a show of earnest seriousness. "I know some people at Government House who may have grant money for your sort of work."

She passed me a sheet of paper giving information and contact details about the St. Jacques Literacy Project. I thanked her, promising to be back in touch and made my way back to the exit. I looked around cautiously but the street was now empty. It had returned to normal. Except it could never look so innocent again. I became aware of a trickle of blood from my right knee. I'd ripped a hole in the trousers. I started back, all the time watching for tell tale signs of being shadowed. Things like a car starting up, someone dashing to be picked up. But nothing out of the usual happened.

24

LATER THAT AFTERNOON AS I sat in my office I could make out two ships approaching St. Jacques. Usually a source of fascination, this afternoon's view went unremarked. I needed to think more clearly about how I was to handle this episode. Obviously, I should report it but I felt disinclined. In a way, was it not a distraction? It may well be that somebody in this labyrinthine building knew of channels of communication with the underworld of Saint Jacques but this was not my business. My task was much more specific. And when completed I would be heading home. I should stick to the straightforward manner with my colleagues, the blunt but effective policeman. I turned to face the mirror and practise my composure; it would be no good to let nerves get the better of me. I'd better avoid local police politics. I couldn't be sure what was policy and what was not. And I was better off not getting involved.

The door opened and Lucy, her face adorned with a smile, approached me. Looking past her shoulder I glimpsed the gangling figure of Tim Quick. He entered behind her. I only gave my colleagues a severely edited version of what had happened that afternoon. It seemed to me that if I had told them how imprudent I had been it would undermine my authority. And then they might feel free to commit all sorts of follies without me being able to reproach them.

"It's no deal boss," Lucy said. "Valentine's leads were hopelessly out of date. We checked out the address he gave us in St. Jacques. It was a dud. Maddox hasn't lived there in years. And you confirmed yourself that Murray had nothing definite."

"It's hopeless," Tim concurred. "I think Valentine is probably covering for him. And, by the way, we both deserve medals for the amount of donkey work we've been doing. We are most surprised you saw him. We think Maddox must have returned very recently. There are certainly no reported sightings to the police, other than yours. Unusual for a man like that. The last boat from Jamaica was last Thursday."

"Last Thursday?" I said so loudly I was almost shouting. "That's the day Quillham was murdered."

"It's conjecture – but a credible one – that he arrived with that boat."

But we had no clue as to where he was.

We held a brief impromptu discussion of possible friends – more like a rogues' gallery, really – who may be putting Maddox up. Lucy and Tim were bandying names about rather in the way football fans can talk airily of players as if they were personally acquainted. But in the end we drew a blank.

"Sorry, Chief," Lucy had said, her sympathy obvious.

"Sorry? I enjoy a good challenge." And I did.

"Sir, I don't want to stick my oar in where it's not wanted," Tim said looking at the wooden floor as if it had become a subject of great interest. "But for a while now you've struck me as looking very down in the mouth."

I ventured a smile. "Well, I daresay you're right. I am feeling a bit low."

"Health problems?"

"Work problems, more like, I'd say," Lucy put in.

"Yes...that's it. This casting about in the shadows, looking for something which may not be there. The wretched procedures...it's all so time consuming and you don't seem to be getting anywhere."

"If you'll forgive me for saying so, what you need is a good night out. A bit of fun!"

Lucy took to the idea straightaway. "That's it Tim. You're quite right. What do you say, Chief?"

And so before I knew it I'd agreed to an evening blow out with my two colleagues at Tim's auntie's place in Babonneau.

GINETTE GREETED US at the entrance to her Babonneau restaurant that evening, pointing to her beautiful cursive writing on the slate which proclaimed the fish of the day in chalk. She drew a friendly nod of approval from a patron, a true connoisseur's gesture of support, then offered me my first lager that I sipped while watching the last boat head off from the jetty. Everything was slowing down, gestures, looks, boats...thoughts...I had got used to this way of life pretty quickly.

Here the sun does not set: it falls, allowing practically no time for a half light to settle down. Tim Quick and Lucy Wainwright, dropped on to chairs opposite me while I was beginning my carefully cooked dish of lion fish accompanied by slices of roast pineapple. But all my attention was on my companions. Lucy was a woman transformed, someone I had never seen before. She was dressed in a sparkling rig and wore it with the flair of the islanders. From her glossy hair held by a golden pin to her bright leaf patterned cotton dress she was as fine an advertisement as you could get for St. Eleanor. Even her manner was transfigured, if you had not known her. She was self confident and assertive, free of the restrictions of rank. Tim was a surprise too. Warm and wary he was more than ever the reliable but hearty companion.

The restaurant was getting quite festive now, the tables full and the decibels of laughter rising. I dare say we fumbled the first snatches of conversation but once we were more settled and the alcohol working its magic we managed to feel totally at ease with one another.

"Wow, well isn't that a pretty little dish," Tim said almost conspiratorially to me, leaning over and indicating one of the waitresses. To tell the truth she looked to me to have rather shifty eyes set in a determined looking face. But of course Tim was more interested in the large bulges under her blouse. Still, it was an evening to unwind and impossible not to respond to the warmth of the occasion. A light breeze made me wish my job gave me more opportunities to work outside, to get the feel of the place. The exact memory of what we talked about is gone now but the faces remain vivid as does the general tenor of the evening. If you've ever been to the Caribbean you'll know what I mean. If you haven't then its hard to describe to you the islanders' conviviality: the lush green of the interior, the bright flowers spilling over everywhere, the abundant fruit ripe for the picking, the ever present deep blue of the sea, the people all companionable, the sun warm on the skin, the nights covered by a sequin shawl of glittering stars. And that's one of the problems of living here. You can forget too easily that it is also home to villains and intrigue. In short, it's a place of illusions. And right now I was enjoying the charm of the evening, the meal and delightful company. We chatted into the evening and as we found ourselves in open relaxing country, I began to unwind. I told them of my youth in New Zealand and about sailing off the coast from Nelson and every day as a joy to behold. No doubt it was an edited version but I half believed it myself and from the south seas it was an easy stride to the Caribbean. They in their turn began to tell me of the fine fishing which was to be had here. It was while they were expatiating on this fishing theme that I caught sight of someone I hadn't really wanted to see. In a seat across the other side of the restaurant, eating his meal alone while staring all the while at me, was the man I'd first encountered at St. Jacques dockside. My first thought was that he must have followed us but then I discounted it as paranoia for wasn't it the second time I saw him in this very restaurant. Perhaps he was a regular. I tried to refocus on the more enjoyable matter at hand. I relaxed, the sense of my surroundings slowly altering. The babble around me seemed to float on the air while all around the distant scents of the tropical forests filled my nostrils.

"It seems to me," Tim was saying after ordering another beer, ponderously at first but then speaking in a rush, "that we might have more of a chance of finding out what we want to know if we bent the rules a little... Sir. Can I give you a tip?"

"Why not?" It pained me to see Tim, normally so bold and upfront, apprehensive and struggling to find the right way of putting things to me. But I must admit I was a bit distracted as I couldn't refrain from snatching glances at our distant visitor from time to time. "Really Tim?," I replied a little sarcastically. "What have you in mind?"

"Well, Sir, as you said Sir, Valentine was holding back on you. He's certainly a flaky customer so he's the most promising line of enquiry. But it's no good doing it the way you and Lucy did – knocking on the front door and trying to sell him a hoover, so to speak, Sir, if you follow my meaning. Now its clear no one actually lives in the curios shop yet you say that there was more than a suggestion from the look of his office that that's where Valentine actually keeps his records, such as they are. Tomorrow night we might – we might explore the place a little bit more in private..."

I could tell Tim was making a great effort to look like a seasoned detective but this was a bridge too far. I was on the point of dismissing the suggestion as a fantasy when Lucy quite unexpectedly reinforced the suggestion. "I think Tim's got a good point. It would be impossibly awkward to ask for a warrant just to get an address but I remember thinking those windows of his looked easy to force. In fact if Valentine had asked for security suggestions I'd have told him forcibly to put a proper robust lock on his windows but he didn't and he hasn't. So I suggest we pay his office a visit one night soon." Good for you, Lucy, I thought, being so affirmative and refusing to be put into the background.

"You could be right." I said. I wondered anew about Maddox and the disproportionate amount of time going into this investigation. Or was it? True, I hadn't a scrap of evidence to link him to the Quillham murder except for the fact that they had met on occasion and at sensitive times at that. Yet I had a conviction that if we could flush him out, we might yet glean a vital piece of the truth. Mulling this over I happened to glance over at our observer again. This time I was spotted.

"What is it?" Lucy asked, following my gaze. I explained about our shadow who kept showing up and staring at us but as they both turned around to see who I meant, he was gone.

Perhaps it was because I was a tad embarrassed by the incident that I decided to smooth things down by agreeing to Tim's suggestion. Or perhaps I just decided to go along with the flow. Maybe it was their cheery faces, the alcohol or the balmy setting but it looked like an easy option right then. "Really ingenious. We certainly need to force things along a little if we are to get our man," I agreed.

WINDWARD'S FOLKLORE AND CURIOSITIES was in darkness and the street lighting non-existent but in case the owner was on the premises I knocked on the door. No answer. I walked around and, to my surprise, saw the glimmer of an internal light showing through a narrow window. I peered in. Sure enough a pale nimbus shone from the little hallway into Valentine's study. I went back to the front and knocked again. Nothing stirred. Valentine was out. It was strange how many people left a hall light on, thinking it would deter robbers. Yet it was virtually an announcement of an empty house.

I signalled the all clear to Tim and Lucy; and returned to the window, thinking that maybe I'd agreed to their plans a little too lightly. After all, if I were found inside what on earth could I say? Momentarily, I had a horrid vision of being pilloried for breaking and entering into respectable business premises. I hesitated a moment before focusing on the window again. External shutters had been roughly pulled over but it was an easy task to jerk them back. As expected, it was the study. At first I couldn't make out much in the darkness, it being hard to distinguish one object from another, but as my eyes adjusted I began to make out a few shapes. A scatter of gruesome wooden charms lay on the floor and Valentine's desk had a drawer hanging half way out as if he'd left it in a hurry. Or perhaps it betokened a quick, focussed search. There was yet another cause for anxiety. A grimy wall, where once the melancholic African picture had hung, was exposed. Below, the Oriental rug had been half-turned over.

The window frame was old and worn, just as we had suspected. Cracks in the woodwork gave it an inviting look. I took out my penknife and pushing the blade through the crack, flicked back the catch. Then I pushed up the window. The first three inches were easy enough but then it stuck fast. It obviously hadn't been opened in ages. I stopped and looked about again. No one. One more heave and at last the window opened with what sounded to me like a terrible squeaking. Then I hoisted myself in and closed the window behind me.

My feet immediately made contact with some inanimate objects and I danced from foot to foot trying to avoid crunching anything. I flicked on my torch and saw that dolls, masks and little figures had been spread across the floor. There was also a scattering of paper and photographs. Materials had been flung from the shelves and from the half-opened drawer. But what were they looking for? And who were *they*? Or was it simply Valentine himself in a paroxysm of rage?

But I didn't have time to dither. I glanced back through the crack in the shutters. Nothing stirred on the outside. For safety's sake I thought it best to put myself beyond prying eyes. I closed the shutters behind me to make the exterior look as normal as possible. When Tim, Lucy and I had been making out our plan we had decided the success of the break-in depended on one thing, knowing where Valentine would keep his confidential material.

We had thought that Valentine was sufficiently orderly that he would probably keep things in their proper place, just as a normal office would. The room's disorder had now thrown this assumption into doubt but I decided to stick with our agreed plan.

So it was that during the next half hour I went rapidly about my task, methodically returning every minute or so to the window to look up the road. I found an address book on the desk. I flicked through it fast but there was no sign of Maddox. There were some folders, clear and neatly labelled but nothing in them which their titles hadn't proclaimed. All the while I was searching for the clue to the whereabouts of Maddox I found myself equally preoccupied with the question of who might have been here before me. In the bottom right hand drawer of the desk I found a dark blue cotton bag. But this find was of no help. It was empty save for a few specks of black grit. The desk top was mainly concerned with correspondence to do with the shop. One of the letters was very interesting indeed. I re-read it carefully and made notes on a piece of blank paper I found among Valentine's stationery. It was a clear reference to Maddox, implying that he was often sojourning in Grand Riviere, wherever that was. But nothing was clear cut. It was disappointing.

I decided to cut my losses and leave. I'd bent the rules quite enough already. There was nothing more I could do without a warrant. Then I thought to myself, this place looks a bit fishy. You can never know too much about a suspect. There was an adjoining room, not leading to the shop. I decided to try it. It proved to be a pleasanter room, a lounge of sorts with a sofa and two chairs. I had a brief look around but there were no likely places for office papers. Suddenly I heard a noise. The front door. Immediately I extinguished the light. Petrified, I lost precious moments before I fully took in footsteps making their way towards me. I heard two voices in low, earnest conversation. I threw myself down behind the sofa only as the door was opening and the couple entered, carrying an oil lamp. Stupefied, I lay low without a thought of how I could get out of this. I could glimpse the rest of the house beyond the open door but all was darkness.

"I was sure I must have left them here," the man was saying. He sounded agitated, jumpy even.

"Well, get them! Such a fuss about a medicine for the digestion," the woman replied.

A bright light suddenly lit the room up. I crouched even lower and missed their next few words. They were speaking in low voices. Little by little a swarm of insects was beginning to build up around my head. It was soon going to be unsupportable. I flapped my right hand to shoo them way but in so doing made a tiny, *treacherous* noise.

"Did you hear something?" asked Valentine.

"No."

A complete silence, lasting an eternity, ensued. I imagined that they were cupping their ears in a theatrical way, trying to capture the least sound.

"I can only hear your stomach rumbling. It's time we were going. I can see your tablets over there, on the side table. Take them. In fact, take two now. That should calm your stomach."

I heard Valentine walk over to the sink, I guessed to a tap to get some water. His tablets taken, he returned to the sitting room.

"Those police officers. what did they want?" The woman asked as they walked back to the door, taking the light with them.

"Maddox."

"You told them?"

"No."

"Why not? He'll be in Libreville. Maddox is nothing to us. You may as well be straight to the police when you can."

"It's a matter of honour", Valentine said in a calm voice, oddly suggesting a strong emotion.

The woman sneered. "And Fernando? Is he still in Libreville?"

"He comes and goes as he pleases. I don't know where he is."

"A fine mess he's made. Why couldn't he take your word?"

"Fernando doesn't take anyone's word. He doesn't trust anyone."

"I wish you'd drop the lot of them. All their fine promises and fancy words didn't add up to anything. It preys on me."

"Listen!" Valentine snapped. "Don't talk like that. We'll do just fine so long as we keep our mouths tight shut!" There was a pause and I could imagine him glowering into her eyes. "Understand?"

There was a murmured agreement before their footsteps retreated into the darkness.

25

"JUST WHAT'S THE PROBLEM?" I asked.

Lucy and Tim exchanged looks. "What isn't?" Lucy said finally. "It's remote and hostile. You can't drive there. You have to climb to get there and there's no saying you will meet anyone. They're not exactly friendly...not that that makes them guilty of anything. They've just dropped out of society. But that's bad enough."

I snapped my fingers. "Look! Why did Quillham have dealings with such as Maddox? That's what I would like to know. Do you have any idea?"

It was the next morning and we were back at the office discussing a projected visit to the rogue village of so-called Libreville, aloof from the rest of the island, perched on a mountain top, its few inhabitants all, apparently, misfits or drop-outs. No doubt we could count on a pretty chilly reception but that wasn't the point. A three hour climb up the mountainside should hardly be a deterrent. But my colleagues were not so enthusiastic.

"We'd be asking for trouble," Tim stated.

"You scared?"

"That's right," Tim replied emphatically, walking up and down the room as was his wont whenever he became agitated. "It's a total pain." He looked around, evidently feeling for more convincing words. "Even if you did meet them, they can be very crude, rude and unhelpful. So everyone says, anyway and I guess it's true."

I gulped. "You mean even you haven't been for a look?"

"Do you think I'm stupid?" he retorted, glowering back at me.

"Well, high time you made up for that deficiency. Besides, you should consider it an order. Any mishap will be my fault." I smiled broadly, hoping to kindle a little self belief in my colleagues. God damn it. We had to get Maddox.

"I have no wish to oppose your idea if you're sure this is the only way," Lucy said, a suspiciously lingering smile settling on her lips.

Lucy proceeded to weigh up our chances of success in that reasonable matter-of-fact manner she had been developing. Personally, I couldn't help thinking that last night I had gone to a lot of trouble and risk to discover where Maddox was probably hiding. It wasn't much to hold on to but it was all I had and I wasn't prepared to set it aside.

"Bruce!" Lucy snapped. I had let my preoccupations take over and her comments had zipped past me unheard.

"Sorry, what?"

"I said: What do you think our chances of success are?"

"Success? Impossible to know. But this is the best lead to Maddox we've got."

Of course, truth to tell, I wasn't too confident myself. I had grown accustomed to viewing the mountains as something rather savage and apart, covered by an exuberance of giant trees, climbing plants and luxurious vegetation. It was going to be like hunting for a needle in the proverbial haystack. Only worse. We wrangled for a few minutes but they must have known that catching Maddox had become an imperative. Besides there was a point at which they were not at liberty to challenge my decision.

So it was that we lost that day in argument and planning but the next morning found us on the coast road heading west in the direction of Soufrière. Soon we turned on to one of the smaller branch roads leading towards the mountains which rose in folds lit by a scorching sun. I call it a road but it was barely that. It was marked on the map and there was a splash of asphalt which looked as if it had been put down a long time ago and now in serious need of repair. After a gruelling climb in first gear, we broke into a clearing where we stopped. The plan was to follow the trembling line of the stream upwards to the mountain top and then on to so-called *Libreville*. I must admit, at that moment looking upwards, even I had doubts about our mission. Mountains, incised by volcanic ridges, towered a good four thousand feet above us.

Right then there was a rumble from below. I recalled immediately that it was normal, they said, nothing to worry about, like the distant rumbling of the London Underground far beneath, if you know what I mean. It marked the permanent restlessness of the island's volcano, the *Grand Piton*. But today it spoke to me as an urgent message, making my hair spike and stand up on end. I stopped in my tracks. Volcanoes, the belt of fire, tectonic plates in motion. No devastating upsurges from below, mind you but permanent moving, a kind of

Parkinsonian shaking. The result was cracks everywhere, sudden potholes, buildings shifting without warning, sometimes reduced to a shapeless magma of flat heaps serving only to grow hibiscus and orchids.

We exchanged looks and after a pause began our trek. Doubtless, the inhabitants of the place knew better routes but we were ignorant of them and had fixed on following the line of the stream. We took our first steps into the foliage towards the sound of the stream. Torrents of greenery tumbled into the ravines while trees hung onto rocks tinted with a shade of red. The air was still and quiet but full of magic; every sound – the chatter of a bird, a hush of water – came with bell-like clarity to ears seemingly made more sensitive by the loneliness of the place. Everywhere was thronged with great green, shiny leaves. Sharp stones cut into the soles of my shoes. Tim was smiling to himself. At my tomfoolery, I suspect. Lucy was utterly focused on her steps when suddenly, we were startled by a muffled cry, two green parrots screeching past.

The ascent proved steep but relatively short, neatly shaving off the worst of the rain forest. Soon we cleared the treeline and struck upwards in what should have been a direct line to Libreville. We made our way up by the side of the stream. The going was rough, steep and littered with bushes which had managed to push down roots in the small earth filled fissures.

Keeping my head down and my eyes on my boots I concentrated on each step but found the act of climbing therapeutic, clearing me of a clutter of ugly thoughts. The gorge grew narrower forcing the stream into a series of rapids, running fast and deep. Above us the water echoed from ledge to ledge tumbling down a rock face as high as a cathedral steeple. More akin to rock climbing now than walking, we had to check each stone in case it were loose.

At last we emerged on to a flatter horizon. We had found ourselves on a kind of plateau, not of piercing peaks like the *Deux Pitons* themselves but a flattish rocky surface. I looked out across much of St Eleanor, a vast panorama of some grandeur, a study in greens and blues. In the distance, green volcanic peaks pierced the sky while the unending sea stretched to the horizon. All around were smaller hills, always hills, covered in wild jungle, fading in graduated subtleties of green, the bottom of which was shielded by a purple haze, so intense that I felt I could almost reach out and touch it. It was a view I would never wholly forget: no man made changes had marred the majesty of the heights, the mountains and the shining sea beneath us. I doubt that I formulated my feelings at the time but I reckon I was conscious of some sort of unchanging permanence of beauty before me in an unstable, ugly and ever changing world.

"The village is just ahead," Tim announced.

His mind had finally cracked, I thought. I looked around. There was only nature, raw and wild. Lucy directed my gaze with a pointed figure. And then a sudden apparition of distant huts induced a quickening of the pulse and a certain mystification in equal measure. About half a mile away lay the little settlement we had glimpsed from below: *Libreville,* a cluster of little wooden huts that looked as if they had grown naturally from nature rather than from the hand of man. They were shaped oddly, full of angles, projections, openings for windows and frankly, falling to pieces. There looked to be some cultivation in its immediate vicinity for the land was perceptibly greener but of the usual rural energy there was no sign.

"Well. Shall we take a look?" I asked, squinting back at Tim and Lucy.

"Time enough for that," he responded. "Let's have our refreshments first."

So on Tim's insistence we broke for sandwiches and short drinks of water from the flask. It was quiet and still. Somewhere a dog barked. After our light refreshments we moved out towards the settlement, searching for any clue that might betray a hostile presence. From the rocks we picked our way on to a thin earth. Nearer the settlement a flock of blue and orange macaws flew overhead, shrieking their metallic cries. Smoke rose from beyond the huts. I noticed some cabbages planted in lines with potatoes between them, a small sign of civilisation. Yet there was one little fact which I found disturbing. Nobody was about. Perhaps it was some buried memory of the war in the Burmese jungle, perhaps it was my Maori training or more likely it was plain nerves but whatever it was I found myself appraising the risk. Risk of what? Of being alone, uninvited, in a remote mountain village? I'd be jumping at my own shadows next.

Entering *Libreville* I found my initial impressions confirmed. The scent had become a stench – human excrement, unwashed bodies, cooking waste coming from beyond the dwellings. Yet it all seemed unnaturally quiet; and we had the distinct feeling that the inhabitants of this secluded spot would not welcome uninvited visitors. We walked up to the nearest dwelling, a dilapidated looking palm thatched hut. The dog's howl rose.

"Anyone at home?" I shouted, banging on the door. No response. Sweat streamed down my face, something the insects seemed to appreciate. I looked around. There was no central village clearing, just an assortment of huts connected by narrow paths. One of the huts had a door leaning open. I went up to it and diffidently rapped on its harshly worked woodwork. There was no reply so I peered inside. A smell of tobacco emanated from within. A rough low wooden table stood on the dirt floor. Suddenly I heard the sound of a baby crying and leapt round. But there was no one to be seen. A splutter of smoke rising from a fire was burning nearby.

We walked towards it and were greeted with a surprise. Sitting on a log, munching on a plate of beans, sat an old man. How old I couldn't say. Maybe not as old as I thought. Probably he had had a hard life. Anyway, he was an arresting sight: a black man with curly hair going white and straggling locks of hair for a beard. His leathery skin seemed to be stretched taut over his skull while his eyes were deep pockets. He wore nothing above his mid riff but sported a faded set of grey trousers. He also wore a warily alert expression.

"It's a fine village you have," I said. And I meant it too because it can have been no mean achievement hauling the timber up here and knocking it into place.

His face did not so much as flicker in acknowledgement.

"What is this place?" I asked. "My name is Bruce Cordell and I'm looking for someone."

The wiry figure lowered his hand and put something else in mouth. He muttered something strange, looking all the while at Tim who responded in Creole.

"English?" The old man replied, incredulously. This gave me a bit of a shock. Could he really not speak English. For a moment I almost envied him his ignorance of the world.

"Is this the village they call Libreville?" I asked.

"You must know that! Its almost twenty years since I last spoke English", he explained with a heavily accented speech. He took a swig of some sort of hootch and invited us to drink with him. It didn't look appealing. In all my life, I have never seen such poverty. We shared a little of his *aqua vite*, strong and fiery on the tongue. You know what he now proceeded to take with his hootch? Leaves! He dipped them in a dish of dirty water, put them in his mouth and rolled them around his teeth before throwing them on the soil. He suggested I tasted them but I declined, not reckoning with his touchiness. He grew so irritable that whatever I did, whatever I offered him he wouldn't offer me the slightest word more. Instead, Tim took a handful of the leaves and followed the old man's example, placing them in his mouth. He kept them there a while and we watched him roll them between his teeth. I thought for a moment he had swallowed them but they resurfaced from his lips and then he too threw them on the ground. It was clear I had to follow suit. The water was flavoured and the leaves left a slight sweet aftertaste. Lucy was doing the same but I saw that she had wisely picked only a few leaves up. As I was drinking I felt the itch of small insects climbing up my leg. Alas, as soon as I swept them off I felt them gnawing at the other.

A door shuddered open behind me. I turned to spot the arrival of men, each carrying a basket on his back. There were six of them, chattering away in a rippling speech. It was plain the young men were very curious about the three strangers who had suddenly appeared in their village. Curious and suspicious. But none of them spoke a word to us. I had a fleeting sense of having recognised a face, an olive complexioned man, paler than the rest. Could this be the man Valentine called Fernando? The atmosphere grew tender as the young men ogled us. Usually I was good at this sort of thing. I'd built up a small fund of experience in dubious encounters, knew the warning signals and had a few disarming tricks of my own. But this was different.

A high cheek boned man with a neatly curling beard and a jaunty moustache pushed himself to the front. I identified him as the ringleader not only by his manner but by what he wore – earrings and amulets – symbols of status, of some sort of experience which set him apart. His attitude was hostile, his lips twisting into a look of disgust as he glowered at me. "What are you doing here?" he demanded. "What do you want? This place is ours. You get thrown in hell. Get on! Go away!"

"We mean no harm," I said with anger boiling inside me at his sudden aggressive way. "Look, I'll come straight to the point. I'm needing help. Some information. Then we'll be on our way." I felt my heart pounding hard and a singing in my ears.

"Get on!" he snapped. "Yuh don't belong here. Yuh a fret?"

As he spoke I heard shuffling, irregular footsteps coming towards us and soon figures of different gaits and ages emerged. The man continued to rebuke me but I paid little heed, focussing instead on the new arrivals.

I guessed they'd been out working the land. As they spotted us, the black figures joined the others, swallowing us up shouting and gesticulating. We were quite a crowd now. Each man looked lean and hard, just bones, muscles and gristle. They formed a circle around us, standing there as young men often do, chatting with hands clasped before them or on each other's shoulders. But all the while their eyes were upon us and I didn't doubt that their conversation was too. Suspicion was natural. No one there would have had any deeds of entitlement; I don't suppose they paid taxes either. Women emerged too, all wearing a similar type of dress with short sleeves and hemmed just above the knees, looking as if they had started life in bright colours but had become a muddy brown.

I'd had something like this happen before, a disquieting moment when you may be in danger if you misread the signs. Often there is a disturbing, violent undertow which might signal they are about to attack but, no, I didn't think so. Lucy had insisted that these people were not necessarily 'hostile', but they were entirely lacking in the usual responsiveness, looking at us strangely. But it was more than them. It was the remoteness of things. Them and the surrounding wild, the rocks and a vague awareness of ancient, secret things. There was a high-pitched noise to my right. I turned, aware a woman had laughed. She was smiling now, a woman with a long nose and an upturned mouth. It was not much but it was enough. The panic left me. Now I was more ordinarily tongue-tied, aware of a new world, and searching for something to say.

But no, a short lean youth leapt forwards brandishing a short upright knife in his right fist. And he had the sort of nose that looked as if it had been broken and not properly set, twisting as it did, slightly to his right. But before he'd taken a step closer an older man had grabbed a hold of him and pulled him back.

"No! Obadiah. No!"

The young man's eyes bulged and he stared at me silently. I returned the look; to start babbling would be to give way to him. Then there was a scuffling noise from another part of the house behind me; and the thread between us, whatever it had been, snapped. A man spoke to us in a very rudimentary English, his tone unfriendly, but hell it could have been a lot worse. He wore a rough T shirt but it was open exposing a muscular chest. He looked confused and I wondered if he was stoned. He repeated something, more abruptly this time, obviously a question. At first I was going to ask him to repeat it again then I just guessed he had been asking me what the hell I was doing here.

"We are looking for someone. A friend of a friend of mine, Julian Maddox," Tim said. "Have you heard tell of him?"

He looked at us blankly, his dark almond eyes set in a still darker skin. Then he said "He not here. Nobody of that name live here."

"No? Could you ask your friends?" I asked. "We know he has been here."

He laughed, incredulous. "No need. I know everybody here. Who the fuck are you anyway?"

"The name's Bruce. These are my friends, Tim and Lucy," I said.

My interlocutor smiled and began to make a small circle in the dirt with the toes of his shoe as he appeared to ruminate. Then he patted me on my left shoulder. "You're quite someone to come here asking questions aren't you?" he said enigmatically and he led us away from the others a few yards towards a more open space. "Well, Bruce and Tim and Lucy. Julian Maddox, you say. I'm sorry nobody here called that."

"Could you ask your friends just the same? Could they have a clue where he might be living?" I asked and produced a tenner. "Maddox – a big, well-built man, about forty. Lots of muscles. Large shoulders."

He looked at the note, amazed, took it, shook his head and walked back to the little cluster which had gathered. He didn't cut a very prepossessing figure. A grey stubble covered his face from cheek to jowl. His shirt and trousers were covered in grime and worn away to a shine at the knees. Perhaps he was about thirty. Our new acquaintance began to explain to his friends the drift of our request. There was a quick buzz of animated conversation then my lean friend returned, a young couple in tow.

"Nobody knows no one called Julian Maddox," he announced, trying to sound casual as if our enquiries were reasonable and run of the mill. The shorter one nodded to what his companion had said, his eyes flitting about, stealing quick glances at us. They edged closer. Then the short one gave me a look that froze the heart.

"Get out!" he snarled, gesturing with his thumb. His eyes were dead, carrying a sense of deep violence. "Leave us!" With a terrifying deliberation he drew a knife from his belt. The evil looking blade hushed us all into a sudden silence broken only by the plaintive cries of gulls circling above and a gentle soughing of the breeze among the trees far below.

Tim Quick recovered his poise first. He jabbed a forefinger at the man's chest. "I would not like to think you are withholding information from us. *Where is he?*"

The man blinked then spoke abruptly in an unintelligible patois, his arms moving in jerky, awkward motions. I recognised then that he was speaking English coloured with Creole. I turned my attention to the woman for it is a strange thing but when local speech is close to indecipherable it is invariably the woman who is easier to understand. Sure enough she grasped my meaning easily.

"Can anyone tell me about Maddox, for God's sake?"

"He's saying no."

"I can give money."

She broke off. There was a long interchange between the two then she returned to me. "He says, how much?"

"Five pounds."

"Fifteen. He says he must live."

I nodded. "Tell him, ten. Take it or leave it. That is my last word."

He signalled agreement and I tore another ten pounds from my wallet. But the man still hesitated. "We don't want trouble," he said simply.

"Neither do we. We just want to find this man."

"He's been here from time to time. He sometimes buys things here. Re-sells them. He seems to have useful friends in the city but we don't know a lot about him. He's secretive. We do not like him but sometimes people do business with him and it means a lot to keep him friendly....but he's not important. A devious man, I would say."

"Where can we find him?" Lucy asked.

"He has one of the houses on the sea front at *Grand Riviere*. I don't know which one."

There was little to be gained, much to be lost by staying so we left and as we did so I was glad to be heading back to *Caille Blanc* and solitude.

26

"YOU READY, CHIEF?" the voice belonged to the irrepressible Tim Quick. My thoughts had been wholly elsewhere. It was the next morning and I was feeling better now with a light breeze from the sea caressing my face. "God! Man," Quick resumed, looking horrified. "You look dreadful. You could do with a good long rest. No point martyring yourself."

"I'm fine. And all ready to go. Anyway a drive down to *Grande Rivière* will buck me up no end!" I smiled as Tim departed for the car park. Truly I felt a little annoyed with Tim, calling me dreadful just when I was feeling a bit invigorated. But perhaps it really was a drive and the adrenalin rush of another interrogation which I needed: not fresh air. Subtly, I suppose, my perspective on St. Eleanor was changing. When I had first arrived I had been drawn by the warmth and mystery of the islanders but now I missed the reassurance of the familiar. For the first time since coming here I was touched by a sense of uneasy isolation. It was then that I heard the telephone. Though it was a humid, stifling day I hurried over to pick up the receiver and place it next to my ear.

"Bruce?"

I was lost for a moment, struggling to place the voice, at once familiar and unfamiliar.

"It's me. Geneviève. You won't remember me. But I remember you. I was there at the Barracuda when you were speaking to Rufus. Do you remember?"

"Of course I do. But we didn't speak. Do you work for Halliday?"

There was a pause and gasps on the other end. She was crying. I was at a loss. The sweat was congealing on my clammy palms.

"What is it? What's the matter?"

"There have been such terrible things going on. Terrible."

"What do you mean?"

"I can't explain on the telephone. We've got to meet."

Her voice became louder and more shrill as she spoke.

"Where? And when do you have in mind?" I felt inadequate to the emotional force at the other end.

"I was hoping it would pass but its only getting worse. I can't take the pressure any more."

My voice dropped in volume : "Okay. Let's meet....I'm busy all day. Can you hold until later? Can we meet tomorrow?" I could tell from the silence that this was far from ideal.

"Yes. But somewhere away from St. Jacques. How about Martha's cafe in Soufrière....one o'clock?"

"Alright. One o'clock."

"Be there."

The phone cut off.

It DIDN'T TAKE US long to cruise down to *Grande Rivière*: but finding the exact location was more taxing. Our analysis of the few houses in the township had identified the likely spot but nothing was certain. Eagerly Tim strode ahead, hurrying by hut after hut, pushing his way past everyone we met before turning at a cross path down a dirty lane towards the beach. Finally we got there. The likely address we had worked out corresponded with a one storey hut, one of many lining the beach and straggling eastwards from *Grande Rivière*. The door was open when we got there but I knocked on the door and peered in. It was dark but I could see only one room with wooden floors and wooden walls covered with cracked paint.

I rapped on the door till my knuckles ached.

At last a woman approached from the beach and demanded to know what I wanted.

"Do you live here?" I replied.

"No, I'm a neighbour."

"Is Maddox in?"

"Jules? No, he left earlier."

"Is there a close relative?"

"No. There's nobody."

Tim rolled his eyes in disbelief. After a few minutes, clearly unwelcome, she gave up her attentions and left. I was starting to sweat. "Julian, are you in?" I cried and started battering the door again. There was a small rumbling from behind the door until eventually it cracked open a bit further. A weary, no longer young, male face stared back at me, barely recognisable as the angry young man I had met at the workers' meeting. Still, he looked tough but with a spare body about to spring, light on his feet, full of energy. His forehead was high and impressive, the line of his mouth cruel.

"You would be Mr Julian Maddox, I take it, Sir?" I asked formally and showed him my ID. Tim smiled as he always did but this time I knew it was devoid of goodwill.

"Yes, that's me." Julian tried to look relaxed but I could see he was suspicious. But then most people were when the police called by. I cast my eyes around the place. There was very little furniture. No carpets, no bookshelves, not even a picture graced the wall. The occupant was not living in any style.

"It's a routine matter but I think you could help us with our enquiries so if you don't mind we'd like to ask you a few questions."

He looked genuinely surprised. "Well, what's it all about. I haven't got long. I'm in a hurry."

"It'll have to wait I'm afraid. You see this is rather important. We'd like to talk to you about the murder of Quentin Quillham..."

Too late, I realised I had hit quite the wrong tone. Julian's eyes had darkened: pained surprise given way to indignation. "Well then, you can fuck off! That has nothing to do with me. I didn't do anything," he spat out, his eyes blazing with an anger whose origins I could not even guess at.

"Believe me, I don't ask questions without good reason. You see Julian, we've been putting two and two together and getting some very interesting results. Do you like arithmetic?" Silence. "If you have nothing to hide, Julian, I think you'd be well advised to speak to us."

After a short pause Julian visibly relented. "You'd better come in," he said, stepping back to make way for us. Closer viewing confirmed his hut was pretty bereft of things. Perhaps not too surprising granted Julian's peripatetic life style. I looked in silence at the man whose face had returned to a private place of security.

He wasn't quite as I had remembered him or what I expected.

"We understand you met Mr Quillham from time to time. Care to tell us about it?" I asked.

"There's nothing to tell."

"How did you get on with him? Did you like him?"

"No. He was too starchy. Too white...hey but don't..."

"Don't worry. It wasn't a trick question. Just curious. Disliking someone is not a sufficient motive for murder. But you did see him? Right?"

"That's right but hardly at all. He liked Afro-Caribbean wood carvings. Sometimes he hinted at the possibility of a big contract but it never happened......I grew fed up with him in the end." Slowly he lit a cigarette, inhaled the smoke and blew it out.

"But you visited him at home?"

"Two or three times but always at his say so."

"And you didn't receive any money. That must have been disappointing."

"I wasn't overly worried. It was a casual arrangement and as time went by I just made other plans. But I did sell him some carvings for his wife's shop. Didn't make much though."

With that he smiled and sat down. He raised his eyes at us and shook his head in a kind of desperation. I thought he had started playing for time. It was not hard to give credence to his reputation. He was a thief. He shoplifted. He picked pockets. He stole wallets or indeed any goods which might be useful to him. He drank. He smoked marijuana. He also fenced stolen goods. He was close to being police property: you could stick anything on him and he would struggle to establish his innocence. Certainly no one would believe him. Something about his very presence even warned me that he could be a killer. Yet still I did not feel that this was our man. He was very nimble minded and in my experience people like that aren't so ready to resort to such crude violence to get their way. They usually had other techniques to deploy. Besides, his support for the plantation workers signalled there was another aspect to his character.

"You were in the vicinity the same time as Quentin Quillham was murdered. You passed by the house?"

"Yes."

"Did you kill him, Julian?"

"What?"

"Did you kill him?"

"Of course not. I don't have to stand for this shit," he said with sudden violence. "Listening to your la-dee-dah accents and you questioning my honest hard work. You whites and your uncle toms are finished here." Julian was almost crouching now, ready to spring like a cornered animal, his cheeks quite inflamed. But I knew such men play act as a survival tool. It doesn't mean anything. There was a practised indignation to his whining. I wondered if he were as secure as he pretended. It had been a long time since I had put anyone through an interrogation for murder; and I didn't like it, being all too conscious that my information was threadbare. I paced up and down the tiny room.

"Look, man," Tim said. "We're not accusing you of anything. We just want some explanations."

"I've already explained it" Maddox said. "I had nothing to do with this. As you can see I don't exactly live the high life. But I don't live off others either. And I don't hide myself behind a mask of hypocrisy." But Julian Maddox was decidedly less cocky now and he went on to explain why he had been in St. Jacques that evening, visiting a carpenter-craftsman who had sometimes supplied him with goods, a man who would vouch for his presence. He had not, however, visited the Quillhams. He was simple, factual in his accounts, his manner almost withdrawn. He was becoming much more composed now, as if he'd somehow summoned a mysterious reserve of strength. Julian genuinely seemed to know nothing about Quillham or what happened that night. I began to doubt Woodbine's judgement, so convincing was his account. I wished I could tell what he thought when he disappeared inside himself. Then I remembered others – and it was always the worst – who were so mired in vicious criminality that they genuinely began to forget the details of their crimes, began even to feel innocent of them, so innocuous and distant did they now seem to them. Criminals have no shame. They have only one loyalty: to themselves. Therefore their testimonies are almost worthless. It reminded me of the ancient Roman rule that no testimony by a slave was valid unless it was produced under torture.

"Tell me a little more about your business talks with Quillham? What did he want?"

He gave me a grimace.

I turned to Tim and we began to talk about St. Eleanor and the West Indies when at its most rugged; and of how the West Indians were so adept in their survival skills. What their detractors said wasn't true. The West Indians were certainly not lacking in initiative nor were they lazy when it came to acquiring business skills.

"If I may," Tim said. "If I may, I can tell you quite a few unlikely characters who managed to turn over a few pounds with shrewd decisions. There are a few who make a lot on the markets. But you've got to know what you're doing. You've got to have it up here," Tim said tapping his head, "to know what to buy and when to sell and who to talk to. But if you do there's good money to be made.... There's fishermen too who know the right spots to catch a great big haul but who are a might canny at telling anyone else. Oh yes...and." He stopped.

Suddenly as if he brought the words up with a hiccup Maddox said: "It was all a bit awkward. He wanted to know more about my contacts and the range of carvings I could get him, where they came from, the costs...He said he had a better idea. There might be a market elsewhere, perhaps in Britain. We could fix something up."

"What did you say to that?"

"I was dead keen....but it petered out. There never was any deal. It's not the first time I've heard talk like that. You know what I mean? Promises, promises..." He let it go at that.

Julian's mood had completely changed from his initial reaction to us. He didn't use his hands to express much. He didn't even raise his voice a lot. He was calm and unmoved. There was, in fact, now a dark introspective look to the man. Yet I didn't feel this was contrived, another piece of play acting. Rather, his moods could change very suddenly. There was a strange power about the man's eyes. A tough nut.

"I need some simple answers to some simple questions," I said.

"But I know nothing..."

"I thought you were used to speaking your mind."

"What do you mean?"

The man was fencing with me. But one thing I'd never do is let a suspect question me. "Your reputation. You usually have a lot to say for yourself. Nothing wrong with that of course. Let's just resume a few facts," I said. "Did you and Quillham have any mutual friends, business contacts?"

"None that I knew of."

"Where were you about midnight on the night of the murder?"

He took a deep breath. "I've told you before."

"Tell us again."

He frowned, then laughed. "Okay. I had gone out to visit a business contact not far from the Quillhams' home. I had had to leave and was walking back to find a lift. It's not so difficult you know."

"I'm sorry. That's not good enough for an answer." I replied calmly. "You must try to be more precise."

"Well, maybe about twelve but I saw and heard nothing special. What did you think I might have seen?"

Ignoring his question I asked, "Who else did you see on the street on your way home? Think very carefully before you answer."

"No one," he replied sullenly.

I looked him in the eye. He could well be telling the truth but police work had long instilled a degree of scepticism into my bones. Here in St Eleanor it was a hundred times worse. Julian's rendering of the truth would be less than perfect. Still, I thought I almost liked him more when he was at bay, snarling at us for being down on him because of his race and class. The British – the

Whites – were still dominant on the island. Anyone in Maddox's position must be annoyed to have to act subserviently, all the while wishing to spit on us and show us how out of date we all were.

"So that's all?" I asked.

"Yes. Really that's all."

"And can I ask, do you drive or own a car?"

"No, that's why I was going to get a lift, like I said."

"Now, let's get this right, shall we? When did you last see Mr Quillham?"

"It would be about my work, the carvings."

"When, I said. I'm not really concerned with Why. When did you last see Mr Quillham?"

He slumped. "I'm not good at dates. They all become a blur. I can't say when."

"You must have some idea. Six months ago, a year...?"

"I couldn't say. I've told you everything. I never killed him. Why would I? Look. I get a lot of shit in life. Just about everything and everyone is a disappointment to me. Everyone lets me down. So what? What do you expect? So people are liars, thieves and hypocrites. Right? Life is shit. Right? But does that mean I have to jump in it just because the police come round and make stupid accusations. No! Of course not. I didn't do it!"

"Did you hear of any relationship he had with the First Minister?"

He looked blank. "I told you. I know nothing about his other dealings."

"And you really have no idea why Constantine and Quillham should have been in contact?"

"No idea." He shrugged and pulled a disgusted face. "Well it's easy to come up with ideas, isn't it? But no,

I don't really know anything." I considered. The sparkle had gone from his eyes. His face was flat and empty. His mind was on...what? Hidden contraband? Colleagues in crime? Checking lies against other things he might have said? Police brutality? Yet Julian seemed to be telling the truth and he had indeed descended into a rather dream-like state.

"Well, Julian, as it happens I do believe you. We needn't detain you much longer. But tell me first, how did you meet Quillham?"

"That's...er..quite a long story."

"Well, we've got plenty of time."

"I don't think I know where to begin."

"He approached you or you approached him?"

"Don't really remember. He approached me, I think... yes, said Valentine had told him about me."

"OK Julian let's go over this once more. You still stand by everything you said?"

"Certainly."

"You understand how unlikely it sounds."

"But it's the truth."

"I will summarise the main points. You live here in comparative isolation. You have no close friends. No intimate female friends. You have no steady job but you sometimes trade small items from island to island. Quillham had asked for some specific wood carvings. You undertook to get them for him. On the night of his death, you were going to a completely different meeting with a wood carver in St. Jacques and only happened to pass by the deceased's house by chance."

Maddox nodded his head slowly in agreement.

We sat a while longer going over the same ground, re-phrasing things, looking for inconsistencies but not finding any. We took down the details of his wood carver contact in St. Jacques. But really I knew it was finished; no more to be learnt here. Finally, I told him to write down his statement repeating exactly what he had said.

I took Tim aside a moment: "What do you think?"

"It may be the truth but it's certainly not the whole truth. He's holding out on us."

"My feelings exactly. There's something very unsatisfactory about his statement."

I looked at Maddox. Frighten him, I thought. That's the best plan. See if he'd spill anything more but I knew we'd have to let him go after a couple of days. "Come along with us. You're coming to the station."

LATER THAT EVENING THE fragrant tropical night and the rhythmic symphony of the frogs was turning me philosophical. I sat a while trying to make sense of it all. Maddox was clearly hiding something but maybe it was not relevant to my concerns, just covering some small time crookedness of great importance to himself alone. So what about Constantine? If we accepted Hennrick's testimony and not the official one, who could have gained access to the First Minister's residence that fateful night? Lucy's latest report had confirmed Dorothy Miller's status as the very model of a loyal retainer, albeit one who was much more articulate and astute than I had originally thought. Mrs Peabody too could be set aside. A dedicated gardener, her employment was of long standing. Like Dorothy no motive for treachery could be discerned. No extreme politics, no particular money problems or vulnerabilities. Surely she was an innocent.

Yet the irritating feeling continued to nag at me. So troubling, so close was the intuition that it was almost palpable, as if I could reach out and grasp it. Then suddenly without comprehending the process, I remembered what it was, like a bubble floating to the surface of my mind after prolonged fermentation. The issue of the unlocked door. If Dorothy Miller was reliable and our researches had confirmed that, indeed, she was then she must have locked the garden door before retiring. It must have been unlocked from the outside. Copies had been made. A copy of the key to the garden entrance of *Anse Chastenet*, an entrance someone had observed, even used, perhaps furtively? He or an accomplice must have known where the key hung. Someone with frequent access to the First Minister or at least frequent enough for him to have worked out where the keys were and probably on a later occasion to have made a print.

A wax copy must have been taken there and then, a matter of only a few moments' work. He had cut a key which was probably used by another, the assassin. The killer himself was a hit man or men, afforded access by someone's complicity. Hennrick's explanation of the First Minister's death opened a wholly new perspective.

Whoever it was, it was most unlikely that they would have acted alone: he must have had powerful backers who would have made it worthwhile for him. There must be a cabal which pursued its ambitions with a relentless determination. This group had generated both the murder plan and the murderer. They had shielded him, they had guided him and they certainly must have promised to reward him. The assassin or assassins must have known that the First Minister was heavily sedated and therefore highly vulnerable in order to carry out his injection.

The telephone sounded.

It was Katie; and the pitch of her voice suggested exasperation.

"Bruce! Thank God. It's me. Katie," she said. "How are things? This is the third attempt I've made to get you. I'm ringing from home. You're impossible to get a hold of." She sounded almost frantic.

"I'm so sorry. The work is making erratic demands on my time. I hardly ever know when I'll be in." I hoped she might be impressed by my implied importance but I was proved wrong by her next words.

"So, how's it going anyway? Any where nearer an end?"

I didn't want to say that so far I had made very little progress so I tried to deflect her by asking after the children.

"They're fine. Laura is really taking to her new school. Andrew needs pushing, you know. He's a bit on the lazy side but he's doing ok too."

Suddenly I decided to run over my ideas with Katie. She was surprisingly responsive. "We must suppose that the intruders are professional," I said. "They have the equipment to make a copy. They must have got someone to use wax to make an impression. It doesn't take long if you know what you are doing."

"Hang on a moment," said Katie, doubtless furrowing her brow. "If you are right how could anyone have got access to the keys in the first place? How was it done?"

"Simple. The key box is so well used throughout the day that it is left unlocked."

"And where is it kept?"

"On the wall, in an alcove off the hall."

"Sounds easy but you would have to know that. So that means people who work there."

"Or are regular visitors. It would be easy to observe. Besides, a frequent visitor would not arouse suspicion. So who fits the bill?"

27

I woke early the next morning, and was immediately captivated by the golden blush of a tropical dawn on a tracery of dark green fronds. Grimly, I remembered my scheduled meeting with the Governor. So it was that later that morning, the clock chiming the hour, that I arrived at Government House. Sentries, smart in white colours, marched before the Governor's residence. A company of young soldiers at bayonet drill, practised a lunge and parry in the nearby square. Strange, I thought, as I entered the Residency that a meeting much needed by myself should now feel as if it were part of a plan pre-arranged by others.

"To the left in the morning room, Chief Inspector," an aide told me when I arrived. "He's expecting you."

I found the Governor relaxing in an armchair. Looking up, Sir Godfrey peered at me through rimless glasses. "Ah, Chief Inspector. Delighted to see you. Please take a seat." Sir Godfrey Thomas Brunton Faed KCMG was a phenomenon. Tall and lantern jawed he must have been ruggedly built in his youth. The pale blue eyes which scrutinised me were as cold as the waters that caressed his native Scottish shores. "I'm sorry to have dragged you out here, Chief Inspector, but I'm glad to speak to you. I've been watching your progress with the greatest of interest."

Sir Godfrey, easily recognisable from the photos, was sitting almost motionless, with a fixed smile, scarcely lifting his eyes from the carpet, drinking from a porcelain cup. Tea with lemon. No sugar and no biscuit. He didn't offer me a cup. The walls were of panelled wood, reminiscent of a captain's cabin. Above a writing desk hung a portrait, a small female face. A family heirloom, I suspected.

"Thank you, Sir, it's good of you to do so but there's nothing much to show yet," I said. "I'm still sifting material, Sir. Checking through things, following lines of enquiry." I was uneasy. I became aware of a third man in the room, Jake Oppenheimer, who was watching us with an amused smile: and he wasn't entitled to the same level of confidentiality as the Governor. "Jake Oppenheimer", the Governor said, introducing the young man. "My assistant. Don't worry. I gather you've already met. You can speak freely in front of him....But what do you mean? What lines of enquiry have you?" the Governor prompted, his words carrying an aura of restrained urgency. He was watching me intently, his mean eyes searching all over me as if looking for every weakness, the better to control me. "Something big has occurred and we need to get to the bottom of it."

"I'm talking to all the victim's associates at the moment." I shuffled uneasily. "A First Minister's death is always 'big' as you put it" I began uneasily, nettled by the implied rebuke.

"But do you suspect murder? It would be an act of war?" Jake demanded.

"Not necessarily" I replied, taken aback by this slant.

"Of course not," Jake replied. "I am sure it would be most unwise to jump to unwarranted conclusions...but you know Quillham's death rather compounds things, don't you think? That same night we had our little chat together. A strange coincidence. Quillham had been close to Constantine for one thing...and he was writing about some very sensitive subjects. Cuba, for example. The Dominican Republic. Here..." I listened as Jake continued with his slant on the English victim, mostly a slant rooted in the Cold War, a time when terrible forces were being set loose, one of which had evidently come to rest with me personally.

"Well, I hear you Mr Oppenheimer but I'm just a detective doing a detective's work. I'm here to catch a murderer. It's as simple as that." I had meant that to sound rather grand and dismissive but it came out more like an apology.

"I believe you think that but think again. There may be a lot more to this. Quillham may be dead but things may just be moving on to the next phase." With that, he smiled, the sort of smile someone gives when they're not used to smiling.

"Getting anywhere at all with Quillham?" the Governor asked, ignoring all we had said.

"Well, Sir, that's what I really wanted to ask you about. Quillham was an influential commentator in many ways. I wondered what the official and indeed, any unofficial, view on him might have been. At the moment I'm still in the dark. The usual motives – vengeance or money – don't seem to apply to this one. Sexual motives don't look relevant either. For that matter, I wouldn't even mind your views on that. Was he a bit of a ladies' man for example...?"

Jake raised his eyebrows. "Could be true. Only time I met Quillham he was flirting with the ladies."

"Thank you, Jake. But if flirting were a motive for murder, God knows where we'd be!" the Governor interjected. "Anyway weren't you going to that Civil Contingencies meeting?"

"Oh, that," Jake Oppenheimer looked disconcerted at the prospect. "Not necessary. That's well covered by the civil administration."

"But not covered by me," the Governor snapped. After a moment of astonishment at an order not expected, Jake looked more respectfully at the Governor who continued in the same tone of natural authority "I'd like one of my staff to keep involved if only to make sure I'm still up to speed on everything."

"Yes, indeed, Sir," and Oppenheimer smiled his sly, sycophantic smile. "Of course, you're quite right," he added with fake enthusiasm. For the first time I glimpsed a tiny rift in their relationship. Faed must be good at manipulating people, I considered; this time pushing, not ordering, Jake towards an action he wasn't keen on. Or was it all a pre-arranged cue? Whatever the reason, Jake rose and with a nod in my direction, vacated the room.

Silence.

Faed looked at me. "Jake's a good man. The Chief Secretary, you know. But sometimes he can get a bit above himself." I was surprised by this confidence, well above my pay grade. I didn't know a lot but I knew that the Chief Secretary was a very eminent official, a true big wig, the next man to the Governor, the man most likely to become the next Governor in times gone by but of course, we were living in the End Days.

"Fancy a dry vermouth? A bit early for anything stronger, don't you think?" Sir Godfrey walked over to a rosewood cabinet with an inlaid top where he proceeded to pour out two glasses before continuing. "Quillham was certainly well known not only here but in much of the Caribbean. He often wrote contentiously about the co-operative plantations and so on. Frankly, it was most injudicious to stir up the Islanders. Right now, the whole place is a stir with talk of joining the West Indian Federation or going it alone. The sudden advent of a Jamieson government has been a shock. It's not only independence and US investment he wants: its land reform and a minimum wage! Well, that's in nobody's interests, is it? I wish to hell I could find out more about his overseas links. We don't like shocks, you know." Sir Godfrey smiled sardonically, his attitude I fancied a relic of an older Whitehall style, conveying the idea that he had more important matters to consider than waste his time talking to me.

"Yes but I suppose new times will need new thinking and new ideas."

"No doubt but they shouldn't interfere with old ideas when the old ones have been right."

For a moment I was about to deny this proposition; instead, I opted for discretion. "It's true these are going to be interesting times for everyone." After a short pause I asked, "Did you know Quillham yourself?"

He allowed a small interval. "Quillham was a strange man...I liked him and I didn't like him at the same time. I serve Her Majesty. I have sufficient to do without wasting time with scribblers. But these are different times – the Cold War exercises its chill even here and keeping good lines of communications open is always important. So you see we did find Quillham useful. But as soon as you show a measure of trust, you provide a little potential for betrayal."

"Betrayal, Sir? Surely not. Or at least nothing to do with Quillham."

"Ah…you see our enemies are always sapping away, looking for our weak spots. And those of our allies. Washington is very anxious that nothing upsets the smooth transition to independence."

"But where exactly could Quillham fit in? He was only a minor publicist."

"Who was talking of publishing? Faed's eyes met mine steadily for something over a couple of seconds and then he went on: "Quillham cultivated a great many people and had his fingers in many pies. He presided over a very well connected social network on the island you know; or at least most people think he did. Actually it was his wife who really oiled its wheels."

"A circle of influence, Sir? I don't think I know about that."

"No. Well, that's something I want to initiate you into. Are you a patriot, Cordell?"

An odd question, suspended somewhere away from any sense of context or landscape but I answered readily enough. "Of course, Sir. I served in Burma; and in Cyprus too in a special capacity."

"Yes, I know something about that. Truth to tell, Cordell, I miss Perthshire. I mean really miss it. I love that place."

"I know what you mean, Sir. I miss South Island," And I did too. It was a wonderful world of coasts and fjords and mountains and forests. I sometimes thought I had never been happier than when I lived there.

"Well, in a way that is part of what I want to talk to you about this morning. It's a delicate matter. You are not the first person to look into this strange affair. There have been others. Like you, they began to investigate the darkness, uncovered aspects but were unable to unlock the main mystery. I want to give you a little additional background and with it a little extra responsibility. You see Quillham was very proactive in his dealings, engaging with new networks and setting up new contacts. He was well known to us. You could say he was even useful to us."

"Are you saying he was our Agent?" I suggested.

"No. Certainly not. But let's say we find it prudent to keep in close touch with those who are ploughing some of the same furrows as ourselves. Sometimes they can help us, wittingly or not, trawling for new information or even finding contacts worth cultivating, and sometimes…only sometimes, mind, in identifying new threats, new hazards. Such people are not agents. They're what we call '*alongsiders*', people who work alongside us. In no sense do they work *for* us, only *with* us. Though we may of course choose to reward them in some appropriate way from time to time." He paused.

"With stories, perhaps?" Information was the commodity Quillham traded in. The occasional helping hand could be a great assistance to him. "Only the other day I came across an article of Quillham's which he published earlier last year. It was well circulated and called *"Time for Intervention in Cuba"* just a month before the Bay of Pigs fiasco. It could have been preparing the public for a big change but there again maybe it was just astute journalism."

The Governor looked thoughtful. "It's a strange coincidence" he finally said quietly.

"It seems to me like a suspicious coincidence," I said.

"Exactly," Faed admitted. "We too trade in information when it suits us. But there were other things. Quillham networked well and his wife organised little get-togethers where people just chatted…maybe let their hair down a bit. He even formalised this a little. Made these 'do's' much more regular, once a month affairs. In time it has grown into a little ring of influence on the island, even on the eastern Caribbean. There was – is, rather – no formal business conducted but often important confidences are exchanged."

"More than idle chat then?"

"I should say so," Faed gloomily told me. "From a little arty group this gathering has grown to include some of the most powerful and influential people on the island. They chat. They talk. They exchange information. Mostly its inconsequential but the social wheels are kept well oiled. It's even possible it may become more important after independence."

I nodded encouragement, dimly aware that what started out as one of my interviews had begun to turn into something else.

"It took us a while to get wise to it. If you ask why someone like me should care about such things I must tell you we are always interested in circles of influence and that is what this has become. It's an exercise in logic, really. If it was going to exercise influence on the transition process we would want to be involved, naturally, perhaps only in a monitoring capacity, perhaps as something more. We decided to get involved in a helpful but potentially manipulative way. Six was planning on launching a magazine in the region. Designed to high standards, glossy, easy reading and reaching the emerging middle classes of the area – could be quite influential, you know. We had discussions with them and decided the initial launch could be here, right here in St. Eleanor. Its called *Caribbean Currents*. Well, we asked the Quillhams if they'd take it on and they agreed. Quentin was suspicious of it, of course. He didn't want to be closely involved. Preferred his somewhat spurious independence as a journalist but Chantelle took to it like a duck to water. Charlotte Gibbs is here right now supervising the first edition. I think they've already run off two dummies. Well, sure enough she soon found Chantelle's group a source of useful expertise on the eastern Caribbean. So far so good. But an odd thing happened which forced us to take a little more interest in this group. We found some of our plans were being leaked. Quite skilfully drawn up preparations were being damaged. Information was leaking out. Not much. Dribs and drabs but that's how a well informed enemy can build up a whole picture. To cut a long story short, our suspicions grew. So we alerted Quillham but he knew nothing. He was keeping his eyes and ears open for us but then he suddenly deceased."

"Could you give me an indication of what was leaked, Sir? It could be relevant."

"An assessment of Soviet military capabilities on Cuba."

I whistled. Was this something I didn't want to get into or, worse, something I should avoid? My pulse began to race and my body became more sensitised to the Governor's gaze, the creak of the furniture.

"Tell me, Sir," I asked, "did Mr Constantine know about this?"

"Ha!" Sir Godwin snapped. "The answer should be: of course not!" He looked at me sharply. "It's none of their business you see. Now look here. This is a serious business. The Colonial Secretary, Iain Macleod, has issued orders that no post-independence countries must ever come into contact with material that could possibly embarrass HMG. That certainly applies to St. Eleanor and any politician here too. No. Constantine should not have known."

"I see, but how could it have leaked? It's too much for Mrs. Quillham's network..."

"Of course it is. It's a sensitive business. You must appreciate that. Our Counter-Intelligence works closely with the CIA, you know. It's really at the heart of the special relationship. Not many people know that. They misunderstand. Laugh at the discrepancy in size of our two countries. They think its British vanity. But its intelligence sharing which counts. The Americans still value our input." This was news to me. Did it mean the Americans had started trusting us again? Perhaps. The Governor continued: "Since Castro took over in Havana, Cuba has rated very high on the American radar. Now, as you know, St. Eleanor is not that far from Cuba though the cultures are a world apart. That helps make Naval intel important here too. That's one of the reasons the Americans want an anchorage here. And that's why we let them have a listening post here and play host to a significant American – should we say – civilian presence here."

"But surely, Sir, there's no threat of communism here. There are no roots..."

"No but you can never tell what may be in store. There's also poverty here. We all know that. And dogma and despair are two sides of the same coin."

I nodded thoughtfully, giving the Governor my full attention.

"So you see, we too are anxious to know if Castro is up to anything in the eastern Caribbean. This disruption to the plantation and now to the shipping threatens the very viability of the island. Of course, Constantine was concerned. Very concerned. And he had our confidence. That's why I sought the Colonial Secretary's permission to make an exception in this one, singular case..."

"The Blue Paper," I breathed aloud.

"The very same you have been so interested in. The document Mr Constantine was reading the night of his death. The paper that has gone missing."

"May I ask the subject of the paper?"

"*An Assessment of the DGI Presence and Activity in St.Eleanor.*"

"DGI, Sir?"

"Yes, there's something more you should know. There is a man, one "Redbeard" Pineiro, a senior aide to Fidel Castro, who we know has drawn up detailed plans for the setting up of a new Cuban intelligence service which he terms grandly the *Direccion General de Intelligencia* (DGI). But there is an additional point of even greater interest. Pineiro's proposals have met with enthusiastic support from Nikolai Leonev, the KGB's boss in the region. Russian backing for Communist agitation in the region is a game changer. So you see there may be much more to the deaths of Constantine and Quillham than is apparent. Armed with the enhanced understanding I have given you I'd like you to keep us appraised of any progress."

I whistled. "I'll certainly keep you closely informed of any developments."

"Good. Well, there's one thing more I must appraise you of."

"Sir?"

"You like it here?"

"St. Eleanor? Well, yes...of course. It's charming."

"Good. A lovely island. I find it very different from other postings. It will be my last, of course. Staff tend to mix more here, you know?"

"Not sure I do. With the locals you mean?"

"No. I mean the grades. The A's usually have quite different tastes and interests. Different people altogether from the B's. But here the Administration Officers often mix with the Executive Officers. Not much difference really. Attaches, secretaries, defence. You find them mixing together more than in a usual embassy."

"I see," I said but I didn't.

"The trouble with that kind of thing is that sometimes roles and demarcation lines can get crossed...Would you like another vermouth?"

"Thank you."

After topping me up Sir Godfrey sat down again, his fingers templed. "On the day in question, the First Minister did have a visitor late that afternoon." The room chilled. "He was one of ours."

"There's no one in the log. Mrs Miller knew of no one."

"That's because Mrs. Miller had agreed not to mention it. You must know we have already carried out a discreet enquiry into this sordid business. Well, as

I was saying...there was a visitor. Not the murderer. At least we are pretty sure of that but a visitor nonetheless. A glorified messenger really. The Chief Secretary was due to drop some cables from London round to *Anse Chastenet* but he got bogged down. You know how it is. So Jahnke volunteered for the job."

"Jahnke, you say?"

"Yes, that's it. Peter Jahnke. Saw Constantine in his office then came dashing out to Dorothy's in quite a flap. He said Constantine needed the spare key to his study. He'd misplaced his. Dorothy has a spare key to almost every room in the building. She said, yes, she'd come immediately and open it for him. But Jahnke said, "Don't bother yourself to come down. Just give me the keys and I'll bring them straight back." So she gave him the keys. He was back in five minutes."

"Long enough for them to be copied if he had the wax ready. Where is this Peter Jahnke now? I need to speak to him."

"No can do, I'm afraid. Counter intelligence doesn't work like that. You see if Jahnke is up to no good we'd want to work him, to unravel all his connections and assess the implications. So nothing must be done to put him on guard. Besides, it's possible he was just doing what he said he was doing. He didn't have the keys long...so for the moment it's business as usual."

"And that is...?"

"Continue investigating the two deaths. You may use the information I gave you to assist your enquiries but don't speak of it openly. Keep us informed of any developments. But if it turns out to be more than just keeping us in the picture, we may need to take action. For the moment if we're going down this road I think it would be better if you make reports to me about your progress. On a fairly regular basis I mean. Of course, we'll help in any way we can." Sir Godfrey had already got his diary out. "The best way to hide a meeting is in a series of meetings, don't you think? Perhaps we could even make a little reputation for ourselves for sharing some pointless, amiable social get-togethers. I could invite others along as make-weights. Not too often. Just now and again. What do you think?"

"Sounds okay to me."

"Good. Well, would dinner at eight a week on Wednesday be too early for you or inconvenient? For our first little get-together, I mean?"

"No. Indeed not. I'd be delighted."

"Excellent," he said, more to himself than to me as he pencilled something in his diary, his movements looking as closely considered as must be his words. "I want this investigation to be quick and decisive. It's already attracting attention from Six in London and we don't want that if we can afford it do we?"

"No, Sir. I'd rather not." MI6, being secret, had its own ways of carrying out investigations which often had different objectives from your own. If you get in the way of one of their operations you're likely to end up being used, squeezed dry and thrown away. At least I thought this is what Faed was hinting at.

"And one more thing, Cordell. If you need to get in touch – if it's an emergency, I mean," and the Governor's fading voice rather suggested that that was a pretty remote possibility, "then you must get in touch. But don't ring me directly, ring this number." So saying he handed me a card which I pocketed quickly. "If you have any more conventional difficulties speak to my secretary. She will be instructed to inform you of my movements. She can be totally relied upon. Now what else is there?"

"Personnel?"

"None. You are on your own. Your cover story is perfect. You are investigating the sudden deaths of the Chief Minister and a leading journalist. This should give you a broad remit to investigate and talk to anyone you need. Your own staff are quite sufficient. But they should have no need to know." He was then all a bustle, evidently with lots of other things to do. I smiled, thanked him for his confidence and as I turned to leave he fixed me with an unsettling steely stare, impressing me with a sense of suppressed urgency.

But that wasn't all. Just as I was closing the door behind me, I saw something else. It was as if a curtain had been abruptly pulled aside to show me what I was actually meant to see. At the end of the shadowed, gloomy corridor, Jake Oppenheimer was sitting at a desk, an angle-poise spotlight brightly illuminating his desk where he was scrutinising some papers. The bold letters at the heading were clear to me even at that distance: MOST SECRET. But surely, I had been meant to see this. It was almost a piece of burlesque. Oppenheimer was not even supposed to be here. Nor would...it was too ridiculous to be anything other than contrived. A mind was communing with mine in the strangest way. As I stepped out into the sunlight I felt a tingling of elation at being inducted into the hidden ways of the masters of power.

28

THE NEXT MORNING FOUND me back at my desk, trying to focus on more mundane concerns. I groaned inwardly as Lucy walked up to my desk. "Here," she said. "All done and dusted." So saying, she plonked a document she had prepared on my desk. I picked the file up but Lucy started explaining it anyway. "You wanted to know about the owners of the proposed *Schooner Landing* site? Well, there they are. I must say this has been one hell of a paper trail but good experience for me I daresay. Initially there were a lot of little local owners but they have all been bought out by five companies, themselves ultimately owned by several others consecutively. There are no listed share owners."

"Sounds fishy, I must say."

"You said it. The paper train ends in the British Virgin Islands with a company called *North Star.* I need to do more work on this but looking at shareholders' names, North Star itself looks to be wholly owned by the much larger outfit – surprise, surprise – *Alpha Omega.* I need hardly tell you Quillham was investigating these links when he was murdered."

My jaw dropped. So *Alpha Omega* owned the whole shooting match from beginning to end. And by accident or design the new First Minister, James Jamieson, had been fronting for this very secretive transnational company. It was hard to believe he didn't know anything of these dubious property deals. "And just what does the Island get back for this largesse to what turns out not to be some small Caribbean businesses but a major corporation?"

"Well," Lucy said. "They are using local labour for the clearance and the construction and I suppose there will be some jobs in the longer run but how sustainable they will be it's hard to say. Certainly all the big money goes elsewhere."

"So let's get this straight. St Eleanor sells valuable land to *Alpha Omega's* little fronts for a paltry sum in return for a handful of jobs. Meanwhile, *Alpha Omega* takes all the rentals, bookings and eventually gambling profits. You must do some more work on this. Thanks Lucy. Keep plugging at it." She turned to go and then something prompted me to ask an unprofessional question. "Who do you *think* is behind this?"

Lucy raised her eyes. "Could be the mob. It's a big operation. The casino suggests it. All the pious talk of helping the islanders is misleading. The ones who benefit will be those who play by the new rules. And you know what that means. Some of them will be getting money for nothing or worse."

"What exactly does this prove?" I asked. "Its legitimate money. I can see its borderline fraud but is it unlawful?"

"The fees themselves may be legitimate but what unseen favours are they rewarding?"

"*Allied Fruits*? I see what you mean. Could we be dealing with the same people? They don't exactly have a reputation for fair play. Another Miami company. It's a tortuous connection but the coincidence of land interests suggests the puppet masters are the same as *Alpha Omega*. Come to think of it, I suppose *Allied* has to report its cash payments like any other company but the details don't show."

"It's a big operation."

"Of course it is. Multinational in fact. That's part of our problem. For far too many people it's just too easy to go along. Why fight it? They are too big. Who has the time and money to figure out how these companies and their associates inter – weave their accounts?"

"And what about soldiers?" Lucy asked.

"Soldiers?"

"As in thugs, leg breakers...people who keep an eye on you. It's probably possible to keep ghost employees – someone who is paid for work in a respectable front but never shows up for work."

I groaned, thinking of the street gang who had pursued me in St. Jacques. Could there be a connection there? "Well, at least that's against the law," I said. The silence grew between us then I asked again: "But what has Quillham to do with this?"

"What indeed? Maybe he just didn't fit the narrative any more. Maybe he knew too much. He was a professional investigator. And he was investigating the tie ups between *Alpha Omega*, *Allied Fruit* and *North Star*."

"There are so many question marks it's hard to know where to begin!"

"How are you getting on with Maddox?"

"Not too well and I'm afraid we have to release him today. We've interviewed him again here but he's still insisting he knows nothing."

"Maybe he doesn't," Lucy said, forcing herself to smile.

"I'm convinced he knows something, something he doesn't want to tell anyone."

"Or maybe he does but daren't."

We left it at that. I pushed my hands through my hair in frustration, fully sharing Lucy's anxiety over *Alpha Omega's* development project. It may well have criminal implications and it was right that the police kept it under scrutiny but it was not in my remit. There was no discernible link to Quillham's death nor to the First Minister's unless you succumbed to the more extreme conspiracy theories. And I was not going to do that. Despite initial appearances to the contrary it looked as if Quillham's murder was probably unrelated to Constantine's. And that meant I would soon be heading home, something which would delight Katie.

But not yet. I wouldn't be doing my duty if I didn't pursue the possibility of a link between the two deaths until it was exhausted. Right now, that meant having a final push with Julian Maddox. There were no evidential grounds for holding him. We had had a number of meetings since his incarceration but Maddox had maintained a steely reticence. I trudged down the steps to the basement where the cells were, breathing in the stale air as I did so. The officer on duty nodded recognition at me as I approached and directed me to Maddox's cell. The key clanked as I was shown in. The prisoner glanced listlessly upwards as I entered without raising his head.

"Good morning, Julian. It's your lucky day. We're going to release you."

"About time too! Ah never did nothing!"

"If you are so sure of your innocence why are you so unwilling to talk about your dealings with Quillham and what you know about his contacts here?"

"And why do you keep asking me?"

"You know very well why. And we'll keep coming back until this is sorted." But by this stage we were already just going through the motions. Maddox knew I had to ask about those links of Quillham's; and I knew that he would still refuse to answer. "Do I have to remind you that withholding information pertinent to a murder enquiry is a very serious matter." No response. I waited. "I can't help wondering," I went on, trying a new tack, "if you wouldn't do better to lighten your burden by talking to us a little."

Maddox kept stumm.

"Is it possible that you've just fallen into a lazy habit with us, that you've kept everything inside for so long that you can't talk now? But it doesn't have to be like this. You could be free of police harassment. All this is partly your own doing and it's so unnecessary."

"So are we finished now?" Maddox asked with vestigial defiance but I noticed his eyes had flashed with an expression of curiosity, almost immediately repressed.

"For the moment. But we may be back. I hope the uncertainty agrees with you." It was a little game. Frighten him. Let him go. Then see where he goes.

Maddox looked up bleakly. "There was one thing..."

"What?"

At last there was a look in his face at odds with his extreme negativity. I waited. Maddox grimaced slightly and focussed his eyes on the ground. When at last he spoke it was in slow measured tones as if he had finally decided I could be trusted.

"Well, I barely registered it at the time. That's why I didn't mention it when you called. I wasn't covering it up but since all your questions, it came back to me."

"What? What exactly came back to you?"

"That night, the night Quillham died I did pass near his house like I said. I remembered it as quiet but that's not quite right. I did see someone. Just this one man and then, very briefly mind you, a figure running down the hill. I wouldn't have paid much attention but he came down through the gardens and jumped on to the road."

Silence sat between us. I smiled thinly. Absently, Julian brushed his hair back with his right hand.

"So please tell me as much as you can about this man you saw running down the hill?"

"I don't know anything more."

"Don't know or won't tell?" This provoked a flash of anger in his eyes. It was so quick I barely caught it at all. Then he spoke, quickly this time, trying to control his anger and succeeding.

"It was dark. The street's badly lit. It was a man. I think he was white. I can't even be sure of that. A youngish man I would guess by the speed he ran. He was fairly scurrying along. He disappeared quickly and I barely registered him. That's the truth. It must have been around the time of the murder."

29

THAT EVENING I WAS glad to be home. To anyone else *Caille Blanc* must have looked a bleak, uncomfortable place but to me it had become home, my ultimate refuge from the heat and the mosquitoes. I was getting into the routines of life here. It began with sharing this tiny home that permitted all manner of insect life to enter; by glimpses of the volcanic peaks and by catching sight of fleeting wildlife. I certainly had my worries during this posting and they had come from all directions, like carrion to a dead carcass. They had started with a dead body which had led to another; and yet others had crawled from the political situation and some had sprung from inside, from my own irrational pre-occupations.

Staring at the blank ceiling which served as a kind of canvas for my thoughts, I saw Laura and Andrew. I had been away too long, perhaps, and the prospect of a happy reunion beckoned, driving away darker thoughts. But this evening I was unable to unwind the way I liked to. Something was bugging me but I didn't know what. Outside it was hot and clammy. All was calm now but an ancient instinct buried deep within my cerebral cortex refused to be fooled. This would end badly, it told me with all the authority of an omniscient, god-like source. But I had hardly closed my mind to the outside world when the telephone rang.

"Bruce? Bruce, is that you?" Briscoe's voice was as familiar as ever despite the winnowing effects of miles of underwater transatlantic cable. "Listen, I've got news for you." "Shoot!"

"I've been asking around a few friends I know in Fleet Street, calling in some favours. Well it wasn't easy I can tell you. Hardly anyone knows Quillham now but then I got put on to this old geyser, Sid French. An old 'un right enough, long since retired but he could remember Quillham when he was much younger, working for Reuters. Well it took a while getting it all out of him but if what he said is true then you may be in a whole new ball game. I had to ply him with a few more scotches than I can afford but what he said in the end was pure gold. He says that Quillham was a wrong 'un. He used to get information from top business people but also used to take perks from them. Not usually cash but free *de lux* holidays, courtesy of business acquaintances, especially *North Star*."

"*North Star?*"

"That's what I said," Ken said evenly. "The very one."

"Tell me more."

"Well, he seems to have been in their pocket pretty much. He'd write little background pieces which were little more than disguised promotional. If anything nastier came out he would edit it down a bit..."

"Censor it, you mean."

"Well, not exactly. You know how these guys work. There are ways and ways of presenting things. Quillham was good at it according to French. Never got caught out but he was a smooth operator. Knew which side his bread was buttered on. He didn't want to lose any of his privileges and immunities. Looked after himself, like. Some of his colleagues were getting suspicious of him but he was getting out by then."

We fell silent for a moment. So Quentin Quillham's reputation for fairness and reliability may have been assiduously cultivated. In reality he was a ruthless manipulator of others' credulity. But how far out of the norm was it? Wasn't a lot of business a kind of confidence trick, getting people to believe things were much more valuable or essential than they really were?

"I imagine a lot of journalists go that way," I said after a while. "They start with high ideals then they take the easy road and earn much more by moving into corporate PR."

"I guess so. It's maybe not such a surprise yet it is interesting: hardly anyone had seen through him. So after that little discovery of course I did a little research on *North Star*."

A pause.

"Guess what?"

"What?"

"They are majority owned by *Alpha Omega*."

I froze, despite the heat. The half thoughts and suspicions which had been floating around my subconscious suddenly crystallised. So Lucy was right.

"Are you thinking what I'm thinking?" Briscoe again.

"I don't think so."

"If I'm reading things right, *Allied Fruit* is a subsidiary of *North Star* which in turn is majority owned by *Alpha Omega*..."

"Which is allegedly a front for the Mob."

I heard a sharp intake of breath down the line. "Does Quillham's death have anything to do with this?"

"Not that I know of."

"You're lying."

"No. Just lacking confidence."

"Take care."

I tried to focus on Briscoe's information. It was difficult not to let it prey on your mind, consider the possibilities. First Woodbine Parish blathers away irrelevantly about the Mob and *Alpha Omega*. Lucy discovers *North Star* is fronting land purchases for *Alpha Omega*. Then before I know it Briscoe confirms Quillham is dodgy and a smart operator to boot. Then there's the *Allied Fruits* connection and more specifically Alpha Omega's ultimate ownership there too through *North Star*'s role. That's one hell of a company, far richer than St Eleanor and quite likely to exert political influence. I felt as if a trapdoor had opened under my feet. But there was no going back.

I opened the door and stepped out into the night air. Needing to sort out my turbulent thoughts, I set out on a short night patrol but I hadn't walked far when suddenly I stopped, sensing something out of place. In my preoccupied state I had left my usual path and was standing in the wild. I felt sure somebody was there. I don't know how long I just stood there. One minute... two. At last reassured, I resumed my pacing. Then I stopped walking, listened again. I turned my head and heard something. The wild seemed to rustle eerily, almost buzzing in my ears. The darkness, the solitude and the soughing of leaves filled me with unease, the more so since I had lost my bearings. At last I managed to re-orientate myself and repositioned *Caille Blanc* in my mental map. By then all I could hear was the hissing of the breeze in the fronds and the sound of my own footfall. I emerged from a screen of shrubs and plants. The distant house itself was in darkness. I stopped and listened. The enveloping silence was complete. I looked around and listened. There was no sign of anyone but the deep shadows could have concealed a whole battalion. Resuming my way, I found myself struggling with the vegetation. Thorns raked my feet and liana tugged at my body. Suddenly, I heard a footfall behind me but barely had time to register what was happening. I tried to catch his wrist but too late: I hadn't a grip when he struck me on the back of the head. The pain shot through me like a starburst, reaching out from my head and spreading through my body. Later I came to, in a fog of pain and confusion. It can't have been long. I must have been lucky. Climbing back to my feet and looking around, I gave myself the once over. I was a bit dizzy, the night sky a whirl. But everything seemed to be in order. Even the pain in the back of my head I found I could lessen if I held my neck at an unnatural angle. But I felt short of oxygen and that didn't help my nerves. That, the throb in my head and the mosquitoes which were beginning to bite, injecting their poison into my bloodstream. I lurched towards *Caille Blanc*. Still in a fog of bewilderment I had a momentary, horribly disquieting vision of myself lying on the jungle floor, missed by searchers, life ebbing away, sinking deeper into the forest mire, eventually disappearing altogether.

A rustling not far away brought me back to my senses, making me stop. What if there's someone in the house, I wondered? Alert now to all sorts of night sounds, coming from all directions, I made my way back to the cabin. The lamp, lit and standing just where I had left it, threw shadows all around the room giving it a faintly menacing hue but no one was there. Furrowing my brows and blinking in disbelief I checked every cranny. *Caille Blanc* was untouched. No one had been in. A cold sweat was forming on my forehead. What the hell had that been about? A warning?

Putting things together to find a new meaning would need a new context. Previously held assessments were inadequate. Once again I checked the door was firmly locked and buttressed it with the heavy dining table for good measure. Then I removed some items from the bedding and made a new niche for myself on the floor against the wall. I placed my service revolver and a torch beside the pillow, doused the light and lay down. From here at least I had a perfect view of my surroundings. I closed my eyes and fell into an uneasy and fitful sleep.

30

THE NEXT MORNING WITH my head, throbbing like a piston engine, I somehow managed to crawl to the sink, to wash and shave. As I did so I put my right hand to the welted bulge that had sprung up on the back of my head and stroked it tenderly, groaning and marvelling all the time at its shape and tenderness. Water did little to revive my jaded senses and the coarse badger bristles proved harsh on my skin. I tried to think. Today was the date of my scheduled meeting with Geneviève Clouin. I wouldn't let last night's sordid episode prevent that from going ahead. In fact, come to think of it, was it possible that the two events were in some way linked? Well, brooding would get me nowhere. If there were a connection between an assault and an auspicious appointment there was only one way to test the hypothesis.

My mood lightened as I dressed. I had risen late but not too late for my assignation. And it wasn't long before I was back in the land rover and wheezing my way down to Soufrière from my hill top retreat. I parked up near the church and began to stroll through the town.

It was a delight to have a normal visit to civilisation again, to see streets, visit a shop, watch the crowds, order myself a meal. It was like an invocation of old familiar rites, strangely missed. Soufrière, after all, was a show place of the Lesser Antilles. I turned from the gate to the white picket fence which surrounded the Church and retraced my steps towards the little café in the High Street looking out on the harbour. The street, already gathering dust under the pitiless tropical sun, wound gently down between squat box-like houses to the shore. Beggars, ragged and listless, sat in the sun as I went by. Women in tight bodices and brilliant hand ties walked down the street. The little houses of unpainted boards were weathered to every shade of chocolate and rust.

It was not long past mid-day but the heat was scorching. The bay below was speckled with white sails. A small blue fishing boat was making out to the open waters, rocking some elegant yachts as it did so. One of them, tall and beautiful, sported a French tricolour. I wondered which port it had sailed from. Near the harbour, the High Street was full of cafés with a froth of little tables and chairs spilling on to the pavement. The aptly named *Café Rendezvous* beckoned. I went inside where, in the shadows it was beautifully cool. The owner, a rotund and smiling middle-aged woman wearing a chequered handkerchief over her frizzy hair, was called Martha; and she welcomed me to a table in a shady corner while indicating a menu chalked up on a blackboard. I ordered some *Carlsberg* and sat down to watch patiently. Of my contact there was no sign.

The café was quiet. The shelves behind the bar were full of trophies, certificates and in the middle, an impressive looking clock with Roman numerals. The wooden furniture, the crudely drawn seascape murals all exuded an innocent feeling of friendly warmth, *bonhomie* and easy humour. The clientele was composed exclusively of visitors who occupied two tables drinking coffee or beer. At one a small group of businessmen were talking volubly about some deal or other; at the other a young couple were totally engrossed in themselves. I knew them to be visitors because after a month here I was beginning to get to grips with some of the wildlife who inhabited St. Eleanor: the functionaries, the artisans, the plantation workers, the white settlers; the schemers, the consultants in all and everything; and the layabouts and misfits. But I couldn't see anything out of the ordinary. My arrival, made to look casual, was timed to perfection. My clothing suggested a tourist but I carried a revolver.

As I breathed in the smoke I looked down on the boats bobbing up and down by Soufrière's pontoon jetty, the sail of the catamaran, *Hélène*, prominent among them. It was a sleek craft, with fine lines and a handsome finish, definitely belonging in the upper range of sea fare. From its transom, I noted its port of registration: Martinique. At that moment a young woman with long dark hair climbed down from it and on to the jetty. She wore jeans and a pale blue cotton blouse. I couldn't tell then but it was going to be one of those moments you never forget.

As she drew near me I hailed her:

"*Bonjour…bienvenue à Soufrière.*"

She turned, intrigued. I couldn't blame her for looking at me doubtfully but she stuck to the charade, indulging in a species of extreme deceit. Then she asked in English, "How did you know?"

"Simple." I pointed towards the pontoons. "Your boat. It's a French registration."

Her smile enlarged. Evidently she could not resist smiling when she knew she was being admired. "Of course. I hadn't thought about it. I am French but not from Martinique, from Antibes. I rent the catamaran to sail around in. And yourself?"

"Me? I'm Bruce….Pleased to meet you," I said. And I was. "I'm not working at the moment. More recreational." Ah, the lies come naturally when you are undercover. For a month now I'd been living here, thanks to government service, who felt they needed another pair of eyes here to cast a light on some of the island's murkier goings on.

I invited her to dine with me. After a show of reluctance, she sat down at my table with its view up a High Street overlooked by the looming peaks of the *Deux Pitons*. A little way away a group of Calypso singers were giving voice to their high spirits. She confirmed her name as Geneviève Clouin. Distantly, I remembered her as the woman in the background at the Barracuda. But somehow, much more striking. And she was beautiful. There was no doubt of that. Her dark hair was drawn back to reveal a clear and open face, her blue eyes sparkled in the sunlight. But for all that there had been some hardening process at work, I thought, as I studied the downturned lines of her mouth, her eyes fixed on some inner turmoil. Something about her manner was harder, prompting a distant siren calling, distinct but still faint. "It's great to get out and about," she said.

"Too long at sea?"

"Not really but I get tired of cooking on board and, yes, you need to stretch your legs again and feel the earth beneath you." Her voice was pleasant, her English good but her accent unmistakably French.

We both ordered vegetable soup followed by fillets of fish, freshly caught.

"Well, I guess it must be the thrill of the new but there's something about a catamaran with its split hull which I find exciting," I said.

"It's almost like a metaphor for life," she smiled.

"What is?"

"Sailing, of course." It was as if she had been reading my thoughts. "One day you're here. The next you're gone."

"*The next you're gone*," I repeated. "That sounds a little alarmist. I don't know what's been going on but you look worried, if I may say so."

"I am," she conceded, unexpectedly. "I am very afraid."

"Of what exactly?"

"That's the difficult part. I don't really know. *Them*, I suppose."

She stopped while the waitress served the soups. There was a difficult pause and as she was obviously finding it hard to elucidate I thought it might help her to relax by altering the tone of the conversation. "You've come directly from Martinique?" I asked as she started to sip from her bowl.

"Hmmm....it's really very good...Yes, I have just started. I've come over from the *Fort de France* and I'm planning a little circuit of the Windward islands."

I stared at her a moment in disbelief. In 1962 it was still most unusual for such a young woman even to dream of sailing alone through these exotic waters. I lowered my head in bafflement. We ate quietly. The soup was thick with chunks of fresh vegetables. I broke the bread and dipped it in, being sure to scoop up the finer leaves. She sat uneasily, looking around at the scene as if a great energy were stirring within her but with a great confidence in her bearing, perhaps from her beauty but perhaps too from her resourcefulness. It was no mean feat to steer yourself around the Caribbean. I'd learned to sail too, on the bays of New Zealand's south coast and it gave me a kind of inner confidence. I knew the signs.

"Plenty of good sailing in this corner of the world," I said, hoping that by being positive I could encourage this mysterious woman to confide in me. There was little hint yet of her previous desperate communication. Why had she rung me so urgently? Who was she afraid of? She told me a little more of herself. She spoke now with hesitation, pausing frequently and gazing into the distance. "My family lives in Antibes now. My father was Director of the *Musée de Beaux Arts* but he has no need to work now. I learned to sail on his yacht on trips to Corsica and beyond. I was very lucky. I had a good yachtsman to learn from. I grew up sailing. It was wonderful. But...that was when I was young," she explained, then hesitated.

"And what are you now?" I couldn't help smiling aloud.

"I do what I wish so far as possible. Now I like to think I am my own master." That I could well believe. To say that she gave the impression she knew what she wanted and did it, might be misleading: it was rather that whatever decisions she had to make were made and dealt with. And that argued for a high level of self-confidence. We chatted easily over our meal and as we did so I passed under the spell of her lilting voice. Her eyes too held me with a touch of coquetry, a hint of friendship and things left unsaid, but I could not tell whether it was spontaneous or contrived. No, not deliberate I decided but an instinctive exercise of charm which was as natural to her as breathing. She had been shown a lot of love.

"But tell me Bruce, do you like sailing?" she said at last.

"Yes, of course, like everyone. Who doesn't? Back where I come from – Nelson, that's South Island, New Zealand, not London – I was always out whenever I could. Footloose and fancy free you could say." And it was true. The pull of the sea was still there, spell-binding in its intensity and in the drifts of stirred memories. "Nowadays, not so often, I must admit…but why are you asking?"

She shook her glass of white wine a little before raising it to her lips.

"No reason," she said at last, then stopped suddenly, her face quickly concealing something I could not read. "Just curious…"

I needed no further invitation and soon found myself talking about my youth spent with Jack Ellison playing on sailing rigs around the turquoise great Tasman bay outside Nelson, all as if it were yesterday. Briefly, a shabby memory of the young Ellison flared up: a thick mop of hair, a rather too rude line of jokes, and a drinker. Most young New Zealanders were boozers in those days. I had a confused memory of lurching down a street in Wellington and something disreputable happening, urinating, something like that.

It seemed oddly natural for such recollections to tumble back into my memory as if this woman's confident nature compelled confidence in return. Here where the sun never sets, only falls, leaving no time for darkness to settle, it was easy to relax. After all, we'd been very young then and the world had seemed to offer us a cornucopia of delicious delights, of uncharted realms and beautiful girls, and alluring lands where, oddly, thoughts of work didn't seem to have featured much at all. Instead, I remembered the rattle of the wind in the sails and the full masts swaying across the endless blue sky.

"I remember it so well," I said, thinking, well, if she wanted to take her time so be it. "We had a rig – my father's really. It was called *The Silver Spray*. It used to turn beautifully and we'd steer it across the swells to North Island. I don't think we'd ever been so happy... but here too, in St. Eleanor, the so-called jewel of the Windward Islands. This is something else." I gestured airily at the world.

"It's wonderful isn't it? I just find it so exhilarating too. I really do. And Soufrière is a gem isn't it?" Her voice just then was all honey. "Ah-" She hesitated and then went on. "This is a wonderful place. I am always moved by these islands....there's such a procession of natural beauty." Her eyes drifted from the wooded hills to the divers in the bay. A little breeze blew in from the bay and she huddled in closer, her knee catching mine.

"*Le vent se lève mais j'espère...*I hope our paths may cross again and then maybe I can take you out and show you the delights of cruising on a catamaran."

"And I hope so too, Geneviève. I sincerely hope so."

And I did too. At that instant, perhaps a Zen moment, I was at peace with the world. Nothing could have disturbed my contentment. The narrow isolated life of St. Eleanor was sufficient for me. I could hear the water lapping against the quay and the sound of an occasional footfall on the pavement. Here at that moment it was hard to believe in human violence or sinister intrigue.

Geneviève's eyes were looking past me at the Calypso singers, bedecked in colours of hyacinth and blood, but then her face suddenly darkened. "You will find it a small island, Mr Bruce. And a captivating one," she resumed. "A word of caution though. The poets are wrong. There is no truth in beauty. Beauty can mask evil. You must tread carefully."

My heart stopped, her words so unexpected. And yet it was not casually spoken for Geneviève's tone was now suddenly slightly awkward, as if her comments had been forced, hard to get out. "You'll find it safe enough in St. Eleanor," I said. "There's no need to be frightened here. People are friendly..." I'd meant it as reassurance, a conversational makeweight, to calm her from whatever was troubling her. But even as I said it, I could see that it didn't work, only serving to highlight her earlier remark about the evil of the place.

Geneviève looked at me in a knowing way; put both hands on the table and twisted around as if checking for someone's proximity. "That couple in the corner...?" she whispered.

I glanced over to the courting couple who were obviously totally oblivious to the presence of anyone else, and shook my head. But Geneviève didn't smile. Instead, she looked at me sternly. "No sign of being followed?" she asked in a low voice, almost whispering, eyes scanning our fellow customers.

I looked at her: "Nothing untoward at all. Maybe if you'd just explain..."

"It's not so easy. There's so much." She looked at me uncertainly. "It was like this – aargh, it's so very difficult to find the right place to start. There's so much yet nearly all in little steps. You will think I'm mad but... I've got to talk to someone. It's a matter of knowing where to begin."

"How about starting at the beginning?"

"*D'accord*. You see I've chosen you because you're my last hope to get out of this. *Il y a de la vie.*"

It's a matter of life and death.

She spoke in an undertone but fiercely, desperately, her eyes swivelling nervously around the room as if someone even here might be watching, listening. Her hands were trembling, as if she were screwing herself up to making a big step.

"A lot depends on you taking me seriously. If I tell you and you betray me in any way I'm a dead woman. You see, once I wasn't afraid. I suppose I was innocent. But I'm afraid now, that's for sure and with good reason. You may think this an idyllic island. Think again. There are hard people here, people who stop at nothing in pursuit of their goals. You won't recognise them, just by meeting them. They walk down the streets like us, live among us and seem like us but they are eaten up by their wickedness." Once again there was that desperate intonation, that meaningful look in her eyes.

"Okay," I said. "I don't doubt you and I don't think this is an idyllic island. Just tell me what is bothering you and I will try to help."

"Look, I'll tell you the truth but you must listen. First, hear everything I have to say. Don't just jump in with questions trying to bring me down to earth, or something simplistic like that. Nothing is as simple as that. There are always wheels within wheels and the world never quite as it seems. What I'm going to tell you is going to sound fantastic but it's the truth...or at least part of the truth...the truth which I've seen. Obviously, much is being hidden from me, concealed deliberately. They know I know something and I'm being watched. How far they'll go I don't know. But I'm in trouble. Big trouble. This much I do know. Believe me; I'm taking a big risk telling you anything. So don't, for God's sake, don't whatever you do, tell anyone else."

A silence. I waited, a little embarrassed and inadequate to the strength of her emotions which were almost palpable. Her face had changed while she was speaking, becoming harder, more trenchant. Sometimes looks speak better than words and this was one of those occasions. I was extremely conscious of her energy and determination to disclose something important. Yet it was impossible to identify the danger of which she hinted. The setting was wrong. The smiling sea, the quaint wooden houses, the lively chatter all spoke of a different story. But she was right: too many people equate beauty with innocence. Threats can lurk in the most unlikely places, all the more dangerous because of their safe-seeming location. Something was holding her up and she needed to have the way eased.

"I think you need to be a bit more specific, Geneviève, but before we go any further you need to know a little more about me before you make any disclosures to me. You are talking of evil people doing terrible things...of wheels within wheels...that sounds like something criminal to me. I may be a help to you. I may not. Either way you have to know the truth. I understand you wish to confide in me as a friend and that's fine by me but it may not be as simple as that."

"Arghhh!" She nodded her head. "I knew it would not be straightforward. It never is. Still it's all just as well....you must have confidence in me. There is much at stake.....if all is verified, it's a certainty. Its more than a confidence I need, it's an understanding."

I could tell she was taking some kind of risk. I should have felt inducted into her confidential world but somehow it wasn't possible. Her anxiety, whatever its cause, was real enough but was there not a touch of melodrama here, a charade? The sympathy I should have owed her was lacking. I needed to know more.

"An understanding?" I said. "That should be possible but I can't be blind..."

She continued, her voice quieter now, less emotionally laden, to tell me a most extraordinary tale, a true story which it's high time should see the light of day.

31

Geneviève had been very discreet when we met at Martha's, dressed simply in a pair of jeans and blue cotton blouse. But try as she might, she could not help but attract attention. In fact she looked as if she could have just stepped out of a painting; and I found myself admiring the painter's technique. The careful positioning of a silver brooch to emphasise the attractive vertical lines of her figure, the strong eyes giving focus to the whole composition, her careful posture suggesting poise.

Geneviève tossed her hair back, letting a few strands fall free before smoothing them back into place. "I don't think you understand what it's like working with these people," she said. We were still sitting in the open. With perhaps more than a hint of melodrama she had broached the subject of evil on the island but it was still difficult to get to the crux of the matter. Whenever she said anything she withdrew it immediately, so tentative was her approach. From time to time she cast her eyes back to the catamaran as if she'd rather be there or did she fear she was being shadowed.

"Well then, help me to understand. You said it's a matter of life and death. Truly, life and death. But why? How can that have happened to you? A young woman with her life before her..." I asked.

"Yes, I am in fear of my life. I have to leave this island and go somewhere where I hope no one can find me." Suddenly the picture of a self assured, decisive woman disappeared, replaced by someone anxious and vulnerable. I would have liked to comfort her but there was no room for tenderness amid the clatter of cutlery and the continual buzz of distant chatter. She gave me a long searching look but then said: "It may seem hard to believe but I think I know who ordered Quillham's death and maybe the First Minister's too."

I tried to turn my face into a mask of disbelief. "And who is it you think did these murders?"

Geneviève leant closer still. Then her answer came in a whisper, faint like a distant sea bird's call borne on the loftiest whiff of cool air coming from the sea on the hottest of tropical days: "Rufus Halliday."

Quietly I answered. "Why? What makes you say such a thing?"

"The strange thing is, it's all so elaborate, it's very hard to pin down," she was saying. "When you are part of a process it's hard to judge what's going on. You are trapped in your own thoughts with no enlightenment from outside. But I'm being pressured, there's no doubt about that." A distant car horn sounded at exactly the same time, as if to emphasise her observation.

"Pressured? How do you mean? Pressured by whom?

"I don't know. That's the mind-blowing thing. There seem to be lots of them but that can't be true...You see there are lots of little things going on but if you highlight any one thing then it just begins to look paranoid or silly."

"Maybe not. I have some experience of that sort of thing. If it's elaborate its deniable. If it's detailed you lose perspective. That all leaves the victim in a difficult position. You feel like someone caught in a game, stumbling blindfolded, while unseen hands push and direct you. But if that's true, it all goes to show how serious and organised your opponents are. You have to try to identify the direction of what they may really be after."

"Well, yes, you have it. I think so too." She fell silent, looking pensive, then resumed "That's good. Maybe you understand these things better than I'd dare hope. You see, they haven't threatened me. Not exactly. But there have been very frightening hints and allusions and disturbing coincidences. The situation is not one that I've been in before. They take their time. They insinuate their way into your head. They blow hot and cold. There's even tact and care…" Just then her eyes gleamed with a rare intensity.

"Sounds like recruitment to me…induction of a very nasty and sinister sort….but maybe I'm jumping the gun…tell me more."

"Where should I begin?"

"How about the beginning?"

Geneviève paused. There are hardships of the mind that you cannot reckon. "*Moi*," she said. "*Je regrette tellement*. It has been two years now though, God knows, sometimes it seems much longer than that. I was staying at my parents' house in Martinique with friends, enjoying the sunshine, the beaches and we had daddy's yacht – at least his old one. I was having the time of my life. But suddenly it came to an end."

Innocently Geneviève painted a rosy picture of a poor rich girl's life on Martinique but I could soon see that maybe she hadn't fitted in to the stereotype image. For though she didn't consider herself so,

Geneviève was something of an adventurer. Most of her acquaintances would never have dreamed of setting up their stall on a relatively remote Caribbean island. They would already have found their place in a society composed almost exclusively of young people similar to themselves. Several had also succeeded in quickly attracting to themselves young men of similar tastes. Yet friends had come; and with them a succession of parties and easy living. It wasn't all to Geneviève's taste but she gave way to the wishes of others, sometimes from weariness, and sometimes from a lingering desire to merge herself in the company of others.

"My friends gradually drifted off into marriage or work" she continued. "And the parties became smaller and finally dried up until I was left alone with, I soon discovered, very little money in the bank. But money was getting tight back home too and Pappa was getting fed up with baling me out. He proposed that if I wasn't marrying into money I would have to make more of an effort to make money myself. So I should let out my little house and live somewhere else more humbly still or even on my catamaran. The idea didn't appeal but I began laboriously making preparations." Geneviève sighed. She spoke with sadness as though for a young woman there really was a time of lost innocence; but, perhaps, for her there was.

"It was painful too," she went on. "I had to get rid of a lot of the stuff I'd accumulated, some of it pretty good quality. But where to put it? I certainly couldn't put it on the catamaran that was for sure. Well, the solution was ready to hand. You see there was a loft there and when I looked into it, it was bigger than expected. But there was another problem. When I opened it up there was already a lot of junk up there. First there were boxes of old clothes and cooking utensils. Also boxes of odds and ends which someone once upon a time had been reluctant to chuck out. Maybe they had thought these things would come in useful someday. Then there were also suitcases with some old watercolours in them, works of indifferent amateur quality probably of my grandmother's.

"Then in the eaves of the dormer window there were three naked mannequins. A bit spooky really and I have no idea where they came from. Behind them, jammed next to the walls thick blankets were draped over what I thought were wooden structures of some sort but turned out to be large canvases. Determined to clear the place of all the old junk I pulled them out. The dust! Oh...la...la. You've never seen anything like it. Anyway I pulled them back to find they were more paintings. In oil this time and obviously not those of my grandma. I decided to take the time to look through them thoroughly. They stood out as different, one from the other, and I think by local artists. Different standards but all well-crafted in their way. Virtuoso attempts, really, to capture the ceaseless flux of life in splodges of colour and line. At that moment I had an idea. Images of dancers, of fiddlers, acrobats and even of farm animals floated into my head. But the style was very different, the colours very bold, more abstract, not realist. I would try my hand at painting. Why not? I had been properly trained and through my family knew much of the art scene. So why not try some exotic oil painting of my own?" She paused a moment, reflective or soaking up the scene.

"Why not, indeed?" I prompted, smiling but intrigued to know where this was leading. It was uncomfortably humid. Even the customary sea breeze seemed to have deserted us. Too warm. Too stifling. "Well, Geneviève, I can't see what harm there is in any of this…"

She just lifted her brows as if I'd said something stupid which I suppose I had. When she started again I let her run as if there had been no interruption. So it was that Geneviève took me on a history of her strange days on St. Eleanor. "It was just after this that I began the first of my Caribbean cruises, bolder than usual. I was looking for new horizons, new inspiration. I took my catamaran across the waters to St. Eleanor and found it so refreshing. *Tres jolie.* Lots of life. Lots of colour. Usually it doesn't take long to do such a small place. But this time I was in a more devil-may-care mood."

She had arrived at St Jacques with a place in her heart for everything. The bright sun dancing on the roof tops: so beautiful! The dark green of the hill side: fantastic! The rows of crooked wooden houses by the quayside: so quaint! At first she had busied herself at the ships' chandler stocking up with new supplies, tins of food and spare canvas. So helpful! Then she had spotted the art gallery, the *Gallerie du Tertre*: so chic. She decided to give it a go. But when she went in, there was quite a surprise. The gallery itself was much larger than expected, complete with an upstairs exhibition room. The canvases themselves were often of a high quality with prices to match. Not especially aimed at the tourist market, then. That was something of a thought-provoker. Additionally there was an ample section downstairs devoted to Caribbean crafts. Again the standard was high. But there were many other things, some very strange, as well as all this. From the ceiling's crossbeam hung a large model ship in full sail with a high aft deck. Farther back a huge shark seemed to be swimming through the air. It all contributed to a bit of a wow factor. This was spotted and Geneviève had soon found herself being taken up by the owner herself, *une madame anglaise*. Nervously but not lacking in enthusiasm Geneviève had invited her to visit her catamaran for some real French coffee down by the jetty. In fact she wasn't moored very far away. A little to her surprise she had agreed right away. The owner of the art gallery proved to be Chantelle Quillham; and she had indeed come along later that afternoon to the *Hélène* to enjoy a coffee and some fresh pastry with her French hostess. Chantelle had been disarming, convivial and easy to get along with. Evidently they had got on well, going beyond the mere exchange of pleasantries and Geneviève being especially pleased to make new friends on St. Eleanor. Though she hadn't liked to admit it, she was already missing the conviviality of Martinique and the pleasures of partying so she took well to the attentions of this middle aged Englishwoman.

"How long have you been here?" Chantelle had asked, her smile widening.

"I arrived on Saturday."

Silence.

"Ah. It must be a bit lonely for you here...Say, why don't you come along to my place this Friday evening. We're having a bit of a party. You'd be most welcome."

Naturally, flattered and pleased and with little pressing, Geneviève had stayed. She'd arrived at the gallery on the appointed time, dolled up and ready to enjoy herself. But immediately she'd wondered if she'd made a mistake. She knew no one apart from Chantelle and hardly her. What would she talk about? She knew little of Caribbean art and nothing like so much as being a daughter of a Director of a *Musée de Beaux Arts* led people to expect. The setting, apparently idyllic, now seemed strangely alien and not so welcoming. The air was unbelievably still and she almost had to push her way through it to the gallery. Yellow and pink hibiscus festooned the roadside opposite and she found herself wondering if a bee would come to visit the neglected pistils. Perhaps, she thought, she was no better than a bee, being lured in to spread the pollen of a different source.

She needn't have worried. Chantelle was there at the gallery to greet her and introduce her to the throng. Throng? Well, this was the first surprise. Actually there were only a dozen people. Geneviève had imagined the gallery packed with sophisticated arts people, a buzz of chatter, free flowing alcohol, laughter. Then this. First she was introduced to a middle aged man going bald, lean with earnest eyes and a craggy face: Quentin Quillham, Chantelle's husband. Memorable but you soon sensed he was not the sort of character you would find it easy to have an idle chat to. Then there was the Reverend Strangeways, likewise an earnest character and an even dourer figure with deeply glowing eyes and a deep tanned complexion. Fortunately, the evening was to be redeemed by others. Amy, a local artist, wowed to be exhibited in the town's premier art gallery. Matthew and Scilla Forrest were engaged in local commerce but she didn't know quite what and it didn't seem right to ask. Then there was Ailsa, a sharp and vivacious local girl who worked in the shop. Her boyfriend, Winston, added another smiling presence to the ensemble. Mr Paul Wang, a Taiwanese businessman, was ceaselessly smiling and affable. Denise Boulton, a dark haired white woman in her late thirties, turned out to be a formidable fine art expert and director of the island's nascent national collection. A tiny scattering of local artists made up the rest of the ensemble.

The gallery itself was laid out much as it was during the day but for the appearance of a large folding table replete with a multiplicity of different bottles offering a varied cornucopia of drinking delights and, of course, many upturned wine glasses. Visitors helped themselves; and this they did with abandon. The walls were changed to feature a new exhibition of local artists. The canvases themselves were a melange of sizes, styles and types but a healthy quota of low cost paintings was more than offset by some impressive canvases of striking originality. The guests looked around eagerly as they chatted and drank. The only small distraction was a fish tank full of tropical fish whose swirling kaleidoscope of colour threatened to steal the show.

Gradually the gallery filled up. Geneviève relaxed. She mingled easily. People wanted to talk to her. People drank. People chatted. This was more what she had expected. People seemed interesting and had something worthwhile to say. It was free and easy. Geneviève was struck by the wonderful feeling that she was being surrounded by some of the most outstanding people in the Caribbean arts world. Could life get any better? She found herself talking again to Quentin Quillham. He knew the south of France quite well and they spoke of Nice, the coast, Antibes....

At that moment, Chantelle, radiating with life, found her again.

"Ah, there you are. You must meet Rufus. He's very keen to see you....Are you enjoying yourself?"

"*Mais oui.* Absolutely super. *Merci.*" And all the while, the fish were flashing their golden sides from the tank.

"Good, well, you know if you're looking for a little job while you're over here I could always do with an extra pair of hands in the gallery."

"That would be *merveilleux.* Thanks."

"Well, drop in again soon after all this is over. Everyone likes you. We'd all like to see more of you."

Then Chantelle introduced her to a rather stern-looking young man with a prominent lower jaw. "Rufus Halliday," said the soothing voice, "will give you an honest answer to all your questions about St. Eleanor." And Halliday had looked at Geneviève appraisingly as if to say that indeed he would. He was fascinated to learn of her trip down from Martinique.

"Now what in the wide world are you doing here? Don't you have to sign up with the Port Authority? Produce a Health Certificate? And won't they be sending out search parties to comb the area once they've found out you've gone?"

"All attended to...and no, no search parties."

"And what are you doing with yourself?"

"Sailing is my passion but I paint a bit as well so I'm delighted to be here."

"What are you painting at the moment?" Halliday enquired.

"An abstract piece," she said though she had not painted for months. "Very modernist. I'm trying to make it thought provoking and entertaining too. I like dualism. The peaks and the troughs, the bad and the good, the beautiful and the ugly."

He smiled. Yet Geneviève must have been in an enervated state because she found it hard to focus on what he was saying, her thoughts running away in all directions, making it difficult for her to keep up her end of the conversation. She felt dazed. Halliday didn't seem at all concerned. He kept up a steady patter of names and places mainly associated with her childhood and family and France. She was taken aback – and flattered – that he knew so much about her. His French was quite good but perhaps there was just a hint of *Québecois*. He asked if she could do with a bit of extra money. He probably knew. He might, he said, have a proposition to make. 'We must talk about it next time.'

32

THAT BROUGHT ME BACK with a jolt. I found it hard to comprehend such an offer on such a brief encounter. Hard but not impossible.

"I take it the offer is the key to why you want to see me," I asked.

"Not the key. Not at all. I have to explain the build-up if any of this is going to make sense. In isolation events just don't make any special sense. There would be no pattern. Nothing sinister. But you see there most certainly is. That's why I need your help. I've thought about the problem constantly. And I've come to a decision. What seemed like a constant nightmare I now know has to be dealt with. *Finalement, j'ai dit la vérité.* It needs shock treatment. Only some unexpected force from the outside can do any good. It can't be seen to come from me. You see I'm watched. I'm a marked woman, I'm certain of it. But these people have got to be stopped." She had spoken with unexpected vehemence.

"Alright. Carry on. In your own words. Take it from there. But I'm afraid I'm pretty ignorant of the arts world. Perhaps you'd better tell me a little more about this strange party. Was it a good one?" I asked feeling sceptical.

"I think so," she shrugged. "I felt very relaxed. They were a sort of party for lots of the top people in

St. Eleanor from all walks of life. The Right people, if you know what I mean. Those who really matter. The movers and shakers of the island. My father always said this was the real division in life. Not rich and poor. Not black and white. The Right people and the Wrong people. He was right wasn't he?"

I nodded encouragement

"This later one was a much more crowded affair. Artists, authors, editors and the idle rich were busy promoting themselves in their usual way. But even here, islanded somehow in this din, Halliday commanded my attention. There was something curious about him. Well, I had a pleasant chat with him about the delights and perils of sailing in the Caribbean. But not as jolly as you might think. Instead, much of what he said was more like a riddle, one that he expected me to understand. It was as if hidden meanings were wrapped up and implied in the familiar words. Well, he left me to brood on his words. I tried to circulate.

"The drinks were flowing and I knew business was being transacted as well but I was just there to enjoy myself when I noticed another curious thing. I had been listening to a bearded European talking about his life on the island. He seemed to think he was inordinately clever living here on very little. But he was polite. In fact they were all polite. Come to think of it, quite a few of them were drifting towards me, more than at a normal party. All polite, unknown faces. They were all strangely serious, in a wheedling sort of way. I didn't see it at the time but looking back I can see that they were deploying a kind of purposeful conversation, as if they were sounding out my opinions. It was almost as if I were being interviewed for a new job. If I gave an answer that went down well then there was a little glow of approval in their faces. If I said something they didn't approve of, a mask of disapproval fell on their faces. Then I noticed another curious thing. The questioners seemed to be in agreement about everything, as if instead of the usual medley of opinions I was getting a consistent whole.

"So I remembered a trick of my father's. One he used to catch people out. The result was clear-cut: their reactions were the same. If I said Castro was a bad thing, a frosty face glowered at me. If I said Kennedy was far too supportive of Pappa Doc and other right wing governments in the Caribbean, a friendly face concurred and asked me to go on. It didn't matter whether it was the latest novel, the UN or my take on the Algerian crisis, everything I said was being measured politically. By the end I had decided to play it dumb in future and stay clear of politics.

"If only it were so simple. It can be a lonely business, living. When I left the *Gallerie du Tertre* it was dark, dark as only the tropics can be but I could make out the shape of a man on the opposite side of the street, a man I thought I half recognised, standing under a lamp post following me with a fixed gaze. It was unsettling. Then I remembered where I had first seen him. It had been down by the jetty, my second morning in St. Jacques. That time I had seen him standing in the same pose, staring at the *Hélène* with an extraordinary stillness and single-mindedness of purpose. It was the same man. I was sure of it. I was being watched."

"Men will find you fascinating for your charms and some I am sure will go too far."

She cut me off. "No. That's not it. You see I am accustomed to being looked at by strange men but this was different and quite unnerving. The same pose, the same fixed glare."

"Did you report it to the police?"

"No. What was there to say? But I can see now everything was done step by step. Each step so small seems insignificant but the whole adding up to a large picture where your own perspective is lost."

"An interesting way to put it. So what was your next small step?"

"I have struggled to remember what exactly it was that happened next that night but when I got back to the *Hélène* I was sure there was something wrong about the look of the craft. Something had been disturbed. I couldn't say what it was exactly but I knew the *Hélène* had been searched. I suddenly felt cold.

"Yet in the next few days, I was able to push this almost out of mind. *Almost* but never quite wholly. I settled in to work at the *Gallerie* easily enough. And I was pleased to make new friends so easily, pleased it had all gone so well. Yet I noticed an odd thing. People were treating me as if I were the most interesting girl they'd ever met. People kept agreeing with me whatever I said about being an artist even though I don't know that much. I lapped it up. Well, it was flattering, wasn't it? It was after about six weeks, that things changed quickly."

"Go on."

"*Eh bien*. Things were getting better. Or so it seemed. I quickly settled into my new working routine at the *Gallerie du Tertre*, finding my colleagues agreeable and helpful, the collection absorbing and, frankly, the work not too onerous. The money helped too. It wasn't a lot but it made all the difference. Chantelle too, I regarded with fresh eyes. Where before I had considered her to carry more than a suggestion of middle age now I could see her figure was still good and her manner charming. I, in my turn showed my ability to be a good assistant and we soon developed a good working and even friendly relationship. I was getting used to the routines of the gallery and I was even shown the contracts with artists and suppliers; and encouraged to understand them.

"Then one evening I returned to the Hélène to find a message had been left for me. It was a single sheet of paper. I still have it here." At that Geneviève handed me a neatly folded piece of A5 paper.

I took it and opened it up.

MEET ME AT THE SAINT LUCIA BRIDGE TOMORROW MORNING AT ELEVEN

Eleven had been circled, unmissable in red. I looked up, mystified, and she returned my gaze steadily.

"Did you go?" I asked.

"*Biensûre*," she replied, her eyes meeting mine in meaning. "That is where it starts…"

SHE HAD FOUND THE bridge easily enough. It is a well known landmark in the capital beside the Waterside gardens. It was impossible to see anything sinister in the arrangements for everything was in bloom, butterflies were hovering over flowers and there were birds hanging high in the air above.

"I didn't know what to expect," she explained. "But there is no doubt I was exhilarated. I was naïve. I should not have taken my visit so casually. No one in the world knew where I was. But I thought the meeting might resolve the mystery of what had been going on, what had been happening to me in St. Jacques. Perhaps it would dispel concerns, even perhaps lead to something lucrative, something exciting. There was no especial reason for concern. After all this is a peaceable island. But there can be no excuse, I know. I had blundered.

"You see, it was absurd, perhaps, but I felt valued. Valued for reasons unknown but valued nonetheless and that might lead to monetary gain. It was foolish. Well, I waited and straightaway it was an anti-climax. You see, the place was deserted. I stood there a moment in silent contemplation and sensed another mood. Just then I felt a tap on my right shoulder. I spun around and found myself looking into the blue eyes of a tall European gentleman, mid-forties or so. Rufus Halliday. Startled, I muttered something silly like 'Oh...you surprised me.'

"He smiled at me but I felt the smile didn't go further than his lips. The look in his eyes told a different story. He was giving me a searching look, committing me to memory. I found myself being scrutinised as if I were a piece of fine art: elegant, desirable and, above all, a good investment. The strange thing was we had already met but he talked all the while as if we were new acquaintances. We got talking. Mr Halliday said he was a businessman. He asked me a few innocuous sounding questions then made it clear that he already knew everything about me. It wasn't the usual line. I am well used, Mr. Cordell, to the amorous approaches of men with an over-estimation of their charm. This was something quite different. He seemed to take our relationship, friendship even, for granted. He said he only wanted what is good for me. Now it sounds almost absurd except that I went along with it. It somehow seemed wrong to question anything. Halliday had let the suggestion of my being involved in something very grand and significant hang in the air. When he had finished he bade me a friendly farewell and departed as softly as he had appeared with nothing more than a vague promise to be back in touch. I recall that I left that day feeling confused but strangely elated as if I had been in contact with a higher destiny." I imagined with what charm Rufus would have related his story to her and was shocked to discover myself suddenly invaded by jealousy. A week later Halliday had phoned her at work.

"Would you like a night out? I know of an excellent restaurant here in St. Jacques. *The Green Parrot*. You've possibly heard of it." She certainly had. It was one of the best and most prestigious on the island. It was only on the next occasion that Halliday came out with his proposition.

"Geneviève, I am authorised to pay you a thousand francs retainer."

"Me?" she had protested. "Why me? I've done nothing to earn the money. I have no special knowledge or skill."

"But you do... You have special skills. Sailing for one. Discretion for another. All you have to do is to take an envelope once a month to the Poste Restante in *Fort de France*. As a resident of both islands you have an impeccable reason for such a routine."

"Well, we met again. The next time on my catamaran by the quayside in St. Jacques. The windows were wide open but there was no respite from the heat since they allowed more hot air in, rising from the burning stonework and melting tarmac. He proposed an easy task for which I would be generously remunerated: £200. All I had to do was to take a thick envelope to a named man at the *Poste Restante* in Fort de France, an easy little journey for me, *n'est ce pas*? And a pleasant one. Money for old rope, as the English say. Of course, I see now that I should have gone to the police straightaway. There was obviously something questionable about this arrangement. But maybe Halliday – or the people behind him – had chosen me because they were sure I wouldn't. I certainly needed the money. I agreed. There was virtually no risk. What I was being asked to do was easy. And the money was good. I must have done two, no, three trips in this fashion. It was a breeze; it really was. Sometimes, I did some odd jobs for him at his office in his home. *The Hammock*, he calls it."

"And what sort of work was that?" I asked.

"Oh. Just odds and ends. Office administration. Filing, that sort of thing. It was dealing with companies, mainly foreign ones. So far as I could see, it was pretty sensitive stuff about commercial risk. Investment risk but also about vetting new applicants for confidential posts. But that was only now and again. Mainly I was delivering messages to *Fort de France* and working at the gallery with Madame Quillham."

I let Geneviève talk on, relaxing more as she continued. I could detect her sense of guilt, of unease at being made a dupe. But I could understand. No doubt Halliday had flattered her, suggested that she was cut out for better things...yet for all that Halliday would have given nothing away, told her nothing. With

Halliday, I knew now, you were always left floundering, looking for a meaning between the words. He was the great withholder.

"Then things began to change," Geneviève explained. "Halliday passed me on to Quentin Quillham and then virtually dropped out of my life. I continued to take messages over to Fort de France but now it was Quillham who gave them to me. And often now on the waterfront mooring at the foot of his garden. They became more frequent too. Sometimes he gave me sealed packages. But these were not for the *Poste Restante*. Instead they were for a named man, a local, Jean Courtois, who worked as a chandler in the port. Once again everything had to be done in the greatest secrecy. Once, they dumped a metallic box on me. God, it was heavy. Secret material, they said. Maybe it was a test. I don't know. I became alarmed but also excited. I wondered who I was really working for then I thought I was letting my anxieties get the better of me, I had tried to get a grip, focus on the tasks in hand rather than let my fears run away with me. But I knew I was their woman, bought and endowed. Their money was in my pocket. Too much of it by now. Their brand was on my forehead. Still, I felt, let's give the Devil his due. He had recognised my merit."

She straightened herself in her chair but she was in full flow, hesitations cast aside. "But I have no doubts now. The stakes are high. I didn't know who Quillham and Halliday were working for nor did I want to but they were obviously serious people and for their own security they might choose to silence me. *Pourquoi pas?* It would not be difficult. It need not even be a blatant murder like Quillham. An accident could be arranged for the *Hélène*."

"You were the voice that night, weren't you?" I said. "The voice that warned me that Quillham was in danger. How did you know he was going to be murdered?"

"I didn't!" she said. "But I *felt* it, felt his fear. In the weeks before his death I met him occasionally and each time was worse than the last. He had become sick with worry. His moods swung violently. He bought a safe. He was keeping a 'special' dossier there, a document he was working on furtively. I mentioned it to Halliday. He became stony faced, told me not to talk about it. That's when I became convinced Quillham was in mortal danger. That's when I phoned you...Later when Quillham was murdered I realised I must do something decisive to get out...and that's why we are here today."

Looking at her, I found it hard to make the connection between an accomplished young French yachts-woman and the Caribbean seascapes with the brutal killing of an investigative journalist. But her story made a disturbing kind of sense. It spoke of "their" trying to get some sort of hold over her, of forcing her compliance. Who?

I must admit, at this point, I was also feeling very annoyed with myself, aware that I had dug a big hole for myself. More and more of my time I knew was being consumed by work for Mr Halliday. But I had found it lucrative too. Was it possible that I too had been lured on with bait skilfully placed to draw me on amid great fanfare until there would come a point when I would find myself hopelessly entrapped? But I knew it was not going to be so easy to bring that particular episode to a close with another substantial payment to me still pending. And Katie would not understand. I would have to seek clearance from the Governor himself.

Or maybe even Oppenheimer. How could I possibly explain my foolish behaviour after the trust they had placed in me? God, what a mess!

I looked again at Geneviève. She was now quiet and subdued but watching me carefully. Yet there were tears in her bright eyes. For a moment I thought she was going to break down and cry. Geneviève was worn out, frazzled by an emotional roller coaster. Alarmed at having encountered something sinister on the island, she could have nothing to do with the deaths with which I was concerned. Yet she was looking for answers and I'm afraid I had none. I felt inadequate to the task.

"Tell me, Geneviève," I asked at length. "What happened to your messages after Quinten Quillham was murdered?"

"They've stopped. That's what's happened."

33

LATER, I RETURNED TO the office to resume the more prosaic mechanics of my investigation. The earlier mood of philosophical *bonhomie* was dissipated. I felt tense and confused. Something was amiss. And no mistake about that. Geneviève's revelations, Straughan's statement and Faed's confused ramblings had completely shaken my assumptions. There was a bigger picture here I was completely failing to grasp. For a while I continued to shuffle papers around my desk but I was distracted and unable to make a concentrated effort when the telephone rang.

"Chief Inspector Cordell," I answered.

There was a moment of silence and then a hint of soft breathing. "I'll talk to you. No one else," the man's voice said.

It was the same voice. Even in the tropical heat I froze at its sound. Maddox. Could it be that he was finally ready to talk? "You know about Quillham, don't you?" I asked.

Another pause. "I'll talk to you but no one else."

"Alright. But where?"

"Go to the corner of Hawke Road and Grey Street in half an hour. Stand on the corner a while. Check that you are not being followed and a friend of mine will contact you and lead you here? Got it?"

"Yes."

"Right. See you then. Remember if you are followed I won't keep the appointment."

I sighed to myself but accepted the stricture. Hurrying outside I jumped into a police vehicle and turned on the ignition. The roads were pretty quiet that afternoon as I drove into the quiet alley ways of the Old Town. Uneasily, I wondered why Maddox wanted to see me. This would be our fifth meeting and we had made no progress whatsoever. Except, that is, that I now believed him to be innocent of direct involvement in either of the deaths. Parking as near as I could to Maddox's designated road juncture I ambled along to be sure of my arrival at the appointed time. It was still early afternoon and many shops were closed but the streets were by no means deserted. Small knots of people, mainly young men, loitered here and there laughing, joshing and blathering. I slipped by as quietly as I could, not wishing to draw attention to myself but not wanting to arrive before the appointed time. There were far fewer people around here but I still wished I'd dressed down a little for the occasion. Then Maddox appeared at my shoulder. Not one of his chums then.

"This is how we'd meet if you were Valentine," Maddox observed.

"Outside?"

"Outside where eavesdropping can't be done and we can see everyone. It would be dark and always somewhere new. You never take it easy, never relax, never drink too much, you don't acquire new friends. You don't even trust the old ones. You only survive by constant vigilance." Maddox spoke as if he belonged to the spy world of Berlin, not the sleepy haze of the

Caribbean. Whether or not I was really doing what Faed or Oppenheimer wanted was a moot point. Either they would approve or they wouldn't but events were unrolling and I no longer had the luxury of worrying about them. I had long ago imbibed the virus of fatalism; and I knew this little operation was my baby now. "I help you and you give me a free ticket. That's my idea."

"Turning Queen's evidence will help you. What have you in mind right now?"

"I'm going to show you a little hideaway they have."

"Go on. I'm interested."

"I bet you are!" He laughed aloud then more furtively, demanded, "You drive here?" I nodded. "Go back to it. I will follow."

I did as I was bidden. Maddox's would-be tradecraft was swiftly rubbing off on me. I found myself retracing my steps back up the hill, confident my man was still nearby. Sure enough, when I looked, Maddox was following at a discreet distance.

I climbed back into the car. Maddox appeared in the passenger seat. He started dishing out his instructions and I followed them to the letter, back down the hill, right at the customs office, straight along the concrete road, past some downmarket restaurants. As we did so, an easier look settled on Maddox's features. He indicated the way and we took off down a narrow, cobbled alleyway. Maddox fell into an unusually loquacious mood but as he talked his whole tone changed. He became gentler, not the Maddox I thought I knew. He withdrew into his youth almost like an old man and forced me to withdraw with him. As we drove through the alleyways he conjured memories from every doorway: the plumber and his wife who used to give him biscuits; Linda, the florist who knew all the gossip; Gordon the carpenter who could whittle any piece of wood into a superb piece of craftsmanship. As we motored along, his talk became more and more vivid and his gestures more ample and sweeping. Without knowing it I had been planted firmly in the town of his childhood. Over there for instance was old Rastus, so old he looked like Methuselah, wheezing all the time and so shrunken, soon he must disappear altogether. For the moment Rastus plodded along, treading on his trouser cuffs and scuffing the ends. Then there was Rachel, so old now her clothes were far too big for her. She looked as if she had just grabbed any clothes when she got up or maybe she had just come from hospital. But it soon became clear that not all of Maddox's ghosts were friends. Many were enemies, some nightmarish. Others he suspected of being police spies. His was a tortured soul, railing against the world. But I could see his street knowledge could be useful to malign intruders.

"Sometimes," he said moodily, "I would like to forget all this...but here we are, Chief Inspector." he said, an air of purpose returning. We had finally come to rest at the foot of some unprepossessing blocks of flats not far from the quayside. Maddox led me into the nearest one. It was a most unattractive building standing detached, faded and run-down. I noticed immediately that all the ground floor windows were barred and that was sufficient to generate suspicion. A light breeze, suddenly rising from the harbour, blew into our faces. The area reeked of garbage, urine and fear. Wild foliage had grown up. The building ran to five storeys, one of the taller ones in old St. Jacques but there was no-one there to show any interest in us as we entered. A fetid smell greeted us in the stairwell. Maddox sprang up the stairs and I followed as best as I could, noting as I did so that there were two flats to each floor. As we climbed the concrete staircase there was no sign of the neighbours, a circumstance which suited me. When we arrived at the top, the fifth, Maddox approached the door on the right, inserted a key, felt the lock ease as he turned it, and pushed the door open.

The flat Maddox showed me looked unlived in, strangely impersonal. A safe flat? It would suit someone lying low very well. The front entrance on to the sea was not frequented heavily, a circumstance which would suit shady purposes. The back overlooked the main road east from the city. The telephone worked. Better still it had an attic window from which you could climb out onto the roof tops provided you didn't mind taking a risk with the tiles. The furniture was rickety but that didn't matter either. But on the whole the place looked impersonal and unlived in except, that is, for a small framed photograph of a small bright-eyed girl of about perhaps five, full of life and innocence.

"Who is she?" I asked.

Maddox laughed and shrugged his shoulders. "No one. The photo is there just to give some plausibility." I took the place in quietly for a few moments. For the first time I noticed Maddox's body smelled of garlic.

"Like to look at the emergency escape route?" Maddox asked breezily as he pushed open the window and gestured to the roof. I took one look at it and froze. I'd done some climbing in my time but this was scary. It was a warren where old and new buildings were all muddled up together. A glance at the roofs told a history of chaos: the tilt of the of the roofs was alarming and there was little I could see in the way of footholds or handholds. Some of the structures even looked rickety and parlous for my weight.

"Interesting." I said. "A safe house? And for whom?"

"Let's get a few of the basics right, shall we? I did not commit no murder. I didn't kill Quillham. I want that to be clear. And I barely knew the guy. It was Mrs Quillham I dealt with mainly. She wanted all sorts of traditional craft work, especially old stuff. Sure, I helped arrange a few fakes but nothing serious. At least, nothing like murder. As for Constantine," he shuddered. "That's way over my head. And frankly it terrifies me....Now, if I tell you about the big rollers on this island, do I get a free pardon?"

I nodded acquiescence. Maddox seemed to accept that but, frankly if purveying a few fakes was the summit of his crime we wouldn't be interested anyway. So, I let Maddox talk. Chantelle Quillham must have been pleased about some of his doings because she had introduced him to Halliday who, in turn, had cultivated him over a few meetings and drinks; and then passed him on to Valentine. Valentine had proved more lucrative, his requirements were peculiar but not criminal. At first Maddox had helped him with a few fakes then with some larger nuts-and-bolts operations, finding this accommodation, for example, and helping organise some street youths. Maddox then got involved in bringing in some illicit goods into the island, including a powerful transmitter. Showing me this safe house was by way of establishing his credentials. Maddox confirmed the flat was used from time to time. Mainly single men who flitted in and out of the island but to what purpose, he had no clue.

"This is all interesting stuff, Julian," I said. "But you must know more than this. It's *Mister* Quillham who was murdered. Are you really saying you have no idea what was going on? Quillham was in the middle of quite an investigation of his own into the *Alpha Omega* business. This stuff you've been involved with reeks of underground work. If it is criminal then it transforms everything. The transmitter? What the hell was that for?"

"I don't know. I delivered it but I never saw it again. That was new. Only a fortnight ago. But, of course, Valentine's a crook. He keeps his distance, mind you. It was he who got me to take an active involvement in the plantation workers' struggles, to keep an eye on it and report back to him."

"Do you mean to tell me all that was a charade?" I almost shouted in amazement.

"No...not exactly. I do care about how they're being treated. It's just that I had to tip him the wink about how things were going. Valentine had all sorts of little tasks for me. Do you know but he's even had me helping him organise some of the rougher lads into a gang in St. Jacques."

Lucy's insight floated back to me. What was it she had warned of? Soldiers? As in thugs, leg breakers... people who keep an eye on you, people who would do your dirty work for a pittance. And I recalled all too vividly my encounter with a St. Jacques Street gang. What else did Maddox know?

"We'll need more details later, Julian. But right now I want to know all the names. You have told me

Mrs. Quillham was the first but that she was mainly interested in buying merchandise. Its the introduction of Halliday which seems to be a step change. So it was he who passed you on to Valentine and all things shady. A transmitter was brought in, you say?"

"Sure thing. It was a rendezvous at sea but we landed it right here in St. Jacques."

"Who took the consignment?"

"Valentine was there but another man did all the heavy lifting. He seemed to have a special standing. I didn't recognise him. Not from here. More the sort Halliday would have hung about with."

"Can you describe him?"

Maddox became clearly disconcerted, uneasy to say much. "It was night and we did the handover very quickly. I didn't get a real good look at him."

"But something surely? Tell me what you can. A European?"

"Yes, sure, he was white. Fairly lean. Young, I guess....There was one odd thing about him though."

"What was that?"

"He wore grey cotton gloves."

"This could be useful," I said. "Perhaps it's time for you to learn a little of what's been going on."

"No! Don't tell me!" Maddox interrupted. "I can see that you've got problems. Big ones. Frankly, I don't want to know. I know how these things get to you." His voice suddenly carried a lot of force of character. Maddox evidently had little idea of what he had been getting into. But who was I to judge? I who had accepted Onslow-Bell's money so readily. At my age I should have known that if it's too good to be true, it's too good to be true. This meeting had been both rewarding and depressing for the same reason. There was much to mull over. I thanked Maddox for his assistance. I told him I'd be back in touch.

Valentine was a bigger crook than the local police realised. I would pass this on, of course, but it was not very strictly my concern. Halliday's role was more problematic. He obviously was not straight but it wasn't clear what he was up to. Some sort of criminal activity or did he just have a taste for the seedy side of life? Some people did. Impossible to know. When I thought about it, beneath his surface charm he was an aloof, arrogant soul. He liked nothing better than to break things down, things which others revered. Subtly he seemed to make the bad good and the good bad. His concern for the islanders' welfare, a pose. As for the young European, who was he? I'd certainly had no reports which might suggest such a person was involved. Was he making damned sure his presence on the island was going unobserved?

Outside again, St. Jacques with its serene seascape and jolly little streets beckoned to me as an appealing prescription. The fresh daylight began to clear my head. I pondered again Katie's letter but there was little comfort in its contents. "*We have all been missing you. You too are missing out on their changes. Andrew is making a bridge from his Meccano set. He really loves that game. Maybe he will be an engineer some day. Laura is the worry. I don't know what will become of her. She is turning into a tom boy, always out and getting dirty climbing trees and the like. I wish you were here to help keep a bit of order. I have to tell you this has gone on too long. Surely, you must have some wind-up date by now...*"

Crumpling up the letter I stowed it in my pocket. Poor Katie. Alone and struggling with Laura and Andrew and all the rest of it. She had made me feel guilty as if I were hiding from my responsibilities. I walked on, looking at the warren of streets ahead which marked the old town, but feeling no better. I noted a grocery shop and a hairdresser's but there was little commercial life. A couple of churches appeared, one Catholic and the other evangelical. The pavements were nearly deserted but not quite. Three men stood in voluble debate on the street corner. Thin, hollow cheeked with almond eyes, they waved bony hands in argument like prophets of old arguing over some fine theological point. Behind them, framed in a shop doorway, a girl watched impassively. As I walked on I heard a gust of ribald laughter as if all at once the argument had collapsed but in the tropics you never really knew when some pit covered with innocent looking grass, green after the rain, might yet claim an unsuspecting victim.

34

BACK AT WORK, THE office was humming with the clatter of distant typewriters but I was far removed from it, trying to concentrate on recording Geneviève Clouin's and Julian Maddox's statements, my mind racing ahead looking for implications. It was proving hard to keep the process steady. One thought led to another. It could mean this or it could mean that but hard facts were in short supply. Yet I had to keep to the bare facts for my briefing with the Governor that evening. I decided to take some air. I had never really been one for office work. But just as I was leaving the telephone jangled. I picked it up brusquely.

"Chief Inspector Cordell."

"Bruce. Glad to catch you." That voice. It was Halliday. "I have some urgent business with you. I need to talk to you. This evening."

"Quite impossible. I have an important assignation this evening. It can't possibly be postponed."

"Six o'clock. My place. Hammock Cove. You'll know how to find it. A man of your abilities."

"Look! I can't possibly do that. I have an urgent appointment, not one I can wriggle out of."

"I'm sorry to have to change your plans, Mr Cordell," Halliday began. "Events have overtaken us. I'm afraid I haven't been entirely frank with you. Its time I told you more of the truth. And it concerns Mr Constantine, a man with whom you must be especially concerned. These things must be two ways. You pull and we pull. Get it. You need a useful steer on the Chief Minister's death. We need a little more confidential information. I think I have something which can help you. But we really must progress this today. All you have to do is just ring the Governor's office and tell them you are ill disposed. Montezuma's revenge or something like that. What could be easier? I'm sure they'll understand. ... Six o'clock. Remember. I will be there. You should be. Alone. You will not get a second chance to learn what this is about."

The line went dead.

What to do? IPA's money was now central to our lives. Halliday almost certainly knew that. In fact he had an almost uncanny ability to know too much. Just how did Halliday know I was meeting the Governor tonight? It had been only newly arranged. Yet he didn't give a damn. In the back of my mind, somewhere in the chaos, was the memory of that wheelchair delivered to my home in Wimbledon. And with that puzzle the thought of my family's wellbeing. Yet, difficult though Halliday was, this connection might yet prove critical if Geneviève's and Maddox's testimonies were anything to go by. So I rang the Governor's office to cancel the meeting. The secretary's shock was almost palpable but she accepted my excuse: she didn't have much choice. I didn't suppose it was normal to cancel meetings with His Excellency. Talk about blotting your copy book. I promised to be back in contact just as soon as I was able. But right now I had to readjust my focus to Halliday and the warnings of Geneviève Clouin. Of course Halliday must be looked at. Now I could see clearly how he'd been pushing me around, drawing me into his web, making it difficult to withdraw. Yet how little I knew of this man when it came down to it. In fact, so far as I knew, he had broken no laws: it was I who had been inveigled into doing things which were not right for a serving officer. It was time to draw a line. Carefully, what was left of that afternoon, I began to assemble as much data as I could on my friend, Rufus. It was vanishingly small. But I did at least get an address. I might have guessed; he lived in one of those opulent villas high on the hillsides, not far from the island's capital, St. Jacques. So, he wanted to see me there? Well, maybe a little visit was in order.

In any case it occurred to me that it might be wise to scout out his house, to study its entrances, to take its measure, so to speak. Besides, I needed the buzz of a little physical activity. You could never get to the heart of things amidst the paper. I was soon on the road heading along the coast. I always liked to drive on my own, letting my thoughts flow unbridled, indulging in all kinds of imaginings without any logical thread to connect them all. To drive was always something of an interlude of liberty for me. My eyes drifted lazily over the horizon, studying the mountains that soared above the dense jungle foliage. I was beginning to find my way around the island by memorising some landmarks: an unexpected bay, a giant fig-tree, a friendly looking cafe or whatever fastened itself into my consciousness. It was a beautiful place, mysterious, haunting and timeless. I pulled off the main road and turned up a track which should take me to Halliday's. The road grew steeper, my arm resting on the open window, the enchanting beauty of the setting in harsh contrast to the unpleasant nature of my task. But God, this heat was becoming awful. I should have been used to it from Burma and the Gold Coast but somehow I wasn't; strange how you completely forget the discomfort until you were confronted with it again. I put my finger underneath my collar and ran it along the perspiration.

I drove into what passed for a lay-by and switched off the engine. For a few moments, I just sat there gazing ahead, then, using my shirt sleeve I brushed away the beads of perspiration which had gathered on my forehead. I had found myself in a pocket of tranquillity facing towards the cooling air from the west. I was still struggling to come to terms with the brilliance of the light, reminiscent of Africa, but so different from the greyer tones of England. The air was oppressive, watchful and sultry, producing a haze around the jungle's fringe. Wisps of mist hung around the forest trees. I sat back a moment, luxuriating in the exotica of the place and listening to the strange chorus of the island's unfamiliar birds. My mind too had become a kind of lay-by, filled with stationary traffic.

From this height I could see a little of the ocean, a jumble of islets and rocks; below, a schooner was cresting its way towards the land, suggesting it may be about five, high tide. The haze haloed mountain peaks looked down on me while all around the riot of greenery marked the dense jungle. The smell of the foliage and the forest vapours should have filled me with a sense of the wild. But somehow it didn't. My mind was elsewhere. It was a kind of disturbed feeling that I sometimes got during an investigation. It was almost like a premonition of doom except it wasn't that either. It was a growing awareness inside me, rather as the ripples cast by a single stone engulf an entire pond, that there was far more to this case than I yet perceived or may ever perceive. I was tired of not understanding what I needed to understand. The thought was helped by my surroundings for around me lay a vast primeval forest, dark and untrodden, hiding the very earth under a canopy of mystery. Something had been bugging me alright. It was Halliday. I couldn't be far now from his house. I climbed back in and drove on.

It wasn't long before I saw a likely house. I stopped again and climbed out, only a short distance beyond the jungle's fringe, to get a better view of my quarry. Sure enough, if the map showed me right, Halliday's house– so-called *Hammock Cove* – was in plain sight now, a one-storey affair but complex and sprawling. It looked opulent but there were signs of neglect too, as if the owners did not come often or had fallen on hard times. Usually a fine house is set off by careful planting but there was hardly anything: just a few dry stalks and fading flowers to do battle against the invasive jungle. But it certainly enjoyed a magnificent vista. And that meant money.

The exhausting heat bounced back from the rocks and I stood there motionless while swarms of mosquitoes and flies appeared from nowhere. Biting ants teemed over the ground surface. So much for reconnaissance. It was time to find out what it was that Halliday wanted, what was it that was so important, so pressing. I emerged from a screen of shrubs and plants and walked up the hill to the house. As I did so all I could hear was the hissing of the breeze in the fronds and the sound of my own footfall on the gravel. The house itself was in total silence. Suddenly, the front door was flung open. Halliday appeared on the steps, shot me a smile of welcome and gestured me inside. I followed him inside cautiously, peering into the hall. He hurried me along a passageway. My confidence in Halliday and his arrangements had been badly shaken. Right now, I felt the difference in our clothes and countenance. Me in my brown fatigues and shorts, Halliday in his cotton suit and brightly coloured shirt. But more importantly I couldn't miss the feeling that we looked out on to the world very differently. I tended to see the world through a policeman's prism; he, well, I didn't know what animated him.

We moved next to a small room, rigged out in study style. To one side was a desk with a typewriter on it and a chair in front. A small wadge of opened letters lay on the table and below stood a bin full of envelopes with foreign stamps on them. Two solid bookcases with dog-eared volumes and a few unused editions looked back at me. A low coffee table sat in the middle of the room. Halliday was the first to speak. "It's good to see you again, Brucie. I know it's not been easy for you but you'll be glad you came. Believe me."

"It had better be good," I replied testily. "I had to cancel an important meeting to come."

There was something malignant in those eyes. Halliday was coldly angry.

Halliday said: "You told me you were going to work flat out and put the First Minister's death behind you. You said the whole business was open and shut. You told me that, Bruce."

"Yes but that doesn't mean I don't keep following up leads."

"What does that mean?"

"It means I try to start afresh."

There was what the novelists call a pregnant pause before Halliday started up again. "You listen to me. You have nearly compromised us. You have set in motion a train of events for which IPA is quite unprepared. Have you learnt nothing? You have been in St. Eleanor long enough now to learn how things stand. You can't do anything of note without being seen. That is the truth of it! That girl's catamaran was spotted in Soufrière and it didn't take long to find out who she was talking to. What do you think you are playing at? Do you really think you can play a one man show here? You should have had her checked out before you agreed to meet her. God knows what nonsense she has been putting in your head."

Questioning me with such directness about my own doings, as if he had any right, angered me. Trying to stay cool I replied flippantly: "Very interesting no doubt but wholly irrelevant. I'm a police officer doing my job."

"Nothing is irrelevant to us, Bruce. Everything is at stake. No matter how trivial it may seem, you should do as I say and we'll get results." He paused a moment before continuing in a more conciliatory mode. "Look, Bruce, I don't know how you stand with her in your work. And you're right, that's not my business. I am concerned about IPA and servicing our clients. It's just I fear she may be a distraction. I have met her and I know what I'm talking about. To be frank she's a bit strange. She is a walking mystery, hiding everything from everyone...including herself. I'd steer well clear if I were you. She's quite capable of saying she's forced to do things she wanted to do herself."

Well, now I had no doubt that I was facing a different kind of businessman to the one I originally thought I was dealing with. A man who traded favours, cut deals, sailed close to the wind and had both high level and dodgy contacts. Halliday turned to look at me as if he were weighing me up. Perhaps I was reciprocating. There could be little doubt Rufus Halliday was engaged in some sort of risk assessment of a very different order from the one his chum, Onslow-Bell, had signed me up for. The first hair line crack in my life appeared right then. Initially it seemed to be nothing of great importance, the faintest of scratches, something easily set aside but I can see now that it was the beginning of doubt, of the dawning of a suspicion whose onset would later split and divide all my thoughts. But right then I simply disregarded it and, deciding discretion was the better part of valour, said instead: "Well, I've been doing as you asked. I've been working with you but frankly I don't seem to be doing anything of such importance. Just fed you a little information on one of our citizens. Harmless stuff. Why are you so haughty?"

"Look, Bruce, you've done good work for us. And you have been well rewarded...well, you must consider your future. You have your family to consider."

"I do. I'm proud of them."

"So why keep stirring up trouble for yourself?"

"How do you mean?"

With an arrogant calm he said: "Have you forgotten that little assignment you did for us. Getting confidential police information for us on Forrest."

"I did as you requested."

"Did I request anything? You did it Bruce." Halliday looked up at me sharply. I was flummoxed but agreed wearily. For a moment Halliday had been angry but now his tone relaxed again. "But you've got tied up with this Clouin girl. Don't let her waste your time."

I looked up. "What has Geneviève Clouin got to do with IPA?"

"Everything and nothing."

"I don't see..."

"You'll have to see, Bruce. You have only one choice. Work with IPA and you'll be doing fine both financially and at work; and in the future. Clouin can only muddy the waters. Time to knock it on the head."

"But you seem to forget I am a police officer with my own priorities and concerns. IPA is for me only by way of a hobby. A well remunerated one to be sure, but nothing more. Nothing has been compromised...If I seem to be an opportunist to you, well, I couldn't care. I, however, work from the evidence I have. Police work is fact based. We always follow up new lines of enquiry. New information is always welcome."

"I imagine that following lines of enquiry can be a frustrating job." He smiled.

"It can be."

"But you've been thinking about the First Minister, haven't you?"

"So? Of course I was appointed to investigate his death and you know it."

"So perhaps I can be of assistance to you in your investigations as well as helping you fulfil IPA's brief, a most lucrative brief...is it not?" Halliday smiled again.

"And what about Constantine? Care to elaborate?"

"Not so quickly, Bruce. You must understand that there are many things about our fair island that I do not know. Especially government thinking. I really value your assistance....but please be reasonable. We've invested a lot of time and money into finding out how this island operates. You can't expect me to dispense my hard gotten gold like a vending machine. I must be sure of your help and compliance."

"What is it you want?"

A small half smile twitched at his lips. "Well, the Clouin woman is certainly not the reason I brought you here."

"No. I didn't suppose it was. So what is your reason?"

"Well, you know how businessmen are. Our clients are practical people not idealists. Though I say this: a great deal of good is done by trade. People...no, whole countries...who were at loggerheads find themselves getting along just fine when they discover they can sell each other goods. That's a fact of life, my friend." He was positively beaming now. "So in a way IPA's work is underpinning the efforts of the government. "

I nodded agreement. "And so? How does this affect me."

"Well, you need feel no conflict of interest. You see, our company needs to know the future trade policies of the soon to be independent state of St. Eleanor. You have established direct contact with the Governor. I gather you were to see Sir Godwin tonight."

"*Was*. I have had to re-arrange it."

"Good. But can't you see, you can't do this without a little check with myself. Together we can formulate the right questions and glean the right information to make sure IPA comes out on top. And you and me with it, Brucie. That's the beauty of it."

"What sort of questions?"

"We need to know St. Eleanor's likely trade arrangements with the UK and the Commonwealth. A preview of the Trade Agreement would be an advantage.

We guess it's at an advanced stage. We would like to know likely arrangements with the US; and of course, Havana. Will any deals with Cuba be tolerated? And what exactly is the likely future of the proposed US base? Is it a certainty? And, if so, when? And what exactly will it consist of? Those are hot potatoes and we need to know the answers."

"Surely, you'd do better talking to Jamieson."

"Don't be naïve, Bruce. Jamieson has inherited a straitjacket. He'll have to follow the pattern laid down by the Colonial Office."

"So it's the Governor who is the key?"

"Yes. He knows everything. And he knows so many secrets all the local politicians are afraid of him. Don't ask too many direct questions. He would get suspicious. But I'm sure if you probe intelligently you will get a feel for things. I'm so sorry if I have offended you but you have now got into a perfect position for exercising a little leverage."

"I think you are a trifle over-confident, Rufus. He wants me to tell him where I am on the investigation into the First Minister's strange death." I elaborated a little on my stalled investigation without revealing anything of Sir Godfrey's assignment. As long as my thoughts were guarded I still thought he could find no entry but I scarcely needed to have been so scrupulous. He was hardly listening.

"But of course. Did I not say I would be able to help you?"

"Constantine's death is a cross I have to bear. Murder? Suicide? Accident? A hard working man sticking his fingers into all sorts of pies...a bit of a conundrum. Who would want to kill him? Everyone or no one. But I can tell you this! The Chief Constable is looking to me to provide the answers. So as you can imagine I have my hands pretty full at the present without querying my pitch with the Governor, asking him all kinds of tom fool questions which have nothing to do with me."

More no listening.

"But, my friend you had all the answers at your finger-tips and you threw them away."

"What do you mean?"

"You see. That pig headedness! That's what makes you vulnerable. You assume Woodbine Parish was ill used because he says so. Has it not occurred to you that he was pensioned off for very good reasons. Let me explain. When Inspector Parish arrived at the Chief Minister's house that fateful morning he found an old lady and faithful retainer weeping into her cups. He asked a few questions and she was too confused and frightened to answer honestly. She thought she would be blamed for not putting on the alarms...so she lied to him. Perfectly natural thing to do. But then she found she had dug herself into a hole. One lie begets another. She found she couldn't easily reverse her testimony. Please don't interrupt...when you visited she tried to alert you to the wider situation but you weren't really listening. You just obsessed about the blue paper he may have been reading. After the body was taken away they performed an autopsy..."

"But there was no post-mortem of any sort...!" I protested, sticking to the official line.

"That's where you are wrong, Chief Inspector. Do you really think they would have a Chief Minister die in mysterious circumstances without some sort of investigation? No. The Chief Minister did take barbiturates but he was not killed by them. He was killed by a lethal injection of air into the femoral artery. The mark of the syringe was clearly visible. So you see Chief Inspector by conniving with the authorities to cover up details of the Chief Minister's death the police are accomplices to murder."

35

So the next morning in a state of considerable confusion, weary, sweating, inexpressibly distrustful but still half convinced that we were on the way to success I told Lucy about the allegation of a lethal injection, making it sound like the merest gossip. To my surprise she took the suggestion seriously notwithstanding the earlier findings.

"But in that case we'd have to identify how an intruder could get into such a secure house without raising the alarm. There was no sign of a forced entrance."

"Maybe he had a master key?"

"Impossible. That would be held by the Police Protection Unit."

"A duplicate then? If it were murder we're surely talking about a professional killer, a motivated man who would leave no clues behind him. Someone cool, calm and collected. Someone or a group who would know how to get a hold of a key if they bent their will to it."

I was reminded of Quillham's warnings concerning close knit conspirators and for a moment we sat in silent contemplation of these thoughts. But as detectives we also knew the pitfalls of speculation. "By the way, there's a message for you from Frank. You've got an appointment tomorrow with the Governor."

I looked up sharply. "What's that about?" I asked, dimly recalling my forced cancellation.

"Think you are more likely to know, don't you?" I shrugged my shoulders by way of answer. "How is Katie?" Lucy asked abruptly.

"Oh she's...she's fine"

Lucy looked curiously at me.

"You don't sound too sure."

"Oh...I'm sure enough. Sorry. I was away..."

"Of what were you thinking?"

"Oh nothing, really."

"Shall I tell you?" She bent forward towards me and gave a slow wink.

"Certainly," I said, smiling. "Why not? You are usually frank with me, aren't you?"

"Geneviève Clouin. You are almost drooling whenever her name is mentioned. You're clearly fascinated by her."

I rather shrank at Lucy's mention of her name. I was on the point of saying something but somehow it was just too deep for words. "Oh, don't be daft!" is what I finally settled on. A bit lame, I admit, but fortunately Lucy had already turned her back. The truth was even worse than Lucy had intimated. Geneviève had begun to haunt my dreams, an impression of her was now so firmly stamped on my mind that I was finding it hard to drive her out of my imaginings. I also had the additional unsettling feeling that Lucy was demonstrating some unfathomable female intuition which I didn't know how to deal with. The truth was thinking of Geneviève augured badly for my relations with Katie. I preferred not to think about it. But it was clear that I must try not to find opportunities to be in Geneviève's company but equally I knew that it would be difficult to avoid completely. I had not created this situation, I told myself.

With some effort at concentration I focussed on the event which had set everything in motion. The normal investigative routes were closed to me. A different strategy was needed. Murderers make mistakes. They all do. The issue is to identify them and to assess their significance. I thought of the whisky glass. No fingerprints had been recovered from them but why was it cleaned? I thought of the timing. Of entrance and exit. Then there was the culprit's past. He didn't come from nowhere. An accomplished murderer was probably one who had killed before. The more I thought about it the more convinced I became that I had missed something vital. It was in this spirit that I returned to the scene of the crime. My police pass assured me of entrance to the grounds of *Anse Chastenet* easily enough but when I climbed out of my car I decided not to enter immediately. Instead I went for a walk along the path which ran around the house and disappeared into the further reaches of its extensive garden. The sun was still low and there was a cooling breeze coming in from the sea. I found it a refreshing exercise to stroll around and enter the front garden proper from the other side of *Anse Chastenet*. The path was narrow as it led past a cluster of specimen trees into the colourful herbaceous area. I was choosing my steps with care when I nearly collided with a middle aged woman wielding a rake. I jumped back in surprise as she turned towards me. A look of sudden alarmed recognition shot over her face.

"Mrs Peabody. Pleased to meet you again." For I too recognised her, now that I'd had a few seconds to process her.

"Good morning, Chief Inspector." She stopped and I put out a hand to shake hers. But she shook her soiled hands showily in front of her, smiling to indicate that this wasn't a good idea. She was dressed in baggy linen trousers and a dark T shirt. A wide brimmed straw hat served to keep the sun from her face.

"Busy?" I asked.

"Of course. The garden always needs a lot of work. We may not be the botanics but there's always a lot to do in *Anse Chastenet*. I like to start as early as I can before the sun really gets going." She smiled. Mrs. Peabody was the real gardener here supplemented by two occasional part-timers and, of course, some *réhabilités*. Though, these latter, Mrs Peabody had already explained, were usually more trouble than assistance. For the first time I noticed that Mrs. Peabody was not the only sign of life. A pile of garden pots and four trowels suggested that others would soon be returning.

"Do you have many youngsters on the horticultural rehabilitation scheme?" I asked.

"Not too many, thank God. They're useless but I have to take them. Everybody – that's everyone else who doesn't actually have to work with them – thinks it's a great idea. But it's not. They have to be supervised all the time. Mostly, they're sloppy and inattentive."

"Lazy?"

"I'll say. They don't understand the idea of hard work. But it may not be for much longer. Mr Constantine was soft about such things. I'm hoping the new regime will take a more realistic view."

"Who put their names up?"

"Youth Justice or some such. All young offenders anyway." I ran my eyes over the garden then informed

Mrs Peabody, for no particular reason, that I needed a word with someone in the house. I was just beginning to walk around to the main door when Mrs Peabody shouted: "You can use the back door here. It's not locked."

I thanked her though it was hard to see her under the broad rim of her hat, followed her advice and slipped inside. She followed. We were standing in quite a brightly sun-lit conservatory with lots of colourful plants and flowers. Reminded me of a greenhouse. There was something about the place which struck me as significant. I stood there a moment trying to coax the thought to the surface but it would not come. Then a thought suddenly struck me. "Are any visitors in the habit of coming in this way?"

"Not to my knowledge. Just staff." Then she paused, evidently thinking conscientiously. "Not since Quentin Quillham, of course, but since him, just us."

"Did he visit this way often?

Suddenly Mrs Peabody stood very still, her face troubled. Then she said: "You must know that perfectly well."

Bollocks. But I didn't say it. "You haven't told the police that, have you? It wasn't in your statement."

She looked pensive. "Do you think it might have been important?"

"Probably not. Do you think he visited that day?" I asked but acutely aware that Quillham had not been entirely truthful in implying he was a more distant friend of the First Minister and an infrequent visitor.

"No, not really but everyone's been talking about it and he did seem sneaky when he came in sometimes."

I was about to press her on this when an inner voice suggested it may be better to let her think about it.

It was time I had some luck. I almost believe in luck, not that you're born lucky or any of that sort of thing, but there is luck which you can earn through sheer hard work. If you keep pushing hard enough, something gives in the end. So, I let it go and, turning, went through another door and found myself in the ground floor corridor attached to the hall. It was busier than on my first visit. It was a little like when there had been a death in the family and the daily routine had been overturned. Which I suppose is what it was after a fashion. People were coming and going with an air of not knowing quite what to do. I heard a woman's voice. Dorothy Miller was attending to some baggage. She looked up when she saw me, smiled and said: "Good Morning, Chief Inspector. A bit of a surprise to see you again." But she didn't look at all surprised.

"I just wanted to check the building one last time, Mrs Miller."

"Well, you just made it. Mr Jamieson and his entourage are moving in tomorrow."

"So you'll be moving out?"

"Tomorrow, Sir. My bags are all nearly packed. My boy, Davey, has a car. He'll be picking everything up in the evening."

"I gather there's a bigger staff than your good self moving in."

"Oh, yes, Sir, there is" she said, suddenly thoughtful. For a moment she paused, her lips pursed together tightly as if they were trying to restrain a burning emotion from bursting out. "No doubt the new First Minister has learned a few things," she went on. "There'll be less opportunity for murderers in the future and no mistake about that."

"How do you mean?" I asked, my antennae very much alerted. She was eyeing me closely, scrutinising every detail with exquisite thoroughness. But of Peter Jahnke there was not a hint. I had certainly underestimated my adversary. Even her pout seemed to say: "You are small fry for me!" But instead she said: "Well, it's always been a mite too easy to slip in if you really wanted to. Warwick liked to relax here. Now there'll always be people fussing about. The police protection unit has been stepped up and they are going to have a permanent presence inside the house." Dorothy stopped and looked around guardedly before continuing, "I'd better get on, if you don't mind, Sir. My bags won't pack themselves."

Clearly busy, she started up the stairs wholly unconcerned about my presence. As she walked away I realised I'd missed an obvious possibility. *A mite too easy to slip in*. We'd asked about visitors to *Anse Chastenet* but we'd never considered the possibility of occasional workers. A trainee gardener, for example, would not be on the permanent staff but might have gained access to the house. Well, it might turn out not to matter about the easy garden access. But it might, as well, and as the investigative officer I should have checked this more thoroughly. This prompted me into the uncomfortable discovery that I knew very little of Dorothy Miller, all too little considering she had been a pivotal figure in Warwick Constantine's private life. Yes, I had known she was the loyal housekeeper of the former First Minister. Yes, she had clearly stated her suspicions concerning his untimely death. It all served to remind me that I knew next to nothing of this key figure. Was she married? Did she have a family? Who else was she networked to? Where did she live? I had made too many assumptions. And why? Dorothy had straightaway given me good grounds to spot her as an intelligent actor in the whole drama. How had I come to disregard her? Perhaps – no, make that a probably – I had written her off too easily as an insignificant factotum, someone who didn't have a lot going on in her head. In sum, I had been stupid.

And Mrs. Peabody. I had judged her too lightly at her word. But perhaps I was not the best man to handle this. A woman's touch was needed here, I reasoned. Lucy would be better able to tease out the details, details which might prove crucial. I had come to respect Lucy more and more as my sojourn here had extended. Yes, she would know how to deal with the Mrs Millers and Mrs. Peabodys of this world. But even as I considered this I noticed Mrs Peabody was busying herself with hanging some clothes on a peg. She looked over to me and said, almost whispering "I'd like to speak to you Chief Inspector." She looked so intense that her mood infected me, inclining me to step towards her almost conspiratorially.

"Well, Mrs Peabody? I'm here now. What is it you wish to tell me?"

"I've been thinking about what you just said and thought maybe I should tell you. On the morning they found Mr Constantine I had come into work normally. Obviously, I found my day seriously disrupted what with the interviews and all that and decided I needed a bit of fresh air. I tried to step out into the garden but when I tried to unlock the door...well, I found it was already unlocked. I thought it was maybe part of the investigation somehow......but found it wasn't. I thought maybe I ought to tell Mr Parish but I never had an opportunity again and then time passed and perhaps it wasn't so important. Especially since the door was sometimes unlocked anyway, maybe it didn't matter. And since I didn't tell the Inspector on the first day it got harder to say anything later on. But it's always nagged at me so when we spoke, well, I thought I'd better mention it in case it was helpful to you."

"Thank you," I said. But it was helpful only in the way grim truths which must be faced are. Then my face must have lightened as an interesting new idea dawned on me. So simple. But the best ideas are simple. Jahnke had made the wax key but it was an accomplice who had used it. "Thank you so much, Mrs Peabody," I went on, my voice quickening. "You've been more helpful than you can possibly imagine."

BACK AT *CAILLE BLANC* I thought about Geneviève again. In confiding in me she had reported Halliday; and strongly expressed her suspicions about the deaths. No wonder Halliday had been so annoyed that we'd been seen together. It occurred to me now that she would surely, if unwittingly, have an idea about other communications channels. It was inconceivable that a criminal ring of such sophistication as theirs would rely on her alone.

The telephone rang disturbing these reflections. A woman's voice was at the other end. Geneviève. Unmistakable. What a coincidence! But what luck too. There was another check I wanted to run on her and this was my chance. At first she expressed her concerns about her continuing work at the Quillhams' gallery but she was not difficult to reassure this time. I had been wondering how to approach my next proposition but now found the way ahead smoothed. She herself wanted to meet up again. She thought she was being shadowed and in response to my request she suggested a relaxing, innocent looking walk on the beach this weekend to talk things over. What could be simpler?

36

THE NEXT AFTERNOON WHILE sensible people were taking a rest, I had my appointment with the Governor. This time I was punctual. I was shown in by a rather stern and, I thought, disapproving secretary but perhaps I imagined that bit. Faed was alone, dressed in a well cut light summer suit with a bright red tie and golden cuff links giving just a hint of wealth. He cut an impressive figure, well dressed, tall and formal.

"Good to see you again," he smiled, walking towards a wooden closet. "Fancy a dry vermouth?" he asked, already pouring out two glasses. "Have you made any progress?"

"I may have a lead. Julian Maddox. He's a rough neck, a Marxist agitator, active among the plantation workers but he had unexplained ties with Quillham. He is keen to turn Queen's evidence and has given us some useful insights into crime on the island. He's been let out for now but when we need him ...I don't see a problem in pulling him in." I was relieved he did not refer to my fake illness or seem unduly put out by it. Instead, I gave him a distilled version of Clouin's tale without any hint of my ambivalent feelings towards her. I also gave him Maddox's limited revelations. Of Straughan's and Halliday's allegations nothing as yet: I wanted to fact check as much as possible in case it was eyewash, as I half suspected. "So Maddox's comments appear to support your suspicions that there may be an underground organisation being used for other purposes but exactly what is not clear," I finished.

"That's why we want you in there. Find out who they are, what they amount to and what they're up to. Observe things a bit. Know what I mean?"

"I certainly do; and I'll give it my best shot." I had said this readily enough but the dark thought that this is what had got Quillham killed, stirred within me. A so-called 'alongsider' Quillham had been working as the Governor's undercover investigator, a double agent in effect, who had gone too far and been eliminated.

"The Clouin girl's testimony confirms what we'd come to suspect about Chantelle Quillham's little get-togethers: a right little nest of fellow travellers. It'll be interesting to see if there's much more to it. But we can cover that. No need for you to take that on."

"And Rufus Halliday? What about him?"

"We are already keeping a close eye on him through his employer, International Project Assessment. Its run by Walter Onslow-Bell, a close confidant of the Foreign Office."

That took me back a bit, I don't mind admitting but I was disinclined to follow that particular avenue. After that we chatted about generalities and I was lavish in my sympathies for the extra work the transition arrangements were causing him, not least a visit next week by the Colonial Minister, Mr Dennis Duncanson himself. After a while, as if on some automatic pilot of Halliday's making, I asked about St Eleanor's likely trading affiliations after independence.

"I'm inclined to think," Faed said, "that changes will come slowly but come they will. Often change which promises so much, just brings new headaches. We're only now getting rid of the worst practices of sweated labour and yet instead of celebration we have the horrors of radical political agitation."

The Governor paused on this gruff prognosis and I moved the topic on. "Very true, I'm sure. But trading alignments...?" I ventured.

"That's all journalists' talk. All a lot of rot," Faed cut me short, making negative signs. "Looking for a story. Most of St. Eleanor's trade will continue as before and that, dear boy, means largely with the United Kingdom. Bananas, sugar, chocolate. Just like now. There may be more of an opening to American tourists as Jamieson wants but that's a matter of simple geography. It's two way of course, Britain will continue to exert a little influence here for a while. The Exchequer grant will continue a bit...though it may be re-labelled foreign aid."

"Has there been any news about Cuba? Any possibility of developments there?"

"I doubt it." Fade frowned. "The Americans would veto it. I daresay their influence in the region will grow, especially when the US Anchorage gets approved which it will. Castro is too pally with the Russians for that to be stopped, even if Harold Wilson gets elected back home."

"Is it such an issue? Maddox has set me wondering but surely there are no Russians or Cubans on St. Eleanor."

"Good heavens no! But then they don't operate like that. They abuse their diplomatic status wherever they are ...pick up *persona non gratias*...like they're decorations. Alexander Sverdlov PNG, Konstantin Pavlov PNG... Bloody outrageous behaviour, the whole lot of them. No, but its not them we're really looking for. You see, there is always the possibility of enemy agents. Men and women of influence. People who may seem harmless, work for us but betray us all the time. Their system of controls and cut outs operates even in the Caribbean."

Suddenly I asked: "How you seriously do you rate the Cuban threat?"

"We take all threats seriously. The Cuban menace is growing every day," Sir Godfrey said. "That's what the Americans tell us, anyway, and since Suez we always have to pay attention to what the Americans say, you know. And who can tell? There may be something in it. There's nothing as yet pointing to serious civil unrest here but who can tell where this constitutional mess will lead us to? The price of liberty is eternal vigilance as we all know."

"Nobody seems to be in a hurry for change," I observed. There was a pause. We were both beginning to feel something of the torpid numbness of the afternoon.

"That's part of the trouble," Faed's manner changed again becoming curt and decisive, giving me a lecture. "A lot of people here think there is no need to change. They think that things can go on as they did before. But they can't. We are getting rid of our colonial responsibilities as quickly as we can, including the West Indies. They even think that the Exchequer grant from HMG will go on indefinitely but it won't. Her Majesty's Government has decided to end its colonial extension in the Caribbean as rapidly as possible. And that includes St Eleanor. The preferred option is a West Indian Federation. But friend Jamieson may change all that." He told me this with an air of dark foreboding.

"You see, Cordell," Sir Godfrey resumed. "There are topics that I cannot tell you more about for fear of compromising sources. I want you to pay attention to the potential political dimensions of these crimes, with special reference to the possibility of Communist involvement, local or external. It's been reported that even Jamieson himself said at the Barracuda Club that it should have been *me* who was over-dosed! If you find the merest hint of a wider political conspiracy let me know and I can wire for police reinforcements or even a platoon of the Green Jackets from Barbados if we need them."

His words all served to remind me that in such a small island, I was living in a world where everything over-lapped very easily: journalism, politics, business, intrigue. We were building our investigation on quicksand where everything was connected and could turn out to be the opposite of what we think. All was fertile ground for betrayals, improbable alliances and double-crosses. How could I be expected to fathom what was going on in Whitehall or even for that matter, what was going on inside the mind of this experienced, intelligent and no doubt devious Colonial official?

"Do you think they have someone on the island now?"

"The Cubans? Bound to. But God knows who or where."

"What do you think he'll be doing?" I'm not good at imagining things. Besides, I was out of my depth.

"Probably weighing things up. Seeing the lie of the land. Waiting to see what happens next. Maybe waiting for instructions from the DGI." The Governor paused a moment. "I don't envy you Cordell. It must be difficult work, tracking down a murderer. I sometimes think it needs a special kind of mind to kill and a special kind of mind to investigate them. The Metropolitan Commissioner thought you were that man."

"I certainly hope so," I said ignoring the innuendo. "But do you trust me fully Sir? Its not as if I asked for this job and I feel I can't get to the bottom of things unless you tell me more."

Faed looked up at me, eyes as bright as pins. "Full disclosure? I'm afraid that's not how it can be. You've done well so far. Maddox's information suggests some sort of network on the island. Halliday is obviously a shady customer but it's not clear that he's involved in crime. And, by the way, I'm impressed that the Clouin girl feels she can trust you. Cultivate that relationship and let's see where she leads us. Leave her to talk to everybody else, to dazzle them with her beauty and with her talk both of which, you say, she does supremely well...You stay back, observe but don't impede her. We'll see where she leads us. Maybe she can lead us to the Cubans' principal agent here"

"What do we know of her?" I asked.

"I'm afraid we have very little on any of these characters. After your tip off, we requested information on the Clouin girl from the French *Surete* and this paper is all we have got." So saying Faed picked up a sheet of headed A4 paper from his desk and passed it to me. I looked at the paper intently, guessing I wouldn't be given a second chance, but there was nothing of great note. A good education but not distinguished; and not much more. As soon as I neared the end of the entry, Sir Godwin took the paper back. It was evidently deemed too sensitive for my low-clearance self to linger on. "Not a lot as I said," Faed went on. "Well...your trained eyes and ears may spot something we haven't picked up yet. It's not as if you'd be walking blind into a wholly new situation. We'll keep an eye on her but I'm counting on you to bring her out"

"No, indeed. I can certainly work with her."

Faed smiled. "Good! Do you really think you can run this? I certainly hope so." He made an expansive gesture with his hands and sat back expectantly. Faed was proving to be more enigmatic than what I'd first thought, impossible to examine all the wires and wheels in his cranium.

"May I ask, Sir, what it is you are most concerned about here? Is it communist involvement in the plantation agitation? Sabotage of the independence process? In short how would this betrayer betray you?"

The Governor's eyes narrowed. "It is virtually impossible to catch someone red-handed. A lot of the actions are almost like thought crimes. You can tip someone off. You can downplay a potentially salient bit of information. You can do a bad bit of research. You can enquire innocently what your colleagues are working on. There are a hundred and one ways of betraying us without leaving a trace."

I pondered. Well, the addition of betrayal on betrayal would certainly have a poisonous effect in the longer term. "That does make it difficult, Sir. Perhaps it would be easier to identify questionable motivations. Is ideology a factor?" I asked.

"Rarely. Usually money but once you get recruited the whole process is corrupting. They fear their overlords but they also have a kind of respect. What their bosses think of them *matters*. Really matters. They are eager to perform, to live like it matters. They don't go lazy on you. And therein is a constant threat...and then there is the completely unknown. Someone, some man, some woman already here under false pretences for purposes unknown."

For a moment I was strongly tempted to ask for more elaboration. But no, I would not ask. I was already being held a hostage to knowledge I did not want. Once the government had decided on policy – and God only knew who the Governor had been consulting with – then it was never going to change. Never. No doubt that was how power is despatched: in quietly sequestered darkened rooms.

LATER THAT EVENING AS I sat at home I felt strangely emptied. Probably extreme fatigue. Whatever it was, I felt stretched thin as if my spirit were an emaciated, attenuated appendage. I seemed to be experiencing life as a series of "shots" streaking across my consciousness, not touching me deeply nor being acted upon. A wraith-like existence. Or perhaps a detective's.

I had become so distracted by the Governor's vague allusions that my mind was in turmoil, looking for meanings and hints in every word and gesture until I even began to attribute a sinister meaning to his offer of a bitter vermouth. What did it mean? Bitter? Bitter betrayal? Bitter death? As I had driven home I had tried to rid myself of these unsettling but hopeless mind traps. After all, no, they were hardly the point. Russian intelligence would never let come to light the chain of links between themselves and their people on the island. They would protect themselves better. But how do they? Cell by cell? Link by link? But the questions hung in the air, unanswered.

Then the telephone rang.

"Cordell." I probably sounded abrupt.

"How are you feeling today?" The same breezy voice.

"Much the same. Perplexed."

"Sorry to have to ring you at such an odd time of day but I just had to warn you."

"Warn me?" I knew Ken didn't speak lightly of such things.

"Your wife has just spoken to me. Put some of those points to me. I'm afraid she's taken it very badly."

"Taken what badly exactly?"

"Yeah. Well hard to know. A bit emotional if you know what I mean. I guess its things you've been saying to her."

"I didn't realise it was that bad. OK. So she's upset. I will speak to her."

"It's not just that. She's coming over."

37

We wandered out along a spit of white sand arching out into the turquoise waters of the Caribbean. We'd done that on an impulse. Neither of us were dressed for it so we had to carry our shoes. Geneviève wore a light blue jacket and pastel coloured skirt which suited her perfectly. It looked like an expensive outfit. What rich people call 'casual' but certainly doesn't mean just what you feel comfortable in. Me? I was dressed in my light wear tropical gear but not beach wear. It didn't matter. I was enjoying the day, soaking up Geneviève's company and the sunshine, listening to the gentle surges of the tide. I was also idly wondering why I am blown about so easily by every sexual breeze but I didn't really care. Supposedly, we were meeting up so that I could reassure her about her strange shadow but he had made no reappearance and I knew nothing more (at least that I could disclose). I made a desultory attempt to find out a little more of her furtive messaging to Fort de France but there was always some awkwardness when we approached the subject. In another I might have thought the aversion a sign of duplicity but I considered Geneviève was simply anxious at being drawn too quickly into exposing her role in dubious activities. Her anxious phone call already forgotten, she was more than ready to put her cares behind her.

Gone were her woes of only a few days before. Instead she was a young woman out to enjoy herself. And she was radiant. When I looked at her she raised only perfect forget-me-not eyes, set in a perfect olive face, to regard me with affection. It was, if I wasn't careful, I knew going to be a catastrophe but one into which I seemed to be crashing irreversibly. For today at least I thought I could put aside my worries. Instead, it was clear to me that Geneviève had brought a new perspective to my stay here; and for the first time during my sojourn in St. Eleanor I truly relaxed. It was impossible to relate Faed's talk of devilish intrigue to the beautiful tranquility of the island. Quite the contrary: it was a joy to be here. We walked along the whole sanded beach barefoot, letting the water and soft particles slide between our feet. The only sounds were the slow wash of the sea and the gentle sigh of the sea breeze which blew lightly into our faces. It was the first time I could remember doing such a thing since childhood. I had kidded myself I was going to find out more about the machinations of Rufus Halliday and the peculiar dealings of her bosses but right now it all seemed a bit pointless...I understood now what it was that had been missing from my life. It is the little things, the frivolity of life's little moments, which were lacking. I resolved that when I got back I was going to spend much more time on the innocent pleasures of life, the mundane, the ordinary.

I liked being there with Geneviève, a light sea breeze blowing over us. It was good to be two for once, not just one. Everything seemed much easier. After a while she said to me: "You will be finishing here soon. But you must promise me that you will never forget this afternoon on the beach together." I didn't answer but must have stood there, dreamily, looking into her eyes. Then I kissed her slowly and solemnly on her forehead. We gazed on the great white rollers, advancing slowly towards us until they beat majestically on the shore just as they must have done since the beginning of time and always would. The water licked our shoes. And right now this struck me as the most beautiful beach in the whole of creation, a place where I could fuse with a deeper reality, easy to believe that God was there, somewhere, in the tumbling foam and the turquoise sea. The sky was clear but I knew the barometer was falling fast. Probably before nightfall there would be clouds and rain and wind. But that would be sufficient unto the day.

We walked through the rough wet sand and glimpsed the coral, which must have been home to half a dozen living worlds. I stopped suddenly, seeing an odd looking shell then I bent down, gathered it up and slipped it into my pocket. Something, ninety-five per cent water yet somehow alive, swished past me, stoutly working its little translucent body. It could neither hear nor see its way but dashed itself into oblivion upon the shore. Momentarily a sliding crab dropped its enormous guard and watched us with its small twin periscope eyes. Was it possible, indeed, that some of these creatures might have had a philosophy of sorts or some delight unknown to mere bipeds?

I looked up to speak to Geneviève but she was scanning a suddenly darkening horizon. "Storm coming," she said, eyes raised to the heavens. The sky was quickly transforming from when we had set out. No longer blue but dark brown it carried malign portents of what was to come. The light itself was dimming rapidly. The sea too had changed from a bright turquoise to a much darker hue. The breeze dropped. Not a leaf stirred. The birds had disappeared, the trees still. Everything was touched by a kind of stupor, a strange calmness.

There was nothing for it but to abandon the beach and seek shelter inland.

Quickly we walked back towards the road but when we reached it I was surprised to find Sergeant Aldridge waiting for me in a Land Rover. The light was purer here, clearer somehow; the edges of the trees and the buildings sharper. Memories of days like that are clearer too. And I remember that day as yesterday. "Sorry to disturb you, Sir. There's going to be a bit of wind," Sergeant Aldridge said laconically. "Superintendent Worrell thought you'd want to do the rounds with me, Sir. Check everything's properly battened down."

"Just how bad is it going to be?"

"Bad enough."

I nodded affirmatively but didn't know what the deuce he expected me to be able to contribute. Just in time I remembered from my notes that among my duties while here would be Hurricane Officer too. Just my luck. "You'd better go inside," I said to Geneviève. "And make yourself at home. I'll be back as soon as I can."

"No. I want to come too." She looked me full in the face. There was something insistent there which I could not gainsay easily.

"Why? It's not going to be worth it," I said. "When there's a storm in the tropics the thing to do is to get under cover. Sergeant Aldridge and I are just going to make a quick sortie to check everyone in the area has battened down the hatches then we are taking cover too as quickly as we can."

"Yes, I understand," said Geneviève. "It's just I'd rather be with you than on my own. Besides, it sounds exciting."

Everything had fallen silent but for the sea which was booming menacingly. After a brief and premature evening the birds had all shut up or gone for cover themselves. Now we felt the first catspaws of wind beginning to disturb the air. The palm trees start to sway ominously.

"Come on then." We all piled into the Land Rover and Sergeant Aldridge set off at a steady speed. If he were surprised by Geneviève's presence he doesn't show it.

"How bad do you think it'll be?" I repeated.

"Just blowy," he said. "Bad enough but don't worry. It's not a full blown hurricane. At least I don't think so." He flashed me a broad smile.

We drove down to Soufrière, past the cricket field and then on past the pier. There were about twenty houses spread out in the vicinity. Nobody was about. I had not seen this before. The whole town was eerily deserted. From time to time Aldridge stopped the Rover, leapt out and banged on the door to draw attention to a loose shutter or batten. Most people were already ahead of the game, accustomed to these occasional problems from many years of experience. They hardly needed advice from the police but still it was part of our job. Up above, the brown sky had developed a menacing look of lead. The flags were beginning to flutter. The wind was getting stronger.

The inspection tour completed, we drove back to my place, the Sergeant not waiting even to switch off the engine as he deposited us and then shot off for his own cover. The gusts were approaching gale strength. We went straight in and shut everything up. As I drew the shutters across I could see the lightning flashes of the approaching storm trembling on the horizon, reminding me of the artillery barrages I had seen in Burma during the War. They hadn't looked good either. The temperature had dropped suddenly and I found myself shivering. Then I changed. When I got back I found Geneviève looking at the woodwork. Geneviève hadn't much in the way of a change but she had brought a light patterned navy blue cardigan which she now put on.

"It's only a few inches thick," she said as she examined the walls with sceptical eyes. They didn't look that solid either, I must admit as I looked at the flimsy timbers decorated with sea shells and an old flint lock.

"Don't worry, Geneviève," I said. "It's only a storm, not a hurricane. We don't need anything more solid. We'll be okay."

We could hear the wind howling around us now, billowing in my eardrums. She looked at me strangely and in her eyes I read both fear and elation. Fear of the storm but maybe fear too of others; and elation at danger shared.

"Like a drink?," I asked speaking in a subdued voice as if in awe of what was developing.

"Yes. Water please."

"You can have something stronger if you like. A gin and tonic perhaps?"

"No, water will be fine. Thanks."

"Water it is then," I smiled as at that instant a downpour of rain hit the roof in a solid ferocious bombardment. Soon we were besieged by a random crashing and thumping, an incessant drumming.

Geneviève put her hands to her ears. "*Mon Dieu*! I've never heard anything like this before."

Wind and rain tore at the roof, the sound of the thunderous downpour amplified into a roaring by the corrugated iron. I peered through the cracks in the shutters. If it was the end of the world, I certainly wanted to see it. Vertical rain fell from nowhere. We waited, eyes staring, attentive. Outside, the storm was filling the spaces with rain and wind, barking wildly against our shuttered home. Water was seeping under the door. Then suddenly it was as if someone had taken a battering ram to the whole cabin, shaking the door on its hinges and setting off a chain of explosives just outside. The wind was getting its act together now, making us prisoners in the cabin, us and a small lizard I hadn't the heart to chase out.

The light had gone.

The violence of the storm made me think of the other islands of the Caribbean who were in its direct path. God help them. Boats could flee. The sea itself could disperse the fury in huge waves cascading towards Europe. But the islands themselves, having nowhere to go could only take the brunt of the storm and wait until morning. The lucky survivors would have the task of mopping up but some would not make it. At least for Geneviève and me the drama would not be the end, just a sampling of mortality. But you could understand why the ancient islanders had worshipped *Urri Kan*, the great Sky god. He certainly needed appeasing whoever he was.

Presently the wind dropped a bit and with it the battering ram relented until it stopped altogether. We had survived. As the rain and wind settled into a steady rhythm but without worsening we were able to relax a little. We discovered a shared hunger and I even managed to prepare a humble meal of garlic prawns and salad. We talked about island life and the tropics even as the rain lashed down outside us in an almost unending cascade, drumming on the tin roof. Flashes of sheet lighting exploded across the sky. Peals of thunder merged into one another like a continuous roar.

At last the storm reduced to a mere stubborn drizzle and distant downpour. The thunder retreated into more distant grumbling thuds. Gleams of distant lightening lingered momentarily as if they were looking for someone. Water dripped from the leaves but the worst was over. We looked into each other's eyes, made cavernous by the shadows. I knew then that fate had caught us. At the thought of our new found familiarity, I was nudged by the memory of Katie and felt a frisson of shame: the kind of shame which makes you want to shut your eyes when you remember. But just then I was able, all too easily, to drive it from my mind and at first we only hugged each other but then I lay my mouth on hers and somehow it seemed natural. The tension drained away. But memories of Katie intervened. That was something else. A great trust existed between us, forged by shared hardships and parenthood. I couldn't betray the lady. Loyalty? But more than loyalty I think; it was very close to something incredibly precious. Whatever it was, older feelings, deeply ingrained, won out. Geneviève took my bed and I slept on the floor by the window.

As I drifted into a half sleep I found myself re-running scenes of the recent past, pleasurable memories mutating into more traumatic siren warnings. Briscoe's words had formed a new suspiciousness in my mind, crystallising the old adage: 'Trust no one!' Yet even at that moment it seemed to ring a little hollow. I thought I heard Geneviève making the briefest of phone calls as I floated off to sleep but then I thought I was wrong. Besides, I guess the line would have been down. At last a pleasing feeling of wholesomeness was enveloping me as I finally nodded off.

The next morning we threw the shutters back. A familiar rich air poured into the house. Above, the angry skies had been replaced by the more familiar cloudless blue covering. The sea too was calm and welcoming. But here and there were traces of yesterday's storm. A battalion of crabs has encircled the house. The dead and living had become intermingled in a mad scramble to find space to breathe away from the upturned roots. The cabin itself had turned a dirty green, being festooned from top to bottom by wind-blown leaves. The water front was strewn with flotsam. Several boats had been upended and flung on their sides; one looked badly splintered. I looked out in astonishment and not a little shame because I felt good, very good. I felt as if I had just rediscovered the core of what it was to be human.

38

THE FROGS HAD ALREADY begun their evening chorus when I arrived the next evening at the Governor's house with its tidy lines of lemon trees and neatly manicured lawns. Outside, soldiers stood stiffly to attention. How much this was down to the Army's love of sentry duty and how much to Whitehall's love of ceremony, I couldn't guess. Although it had been presented as a quiet 'at home', Faed welcomed me with the courtesy and decorum more befitting the High Commission. Indeed, I was beginning to suspect he only wore freshly starched suits. Royal Doulton green and gold china adorned the table which was set for five. Lit candles sat in the silver candlesticks. The room itself was a little more surprising. African tribal masks stared down at us from white walls and gigantic elephant tusks adorned the mantelpiece, relics no doubt of the Governor's former diplomatic postings.

The dinner itself was to be a relatively small, intimate affair consisting of Sir Godfrey Faed himself and his wife, Lady Jocelyne; Jake Oppenheimer, and his wife, Ursula; and myself. I was glad. As a Kiwi I always felt socially disadvantaged at these 'do's', ill at ease in a world of subtly shaded social distinctions. Still, it didn't seem like it was going to be the sort of dinner where everyone got on like a house on fire, knocking back the drink and gossiping like old time friends. Conviviality had of course prevailed as it always does on these occasions but it was conviviality of a brittle sort. Naturally, I got on with it, and it proved an excellent dinner though not one I would have expected in the tropics consisting as it was of soup, fish, roast beef, various vegetables and side dishes of tongue and game. The only distinctive Caribbean trait was the zingy freshly squeezed grapefruit at the start. All was washed down by some excellent burgundy, only slightly marred by the heat.

But although the food and the drinks were of excellent quality the occasion was not a great social success. Everyone seemed a little on edge. Jocelyne spoke too much, myself too little. The Governor spoke with knowing insight about the development of the Caribbean; but his mind was closed to every logic but his own. Jocelyne spoke of the delightful house in Perthshire which they were going to retire to; Ursula spoke with mock humility but evident pride of some of her investments which had proved to be remarkably shrewd. Only Jake made some attempt to be the wit of the group with a rather malicious grin and a fund of scandalous stories. I took my cue from the prevailing mood and chatted perfunctorily while keeping a subtle watch on all of them. But I didn't get it. Why had they invited me to this dinner? It wasn't really necessary. The Governor's explanation did not ring true. There was no opportunity for me to provide him with a confidential update. Was a detective really expected to brighten up a dinner table? No, there had to be more to it than that.

Sir Godfrey was playing the role of host well, being chatty and friendly. Yet his style of conversation had something of the interrogator's guile, punctuating long relaxed periods of entertaining conviviality with leading, pointed questions. I tried to be both forthcoming and discreet. Jake Oppenheimer meanwhile played a lively part at the table, producing some spikey retorts and interrupting others to remain the centre of attention. Ursula proved to be a down-to earth woman with lots of anecdotes of local life.

If ever the conversation got a little dry Sir Godfrey would oil it with a well-honed anecdote from his tribulations of life as a Colonial Officer, Jake agreeing eagerly with all his observations, his attitude a subtle blend of unctuous admiration and secret cynicism. The intertwining connections of old schools, similar upbringings and shared values were a stronger bond than any shared ideology could ever have been. Everything seemed normal, convivial and pleasant. But nothing was. I was seated next to Ursula and she spoke to me more than anyone else. The Governor, Lady Jocelyne and Jake became immersed in a conversation about the progress of Fidel Castro's revolution. I felt side-lined by this turn, being pretty ignorant of the whole affair.

"It's good you were able to come," Ursula said to me in an aside. "We need the occasional breath of new life in our corner."

I didn't doubt that this signalled a false modesty on her part. "I'm sure you are kept busy here."

"Mainly formalities here, you know. But I specialise in getting to know the local political leaders."

"I didn't know actually but I suppose you must have to socialise with them quite a bit."

"Yes. But that doesn't tell you much. I have a schooling in psychology. It's useful in this line, you see. How their mental states react to extreme pressures is very interesting to us. It's important if independence is going to amount to much, you know. Do you mind by the way, if I call you Bruce. Chief Inspector sounds so formal."

"Bruce is fine. But I hope you're not planning to psychoanalyse me."

"Certainly not." Ursula smiled but in such a way as to give me the disconcerting sensation she knew a lot more about me than she should have.

"And what's your opinion of the new Chief Minister?" I ventured.

"Well, as a man he has many qualities to commend him but I fear he is embarked on a highly dangerous policy."

"And what policy is that?" Lady Jocelyne asked, all innocence, while turning her head towards us.

"Palling up to the Cubans, I fear. That and lining his own pockets."

"Surely not," I exclaimed, shocked.

"No indeed," Faed interjected smiling genially. "I think Ursula is teasing or making a morbid pre-judgement. Why don't we change the subject, Ursula. No offence meant but I'd rather you didn't spread alarm. You really mustn't tease our guests."

We all chuckled politely and the tension relaxed.

"Quite right," Jake was saying. "Just a little jest. Besides, murder, not corruption, is the Chief Inspector's concern," Jake added. The reference to myself brought me back to the wider table.

"But have you found corruption to be a problem?" I asked.

"A small one," the Governor interjected. "But it's not one for you. Leave it to us." It was only as the

Governor hesitated that I sensed a different thought in his sparkling, deep-set eyes; a sudden expression at variance with his easy manner.

"I've heard of no arrests," I pointed out.

"Nor will you. We don't operate like that. We have other ways of dealing with such people. Some we pigeon hole, others we work until we can expose whole networks. In such cases we need to know how high up the rotten apples go."

Jake interrupted: "Chief Inspector, allow me to bring you up to date on some developments which may have a bearing on your case. We believe there may be a link between the Quillham murder and certain developments in independence politics; and that is why it is helpful to have exchanges of information and, if necessary, active collaboration on this issue."

I can't deny I was taken aback by his openness but let Jake continue: "Quillham was heavily engaged with questions about the plantation workforce, the US anchorage, the new recreational area and, of course, he was pally with Constantine." Jake was licking his lips almost continually as he spoke. Then he made a dismissive gesture. "I must admit," he said. "I didn't care for Quillham. But then why should I? He made no secret of his loathing for the British....or the British Establishment at any rate. He tried to cultivate Jamieson too."

Speaking of caring for people, I'd never really taken to Jake for that matter. He was one of those necessary cogs in the machinery of government whose work is sometimes dirty but of whom, we usually say, the work has to be done by somebody.

"Would being pally with Jamieson be such a bad thing?" I asked, forgetting my vow to steer clear of politics. "After all he was always likely to be the next First Minister. I have to say when I met him he seemed to be genuinely concerned about the islanders."

"*Pah..*" Jake began. "Politicians always make out they genuinely care. Strutting up and down, making out they are indispensable. They make me sick."

"Ouch!" I joked. "But I suppose you know him better than me."

"Well," Ursula conciliated. "I don't think you are wrong Chief Inspector. Jamieson's just idealistic. That's making him bitter. Always disappointed with what he's got. Always restless. Always chasing dreams. The abstract is real. The real is invisible. It's absurd of course."

"We let them get on with their tiny lives of course," Jake resumed. "But we don't want his sort interfering too much with the independence process." I sensed Jake was expecting me to cap this but I had no intention of capping anything. Instead, I just remarked: "I must admit I never was one for politics. I leave that to others."

"You make a mistake there," Ursula said almost with a sigh. "History and politics is why we are here today. After all, if Admiral Hawke hadn't cast anchor here when he did, why then, none of us would be here tonight discussing the price of bananas....Still, politics is more Jake's baby than mine," Ursula said but gazing at me.

"No, I would hardly say that," Jake interrupted. "Not Caribbean politics at any rate. You see I'm baling out. I've been recalled to London."

"What? You can't be serious!" I said, still wondering who Admiral Hawke was.

"He is I'm afraid. He came here on a fixed assignment. Now he's going home again. You'll be a great miss, Jake." The Governor smiled. "He's finished his work here, drafting protocols and procedures for the new government." Somehow I didn't believe all this. It didn't ring true. Jake Oppenheimer was intimately bound up with the government's red tape and I knew governments never really came to the end of red tape; it was just that, sometimes, the tape got wrapped up in other mysteries.

"What about the Communist threat?" I asked, recalling the Governor's warnings. "What with Cuba and the growing Soviet presence in the Caribbean I thought there would be a lot of work to be done and I thought Jake handled that kind of thing."

"Communist threat?" Jake put on his mocking voice. "There is no communist threat. Just because Cuba has gone over the top doesn't mean the whole of the bloody Caribbean is going Red. Cuba was always different anyway."

"All nonsense then?" I asked, casting my eyes towards the Governor.

Sir Godfrey Faed looked irritated. "We are not saying there aren't any troublemakers around. I imagine there always are. But they're not a huge problem. The Communists strike when you are weak. Terminally weak. Then they come in like hyenas. That's hardly the situation here. Nonetheless Castro and the Cubans make for an uneasy situation. It's not enough that we have the normal issues of independence to grapple with but there is a new dynamic in the East Caribbean as well." He shot Jake a look. "One which we'd all do well to ponder. I'm afraid the Russians and the Americans between them will bamboozle us with their wider Caribbean and Latin American concerns. But the life of the island must go on, regardless of exogenous forces or fashionable ideologies. If there is a threat to the realm I'm sure we can count on the police – backed, of course, by the discreet support of the security service." Sir Godfrey smiled broadly at that.

Jake seemed to sense my lack of enthusiasm for the implied mysterious bonding of police and intelligence work. "Tell me," he said, "as a soldier did you ever get into dangerous situations where you had no back up, no partners, no one who was responsible for your safety and no one who would help you if things went awry?"

"Of course not. I'm not a bloody fool."

He laughed. "Sometimes you have no choice in life. If that sounds unfair, well welcome to the world of counter-intelligence. They are separate but parallel lines of work. We are never far away." There was no proper answer to that. Was it a kind of induction? But induction into what? I couldn't raise an objection to this line of conversation though some instinct told me I should. There are times, and it's funny that they always stay in the mind, when jaunty, easy-going talk turns deadly serious. And so, it was then. I can picture it now, the men in their formal dinner attire, the ladies in their vivid summer frocks, the gentle torpor of a tropical evening, the subdued sounds of servants working in the back, the polite laughter, Jocelyne smiling across the white tablecloth, and the Governor with his thoughtful, piercing eyes.

"I understand you may be getting a new job soon, back in London," Sir Godfrey announced, smiling quietly to me. "A desk job. Bigger and more lucrative."

"I know nothing about it," I answered. Was something being dangled before me? Faed had made it sound like a golden opportunity.

"That's the way of the world," Faed continued. "Upstream, downstream. One's career is vulnerable to strange caprices. Still your lovely wife will be pleased. More money. Less gallivanting about. Less capricious. Attractive, bright and altogether a lot of energy about her. She deserves better." How the hell did he know anything about Katie?

"You've done well Bruce," Faed went on. "I understand that you have spent your time intently going over all the information, hunting for the new, and ready to take risks, all to find information about the causes of someone's death, now long ago. All very commendable. Yet you still haven't the full story! Tell me, Bruce, what did you expect to achieve when you accepted the assignment to come to our little island?"

"I came here to determine the cause of the First Minister's death."

"And that, dear boy, you have settled. Death by a purely accidental overdose of barbiturates, just as the Dr. Fortescue found."

I was a tad flummoxed by this presumption and continued thoughtlessly: "But of course this has expanded into an enquiry into the murder of an innocent journalist."

"Innocent? Is that what you'd call Quentin Quillham?" Faed almost snapped at me. I retreated a bit, conscious of having committed a *faux pas*. Fortunately, the ladies stepped in with some diverting conversation but I wasn't paying much attention. There was obviously something else involved but no one was telling and

I could hardly pressure the Governor. As I sank into my chair, gloom enveloped me like a sheet. I found myself asking: could I be wrong in everything I had discovered? Was I wrong in assuming that Quillham was not bashed to death in an excess of force but by a trained assassin, commissioned to get rid of him? What were the scarcely veiled references to intelligence? Was I being inducted or was I being discreetly warned off? Or both?

Jocelyne, turning to Ursula, said in a loud aside: "Oh, Ursula, I was going to tell you I've found a divine little restaurant in Soufrière, just a little place in the High Street there, run by a local woman called Martha. Quite ordinary to look at....but so charming, don't you know...excellent food."

I was astounded. She was talking of the place I'd dined only the other day with Geneviève. But before I could say anything Ursula was replying nonchalantly: "Oh, I don't know. One day they're here. The next they're gone. I prefer to be sailing myself. A little circuit of the Windward Islands is more my kind of scene. Plenty of good sailing in this corner of the world... wouldn't you agree, Bruce?"

This was too much. They were mocking me, taunting me, using my exact phrases from our meeting. So, we'd been bugged. What an ass I felt but what the devil was I to do? I was deeply confused and bewildered but nodded, grinning idiotically. Everything faded into the shadows as my mind struggled to accommodate new realities. It was a warning, of course. I was being told no matter what I thought or did, they were always several steps ahead of me.

"You have to be careful," Jake put in after a moment, toying with his wine glass. "You mustn't be too footloose and fancy free, don't you know? You might think it a daft notion, I daresay, but people do have nasty accidents even in these lovely parts. I had a friend once. He was a Kiwi too. Loved sailing. Thought he could breeze around but hit a skerrie. Nasty injury... very nasty. Crippled for life I regret to say."

I was stupefied. Bugs? Surveillance? Threats? Rewards? But the St. Eleanor government could not have many people trained in unobtrusive surveillance so this must have represented quite an effort on someone's part. But why? No answer came to my rescue, just a dark foreboding. Instead, I remembered the black sedan car and the mysterious man who seemed to dog my footsteps. Unpleasant invasive thoughts swarmed through my mind; my skin grew cold. How could I dissemble when I was so outraged and so confused?

"Let's turn to more pleasant thoughts," Sir Godfrey broke in. "I propose a toast to Bruce and his good wife in their new assignment in London. I hope it goes well, Bruce. I really do. Everyone likes you, you know. It's up to you to make the right decisions. I'm sure you will." He raised his glass and the others joined him, the mocking tone now forgotten; but I would be glad to be gone.

It was only as we were actually leaving that Faed motioned me aside and asked explicitly how the investigation was now going. What I had been led to think was the main reason for my being there was now being treated as a mere perfunctory finale to the evening. "Just a device to move things along a bit," he had said. But it had become something different.

Briefly, I gave him my prepared summary of events including Quillham's strange liaison with Maddox, and so on. But didn't he know anyway? Faed took it all in but his features remained expressionless. He was holding a slim file in his right hand.

More to the point, no steers were forthcoming. No help at all.

"Well, that's fine, old boy," he said finally. "Keep me informed. Don't do anything drastic without telling me. Otherwise it's strictly your baby....But here, take this with you. It might give you some food for thought." He smiled brightly. I took it lightly as if it were a matter of no consequence and tucked it under my arm. "Rastas will help you out. Goodnight," Faed concluded. A servant, presumably Rastas, duly showed me the door but it was scarcely necessary.

As I stepped out I heard Ursula bawl out: "Take a look at this!" But it wasn't evidently aimed at me though I certainly felt it was. So I was especially observant as I stepped down the steps towards the waiting car when a soldier, presumably serving as some kind of sentry, slipped the rifle off his shoulder, raised it and pointed it at me. He fixed me plum in his sights, made as if to fire at me. For a second or was it milliseconds our eyes locked; and I didn't doubt the threat. Then he dropped the rifle down again, standing to attention as if nothing untoward had happened. I felt the goose pimples on my back. The night air seemed a mite chillier. Another warning? And what could I do? Come to that, what was I *expected* to make of it?

THAT NIGHT I WAS woken by a sound. I found myself immersed in total darkness. I was suddenly aware of a movement in the house. Had an intruder come in, moving about, just out of sight, in the living room, perhaps around the corner but somewhere, right here? I lay there in the darkness, trying to make out what it was but heard only the wind soughing in the trees, somehow subtly different from the noise it makes at home. It was two in the morning, that darkest of hours. There was nothing but wind and the unending shriek of the frogs. The room I could see now was tinged by only the palest of moonbeams. As my eyes adjusted to the gloom I could see and sense everything but somehow even the familiar was strange to my jaded senses. I got up, nerves honed by fear, very unsettled but not knowing why, walked around *Caille Blanc* then to the window and pulled back the blind. I looked up and down but there was nothing. There's no one here, I thought, it's just my imagination. Momentarily I fancied I caught sight of a movement in the wild but nothing more. I stood and stared. The jungle lay in a misty hue of indigo and seemed to hold all the mystery of immemorial age, changeless and indifferent.

39

MUCH OF THE NIGHT was spent in such painful cogitations. But everything has an ending. Even the night. I was awoken by a pain in my back. I had probably slept in an awkward position. My cervical vertebrae felt ill-used, the brain bewildered.

Most mornings when I awoke I listened awhile to the drops of water falling from the overhanging trees onto the Rest House's wooden roof. Not today. I was too preoccupied by the previous evening's strange goings-on. To ignore the message, disregard the warnings and to carry on as normal was not an option. I was confused but also euphoric as if I had been marked out by destiny for great things. After all, had I not been inducted into something of their "codes"? I had glimpsed too something of the Counter Intelligence cloak over the island and felt I had been introduced to their recruitment process. A better future beckoned. Or did it? The only concrete suggestion was that I confirmed that the First Minister had died from an overdose. Whether I liked it or not I was still in limbo, in a wait-and-see position, an attitude which concentrated what remaining energy I had to the task of simply holding on.

But I was cautioned by that deep internal voice. "Be careful," it said. "Take nothing on trust. You need to take stock. Look inside." The primeval organism had an infallible sense of danger. If it was prompting me to think, I'd better do so. And suddenly I was two people: an outward figure which the world encountered and an internal me, a rather desperate character, trying to think myself out of a fix. A shadowy power whose outlines I could only dimly discern, loomed up before me, as a collection of immeasurable attributes and tentacles. This power appeared to demand something of myself that no one else possessed. A territorial, a political, a military complex had decided to draw me into its orbit. A certain instinct told me to resist, warned me that there was a severe risk to my very identity here and that I should retain an orbit of my own. My integrity would matter not a jot to Power. Yet more thoughts jostled for attention. They told me that I might do very well for myself to trust such a matrix of power and that it would be most interesting to see something of this system from the inside. But on the other hand it would complicate and overturn every hour and that it would only be a burden.

Whatever was meant by that carry-on, it must have been intended to have some sort of meaning. Clearly, they work for the intelligence service or some sort of deep state emanation. Doubtless that too was the explanation of the mysterious shadow who had been dogging my every step. I did not know why such an organisation should choose to deliver its message in such a way but presumably they have their reasons. It was a sort of "announcement", deniable of course, of their presence. More than that, it says they are watching me and that presumably I should be careful. Yet did it not also imply some level of qualified approval? Was it then the first step in an induction process? But if all the play-acting were partly by "way of an education" that was only the half of it; what was being implied was much, much more, a means deliberately calculated to instil fear. It was threatening, almost bordering on cruelty.

I like writing down headings to focus my thoughts on if I'm to think constructively. I grabbed a pencil and a disused envelope. Quickly I jotted down a few words:

1. Recruitment?
2. Warning?
3. Constructive dismissal?
4. Political murders/ Independence issues
5. FM accidental death = career development
6. Watch out for the xx.

Nothing made much sense. It could be part of a process of recruitment to an intelligence service. A sort of graduated, encoded and untraumatising apprehension of their presence. But it was equally clear that they wanted to keep me at arm's length. Warning – well that was for sure – but about what exactly? Presumably, to keep my mouth shut about this new knowledge. Constructive dismissal? My day job certainly had a different look to it and I was not now in a good mental shape for it. But dismissal was not the right word for this. It certainly looked as if Counter Intelligence viewed the murders as political. Could this be taken as a fact even though I had been shown no evidence? But presumably that's part of the point of intelligence operations: to find out the truth beneath the surface and then secure advantage. As regards the independence question, this was fundamentally above my pay grade and I didn't intend to adopt new attitudes myself.

I would observe but nothing more. I had given up on politicians and all that sort of thing long ago. So should I close the FM file? Certainly looked like the right course of action. Quillham? God knows. Maybe a new steer would be forthcoming. Double cross? It certainly felt like I was dodging bullets but again, God knows.

But one thing I can now say with certainty though I didn't fully appreciate it at the time was that my life had been irredeemably changed and not for the better. The previous night's goings-on, the culmination I could now see of a long process, was to prove traumatic, catalytic. At the time I had let them and their tricks wash over me, accepting them as if they were a kind of new normality. But I can see now that from that evening things were never to be the same again. I had begun to live precariously in a new dimension I had hitherto been unaware of. I was now a man incomplete, haunted by other spectres, out of balance. Worse, I was a danger to all who came into contact with me.

The way ahead was far from clear. I had better choose my steps with care. I still needed to establish facts. I could let the FM case go for now anyway. Death by overdose was still my best working hypothesis, anyway. But what about Quillham? If Faed was right, Quillham had been on the rocks. But how badly was he on the rocks? Listing dangerously close in a heavy sea? Or was he lying atop them, timbers screeching and breaking on solid rock? That he was a difficult man I didn't doubt. Also brilliant in his way. People deferred to his judgement and sought his counsel. But he was also used to getting his way, to having the world around him ordered to his wishes and convenience. And if he didn't get his way then the resentment would bubble inside him. Where would this lead him? Quillham had taken a significant moral risk for his beliefs, something which may have marked him down with the intelligence services. They would never wholly have trusted him. Somehow, he had got caught in the power struggle between Moscow and Washington. They would have moved him up and down the board just as it suited them. Thinking about it began to make me feel insecure. If Quillham had really been involved in all this I was surely out of my depth.

I knew it now. Quillham had failed to reckon with his adversary's ruthlessness. He had worked out his plan behind his neat, rose wood desk and hoped to bring it to a successful and speedy conclusion. But he had not understood that the Russian secret intelligence service did not think like that. To the contrary, it too would seek to bring matters to a quick conclusion but in a very different way. Their tried and trusted method would be to hire a local criminal, a man who for a startlingly trifling sum would commit murder, leaving the people who paid him anonymous, distant and untouched.

BUT WORK WOULD NOT wait. My head still brimming with these new concerns and possibilities I took myself in to the office clutching Faed's small file and looking, I hoped, no worse for my distress. I was determined to reveal nothing to my colleagues. Once there, quietly ensconced in my room opposite a preoccupied Lucy, I opened Faed's report. At first I was nonplussed by its brevity. Then I was more struck by its sheer anonymity. There was nothing in this brief memorandum to indicate that it had emanated from Government House yet it alluded to comings and goings there. Peter Jahnke, evidently a pivotal figure in the *Anse Chastenet* keys mystery, was now confirmed as having returned to the UK. There, I now knew, he was to be viewed as out of bounds. With that lead gone I fancied (and Government House must have known) I could not hope to identify the assailant. But there again the rest of the memo was simply a regurgitation of the earlier now disproven findings: the First Minister died from an overdose of barbiturates. And was this not exactly what they had all, in an ever so deniable fashion, been hinting was the conclusion I must arrive at?

Opposite, Lucy was pulling faces at her paperwork. "How are you getting on?" I asked. "The figures driving you mad?" Lucy nodded slowly. I knew she was trying to get to grips with the shadowy plans the corporations were preparing for St. Eleanor.

"Well, there is one more angle. The only outstanding question in my mind is how much public money they can get their hands on."

"That's Jamieson's department. He reckons there are going to be all sorts of spin-offs for the islanders."

"Don't make me laugh. These people don't give a damn about the Islanders. Oh, they say they do, of course, but that's a joke. They'll learn the hard way. These people like the climate, they appreciate the beautiful people. But they don't need them. You know what I mean. They'll just gut the place. Take the local resources, blight the coastline and the Islanders will let them. They'll swap it all for a few cans of Coca – Cola. As for the balance of payments the politicians talk about, don't make me laugh."

This shook me, I don't mind admitting. I had not being paying sufficient attention to her commercial researches. Lucy had obviously been giving this a good deal of thought and I was listening to its fruit. "You see the beach developments will make a lot of money for some rich people. So far as I can make out it's going to be a gigantic theme park filled with shops, mainly aimed at wealthy American visitors. High end shops, a marina, fancy restaurants – all that appeals to the affluent. First there is the price of the land. Cheap now but bound to skyrocket if it is ever sold on. And it will be. But only after the good old tax payer has provided the extra funds for new access roads, street lighting, car parking, bus services, stepped up policing...you name it. And then there's the extras. The construction alone is worth millions. Hotels will follow. Consultants galore will take a fortune. These projects are bound to become political. What then has to be gauged is how beneficial they really are and to whom. At that point you really need to know the decision makers well."

"Jamieson," I said, aghast. "He's in their pocket."

40

THAT EVENING I HADN'T been in *Caille Blanc* long when the telephone jangled. It wasn't Geneviève phoning in a plight, it wasn't Frank to dish out new instructions, and it wasn't a new lead from one of the great unwashed. It was Katie.

"Hello, Bruce, it's me," she said.

"Hello Katie. How wonderful. How are you?"

"More to the point, maybe you should be asking, 'Where are you?'"

"What do you mean?"

"I'm staying at the Trafalgar Hotel in St. Jacques."

"How...on earth?" I really was dumbfounded.

"The Onslow-Bell money. How else?"

I began to understand, but only barely. "Well, that's great...but the children?"

"Mum's looking after them. Don't worry. I simply had to come. There have been no recurrences?"

"Recurrences?"

"Don't repeat everything I say. You know. After you were attacked I simply had to come out."

For a fleeting moment I didn't know what she meant but then I remembered that horrible incident at *Caille Blanc*. "No...nothing like that. Nothing at all. I'm fine. Look, it'll be great to meet up. Let me come over and we'll have dinner together. OK?"

"Superb. Come right over now."

Straightaway, I spruced myself up before taking myself off again to the capital. When I got there my nerves, tenderised by Faed's mysterious pantomines, were relaxed by the sight of Katie, looking bronzed and in holiday mood, sitting in a reclining armchair in the reception area. I could hardly believe my eyes but immediately we put our arms around each other and closed our eyes, basking in the moment. I knew I would never tire of it. I stood there drinking in her fragrance. Her long chestnut hair hung shiny, loose and wavy. Maybe the passionate desire of the early years had waned a little but we had something better: a steady, calm and enduring love.

The hotel was evidently in the throes of being redecorated. The workmen had left but there was an opened step ladder and many pots of paint of sundry colours standing around. Steering around these obstacles, we took ourselves in to the hotel's restaurant, myself still wondering at this wholly unexpected but pleasing change in the course of events, and soon snuggled down for a light meal. Katie had lost none of her youthful charms. The strong eyebrows arched over her large almond eyes lent her face a distinctive individuality. Yet Katie's allure notwithstanding, I was unable to brush my worries from my thoughts. I can't remember what we ate that evening but I'm afraid our conversation at first was pretty desultory despite the long absence. I had been so burdened by police investigations and the attendant confidentiality that I simply couldn't unburden myself. Instead, after the mandatory children's report, we flitted from one trivial topic to another. It looked rather as if our relationship were creaking which I don't think was the case.

Katie shuffled uneasily in her chair. I could feel her eyes boring into me.

"Why do you think I've come out here?" she asked. "You do realise I've been trying to manage everything back home? Do you know how hard it is?"

"Are you telling me you've come here to be amused and you're unhappy in the house!"

"I'm telling you I'm unhappy. The children are unhappy. You know you are very stubborn. You wanted your way but when it's clearly got beyond you, you can't let go. So here we are."

"I've been thinking of you..."

"I beg your pardon."

"I have a job to do but don't imagine I'm not thinking about you and the children all the time."

Eventually, I found myself almost against my will talking of Geneviève Clouin and her strange approach to me. I explained nothing about Halliday, the Governor or Oppenheimer, presenting Geneviève rather as she had first appeared to me as a rather bewildered but essentially innocent victim of intrigue.

My preoccupations resurfaced and Katie, no doubt disgruntled by my unresponsiveness, offered me a penny for my thoughts.

"Would you believe me if I told you?"

"Try me," she said.

"I'm confused myself and I'm scared."

"You? Scared?"

"It's far from clear where this business is going to in the long run..."

"In the long run we'll all be reduced to atomic waste so why worry."

I thought of the hours I'd spent replaying things over and over in my mind, the meetings, the deep unease...the last thing I wanted was to introduce melodrama. So I told her about Faed, his phone call and assignations. Bit by bit, I hinted at the strange goings-on around Government House. And all in as a matter of fact manner as I could muster. She was genuinely very surprised at this development and asked questions about Oppenheimer, his intentions and whereabouts which I couldn't possibly answer. When I expressed my reservations about meeting him in such a furtive manner, she brushed them aside, reminding me who was my paymaster. She was clearly getting exasperated with me but then she was not fully aware of the web which I had been drawn into. Just at that moment a waitress came by, swinging her hips. Katie called her over. "Same again. The house white," she ordered as she handed her, her empty glass. I watched her sashay away for a moment then my eyes returned to Katie.

"But surely," she was saying. "You are over-reacting Bruce. There are other possible reasons for government officers going on like this, for not wanting to draw attention to themselves. Some things have to be done discretely, deniably. Don't worry. After all you are the Chief Inspector. The man in charge."

"Ha! Formally, perhaps but the masters of power don't operate like that. I do what I am commissioned to do. But, boy, am I unhappy? I don't like being manipulated. I would like to know where I am being directed and why."

"You think the First Minister was murdered don't you? But you still don't know who or why. From what you say, they suspect this fellah, Jahnke, and they have recalled him the better to put round the clock surveillance on him. But no hint is to be made public.

The official line is that there is no cause for alarm: the cause of death is an accidental overdose. Leave it at that. Whereas you think you can and should unravel the whole thing and that this French mademoiselle is an innocent victim of some sort of criminal scam which may be related?"

I looked up sharply. "Well, I suppose that's not a bad summary."

"Aren't you presuming too much? You want a free investigation but you can't have it when matters of state are involved. Whenever they move, you are just a pawn on the board. Such is life. Accept it! Get on with it! You're dreaming!"

"And what guarantees do I have?"

"None at all, of course. But what do you expect in this mad world. I've heard you say it a hundred times. The law is just a thin crust over a nest of vipers."

"But I have to trust someone."

"Let's say you can trust me. Now, can we just get on."

"I suppose you're right. It's just I like to be in the driving seat, not a pawn."

"Now look. Consider it a moment. None of us know how things are going to work out. Every decision we make is a guess. We never fully know what the consequences of our actions are going to be."

"I know. I know. But I'm getting closer now."

"You are, are you?"

"Yes. But these intelligence people have sown confusion everywhere. I thought Constantine had died of natural causes. Now I am sure he was murdered. That makes me wonder about it all. You see, I was pretty sure Maddox killed Quillham but this intervention has changed everything. These people don't tell you much and it erodes confidence."

"But we've heard odd stories about Security before. They have a peculiar way of doing things. The First Minister has been murdered at a sensitive time. They want things hushed up but they want them investigated at the same time. They wonder – they always wonder– if the communists are involved. You can never tell. They have plenty of unlikely recruits. Why do intelligent people believe in communism?"

"I hadn't been thinking of communists. More like racketeering. You know the sort of thing. Defrauding the revenue, gambling, pimping....The whole thing about blacking St Eleanor's banana crop sails pretty close to the wind."

"What about the woman, Clouin? What do you know about her? Is she honest? And would you honestly swear to it?"

"Depends on what you mean by honest, Katie. She strikes me as telling the truth. But if you asked me about the woman's political opinions, well, I don't honestly know. I'd be surprised if she wasn't pretty orthodox but...well, I never thought to explore that."

"Is she more complex than you thought?"

"Perhaps. You know it's always hard to know what's going on inside someone's head but I'd never have put her down as a communist."

"Bruce, what's the matter with you! What do you know about this woman? Surely you have learnt not to go by appearances. Nobody is quite what they seem. Everyone has their private passions. So this woman bitches about her boss. She makes eyes at you and you don't pay attention any more! This woman is sick. Worse, she knows it and doesn't give a damn! So she's good at spinning a yarn...better than Daphne Du Maurier even!"

"Yes but..."

"But nothing. Listen. She sees you as a challenge, maybe. She has to prove to herself that she can pick you up and make you eat out of her hand like others before. Now she has something you want and she's going to make you sit up and beg for it. But sooner or later she'll show you the whip."

"Ok, ok but you don't understand. She has information I need."

"Where has she got it?"

"In her head."

"Who does she share it with?"

"Eh?"

"A woman with a story like that will need to share it with someone."

"Perhaps it could be me."

"Well then. You have the whip after all. Tell her to spill the beans or you'll hand her over to the heavy brigade."

"It would never work."

"Then you don't understand people! How you became a police officer beats me."

I looked away and started to drum the table with my fingers. "You're annoyed with me?"

"No. On the contrary. I'm glad you have explained more about yourself and what's going on. I was beginning to think a wall had been put up between us but now I can see it's more like a door."

I didn't say anything, feeling that it was more like a locked door.

"Well," Katie said emphatically, as if inviting me into her confidence, "this is what I think. There is a tie up between *Alpha Omega* and the KGB. I don't know where exactly but it must be at quite a senior level, certainly so far as this island is concerned." Katie's eyes were shining with an inner luminosity that quite transfigured her at that moment. She was quite beautiful. I nodded in acknowledgement and let her continue. "And your dear little Geneviève is in cahoots. Maybe she did try to run away at some stage but something or someone has drawn her back. It's probably money. Usually is. Why else hasn't she just upped sticks and gone back to Daddy in the south of France? Have you thought of that?"

"Look here," I said, feeling my professional competence challenged. "I've thought of just about every explanation imaginable."

"Look at this possible scenario. The Russians are wanting to extend their foothold in the Caribbean. They have suborned Castro thanks to America's blundering. But they feel insecure and are looking for other footholds. America has shored up the obvious weak spots: Haiti and the Dominican Republic. Do you seriously think they would not have noticed Britain's withdrawal from the area and considered these very weak and vulnerable statelets?"

For a moment I looked on at her in wonder then an idea dawned on me. Our eyes locked and I held her in my gaze, my vision of her suddenly enlarged. Katie must have misunderstood my thought processes for not getting a reply, she said, "Well, it's getting late. I will leave you to think about it. Right now I'm utterly whacked. I'd better go to bed now and we can talk about it again in the morning."

"Don't go! Look, God knows, you could be right but that's hardly police work..."

"Exactly! Do as they say. You have no real choice. You are torturing yourself unnecessarily....Anyway, I'm off to bed now. I'm dog tired. Goodnight. We'll speak again soon."

"Yes, of course. Goodnight."

She left the table then and, after a fleeting kiss, left me to my thoughts. It wasn't exactly Oppenheimer or Onslow-Bell who were troubling me. More that I was now out on a limb, carrying on with an investigation into Warwick Constantine's death when I had been all but told to drop it. Only my conscience had kept me from doing as Faed had prompted. Yet a small part of me could hardly believe that I was contemplating such defiance. But I had to. At no stage did it matter to them about others, only them, their plans and their covers. I had to show myself I was better than this. The Oppenheimers of this world who at heart, I didn't doubt, despised me and my ilk had inspired me to tilt at fate, to defy all their hints and blandishments, to see this thing through, even if it was with the desperation of those with no alternative. That's how I felt.

41

THE SURPRISE, NAY SHOCK, of meeting with Katie had left me with a warm after-glow. It lasted until the following morning when I awoke, still in my own bed, feeling unusually pleased with life. It had been raining for two hours but had stopped as abruptly as it had begun. Flocks of fluffy white cumulus still lined the sky but I knew that the sun was already in the ascendant, glinting on the dappled landscape of banana and sugar plantations; and behind them, the tall jungle. Faed's elliptical explanations left much to pursue. One man, in particular, was well placed to understand where all the threads were leading.

Getting an interview with the new First Minister had proved once again to be easier than expected. We could say what we liked about a policeman's innate suspicion of smooth politicians but Bob Jamieson was certainly very approachable. He had a busy itinerary but sandwiched meeting Lucy and I between his opening of a new jetty in Soufrière and a Chamber of Trade meeting in St. Jacques. We met him in Soufrière that morning just after he had concluded the formalities.

Energy was in every line of him from his firm jawline to his smooth fingers so I asked him straight out about what he knew of Quillham's researches. He didn't seem surprised but then he never did. "He found out,"

Jamieson said, "that there was money for him in reporting on Cuban activities, real or alleged. You know the sort of thing. Arrivals and departures. A little background intelligence. If you have good contacts, you have high grade gossip and that's stuff you can sell to the Americans. There's nothing wrong about profiting from anticipation, he did that alright.... Sure, that and Haiti like I said. But you don't have to ask me. Just look through the recent issues of his newsletters – *Caribbean Confidential* – that's what he called it. And you'll see there lots of stories about comings and goings in the Caribbean, new trade deals that sort of thing. I'd say it had become his bread and butter."

"Where did he get it from?" I asked, my throat dry.

"Come again?"

"The information I mean. That sort of thing would need its own intelligence network. Quillham could hardly monitor all the airports and harbours in the region from his mansion in St. Jacques, could he?"

"Search me," Jamieson looked suddenly puzzled then his confidence began to reassert itself. "Well, I guess he had his own contacts around the region. Costa Rica, Florida, Cuba I wouldn't be surprised. They must have fed him a lot of gen."

I let it go. Jamieson didn't seem to know anything much about Quillham's sources but it struck me as highly improbable that you could provide a convincing profile of diplomatic and trade comings and goings on the basis of a few friendly contacts. So I pressed Jamieson again on his personal links to Quillham but though Jamieson's exposition was all very polished, it served only to minimise his relationship with Quillham.

Lucy was beginning to get agitated and she stepped in: "Quillham was interested in *Alpha Omega's* proposed development at Schooner's Landing. Did he speak to you about it?"

"Sure did. Who didn't? It could bring a lot of jobs to the island. But as for *Alpha Omega* itself, there was no news as yet at all. Certainly none I was aware of. And I was acquainted with *Alpha's* Project Manager quite well."

"Project Manager?" Lucy queried.

"You know. The guy who was handling the ground stuff. Dealing with the planning department, getting all the topographical surveys, permissions, that kind of thing. He was an American, from Florida. Quillham wasn't the kind of contact the company especially needed or wanted." So, I thought, that was what Quillham's trip to Miami was all about. Probably.

"What was his interest in the company then?" Lucy asked.

"The usual. What were they going to set up? How many jobs were we going to create? Who had we bought the land from?"

"And who had you bought the land from?"

"Several small concerns but mainly one big one, North Star. It turned out that they had only recently purchased most of the land from a plethora of local companies. It took quite a while for me to sort out all the sales and transfers. But like I said, I only handled the conveyancing for *Alpha*. Nothing more. After I became First Minister, I ended all ties though I openly welcome their proposals." Jamieson left me a touch uneasy, his words faintly manipulative but I continued to listen to the brisk, impersonal voice.

"Do you know anything of Quillham's contacts here?" Lucy asked.

"Here? As on here in the island?" He smiled.

"Sure. Where else?"

"Where else? I just told you he had contacts all over the Caribbean. Maybe not that close but they seemed to do the job for him. But here on the island...I don't know so much about them. Mary Beale of course. You could try the Barracuda Club. Most Europeans hang out there sooner or later. All sorts of business people there... And Rufus Halliday. I've seen them together."

"Who is Rufus Halliday?" I tried to dissemble ignorance as well as I could.

"Risk Assessment Analyst. Right here in Soufrière. He works for *International Project Assessment* in London but his principal client here would be *Alpha Omega*. Maybe he could help you."

I jotted down the name.

"And you personally? Are you sure that's all he was questioning you about?" I asked.

"I am sorry. I'd like to help the police on this, Chief Inspector, but what I know amounts to zilch." Jamieson sounded nonchalant. "I ran into Quillham on a couple of occasions recently, I'd say. But he said nothing out of the ordinary, nothing very memorable. I *do* recall him asking how our development plans were coming along, like I said. But that was nothing special. He was just picking up the threads. You know how it is. Ah dare say just about everyone on the island asked me that when they got a chance."

"I understand. So nothing special?"

"Nothing special. No. Not leastways that I can recall. Well...I suppose he had a preoccupied air. But he often did. Always turning stuff over."

"Any other projects in particular that you recall he was working on?" Lucy asked.

"He'd been reading up some special business report on Haiti and the Dominican Republic for some US company. Don't know any details except I gather that it didn't rate either Trujillo or Papa Doc as good investments. Who would? Awful people. Long time since they should have gone. But if someone comes along and is prepared to pay you good money for telling them what they should know already, then good luck to you. That's how some folk make their money. I think a lot of Quillham's work was like that. Just putting a few facts and figures together to back up an assessment you could have got from your morning newspaper."

"Mr Quillham sold information to clients?"

"That's his business. That's his speciality."

"So he was more than a straightforward journalist. Did he sell to your clients, *Alpha Omega*?"

Jamiseon shrugged. I wasn't taken in but if he was staying shtum I could leave it for now. Maybe it wasn't purely business. Maybe Quillham was an informant.

"So Quillham didn't rate those governments anyway?" I asked returning to his point.

"Naw, of course not." Jamieson almost spat the words out. "It wouldn't be a bad thing, if you ask me, to get rid of those bastards. Castro is far better but no one seems interested in justice. It's all got mixed up with the Cold War. Castro means Red means the Russians – that's what Washington thinks and that means they've got to be stopped at any price. A shame really. I ask you who would want to pick up Haiti's problems anyway? It's absurd. Of course the Cubans aren't doing anything. But the US is totally paranoid!"

"And Constantine?" I asked.

"Ah, Constantine! Well, of course, he would sit on the fence if he could. He kept an eye on Cuban goings and comings you know."

"That's what he was working on at the end?"

Jamieson nodded emphatically.

FILLED WITH A RENEWED resolution, I deposited Lucy back at HQ and then flew down to St. Jacques, parked near the quayside and walked over to the marina where several yachts and vessels were moored. A cooling breeze ruffled my hair and tugged at my clothes. A gentle creaking of ropes and wooden decking greeted me as yachts and boats stirred uneasily in the gently heaving harbour. The marina's gate was open when I walked in and down the pontoon. It didn't take me long. There was the usual clutch of speedboats, a scattering of yachts but only one catamaran. Its name, *Hélène*, painted clearly and elegantly on the prow of her starboard side. I felt a glow of relief at the sight of such a beautiful vessel, all fashioned from oak timbers.

Geneviève was working on the deck as I approached. Even sporting a straw hat she seemed to me a kind of vision of loveliness, possessing a poise that defied the elements. I gave her a breezy "Ahoy there!" as I strode down the jetty. She turned, beamed a smile and welcomed me aboard, gesturing towards a capacious cabin. Even before I rattled the door handle I was clocking the extravagance of the vessel. It certainly didn't lack for gear. Well equipped with a sextant, chronometer, spare sales, oilskins, barometer, tool box and the other essentials it could undertake long voyages.

"Quite a home from home you've got here," I said.

"*Eh bien*! All mod cons," she said. "I'll say that for Papa. He never skimped on things. Do you desire some coffee?"

"That would be great. I don't want to be a nuisance but would a sandwich be possible? I'm starving. I had to skip breakfast." I said.

"Sure. Not a problem. I could make up something more interesting than that easily enough, alright?"

I smiled my acceptance and in a moment she had disappeared. Soon I could hear the clanking of pans and crockery. Quickly, glancing over my shoulder, I checked that Geneviève was still preoccupied in the scullery before searching through the lockers, my heart pounding in case she suddenly returned. In the time available, I could do little more than glance at things before pushing them back into place. Clothes of all stripes were in evidence, more than a male mariner would have taken, also quite a store of spare films but innocent enough and a box of spanners, no doubt to supplement the tool box and to meet a variety of needs. Very little paperwork of any sort was in evidence. Nothing from home, no letters, no bills, no insurance policy, no photographs, no writing paper come to that. I hesitated again, wondering if I had time to complete my search before boldly opening the last locker. It clearly held extra blankets and I was about to shut it down again when my policeman's training kicked in and I reached inside, running my hands carefully over the contents before hitting something very solid and metallic. Gingerly, I unwrapped the blanket to uncover an old rifle. Wow. Now this was interesting. Weighing it in my hands it looked to be in good working order too though

I could see no ammunition. Still, this could be stored in some redundant cranny easily enough. A distant memory of an arms identification class stirred in my mind. A *Fusil à Répétition modèle F1*, the standard French army rifle. That was enough. I made haste to put everything back and was just in time as Geneviève emerged with two plates of *fruits de la mer* salads. She looked like an angel at that moment.

"So pleased to see you, Bruce," she smiled up at me, rather smugly perhaps. "Do please take a chair."

I did so and it was hard not to feel seduced by the easy calm of the setting. The luxurious cabin looked out on to a leisurely sunlit marina. It was difficult to imagine crime in such surroundings, impossible to believe that Geneviève could be involved in an espionage ring. She, on the contrary, seemed to be so relaxed and natural. Right now Geneviève was wearing casual clothes and earrings. Her hair was done in a softer style and fell over her shoulders. I must have looked excessively pleased because she asked me what was entertaining me.

"The views make me happy," I said, looking out the cabin window at the bobbing boats.

The eyes which suddenly held me were suddenly severe. "And are you not usually happy?" The abrupt change in her mood threw me completely. When, after all, had someone last asked if I were happy? She smiled. "Well, Bruce, may I ask if you are any nearer a resolution of your investigations?"

"We are making progress. You know I can't divulge any details."

Geneviève looked downcast but something was obviously on her mind. Of course, I had a pretty good idea what it was: the fear which beset her had congealed into a static melancholy at the base of her mind, trapping all her youthful longings and zest beneath it. Yet I couldn't stifle the wave of affection for her which washed over me at that moment. Right now she was in even more of a quandary than ever.

"I understand there's something more you want to say," I reminded her. "The other day we met to talk but events overtook us."

"Well, not really. Sort of. But you know how it is. I thought maybe I ought to mention it."

"Mention what exactly? Could you explain a little what you mean?"

"I think somehow I have annoyed them. Somehow I am not doing what they want. I have missed a signal, failed some induction test...something like that. Now my life is always on the edge. Last night, there was a car parked outside the *Tertre* when I went in to work...Well, that's nothing. But then when I came back it...the same car, I mean...was sitting outside at the head of the marina."

"Is it there now?"

"No. It left just before you arrived. It's so maddening. It's as if they knew you were coming. It makes me look paranoid."

A taut silence fell between us. Well, was she being paranoid, I wondered? But it was too much like my own experience. "Was it a black sedan?"

"Yes...but how did you know?"

"I've had similar reports."

She returned to a gloomy silence, glum in spirits. "What do I do? Take my chance? With you? ...With Halliday? You don't trust me, do you? I came to you for help and you have put me under investigation? No?"

"No!......Well, not exactly. You may have fallen under observation but I very much doubt it's that intensive. And the police budget doesn't run to sleek sedans."

"So who is it?"

"I just don't know. But they don't seem so threatening or so discreet. Maybe they want to spook you."

"And you? Why am I under observation," she asked.

"It's for your own protection."

"Paah!.....Do you expect me to believe that? I do wish I could know what is going on inside that head of yours. Why do you think I'd do such a thing like going to you if I wasn't sincere? Do you think I'm the sort of woman who likes to play games of deceit?"

"Don't you understand? There are no sorts of people. No one can be wholly trusted." She was silent. I could see she was suffering. It wasn't just a chance disposition of her eyelids. She was on the point of tears. "Geneviève, tell me what you wanted to say to me."

She shut her eyes but said nothing. I had the uneasy feeling that if I said anything more she'd get hysterical or break down into floods of tears. Instead she began to laugh quietly.

"What is it?" I asked.

"You," she said. "You are so predictable, its hilarious. Or terrible." Then I saw that tears filled her eyes and she was shaken by a terrible emotion before which I was both startled and ashamed. Geneviève picked up her glass and resumed. "You'd never guess what I'd been thinking. You know how what you expect never quite coincides with what actually happens? Well, as a girl I used to try to imagine the worst things that might happen in order to stop them from happening.

And that's what I have been trying to do now, to prevent bad things happening to me…Only now I fear they are maybe a prophecy." Then quite suddenly she threw her glass across the cabin, smashing it into shards. She put her face in her hands and began to sob. "It doesn't matter now," she said.

I felt helpless before such raw emotion, uneasy as a stranger must always be in the presence of an open heart. This was too much. Geneviève's suffering had been exacerbated by my failure to resolve her problem. I concede that readily. I was partly to blame. I had taken from her more than I had given and that had damaged trust between us. But my intercession might have had one good effect: had it deepened her resentment of Halliday? She was no longer in thrall to him. The more she hated him, the more she would turn to me for support. So it seemed to me that all I had to do was bide my time and avoid giving anything away. She wanted to break free of something, whatever Faed and Oppenheimer thought, but something was in the way. Fear, I guessed. A longing for protection, for some sort of explanation, a feeling which is all too close to the stirring of dependence. All I could do was promise to look into the black sedan and made arrangements to meet again to let her know of any developments but she looked doubtful, cynical even.

Right now, though, I had a rendezvous of a different sort to make, one which the demands of etiquette insisted I make. Duncanson's visit was due today.

42

IT'S NOT NORMALLY my scene but sometimes I have a secret yearning for the pomp and ceremony which goes with an important diplomatic visit. Perhaps it's something to do with being a part of something much bigger than yourself, of having some sort of living link with the past and the future. Whatever it is, that's why I hadn't felt discombobulated when I had found myself later that day standing to attention, like an old trooper, on a sandy strip next to coconut palms as the national anthem was being played to greet the arrival of the Colonial Minister, the Right Honourable Dennis Duncanson MP. He had just descended from a BOAC *Comet* with, of course, all the customary clearance procedures duly waived. For a moment the minister looked quite dignified as he stood there, his solemn features, decorous against the light sky, lending him an authoritative air even as the ocean waves crashed close by.

Afterwards, I walked alongside Superintendent Worrell to a rather sleek official and uncustomary sedan, to join the official cavalcade to Government House for the diplomatic reception. But before I had a chance to say how good the welcome had been I felt a tugging of my elbow. It was an airport official with a message or actually two messages. We stopped to examine them. The first was from Tim. They'd lost all trace of Maddox. I knew immediately that Maddox was gone. He was not simply visiting someone or out on an extended trip of some sort. He had fled. The second was from Halliday, demanding an urgent meeting down by the waterfront gardens. I felt I had to find out what he was offering. I explained that to Worrell.

"I was not aware he had become such an important informant. But if you must, Chief Inspector, you must. But I'm warning you, you must be at the official reception or there'll be all hell to pay and we'll know who to blame."

I PULLED UP AT a parking lot close to *Waterfront Gardens* and got out briskly. Whatever it was Halliday wanted to talk about, it had better be good. If I were late for the Governor's reception my reputation would be in tatters. But right now, a press of people nearby was making it well nigh impossible to spot my erstwhile mentor. Lingering looks from passers-by slowed my pace. Did they suspect something or were they just gawking? An agitated white man loitering by the park's entrance must have presented an odd sight.

"I'm over here." A disembodied voice rang through the ether before I saw its owner. Halliday slipped out of the shadows of a pine tree, a faint sea breeze ruffling his hair. An easy smile sat on his face as he made his way towards me. "Fancy a walk, Bruce?" he asked. "That alright with you? We've one or two things to chat about. I find a bit of exercise helps to clear the mind, helps you to see things properly."

I nodded agreement, without a lot of enthusiasm, and we started through the black railed gates into the little park. Above us the fronds of palm trees chuntered in the warm breeze. We should be in no danger of being overheard or even noticed. But what of my suspicion of being shadowed? The shadow I never saw, only sensed in the passing cars and strange looks.

"What's all this about?" I asked, looking at my watch. Bang on six o'clock. "I have an important meeting." Even if Halliday were quick about it I was almost bound to be late for the reception. I really shouldn't have let him mess me about. And yet there was his message: *You will not get a second chance.*

"It's good of you to come," Halliday continued. "I know about your meeting, Bruce. That's partly what I want to talk to you about." He stopped and looked at me meaningfully.

"Well," I asked, unable to keep a note of impatience from my voice. "What's it about exactly?"

"Something's happened. We...that is to say, our clients need to move quickly."

"Clients? Do you mean these special clients you spoke of?"

"Yes. That's right. I'm sorry about the inconvenience but these things can move fast. So many issues are interconnected, it can be hard to keep track. You see our clients are poised to make their investment but they have to move with care. Their rivals must not know anything. But there is still one difficulty. When that is resolved they will reach out their hand and seize the opportunity. But right now they must take precautions."

"That may well be but what's it got to do with me? And why now of all times?"

Halliday smiled and we resumed our walk. "In a minute...In a minute. First, that reception. There's an assistant with Duncanson, a man I know quite well. I want you to give him a letter. I've just received it myself. I had promised faithfully to deliver it. Now I can't. I'm not going to be there. So would you mind handing it over for me."

"What sort of letter?" Halliday produced a long white envelope and handed it to me. A name was written on the cover in an elegant hand: *Jake Oppenheimer*.

"That's it? Hand this over? Why didn't you say on the phone instead of all this cloak and dagger stuff," I said as I thrust the envelope deep into my jacket pocket. "You know I'm only a dinner guest. Not exactly one of the Minister's men on the spot, sort of thing. But I daresay I'll be able to hand it over."

"I should think so. You'll find a way, a man of your ingenuity. Thanks very much. You're a real star, Bruce."

I looked at him, puzzled. "Is there anything else?"

"Well, yes, there is. As I said, it's to do with our clients. You see, there's a little problem occurred and you can help us sort it."

"What sort of problem?"

"I'm talking about the little enquiry some of your colleagues have been making into Schooner's Bay. Drop it Bruce. Just drop it."

"No can do, Rufus. I can't stop an official police enquiry even if I wished to."

"I'm not asking you stop it, Bruce. Nothing so crude. There are other ways. Sideline it. Lower the priority. Put it on the back burner. Put your sidekick on to other duties."

We fell silent a moment as I absorbed this proposal then, deciding discretion may be the better part of valour, I said: "Maybe. It just might be possible. I'm happy to help so long as it doesn't involve breaching any investigative procedures or confidences."

"There's something we need to be clear on," Halliday went on, entirely unconcerned about my tone. "Are you with us? Wholly committed I mean. It's important, you know. Misunderstandings can lead to mishaps. And we wouldn't want any accidents would we?"

I disliked his insinuating way of talking. He was trying to get a hold on me. People who hinted at hints usually had something to hide. But I also didn't like the debts besieging my family and the thought of the £5,000 newly paid into our bank account was still fresh in my mind. Besides truth didn't always proceed in a straight orderly line but often by way of detours and circumnavigations. There might be something of use here. It was time to tread warily but not overtly suspiciously.

"Of course," I replied. "I'll fulfil my side of the bargain. Do you doubt it?" I remember at that moment drifts of foreign languages floated across from other pathways and the broad leaves of the palms were spotted with droplets of rainwater.

"Thanks Bruce. I knew we could count on you."

"OK. One thing, though, please don't make a habit of calling me out of the blue. I do have some important work to do. I can't just drop things and come running every time you decide you need some info on someone. It's really most unnecessary and time–wasting. You've made me late tonight for the Minister's reception. And another thing Rufus. I'm still puzzling over what you meant in your message. You..um..suggested you had something terribly important to tell me."

"Oh that! Yes." Halliday looked up at me soberly, his face a picture of sombre lines beneath a jutting brow. He took his time as if weighing his words. I must admit I have a fear of men who act as if they had a direct line to God Almighty. A suspicion they may have one lurks somewhere inside me. "Well, you know this is all about commitment," he went on. "We like people to show commitment. What about you Bruce?" he went on, seemingly ignoring my question. "I've been doing some thinking about you and then some. We've done some checking up on you. Where are you going? Things don't look too bright do they? This *North Star* business has completely derailed your career, hasn't it?"

I recoiled momentarily as if I'd been the sudden victim of an unexpected attack.

"It's certainly caused problems..."

"Problems! Face it, man! There's no point in burying your head in the sand. You're finished. And this little assignment is just a few crumbs from the rich man's table."

"I don't..."

Halliday raised his hand. "No. Don't bother with the excuses. We know all about you. We've had our eyes on you for a long time. A man of your ability ought to be going places. We believe in you. You certainly deserve better than this, don't you think? You've just been put in as the patsy, the fall guy, the utterly disownable man who comes up with the convenient verdict. The point is that we can make careers. And break them. It's true. In Britain. Elsewhere too. We play for big stakes."

I looked into Halliday's face curiously but it was expressionless. This was now all a far cry from the sober and socially minded businessman I'd met the other day at the Barracuda. He was hard to work out, his mind resembling an aquarium with different coloured fish swimming in different directions at the same time. Was he some kind of madman? Or was he simply a consummate actor. What in God's name had got into him? "OK, Rufus, what is this all about?" I asked rather lamely. It seemed Halliday knew a lot about what had happened to me.

"This could be about so much more than a neat little report on St. Eleanor's prospects. We can make you. We can put you back on track, in the big time where you belong. You see *International Project Assessments* represent much more powerful consortia. We have fingers on the levers of power worldwide. You will find that what we say often goes. You could be part of that process, a positive part." He sounded as if he meant it. The hint was as stark as could be. Overdone if anything but spoken words drift away into the ether. Halliday made it sound like a business deal. Making offers. Profit and loss. "Nothing to say, Bruce?" he went on. "You see we want to be sure you are a team player. How committed are you to your career? Or perhaps there are limits to your perceptiveness. Perhaps you should take more care."

I met Halliday's eyes with a steady stare. That a threat was implied, there was no doubt, the ultimate hint of a superior, hidden strength. I felt he was trying to convince me, dazzle me even so as to prepare the ground for a proposal of some sort. "That sounds very interesting," I said not giving him too much encouragement or discouragement either. "But I don't know what to make of it."

"I hope you don't feel its been a bit of a charade...but we can do much better for you..."

"It's good of you to be so concerned on my behalf but it seems to me that risk assessment has a limited future for me..."

"Think about it. Mull it over, Bruce. This could be your great opportunity. Kill the investigation into *Schooner's Landing* and I think we can give you the First Minister's killer," he said. The bottom line.

43

I ARRIVED LATE BUT not too late for the reception. The general hubbub indicated things were well under way. Outside, a rabble of cars and the sound of doors slamming indicated small groups of people were still making their way inside. Crepe, wound round the lamp posts, was streaming in the breeze. The gravel was unpleasant under my evening shoes as I followed to find the island's Governor Sir Godfrey Faed and his wife, Jocelyne, busy greeting the guests with a tireless aplomb which must have been very wearying for them on account of the heat and their age. Their roles, dress and age identified them and their unswerving devotion to the standards of a bygone age. Godfrey Faed's grey whitening hair was clipped short in a way that was faintly reminiscent of a poodle. His face was long and though lined it still had warm and well defined features, unspoiled by fat. He also sported a blue sash whose meaning I could not tell but doubtless denoted membership of some august order. While he must have been in his mid-sixties, Lady Faed was a good fifteen, maybe twenty years, younger, her hair dark and curled, and her manner suggestive of a woman given to natural exuberance.

The Governor greeted me warmly, even identifying me by name, in a way which was quite touching as if he really did especially value making my acquaintance. It was a trick which left a warm glow with the recipient and one I wished I could perform. Now I moved on into the hall where there was already a low din of human chatter. A smiling waitress presented me with a glass of white wine and another with a choice of nibbles. Shouts and laughter erupted from a continuous din of human voices. Feeling duty bound to circulate I soon find myself chatting to a young man, an islander who turned out to own the largest garage in St. Jacques. Looking over his shoulder, past the voluble crowd I could see a few tables neatly laid out and covered with starched white table cloths. Various luminaries of St Eleanor's social sphere, leading business figures and a surprisingly large Christian contingent were also present. Of the thirty three churches and twelve religious sects which existed on this tiny island the Presbyterians led by Murdo Macleod had sent the largest group. Many were women, adorned with flowery hats, and they sat close to the federalist supporters. I tried going through the names of people in my mind, people I needed to see; then asked my companion, a young man in a light tan suit, if he knew anyone here from the press.

"Press?" he laughed. "There's no press here unless you count the *St Eleanor Gleaner*."

"Well, what of it? Where are they?"

"That's it over there." He nodded his head in the direction of a large ebony woman sitting at the reception table, pencil in hand. I walked over and was about to introduce myself when she started yelling at a waiter: "Do I have to wait half an hour just for a drink?" The waiter, perhaps habituated to being shouted at in a day's work immediately turned and left, presumably in search of a replenished tray. She saw me and turned on a pleasing smile. "Ah, Chief Inspector Cordell, so pleased to see you." I observed her properly for the first time. A striking face and one suddenly illuminated by a broad smile. She said something which was hard to catch amid the hubbub but I did: "Mary Beale."

There was a moment, only a moment, when I thought I had made a new friend then I realised she was the open type, suddenly expansive to all new acquaintances. With only a little secretarial support and some very erratic contributions from a few freelance stringers she managed to bring out a weekly paper for the island almost single handed. She had built up a formidable reputation. Though of course the occasional error slipped through, she had succeeded in making the *Gleaner* a respected paper, sought after for its news and comment as much as for entertainment and its calendars of events. It struck me that the accumulated gossip she could pick up at a meeting like this could be eked out for weeks in her columns.

She already knew I was here to re-open the Constantine inquiry and when I hinted that there was maybe more to the case than had initially appeared she looked duly solemn before tossing me an open invitation to drop in on her any time at the *Gleaner*'s offices in St. Jacques, an invitation I promised her I would be taking up.

"Come to see me," she repeated quietly, insistently.

"Yes, I will." My tone was altered, mystified by her insistence .

I was just on the point of asking her if she had known Warwick Constantine when we were summoned to our seats and the head table too began to pack out with local dignitaries. A loud knocking of a spoon against a wine glass silenced the room. Jake Oppenheimer got up with the ramrod straight stiffness a certain type of official used on these occasions, coughed loudly, and then announced in a loud voice that the Governor wished to speak. At this, everyone *oohed* and *aahed* and then fell silent as H.M.'s representative rose to his feet and began a ponderous address, the whiteness of his starched shirt contrasting oddly with his weathered face and lending him the slightly sinister look of someone who doesn't really belong here. He started by welcoming everyone present. Around the room there was a wave of warm assent. His voice was agreeable, hospitable and anonymous.

"It is customary for the Governor to say a few words on these occasions. While I don't want to keep you from the refreshments for long, I just want to say that Mr. Duncanson's visit simply demonstrates once more the high seriousness with which Her Majesty's Government views St. Eleanor's prospective independence. It is 1962. The world is changing fast and we have seen most of Britain's colonies attain independence in recent years. It is now time for the countries of the West Indies to take their place as independent nations." The times, the Governor said, were extraordinarily difficult. He sketched in some of the island's well known difficulties. But, he said, there were opportunities too. He didn't actually mention a name but he said that St. Eleanor was fortunate indeed in having a large corporation, so committed to the advancement of the island's prosperity, working here. He appeared to be losing some of the audience's attention; a few people were even muttering among themselves. We were lucky too to have Mr Dennis Duncanson present who knew so much about the Windward Islands and had taken great care to study realistic options for economic development. The audience was very kind, applauding every over simplification and half-truth as if they were insightful perceptions.

"Some changes," Faed went on, "will be easy and much welcomed. Others will be a good deal harder. Let's hope that by working together we can overcome them together. Thank you." His purpose seemed to be to garner support for some far reaching changes HMG had in mind, and to give support to US investment in the island. The audience had listened politely. Perhaps they took the view that nothing was about to happen too hurriedly. I wasn't so sure. I knew these mandarins were not as harmless as they looked. They considered themselves to be lords of the world, dispensers of fate.

Finally Sir Godfrey raised a glass of champagne in an extended right arm. "The Queen," announced the Governor. His guests, gathered all around the long tables, dutifully echoed his toast clinking their glasses, drinking the champagne and repeating the refrain: "The Queen!" To my surprise the Governor looked touched by this display of loyalty to the Monarch. Everywhere the Empire had crumbled and often into dissidence at that but the unexpectedly positive reception had evidently given him a warm afterglow of nostalgia. The Governor now sat down to applause. His delivery had been excellent even if the exact import of his words remained opaque.

I looked at Dennis Duncanson, the Minister of State at the Colonial Office, a thin spry and elderly looking man but I was too far away to read his expression well.

Something about his posturing manner suggested superciliousness. Yet I knew better. He already had Jake Oppenheimer in place, a much more incisive man: the Colonial Office's fixer, the eyes and ears of the department of dubious tricks. Lean and efficient he would attract others of the same stripe.

Duncanson himself now rose to speak, looking very grave. He obviously fitted his demeanour to his responsibilities. When he spoke, he stood straight and gazed into the middle distance to give himself a little more *gravitas*. No doubt about it, it was his ministerial stance. He talked in some detail about the budgetary problems Britain had at the moment, rather implying there would be damn all for St. Eleanor but not actually saying that. Yet his audience listened politely, their manners impeccable. He too hinted at a growing role for the US. And who could deny the importance of the United States' defence shield? It was unlikely that such a small island as St. Eleanor's could be truly wholly independent and now that there were serious doubts about the future of a West Indian federation, the role of the United States in the Caribbean was only likely to increase. After all, Britain itself was a small island dependant in many important respects on the United States. Why should the islanders of St. Eleanor be so surprised at such a development? But exactly what development, he didn't say which must have been as irritating for the audience as it was to me. Did he imply there might be a US facility here as there had been during the Second World War?

If so, *what* was the Government's position? The Governor himself had never indicated such a thing and he would see things out, I didn't doubt. He still had a few years of service to go. He could retire now at the top of the tree but I fancied something about that face – dry and determined – suggested he still had plans to fulfil himself. Mr Duncanson was continuing, now patronising his hosts with heavy compliments about the beauty of their island. His audience accepted it stoically and applauded politely while I affected outward nonchalance and squirmed inwardly.

Next and last the new First Minister, Jamieson was invited to speak. Like most of the genuine Island natives he pronounced his "th's" as "d's" and I couldn't help feeling he was a true Islander. Jamieson evinced considerable respect to the visitors from Whitehall but in a self confident manner. And why not? After all, no one knew better than he the eighty six square miles which made up the tiny island of St. Eleanor. Now he enjoyed considerable popularity and occupied the post of First Minister, though his political preference was to support independence rather than the wider Federation of the West Indies, which the British encouraged. His experience was expansive and his intelligence outstanding so I had expected a more thoughtful peroration from him than the one to which we were now subjected. Like an experienced doctor in front of a tiresome patient he had listened patiently to the two British speeches while he prepared his own judgements. When he spoke, however, it was rather to congratulate the previous speakers on their acumen rather than to judge them but buried in his short address was a message uncomfortably direct to the British.

"We are few in numbers, perhaps," said Jamieson, "but we are proud of our long history going back to the days when Christopher Columbus recorded seeing our island on the way to the Spanish Main. Descendants of slaves and also of shipwrecked sailors, fugitive thieves and others we are nonetheless proud of our ancestry; and we are a God-fearing people who have lived peacefully here for many centuries in these tropical islands which are cooled by the trade winds.

"What perhaps we are most anxious to preserve now in these new and exciting days is our simple way of life and the continuance of large grant aid from Britain."

To conclude, the girl guides who were assembled at the back of the hall, in their light blue uniforms and red scarves, began to sing *"God Save the Queen."* Everyone cheered and there were not a few moist eyes in the hall. There was something a little forlorn about this end of Empire stuff. People didn't really believe in the Commonwealth. The eccentricities of the British just seemed absurd now that their power was slipping away.

44

IT TOOK A LITTLE while for the crowds to begin to disperse, everyone seemingly reluctant and enjoying the free refreshments available. The European guests in particular obviously felt more at home here. Cotton Horrocks frocks shimmered with bright floral colours and middle aged men sported medals and ribbons from the wars as everyone laughed and the music played. Even the sweat of bodies mixed with the odours of tobacco smoke smelt differently from home, adding to the lustre of the occasion.

I found myself buttonholed by a loquacious suited Englishman, one of the delegation, I fancied. Then suddenly I realised who he was. Damned fool that I'd been: It was Dennis Duncanson himself. I hastily introduced myself. It was easy to see that he would have had big plans for the island and would try to push them through. I was very struck by his style. While others scoffed their refreshments with almost unseemly haste Duncanson took his Chablis with a distinctly French self-possession, rolling the wine around his glass to release the full bouquet and holding it up to the light to study its colour more precisely. Yet he was a forceful man, I could tell at a glance, and not one, I imagined, who would suffer fools gladly.

"Ah yes," he said. "I've heard a lot about you. It's a difficult job you've got but I wish you every luck. I liked Warwick personally. Bad business." He shook his head ruminatively.

"You knew him?"

"Of course. I know everyone here!" He laughed.

"Do you have anything to say about Sir Warwick which you think might be helpful to me?"

"Not much to say, I'm afraid Chief Inspector. I didn't have a great deal of time here. I had met up with Warwick on occasion. You know how it is. It's a small world." Duncanson spread his palms outwards in an expansive gesture. "But there is nothing special to say. He was always concerned about developments in the Caribbean. Recently Cuba, the Dominican Republic and Haiti had been at the forefront of his mind. You know how it is? Kennedy and the Americans are obsessed about Cuba and the Cuban threat. Trujillo and Papa Doc – Duvalier that is – play on their fears incessantly to get aid from the States. And you know what?" Duncanson stopped in mid flow like a theatrical performer, eye brows raised.

"You tell me."

He smiled. "It works!" He spoke emphatically. "Maybe we should do the same in St Eleanor! The Yanks pour millions into those corrupt dictatorships to keep them safe from Castro. But is Castro interested, I ask myself? There is absolutely not a scintilla of a reason to think that he is. Maybe that way we could get more than *Alpha Omega* are offering."

"*Alpha* who?" I asked, not wishing to reveal my knowledge.

"*Alpha Omega*. That's the US corporation the governor was talking about in a roundabout way. Its the same company Jamieson had been acting for so we'd better take an interest."

"Well, perhaps you are right," I answered after some hesitation. "But politics are not really my line. Now, Mr Duncanson, Sir, its just as well we met. I have a personal letter I need to give to a member of your team. Mr Oppenheimer."

Duncanson suddenly looked around the hall, rather like a startled owl, eyes scanning the crowd. "Oppenheimer, Oppenheimer...yes, of course, ...there he is." He pointed to the staircase. I spotted him now: a solitary figure climbing a few steps to a gallery overlooking the hall. Giving my apologies and thanks to the Minister I made my way over to him. Easier said than accomplished. It was an absolute crush. To get through I had to elbow my way along in a most undignified manner. People I was passing were talking of the Governor's speech. It had gone down well, it seemed; there was some excitement at the imminent prospect of independence. There were not many steps but Oppenheimer was now standing alone, self absorbed, studying photographs of old St. Jacques hung in frames alternating with mirrors between the windows. He was smoking a cigarette, the tip of which shone red.

"Fascinating, old photographs, don't you think?" I ventured. "Sometimes its as if only the costumes have changed. So much is still as it was."

Oppenheimer knew instantly that this was an attempt to establish contact rather than an innocent observation. "Chief Inspector Cordell, if I'm not mistaken, isn't it?" He looked at me with a feigned surprise, searching my face for some sort of recognition. Anyone observing us would not have guessed we were already acquainted.

"Yes," I murmured hesitantly. "Cordell. Bruce Cordell. Very pleased to meet you again."

"Jake Oppenheimer," he continued and we shook hands cordially. "Pleased to meet you I'm sure, but you have the advantage on me. I'm afraid I..."

"No need to apologise. I'm on a bit of an errand. I think we have a mutual acquaintance: Mr Rufus Halliday."

Oppenheimer continued to look at me blankly, even suspiciously, as if a further clue as to my intentions might be found in my features. "I'm afraid not. Have you got the right man? Is there anything I can help with?"

I was flummoxed to say the least but cursing Halliday inwardly I put my fingers inside my jacket top and drew out the envelope and handed it over.

"What is it?" he whispered quickly, whisking it unopened into an inside pocket.

"I've no idea. He said it was urgent but for the delegation only."

Oppenheimer smiled. "Ah, let me think. Communications you have no explanation for, eh? I'd be careful if I were you. Were you followed?"

"Maybe."

Jake raised his eyes to look around the throng while slowly and deliberately he pulled the envelope out, opened it and read its contents. After he did so, he fixed me with steely eyes before bursting into laughter. Turning to go, he said *sotte voce*: "We are a pair! It's an official letter from the Council's Works Department. They've dug up some of the road and we have a small diversion back to Government House. We'll be obliged to take the coastal road. Ah, well, I'd better tell the team." And on that dutiful note he blended back into the crowd.

I was left speechless. After all that palaver Halliday had used me as a mere messenger boy for a third party. It was typical of the man. What a lot of the theatre there was about him! I expected nothing of substance from his alluring hint about the identity of the First Minister's killer. More likely it would prove to belong to that familiar category of 'bait, lure and switch' which I could now see Halliday was a past master of but which for me was fast losing its magic. Yet I did not doubt that his wish for me to sideline an investigation was real enough.

Then I too joined the crowds who were beginning to seep towards the exit. As I was just descending the Town Hall steps I was surprised to be stopped by Mary Beale in person. "You don't waste your time," she said.

"How do you mean?"

"Getting to know all the island's rogues already."

"Jake Oppenheimer ? He looked solid to me."

"Yes he looks good. Most people here tonight look good. You can say that for them. The ordinary folk may not look so good but mostly their 'yes' means 'yes' and their 'no' means 'no'. You can rely on them, pretty much."

"But not Mr Oppenheimer, perhaps?"

Mary gave me a sour look then whispered quickly. "These people lie so naturally it's easy to fall for them if you don't constantly scrutinise their messages and their real import. Most disturbing. Perhaps you'll telephone my office and we'll have a fuller talk some time."

"Why yes, I'd like that. Of course, I will," I said as I stood there rather clumsily watching her get into her motor car and glide away through the poinsettias to the main road and a horizon dotted with lights. Something of the spell of the place lingered into the night: the purple sunset, the picturesque coastline, the distant murmurs of the wild, the charm of the people...the kiss of intrigue.

45

WHEN I LEFT THE RECEPTION I felt my job was done, my work had run its course. The official report would confirm that the First Minister had died of an overdose. If it transpired Jahnke has played a role, this was to be left to secret agencies and it was most unlikely that a word of it would break into the public domain. Perhaps it was all for the best but I was uneasy with all this. It's just not how justice should be administered. But I knew the secret organs of power had their own rules and one of them concerned jurisdiction. Counter Espionage was not our game. It was now time to hand the investigation over. In hindsight I suppose I felt Intelligence was wrong to appeal to one's sense of loyalty and trust. Should these not be the building blocks of the stuff of life itself? Yet it is hypocrisy in a political context. Political establishments do not, can not, work like that. What honesty had these people ever displayed in all their behind the scenes dealings? What right then had they to assume my fidelity?

Faed had told me that my work was done, that I could go now but I was too unsettled to return to *Caille Blanc* and wouldn't be able to explain my tormenting thoughts to Katie. Instead, I drove back down to St. Jacques to try to collect my ideas. I looked at my wristwatch. It was nine o'clock. For the first time in a long while I suddenly felt really frightened. Something, something really bad, I was sure, was going to happen and happen soon. The rains had stopped but water was dripping furiously from the leaves and the road was marred by deep puddles. What had this criminal ring wanted? Why had they been so sure of themselves? Understanding was impossible: it was like grasping at a cloud of gas, a hopeless task. I had run into an official enigma which I knew instinctively would never be explained to me. Yet I could not still the questions my very unquiet mind was seething with....Then something unexpected occurred to me. It was just an outline of an idea but it was sufficient. The main road was blocked by unexpected highways work. The Minister's car would be diverted. The small police watch on the roof tops were redundant. And suddenly I remembered Mary's stricture about the real import of messages.

I shot back to St. Jacques.

The night sky had darkened but the coastal road remained brightly illuminated. I reckoned I would only have half an hour at most before the Minister's car was due. I swung off the main road, down the foetid little alleyway to the dockside. The car purred to a halt. There was no time, no opportunity to call for assistance. I would have to do this alone. It was something I had to do. Never had I felt more vigorous as then, when I climbed out of the car, exhilarated and drawing the salty air deep into my lungs. I ran at the block of flats, through the squalid alley in an all enveloping darkness. Everything was as normal but I knew it wasn't. I crashed through the doorway and up the staircase.

Arriving at Maddox's flat I had a moment of doubt. The place was quiet, the door locked. I drew my service revolver and shot the lock off. Bits of wood and metal spattered on the landing. Putting my shoulder to the door, it rolled inwards. The sniper gave me little time, swinging his rifle from his vantage point at the window and firing from the hip in one quick smooth action. Fast but not fast enough. The revolver was already in my hand and I got off a single round before he fired. The echo of the gunshots were still ringing in my ears as I bent down to examine the body. Blood was already soaking through his shirt. He was certainly dead. A not so neat bullet hole was blasted through his chest. I fumbled my way over the clothing but the body refused to give up its secrets, its pockets empty of all documentation. Nothing. Then I picked up the rifle. A *Fusil à Répétition modèle F1*. Well, well, well.

Standing back to reflect I knew we'd had a dash of luck. But maybe inspiration too as I savoured my personal triumph. I didn't kid myself that my work was over but it was as near to completion as I had hoped. Now, looking at the rifle I knew that a new phase of my labours had just begun. But who was he? Despite the gun shot there was no stirring from within. All had returned to silence. The window was ajar and a faint gust of air touched my cheeks. Below, cars rumbled along the coastal road. As if from great distance I could hear the gentle soughing of the sea. I moved around the apartment, checking for things but not quite sure what I was looking for. I started in the front room where I was standing, went through to the bedroom and then the bathroom. I opened each cupboard, every drawer. I had to do this methodically. But there was nothing. Satisfied at last, I went outside in search of a call box.

"THE MAIN THING IS you have removed the threat," said Jake Oppenheimer later that evening when he arrived with a back up team of burly, suited men. "It's interesting, of course, that you remembered this man from Libreville but maybe not that important. He's probably Cuban but they'd deny it. There will be no publicity. And thanks to your quick reactions, there will be no trial. So far as you are concerned, it's all over. The case is closed."

Reluctantly, I left the scene to Counter Intelligence and made my way back to *Caille Blanc*. Oppenheimer had told me that my work was done, that I could go now but I was too unsettled to sleep and wouldn't be able to explain my tormenting thoughts to Katie. Much, too much, had been left unsaid. Instead, I drove back down to St. Jacques to try to collect my thoughts in the breaking light of dawn. The rains had stopped but water was dripping furiously from the leaves and the road was marred by deep puddles. My thoughts were elsewhere. I had run into an official enigma which I knew instinctively would never be explained to me. Yet I could not still the questions my very unquiet mind was seething with. I could not understand why Geneviève had smuggled this deadly sniper's rifle into St. Eleanor.

In search of an answer I drove back to the port. But the mood was to be one of anti-climax. The postage stamp harbour remained as pretty as ever and I found the Hélène becalmed at her usual anchorage. A light breeze was blowing from the West, carrying with it a tang of sea salt. Walking down the jetty I picked up on the first harbingers of change, an air of bustle, as if getting ready for departure. Wrapped and boxed goods of all sorts stood on the quayside; and Geneviève's spry figure soon appeared organising the catamaran's quartering. She smiled when she saw me, her face registering no alarm.

"You look, as if you could do with a hand. Can I help?" I asked. She didn't demur and I was soon at work loading the vessel and wondering how to approach my enquiries but it was she who initiated things. When we'd cleared the quayside she invited me in for a coffee. She fixed up an early morning cocktail for herself. When we started to drink Geneviève clasped my wrist with her hand.

"Tell me Bruce, you said you liked to sail. Is this true?"

"Of course it's true. I'm a bit rusty now but why are you asking?"

She took the straw from her cocktail then sucked it while rounding her lips.

"Rufus has asked me to deliver a letter to Belle Isle. It's not far from Martinique. It's an easy run but it will take a couple of days. I thought perhaps you could accompany me."

"When do you plan on sailing?"

She laughed with a natural laugh that made her shoulders tremble and shook her breasts. "I can't tell but as soon as possible. It's going to depend. I have to get the weather vane-anemometer mended. It could take three of four days."

"Otherwise?"

"We're fine for departure. We have plenty of water, food, stores...and so on."

"Are you happy to do this for Halliday?"

She smiled thinly. "One last time. Then it's over. I won't be coming back."

Then she put her hand on mine in an act of reassurance. Looking into her face it would have been easy to believe her, to accept her innocence. The would-be hit man, the presumed Cuban fugitive glimpsed in Libreville, the twice murderer were in all likelihood the same man. And I knew who had smuggled the rifle in. At this moment Geneviève seemed oblivious to our night's work. Was it possible that somehow the ring had got a message to her, that she was in fact planning an escape from the island? The boards swayed gently beneath my feet as I made my exit that morning. I'd have to think about it, I said. How long had I got? Three to four days she suggested. Well, I wasn't going by that. Three to four hours maximum but that should be more than enough I figured as I looked at the darkening sky. Only a madman would put to sea with another such storm imminent.

How far had she entangled me in some covert design? Those 'urgent' summonses first to Martha's and then to the beach, mere *ruses de guerre*. Halliday's fury at their meeting, a blind. Were all her anxieties a sham, designed to channel my thoughts in the wrong direction? I dropped into the Blue Lagoon Hotel and put a phone call through to Oppenheimer. After a short wait I was connected. Briefly, I explained the situation. He listened and spoke in that oily voice as if all this had long been evident to him. An arrest squad would be around immediately. With that in mind I decided to absent myself. I didn't want to be around when the arrest was made. My feelings had grown too complicated, pained at the thought of my infatuated complicity.

Not without sadness I made my way back to the quayside. I thought of what Jake appeared to be offering: a better-paid position; a very senior rank; and the money with it. Part of me wanted to tell him where he could stuff it but deep down I knew Katie was right.

Just then I noticed the scowl on the horizon, the sky darkening again with black and violet rain clouds. Already, the temperature had dropped precipitously and I grew alarmed at the prospect of a storm sweeping across the water from the Americas. I had half intended to give Geneviève a wave as I made my way to the car. But I was too late. Only by a cat's whisker but too little, too late. The *Hélène* was already pulling away from the dock side heading towards the open sea. I could see Geneviève clearly enough standing at the wheel, her long black hair drawing out in the wind. Her lips were hard set yet half smiling, her eyes wide open. Ah...A lovely woman stooped to folly. But this was madness indeed. All morning the news reports had been repeating warnings of an imminent storm. What was she doing? Risking her life for a short term escape or even to report to God knows who.

I ran to the end of the pier to watch the vessel pull away, away and into the incoming storm. Even as I watched, the darkening sky seemed to lower. The spray dashed over the catamaran as the *Hélène* tore across the water's surface. There was wind but not yet especially menacing, coming in short sudden puffs and then receding. Geneviève was now truly launched upon the waves which were breaking in a long, menacing roar. It was not really rough yet but I could see that even in the short time since I had reached the harbour the weather had deteriorated with gusts of wind blowing much more frequently and violently, whitening the water's surface and tearing off the tops of the waves into fountains of spray. The dark clouds above were breaking up as great rents seemed to appear in the dark curtain only for them to close up again just as quickly. The *Hélène* was rolling heavily on the rising waters.

I looked at Geneviève to see if there was any change in her determination but the diminutive figure gave no such indication. In another few minutes the small vessel was far out at sea, ploughing its furrow through the ever increasing waves. The wind blew with a hoarse roar across the water. It was madness to continue. The craft quivered under the shock of each succeeding wave. Did she understand the real state of things? A fresh gust struck her with even greater force than ever. The vessel keeled to the side and surely must go under but she seemed to right herself. Then the drifting dark clouds and heaving sea took her utterly from sight and she vanished into the darkness.

Epilogue

THE RAIN HAD JUST finished, releasing sweet fragrances from the leaves and embracing us all in the moment. St. Eleanor with its burden of deceit and injustice still preoccupied me. That afternoon the two of us – Katie and myself – were sitting by the riverside at Richmond, the children playing and crying nearby. Not far away two women of colour were sitting on a bench talking to one another. Once the riverside might have seemed the acme of British life. But the new Britain was asserting itself even here.

Katie pushed a newspaper under my nose. A garish headline screamed: **CUBAN MISSILE CRISIS: KENNEDY WARNS RUSSIANS**. US reconnaissance aircraft had identified several Soviet Missile silos on the Caribbean island. Washington was demanding their dismantling and mobilising against them. Quietly Katie nudged me, pointing to a different headline: **A LONDON ARREST**. I read on:

> The Metropolitan Police face accusations of using heavy-handed tactics in their investigation into a member of the Colonial Service. A civil servant's wife has revealed that her husband, Mr Peter Jahnke, was arrested under the Official Secrets Act as part of the operation. Just before 6am on a cold morning on

21 October 1962, the civil servant was asleep in bed when 14 armed police officers battered down his door, stormed into his flat and arrested him. The armed officers swooped in under the cover of darkness, detaining him under the Official Secrets Act, a law meant to be used to hunt down hostile spies and enemies of the state.

"They dragged him from our bedroom to the living room and started interrogating him while he was utterly disorientated," Mrs Jahnke said. "The police crowded into the house. It was totally humiliating and disorientating – he was treated like a criminal."

In her first interview since the dawn raid, Mrs Jahnke accused the Met of acting like a "secret police in a tinpot state" and of breaking multiple human rights laws in their investigation. The house was ravaged: cupboards were ripped out, panels were torn from the walls and the police even emptied a cereal box onto the floor in a desperate hunt for evidence.

I shrugged it aside, feeling strangely disconnected from this denouement to the Constantine affair. I had been ordered back to London to give some evidence in the *Alpha Omega* corruption case and when the trial ended I was not likely to be returning to the Caribbean. It was a bitter sweet moment for I can't deny the prospect of leave with my family was a welcome one. You need companions of the heart when you feel like a convalescent: vulnerable and highly sensitive. It was strange to be back in the big smoke. London is so vast yet it is only a conglomeration of innumerable private cells. I could not pretend to belong to a community here but yet part of me, I know, actually likes the impermanence, the total absence of sentiment.

"I must have hurt you, Katie," I said. "I'm sorry but I made a mess of everything from beginning to end."

"Hardly. You didn't. You got there in the end. It's hardly your fault that you were deceived. It's always so difficult to know other human beings well, to guess their thoughts and feelings. Our minds are like separate little black boxes."

"Perhaps but sometimes I don't like the person who lives in my skin."

"I like him well enough. Sometimes, anyway."

"Life is a lonely business."

"Philosophy?" she smiled.

"No," I laughed. "It's all part of my line of work. I guess we'll just have to try to explain to each other more of what we're really thinking, to get to know ourselves deeply enough so we can give each other honest answers. I just feel I let myself down when I fell for their wiles."

"Forget it," Katie said. "We've all been taken in at one time or another. And it always hurts." She smiled. "Besides," she said "you are out of it now and you're better off without them, that's for sure. What's the point of living your life with plots being woven around you every day and no one telling you anything?"

She was right, of course. No more words for me, except those I hereby set down long after it matters. I have had my fill of intrigue. I no longer care who lives in the anonymous houses, their lives, their beauty, their ugliness. Now I had learnt from Frank that the Constantine case was closed. Death by accident.

An overdose of barbiturates. The Quillham case too was closed. Maddox, a man under the darkest of suspicions, had come to an untimely death in St. Jacques. No other line was to be followed. Geneviève Clouin too had vanished from the scene like a puff of air. Valentine had been arrested for fraud. Of the Cuban assassin, nothing at all. As for the intrigues of *Alpha Omega*, this had been left in the hands of Superintendent Frank Worrell and his capable assistant, Sergeant Lucy Wainwright. Proceedings were continuing but at least *Anchor Marine* had been persuaded to drop its blacking of the plantation produce.

"So was IPA a phoney?" Katie asked.

"Not exactly. No. In fact, certainly not. The report is real. Their clients are real. It's just that IPA is not quite the freestanding body it seemed."

"Always wheels within wheels."

"Always. Onslow-Bell is one of *them*. He's on a long lead from Whitehall but he does what he's told. And I did his bidding. They thought I would be a useful tool to stir the pot. But Halliday...I don't understand why they didn't arrest him."

"Why should they?" Katie asked in her forthright way. "He's a controlled enemy agent. More use controlled than muddying the waters in a trial. Besides, it's not clear he has broken any laws. He probably wasn't aware of the ambush or the contents of the envelope. Being an Agent of Influence is not against the law, contrary to what most people imagine. Its not espionage."

"So what do you think their interest in *Alpha Omega* was? I'm sure that was principally the Mob, not the Russians."

"Yes but they always like to use both ends against the middle, don't they? They deliberately provoke labour unrest by encouraging the more exploitative owners and fomenting the resulting unrest. Meanwhile, they have also compromised the First Minister. Either way, they think they win. An assassinated Colonial Minister would have been the spark for the whole thing to blow up."

"You think so."

"Know so."

We lapsed into silence. The grey eminences inhabited a different world without boundaries, dark, lit only by a faint moonlight in which they all moved, not people but creatures, numbers, signs; all features whose meanings changed every day. I was not forgotten yet. From now on I would really understand the meaning of the phrase, a "cold sweat". It was terrifying just to have become one of the Aware. Now I wished I could wander among the nameless multitudes who didn't figure in these people's calculations.

END

Milton Keynes UK
Ingram Content Group UK Ltd.
UKHW010620280723
425939UK00004B/156

9 781803 814551